Then They Came

By
Keith R. Kirkwood

PublishAmerica
Baltimore

ISBN: 978-1-4489-9141-9 (softcover)
ISBN: 978-1-4489-6658-5 (hardcover)
PUBLISHED BY PUBLISHAMERICA, LLLP
www.publishamerica.com
Baltimore

Printed in the United States of America

A fictional tale of events along the American/Mexican border with the problem of millions of Mexicans entering into the U.S. each year in search of a better life, illegally and how many terrorist sneak in with them is unknown. It tells of the billions in illegal drugs and of cartels smuggling drugs in to the U.S. with what seems the blessings of the federal governments on both sides.

INTRODUCTION

In the years, two thousand seven and eight the mass of Mexicans fleeing from Mexico was amounting into the millions. The congress and President of the United States, George Walker Bush was only going through the motions, in an effort to fool the American people they were trying to close the borders. This phony scheme fooled no one. The people knew that big business was applying pressure to keep the border open. Profits in the billions were being made on the backs of these simple people coming for a better way of life. Cheap labor blinded the moneymakers as to the results of this horde of illegal's streaming across daily. They cared not for the American worker.

The Mexican army was even transporting some across the border deep inside Arizona. Congress finally decides to build a fence to help control the tidal wave.

Now that does bring back memories of the past. President Nixon, after he left office convinced China to remove the bamboo curtain. For fifty some years, the U.S. worked on Russia and the East Germans to remove their iron curtain and join the world community. These items did not work and a fence will not solve our problem. People still escaped, many killed, but still they did nothing, to very little, to dampen the need for people to be free. In the Mexicans situation, it is jobs for making a living.

The stupidly of congress and Bush and their lies have almost destroyed our constitution and what we stand for. Iraq is a good example of Bush's lies.

Even a child knows that ladders can be made to breach fences. The taller the fence, the longer the ladder will be. The deeper the fence under ground, the deeper holes under it will be. It looks like congress has totally forgotten whom they work for, the American people. Apparently, the only reason you run for congress is to get wealthy. It certainly was not to serve the people. Term limits might just solve this problem. Repeatedly congress has proven that.

The disgusting thing about all this is there are three hundred thousand Mexicans who have applied and have waited years to get into the U.S. legally. They still wait because of the blindness of greed for the unlawful.

The bottom line to this mess is that when nations of laws ignore the same laws that have kept them free for over two hundred years, our freedom is gone.

When the lawmakers become lawbreakers, we are drifting into anarchy. If our leaders continue to do nothing but spend money, America may go the way of the Roman Empire and implode from within. It has already started.

IS THAT HAPPENING TO US???

A courageous General and four U.S. Senators decided to send six men and a woman undercover to the border area. Their mission is to go into Mexico along the border in an effort to identify terrorists coming into the U.S. with the hordes of Mexicans seeking jobs. All of Mexico knows the American government no longer cares and in fact encourages the illegal migration. With the honest ones, come criminals of all sorts. These six are to identify terrorists coming in to attack us where we live. If not stopped the U.S. will soon look like a war zone after their attacks. Their mission was to kill those located and report these actions to the General. They were to gather facts of just how many Mexicans was crossing over. Hard to do, but tried.

Then They Came

CHAPTER 1

Lying in the tall sagebrush, on the Mexican side of the border, Nate was soaking wet. The rain hammered everyone, both man and beast in the early spring rain. The Rio Grande River had risen two feet in the last ten hours. His night vision binoculars becoming blurred every couple of minutes from the moisture. It was hard to keep them streak free. He peered thru them until his eyes burned. He feared he would miss something, but it could not be helped. It was still in the wee hours of the morning and should be light in a couple hours.

Dark figures, all at once appeared going into the river. They were about thirty yards from Nate's location. He hunkered close to the ground for fear they might see him. They were upstream from him and they were the ones he came to see. In the group, he could barely make out women and children. Some he recognized by the way they walked. Others he could distinguish, a couple carrying what looked like children. Altogether, he counted sixteen. A couple of the men helped a few of the women but not all. Nate decides this is because they were a family. Three of the women had no one helping them and struggled against the current. The water was waist high on the men and maybe four inches higher on the women.

Nate had to admire people like these who would risk everything to get into the United States.

As he watched, one of the women seemed to slip and almost fell. She had released the grip on the child she was carrying. It fell into the water and was swept away before she could reach it.

Damn, Nate thought, *now here goes my cover.*

He knew he had to move quickly or the child was a goner. With the binoculars around his neck, he ran the thirty feet to the water's edge. He waded in with disregard for his own life.

His eyes pierced the darkness for the child he knew was coming his way. All at once, he heard a faint scream, as from a child, and spotted a blur of white.

That had to be the child; he thought and lounged for it. He knew he had guessed right when his hands grabbed cloth. The white he had seen was from the shirt the boy was wearing. Righting himself, he walked back to the bank, slipping, and sliding he made it to safety. He sat on the ground and tried to comfort the child. The crying could be heard for some distance over the noise of the river.

Nate could hear a woman's voice yelling as she ran down the riverbank toward him, trying to find her child.

"Over here, we're over here," he responded to her yells.

In a minute, she ran up to Nate and took the boy from his arms. The child gripped her as if life itself depended on it.

"Thank you, oh, thank you, mister," she said in poor English.

A little fatigued, she sat down to rest as Nate struggled with what to say to her. He spoke little Spanish and it was clear she spoke little English.

Both sat there in silence, catching their breaths and noticing the rain was subsiding. The rain stopped as quickly as it had begun which is common in this part of the country. The sky was starting to lighten. Soon the sun would be up and their clothes would dry. The chill will be driven from their bones.

Nate felt he needed to be out of there before the daylight. He did not wish to be discovered. People might start to wonder what this white man was doing. Many had died along this border and he did not wish to join that group. If anyone suspected him to be an agent of the American government, he felt he was dead.

He reached the conclusion he could do no more for this woman. He rose from the ground and turned to leave.

"Senor, senor, please, oh please," she said and pointed across the river.

Nate shook his head and said to himself. *What does she want?* No more had the thought pasted thru his mind than it dawned on him. *She wants me to help her across the river. No, by God, I cannot do that. I cannot break our laws but how could he tell her.* He knew if she tried on her own, she would likely die. He could not have that on his conscience. Damn he was in a catch twenty-two situation. He struggled for excuses that would not help but was having trouble finding one.

The woman rose from the ground and walked up to him. She kissed him on the cheek. She then opened her clothing down the front exposing her breasts and crock. She smiled at him and pointed to the breasts and the hairy place between her legs. Tempting, very tempting, she was offering to repay the kindness for saving her child. She had nothing else to offer. She was in her twenties and had a beautiful body.

She pointed to her body, to him and then across the river. She was smiling brightly waiting for a response.

Damn, he thought, *she is offering me her body if I will help her across the river.*

He resented himself for being there; wishing he'd never came to this place, on this night.

The sky was getting lighter and he must decide quickly on a course of action. *What the hell, two more will not make any difference.*

He took the child from her and took her by the hand. The three waded into the water. Nate struggled to maintain his footing as he inched his way the thirty yards across the river. Minutes later, they walked up the bank on the U.S. side.

The woman was so excited she again offered him her body.

"No, you don't have to do that. Get going it will soon be light," he told her not knowing how much she understood.

She smiled and taking her child from him, she turned and hurried up the bank and out of sight.

Silently he hoped she had made it.

Hurriedly, he waded back across the river and walked the hundred yards or so to the pickup truck he came in. It was well camouflaged in the tall sagebrush, as tall as a man was.

It was but a ten-minute drive into Ciudad Juarez over what passed as roads, here in Mexico. *In the U.S., we would call these trails, not roads,* Nate was thinking. He bounced around over rocks and soil for a good part of the time. He was relieved and thankful for the rain for at least there was no dust.

The sun was up and it already felt like a very hot day coming up. Nate drove into the courtyard of an old hacienda just after six AM. Dismounting from the truck, he walked to the porch and entered the house. The others were up and seated around the huge table that once fed twenty men. Ranch hands when this was a thriving cattle ranch. Drought and years of low cattle prices had taken its toll. The young people had left for the cities and only four ranch hands and the old man and wife who owned the property stayed. The ranch hands were loyal to the old man because some of their family members had worked there for decades. If you asked them why they stayed, you would get the same answer from everyone of them. They would say they did not like the cities and preferred the open range and clear air. Beside they had nowhere to go. This place was as good as any, you would hear.

Delbert, Katrina, Bradley, Carl, Ed, and Don were all sitting around the table waiting for breakfast to be served.

"How'd it go boss," Ed asked.

"That's just fine. I am soaked to the skin, had to wade the damn river and nearly drown. I did find a crossing used by the Mexicans and it will be worth watching. I saved a child from drowning when his mother dropped him in the river. I ended up helping her and the child cross the border and it is not eight yet. Hell of a day coming up," Nate replied, "damn I'm hungry."

"Damn boss, I thought we were here to stop illegal's from crossing not help them," with a cheesy smile on his face, Delbert responded.

"Ah, go to hell," Nate replied as he flung his hat at Delbert.

The old man and his wife came out of the kitchen carrying platters of pancakes, eggs and bacon. They deposited these on the table and hurried away. They returned with two pots of coffee and sat one at each end of the table. They all sat down to eat.

The General had told Nate, the old man's name was Pedro and the woman Lorena. This thought brought a flashback of how he had gotten to Mexico.

Nate was sitting on the patio, in Colombia, enjoying the sights and sound of the city. A rain last night cleaned the air and it smelled oh so good. Loretta sat next to him as they finished breakfast. These two had been married a year and had gotten use to the ways of each other. They were very happy and Nate thanked God every night for his blessings. His life was complete and he looked forward to growing old with his wife. He had gotten use to the quiet life, but missed the excitement of covert work. He did not miss the killing. It was more the challenge of not being caught. It also had a lot to do with patriotism. He loved the U.S. and had always been willing to lay his life on the line. At fifty, he knew he was slowing down and had to quit. He had also fallen head over heels in love with Loretta. She had this restaurant and bar in Columbia and everything was perfect. He looked to going home.

He often wondered about his friends. The ones he had served with in Nam and who had helped him with slowing the drugs coming out of Colombia. On that caper, they had all earned enough to retire on when returning to the U.S.

They were just finishing their second cup of coffee when the intercom phone rang.

"I'll get it," Nate said, "and I'll get another pot of coffee. It's too nice a day to hurry into."

"Yes," Nate said into the phone.

"Nate," said the bartender, "sorry to disturb you but there's a two star general here to see you. Says his name is Scofield. Should I send him up?"

"Yes and another cup and more coffee. Thanks," Nate replied and hung up.

Nate returned to the table with a puzzled look on his face that was noticed.

"What's wrong?" she asked.

"Nothing Honey, there's a general Scofield here to see me. You remember the general I told you about when we were sinking the drug ships. He must be on vacation and decided to stop by. There is more coffee on the way and another cup for the general. I'll go wait for him at the stairs," Nate told her.

He walked back inside and to the door. Opening the door and looking down the stairs he saw the General coming to visit.

"Hi, General, come on up. We're having coffee," came out as the General reached the top stair.

"Hello, Nate," said the General as he held out his hand.

The two men shook and Nate directed his guest back to the table. Reaching it, he introduced Loretta and the General.

"General Scofield this is my wife and honey this is General Scofield," Nate said.

"Well what a beautiful woman your wife is Nate," he said and reached down and shook her hand.

"Sit down General and have some coffee," she invited him.

As she spoke, the door opened and an employee hurried in with a big pot of coffee. Placed it and the extra cup on the table then departed.

"Now general you're in for a treat. This coffee is real Colombia coffee. It is nothing like they sell at home. This coffee bites back," Nate, joked as he poured the General's cup.

The General lifted the cup to his lips and took a sip.

"My lord this is great coffee, Nate. Remind me to pick up some on my way out today."

"Sure, in fact we'll give you a couple pounds. What brings you down here General? You look dressed for vacation. If you need a guide around town, I can do that for you. Forgive us for being so slow to get around but we do not have to. Night time is our working time and we love it," Nate shared with him.

"Yes, I have a few days off and wanted to see how you were doing. I have always loved this part of the world so I keep coming back every few years. My Nate, you folks have a lovely place and the view of the city is great. To sit here in the evening, sip brandy, smoking a cigar, looking at the lights of the city must be grand," was the response.

The next hour was spent catching up on news from the U.S. and changes happening in the military. Loretta caught the General up on Panama and Colombia as far as politics, way of life, etc.

Nate had a nagging feeling the General was not here on vacation. He was sure he would find out when he took the General on a tour of the city. He seemed cautious around Loretta, but when the two men were alone, Nate would find out.

After the morning coffee, it was decided Nate would take the General on a tour of the city.

"Honey, you don't mind if I take the General on a tour do you. We'll have lunch somewhere and talk over old times," Nate politely asked.

"No, course not. You two get out of here and I will concentrate on the menu for tonight. How long do you think you'll be gone?" she asked.

"Don't know, but maybe three or four hours. Why don't we have the General for dinner tonight and serve one of those delicious steaks," Nate answered.

"How about it General, would you stay for dinner. No vacation here is complete without having one of our steaks," Nate turned to the General.

"Well, yes I'd like that if it's not too much of a bother," he said.

"Then that's settled. We'll be off then and honey, I'll take the pickup," Nate said directing his comments to his wife.

The two men walked down the stairs and out the front door. Nate led the way around the end of the building to a small graveled area. He climbed into a brand new Chevrolet pickup truck. The General followed suit and they were soon moving through traffic.

"Ok, General, tell me just what the hell you're doing here and don't lie. You've got something on your mind and I want you to spit it out," Nate started the conversation.

"Not while you're driving. Is there somewhere we could have a conversation without being overheard? Perhaps over a cold drink," the General answered.

"Yeah, there's an American place down the road a piece. They are friends and he is a veteran. They have a couple enclosed dining areas for young lovers. They will not be busy this time of day. We'll go there," Nate said.

It was quiet for a couple minutes when Nate just had to say what was on his mind.

"I'll tell you right now General if you are down here to get me back into some damn covert scheme, the answer is no. I have a beautiful wife and nice quarters. Katrina and I have the world by the tail on a downhill pull. We have a very good bank account for our old age and the club makes us a damn good living. We have more money than we can spend so do not give me no jive about the flag, our country, etc. I have done my duty and my time, so get someone else. If you are just on vacation that is different and I am glad to see you. I have often wondered what you were doing, etc. You are always welcome here and you know that but no business. Understand?" Nate finished and anxiously awaited a response.

The General stared out the window as they moved thru traffic. His thoughts were on how he could get Nate to sign onto the dangerous mission he came here for. He knew it would take some doing but how. That was the question.

"Let's talk when we get to the bar you mentioned," was his response to Nate.

Nate pulled into the parking lot of a nice looking place. The color of the place and a sign showed it was an American bar. The name was The Rio Grande. The General assumed the owner must be Texan.

The two walked in and found it to be cool and quite quaint. The bandstand and dance floor was small and on your left as you entered. The hardwood floor shined in the dim lighting. Nate spoke to the General,

"Let's take that enclosed booth at the rear," he said as they walked along the bar.

The bartender nodded to them as they pasted his station.

The two sat down and shortly a cute little blonde server appeared in a mini-skirt. She smiled at them as she spoke.

"Good morning gentlemen, may I take your order?"

"Hi beautiful, how are you this morning. Bring us a couple mugs of cold beer. We have business to talk over so we will wave for any second rounds, Ok. Tell Tex I said hello," Nate offered.

"Will do handsome, how's the wife."

"She's fine, now of you go for the beer," Nate said as a way of nudging her away.

"Mind if I smoke, Nate. I still have the cursed habit," said the General.

"No, go ahead. I kicked the habit when I married. I now have better things to do and need all the breath I can muster," Nate replied with a big grin.

A couple minutes later, the server returned with the beer and Nate gave her a five and told her to keep the change.

"Thanks," said the General as he tipped the mug towards Nate. A jester of thanks seldom used any more.

"You're welcome, now let's have it. Are you on vacation or here on a mission to suck me into another covert action? Now do not lie to me General. We have been thru too much to play those silly C.I. A. games. Come on I'm listening," Nate said.

"Damn it, Nate you are going to have to trust me and not assume these things. Maybe I just wanted to see how you are doing. You've done some fine work for me in the past and we respect each other," returned the General.

"Respect yes, but we both know if you have some dirty work that needs done, you're not above being sneaky to get so called volunteers," Nate replied.

"Ok, Nate, you're right. I suppose you have read about or saw on TV what is going on up north. The Mexican /U.S. border is burning up with the Mexicans trying to get across into the U.S. In one month, eleven hundred people killed by the drug cartels. Some were police officers from both sides and several innocent people. Every since the President decided to not close the borders they came. They were criminals and dopers. The same group of men you talked to before your last mission. Remember, at the C.I. A. headquarters in Washington. Remember?"

"Yes, I remember," Nate, replied.

"We treated you well then and will this time. We need to put about a six-man team up there as our eyes and ears. Thirty days should do it. It's not so far you couldn't come home for a weekend a time or two, interested," the general inquired leaning across the table as if trying to insist on a yes.

"No, I'm not. You have not told me a damn thing that would take me from this life for a little excitement. Besides, you say as your eyes and ears are baloney. Am I to assume there will be no killings, General?"

"Yes, but only when you have to protect yourselves. If it becomes necessary, it is your call, not ours. Different from last time, huh," said the General.

"Go on General, there's more to this than you're telling," Nate said leaning back against the cushion.

"Well, yes there is. We need people at three or four locations to count the people coming across. We need to know if the Mexican army is assisting people getting across. We suspect some army officers are also drug dealers and we need to know their names, etc. It would be helpful if we knew the Mexican police were also involved. We know they are, but not sure who or how many. You know stuff like that. We need this information for the congress. We feel they would take action to close the border if they had this kind of information. The White House is lying to them and they are not sure what to do or who to believe. Nate, it will be a little dangerous just because of the location. You and your team should have no problem there. You have always been good at ducking trouble. We will make it worth your while. What do you say," finished the General.

"You mentioned my team. Who would that be? My boys have all gone home and started a new life after that last mission. I'm not even sure where they are right now," Nate said.

CHAPTER 2

"I do and I've talked to everyone of them including Katrina," the general said smiling, "you should know I would."

"Oh, and what did they say. Thanks but no thanks, I'll bet," were Nate's answer.

"You should also know I'd never come here unless they agreed to my offer. So far, Delbert, Ed and Don have agreed and the others are thinking about it. I think they are waiting to hear if you will lead them. In fact, the three will not go unless you do. So Nate, my boy, I need you. Your country needs you. Will you at least hear my offer," said the General with a solemn tone.

"Oh, what the hell, Lay it on me and it had better be good but let's get another beer first. I have a feeling I'll need it," Nate said as he raised his glass to get the attention of the server.

The offer was a cash wage of one hundred thousand dollars for one month's work. If by some reason this team was to kill a terrorist or two, Uncle Sam would pay ten thousand each if killed in Mexico. Of course, as in the deal with Colombia, the government would not be able to help get the team out nor would they admit to knowing anything about these Americans. In exchange, all the government wanted was how many terrorists were infiltrating with the Mexicans. If they came across information on where and when an attack was to occur, they would want that.

"The money's good, but I have enough so why in the hell would I risk my neck for the U.S… I have paid my dues to my country and I do not even live there. One of theses days, someone is going to die on one of these covert missions. All my team, around fifty years of age, should stay retired. The war game you guys play is for the young and foolish not us older people. No, I cannot help you General. I have got too much to lose. Thanks but no thanks," Nate informed him.

"Remember your old buddy Sam; Sam Brown I believe. You knew him even before Nam. You grew up together didn't you," responded the General.

"Yes, I remember Sam. He saved my life a couple times in Nam. I owe him big time. What the hell does he have to do with this?" Nate asked.

"I recruited him over a month ago and he's somewhere along the border. I was hoping you would go in there, do the job, and bring him out with you. We have lost track of him and he may be dead. If so, we need to know that also. Nate you and your crew are the only ones who can do this," said the General.

"Why don't you use Special Ops for this sort of mission? They are trained for just such a job," Nate reminded him.

"No, they are more for going in quick and coming right out. They are also good at tracking and attacking the enemy like in Iraq. The Mexican/American border is not Iraq. See my problem," answered the General.

"You bastard, you bastard, you recruited Sam just to get to me. You sneaky bastard," Nate said with a raised voice.

"Well sleep on it. I do not need to know until morning. I will be leaving around ten o'clock. There will be no hard feelings if you're turning me down. I would not want to leave such a beautiful wife for a month. Come on lets see the rest of the city," the General said as he stood up to go.

Nate rose to his feet and tossed a ten on the table, departing with his friend.

The rest of the afternoon was pleasant and passed quickly as the two recounted war stories.

"Nate, do you ever wonder how we've gone thru so much and survived?" asked the General.

"Sometimes," Nate responded after a slow pause. Pictures of the dangerous times sped thru his head. He had always been lucky but never more so than in life and living. The narrow escapes recalled and besides luck, he knew it was because he was always prepared, even to die if he had to.

Nate glanced at his watch and saw it was four o'clock.

"Time to head for the barn and I'll discuss your proposition with Loretta. I really don't want to go, but let's see what she says," Nate said.

"Listen, Nate if you don't want to go, I won't hold it against you. I envy you and wished I was retired and living the good life. Another year and I will be. Oh, I almost forgot. I need to stop by a hotel and get a room. Can we stop and do that before we go to your place for dinner?" asked the General.

"No, you don't need to do that. We have a guest room and you can stay there tonight. After breakfast in the morning, we will talk again. You don't say a word to Loretta, understand?" Nate threw at his guest.

"Sure, I understand," came the reply.

Arriving at home, the two joined Loretta on the patio.

"Hi, honey," Nate, said as he kissed his wife, "we had a splendid afternoon. I even saw things I'd not seen before. We need to get out and around the city more. Oh, I told the General he could stay in the guest room tonight. He has to be at the airport by nine thirty. His plane leaves at ten. One question, when do we eat?" Nate said with a grin.

"That's all you men think about is eating. Not till six. We have other guests coming. They should be here any minute now. We will have drinks before dinner. I've already talked to the kitchen staff about what we're having and I think everyone will like it," she advise he mate.

"Who's the other guests and do I know them?" Nate inquired.

"Yes, I think you know them and I'm not telling. It is a surprise. You and the General freshen up and I'll call down for the drinks. Now hurry, the others will soon be here," Loretta said.

"This way General, the boss has spoken," said Nate as he smiled at her. She winked at him in a returning jester.

Returning from the bathroom, the doorbell rang.

"I'll get it honey," Nate volunteered.

Reaching the door, Nate opened it to look into the faces of old friends.

"Hi, Nate can we come in," said Carl and Katrina at the same time.

"Of course you can. Come in here," Nate replied and gave both a big hug.

Recovered from the shock of seeing friends that he never expected to see again, Nate addressed them.

"What the hell are you two doing way down here?" No don't answer that," he continued, half turning to look at the General. The General just shrugged his shoulders.

"God, it's good to see you. Where's the baby?" he asked with a grin.

"We can't have one and really we're too old to want one so we take steps not to have one," was the couple's response.

"You remember Loretta, don't you," Nate asked Carl.

"Yes, of course," nodding her way, then he introduced Katrina.

"Katrina, this is the General who bailed us out on the mission down here," Carl said.

"Well, sit down and I'll get the bar to bring up some drinks. Margarita's ok. Do not be shy we have anything you want."

"Well if it's not too much of a bother, could I just have a beer and whiskey for a chaser?" Carl asked. Nate and the General asked for the same.

"Carl and Katrina called a couple hours ago from the airport and asked for you. I remembered the names and so I invited them for dinner," Loretta said as them all settled for a great get-to-gather.

The door opened and in came the bartender and a female server. They brought a bucket of ice and a case of cold beer. They went to the small bar and set it up for serving. The bartender stayed and the woman left by the stairs. A huge pitcher of margaritas sat on the bar.

"Who wants margaritas," he asked.

Both of the women raised their hands and were served first. Next bottles of beer opened and straight shots of whiskey served. A bottle of whiskey was set in the middle of the table for service purposes. The evening was a pleasant one as the men hashed over old times and two women kept up on the latest fashions and gossip. Around seven o'clock dinner was served.

The very best of steaks served to each other's taste. Red boiled potatoes, fried rice and creamed broccoli. A platter of fresh fruit placed on the table. Grapes, melon, peaches and oranges, all prepared to eat. The oranges were without peeling and sectioned, peaches peeled and sliced as was the melons. A meal fit for a king.

The meal went slowly as if no one wanted to break up the atmosphere of the reunion. Once the meal was over and the table cleared, wine and a brandy served. Everyone sat admiring the lights of the city.

Carl and Katrina were the first ones to move and say goodnight.

"We need to get to bed. It is late. We will see you in the morning Nate for your decision and thank you Loretta for a wonderful night and great food," Carl said as Katrina nodded in agreement.

Nate rose up and walked them to the door.

"Come for breakfast in the morning at eight. We can talk more then. There's a pay phone right at the bottom on the right to call a cab from," Nate said as the two started down the stairs.

"Sure will and thanks Nate," Katrina said as the two reached the bottom of the stairs.

Returning to the table Nate found everyone standing and saying good night to each other. They all felt it was late and they should go.

"Everyone is invited back for breakfast in the morning at eight. The General is leaving for the airport at nine for a flight home. See you all then," sounding more like a question than a statement.

"See the bartender General and he'll show you to the guest room. It is on the lower floor. If you need anything, just ask. Ok?" Nate advised.

"No, I don't think I'll need a thing and thanks for your hospitality," said the General as he started down the stairs.

With the goodnights all said, Nate turned to face Loretta. She was a few feet away and had a frown on her face. Nate knew what was coming and was not quite sure what to say.

"What did they mean by your decision in the morning," she said.

Nate decided that honesty was the best policy so he started his story.

"Well you see the General wasn't here for a vacation. He came here to see me," Nate said.

"I had that figured out when he first got here and I'm sure you did too. He wants you to go on another one of those damn missions, didn't he," she said with a hesitation in her voice. She was almost starting to shake and so Nate hurried on.

"Yes, honey he did and I told him no. Those days are gone forever and I am happily married and like my life here. No more damn dangerous missions. I want to live out my life with you. No more taking chances like in the past. I am too old for that sort of thing anyway. Don't worry honey, I'm not going," he stated a very direct statement.

He walked over and put his arms around her. He could feel her trembling and he hated this had affected her this way. After a couple minutes, she raised her head and kissed him, a tender kiss.

"Come on honey, let's hit the sack. Morning will be here before we know it," Nate cooed in her ear and hoping the matter was closed.

As they reached the bed, she turned and pulling his head, down kissed him long and passionate. He could feel her need thru his clothes. His hands started unbuttoning her clothing down the back. As he undid the bottom button, he slid his hand down the rounding of her buttocks. He pushed her panties aside placing his hand firmly in place. He gently rubbed her butt with tenderness.

God, she feels good, he was thinking. As he rubbed in this area, she pushed closer to him. A faint moan rising from her throat was telling the story. He moved his hand lower. Now anxious to get to making fantastic love to this woman was all he could think of. This of course sped up his fingers. They moved to her shoulders and lightly lifted the dress, then pulled it downward over her breasts and on down until it lay upon the floor.

As he looked over her body, his feelings intensified. She pushed away for a minute and helped him remove her bra. He then had to kneel to remove her panties as they were still standing. As he straightens up, he again realized what a woman he had for a wife.

Their lovemaking was more intense this time, than before. It was as though both knew Nate would be going. The love flowing between was from one side trying to keep him and from the other side convincing her he had to. Sam Brown kept coming up as if a ghost between them.

Sam was an old friend from Nam who had saved Nate's life a couple times and he always felt he owed Sam.

In his heart, Nate knew that Sam himself would tell him to stay home. Sam himself would never ask Nate to jump into this kind of danger for him. Of course, it was not Sam asking. It was the General. Nate was keenly aware the General would tell him anything to get him to help. The General would not out and out lie but maybe shade the truth a little.

After Nate and Loretta made love three times, she fell asleep exhausted. Nate could not sleep because of the nagging image of Sam, the danger he was in and should he go help.

After an hour or so, he got up and went to the bar. He poured a healthy brandy, picked up a cigar that had been there for months. Walking to the patio, he sat on the railing and lit the cigar. He could always think well when smoking or at least he thought so. This was the first smoke he had had in months. The sharp taste of the brandy warmed him from the inside out. For once in his life, he did not know what to do.

Nate finished the brandy and was about to put the cigar out when he heard someone behind him. Loretta put her hand on his shoulder, saying nothing for a long time finally words came out.

"If this Sam means so much to you, go help find him. I will understand. I do not want anything coming between us. I'm so in love with you, I can think of nothing else. To be honest I am afraid to let you go and yet afraid to keep you home. Either way might be disastrous. How long will you be gone?" she asked with a slight shiver in her voice.

"A month and it is not like the one here. We will be like spies and report what we see. We are to take no actions on our own. The General needs to know how many terrorists are coming into the U.S. thru Mexico. If we can find out where they will strike, he also needs to know. No killing except is self defense," Nate told her as he put his arm around her, pulling her close.

"Go Nate, I want you to go, but come back alive. Our love can handle it. Just do not get killed. I would never forgive you if you did. In fact I would become and undercover agent and kill the bastards who killed you," expressing herself.

Nate was shocked because he had never heard her use this kind of language.

He turned, kissed her and they walked back to bed hand in hand.

Two weeks later Nate and his old crew, crossed over into Mexico at the border town of Ciudad Juarez. They arrived one by one so as not to arouse any suspicion. A group of seven Americans would not only get the attention of drug cartels, also the Mexican Police. They wanted to do neither. Covert mission means just what it says. Once in country, they were on their own.

They all posed as tourists and dressed that way. Carl and Katrina crossed over as man and wife, which they were, but the rest as single sightseers. Their plan was to meet at a hotel on the western end of town. Its name was Las Verdi. An older but beautiful, two story hotel. It was spread out over several acres. It contained sixty rooms, always in demand. The group was to arrive two or three days apart.

This city was a jumping off point to the border in all directions for illegals. From here, they could go in different directions. Some Mexicans, mostly women and children would merely walk across the bridges into El Paso, Texas. They could also travel west to Arizona, New Mexico or California. Between El Paso and the Arizona's western border was the area of interest to the federal government. This was the assignment. It was a long border and desolate land. There were areas for farming where there was enough water to support this sort of industries. There were miles and miles of dry forebode land next to Arizona, New Mexico and Texas. This was a hot spot for concealing what may come across the border.

This area had little border patrol to worry about because they were stretched so thin. This, it was rumored, was where the Mexican army assisted illegal's crossing. This the more likely spot for terrorists to sneak in bombs, bomb materials, dirty bombs and all types of arms. This was their target area. Hot and dry land that can kill you in a couple days, if you are not prepare for it.

Now, in August, the heat was about as intense as it can get.

Nate was one who walked across one of the bridges. Some of the others took taxis, rented a car, etc. Nate's vehicle would be waiting at the hacienda.

Their meeting date was August 9. Nate was the first to arrive on the eighth, early in the day. Carl and Katrina were next then the others came by car or cab. By five PM, they were all registered and hungry.

Nate called the others and asked to have dinner at six. They could eat together but to act as though they had just met. Try to look stupid as was American tourists. Nate drew on his experiences from the past to arrive at the conclusion that when on vacation, Americans seem to leave their brains at home.

Just prior to going down to the bar, Nate received a call from the General.

"Hi, Nate glad you could make it. How about the others? Are they there and raring to go," he said in a cheerful voice.

"They are all here General and seem to be in a good mood. This damn heat might change all that by nightfall. How are you and why the call. You knew we would be here," Nate answered.

"To the west and within minutes of the river and town is an old hacienda. Your team has to go there in the morning. It has been leased in your name and you have it for a month. You will be more comfortable there and you can plan, talk without being over heard. A young man by the name of Jose will pick you up at nine and run you out there. It has a cook and a man who takes care of the grounds. They will not be in your way except at mealtime. The woman will do the cooking and serving. The old person can get you anything you need accept guns. That is my job if you need them. Both these people hate the drug runners and the others causing trouble on the border. They also believe the Mexicans who wish to come to the U.S. should do it legally. Play the act of being tourists and they may feel comfortable talking with you. They have many stories of people sneaking across the borders and they may give you tips on just where the best areas are for bringing in guns, etc. Jose will also have a package for you. It contains cell phones for each of you. Only yours and Delbert's have my number entered into the speed dial system. The phones are fixed so no one can intercept calls but you. Just like before. Any questions Nate?"

"No, not right now but soon I'm sure. Goodbye General," Nate signed off and hung up.

About six, they started drifting into the bar and found Nate and Delbert already there. They were sitting at a huge table that seated eight. This was the reason Nate had picked it.

Carl and Katrina were the first to arrive. As they entered the bar, they saw Nate and Delbert.

"Hey, look honey. There are some Americans. Let us see if we can sit with them. They may know of some places for us to see that we overlooked," Carl said loud enough for the bartender to hear.

The others came in one by one and soon all were there. The same type of conversation took place and they were told they were welcome at the table. This is not unusual because Americans seemed to flock together when overseas. There is just something about being with your own people that makes you comfortable. They all shook hands and acted as through this was the first time they had seen each other. The conversation was on, how are you, where you from, etc. There was absolutely no conversation that, if over heard, could be interpreted as their real purpose for being in Mexico.

When a waiter appeared, beer and whisky were ordered all around and a margeritta for Katrina. Questions were asked about what was in some of the food listed on the menu. Nate was proud of his little group because they were acting like tourists, pains in the butt. It seems everyone at the table ordered something different. The waiter was patient but you could see he was a little strained by all the questions. In addition, they all asked for separate checks except Carl and Katrina. Inwardly Nate was laughing but he was careful not to smile.

Soon afterwards, salsa and chips arrived along with a server who brought the drinks.

After a two-hour, dinner and several drinks, each person seemed to go their own directions. Some went for a walk, some to the bar and others to their rooms. All knew tomorrow would be a long day.

Nate walked to the bar and sat down for a beer. The bartender was very friendly and Nate was thinking he might have information they could use. He had to be careful not to be too curious about what was going on along the border because you never knew who was listening. He decided to start out with what had been the papers.

"Senor," Nate started, "the papers say things are bad and dangerous along the border. I have a rented pickup truck and wanted to drive west up close to the border. Is it safe enough for a tourist who only wants to take pictures?"

"Si, senor," was the reply, "things are bad up that way but if you don't get involved perhaps you are safe. Many murders committed of police and drug dealers. Drug dealers are battling to hold their territory others want. If you go that way, be sure you are not out there after dark. Horrible things happen after dark. Better be here, senor."

"Yeah, that's what the papers say. I guess many honest Mexicans are also being killed who just want to go to the U.S. for work. Feed their families and such. That true also," Nate asked.

"Si, many pay hundreds and thousands to be taken across to America. Many die on the other side in the desert because of the greed of those who take them. They drop them off in the desert with no water and they die. Yet more come everyday, this is a bloody time in history. In addition, people say terrorists come this way and sneak in with my people. They take hostages and force them to hide them within the group. No good sons-of-bitches."

At this point, the bartender walked to the other end of the bar to serve a couple men who had just come in.

Well, Nate was satisfied they were in the right place. In the morning, they would be moving to the hacienda. Then they could make their plans and began their spying. He hoped that spying was all they had to do but something inside told him it would not be that easy. He would bet his bottom dollar the General put another one over on him.

At six AM, the group all settled around the large table to have breakfast. At least that was what it was going to look like to anyone watching.

They all had a regular ranch style breakfast, lots of coffee and a few minutes to say goodby and exchange addresses. Nate marveled at how good they were at this. They took their time have the meal because all knew that Jose would be there at nine. Once breakfast was over, they paid their bills and left one by one. Each one came separately except for the man and wife. They had all rented Ford Bronco's because of the terrain in which they would be working.

Nate had told them to move out west a little ways out of sight of town and wait. By a quarter till nine they were all gone except Nate. He sat on a bench outside the door and waited. He was smoking a slender cigar when a young man drove up and stopped in front of him.

"Senor Nate?' he asked.

"Si, that's me," Nate replied, "is you Jose?"

"Si, follow me. Where are the others?" he asked in broken English.

Nate got up and walked the couple of paces to the kid's vehicle. Leaning through the window, he answered.

"They are just out of town to the west. They will follow when they see us pass. Remember Jose, we must keep this secret. If word got out, we would have to fight for our lives. Savvy?" Nate asked.

"Yes, I savvy. Follow me," he said and started slowly moving down the street.

Nate had to run to his Bronco for fear of losing him. In a matter of five minutes, they were traveling thru the sagebrush and bounching over dirt roads. As they put more distance between them and town, other vehilcles fell in behind them. The team was all there.

Thirty minutes later, after winding thru the countryside and dusty, dirty trails, they pulled into the courtyard of what was to be home for the next month.

As one just arriving, the place looked old but in good shape. The caretaker had done well in keeping the place in good repair. The entire group was pulling in as Nate dismounted his vehicle and stepped over into the shade. He waited until they were all out of their Bronco's before he spoke.

"Let's go in and introduce ourselves and meet the help. As soon as this is done we'll pick out our bedrooms," Nate said.

The main doors were massive and heavy as he pushed thru them and entered the living room area. The group was awe struck with the beauty of the place. The lighting was all attached to the walls in beautifully made lamps. They were electric but Nate would bet they were candles or oil when first installed. There were no overhead lights at all. There were three colorful blankets hanging on the stucco walls. The furniture was hand carved wood for arms and legs. Two couches faced each other in the middle of the room. They were about eight feet apart. At both ends of the area were two chairs. A huge coffee or perhaps an old style serving table divided them. Ten people could sit comfortable in this area. The floor was covered with eighteen-inch tiles of various colors. They were laid out in such a way that was beautiful and made the room quaint and yet comfortable. The windows were large and set to get the best of the sunlight in both the morning and the afternoon. Several lamps sat on tables around the room. The room was huge according to what was built today. The room itself was about sixty feet by sixty. All the lamps were old and of mexcian style. Knick-knacks were placed around in such a way they gave the room charm.

As the group was still standing, Jose said he would get the caretaker. He took a right turn and disappeared through a door on the backside of the house.

Approximatly five minutes passed before the door opened and a Mexican, dressed in white, appeared.

"Oh, you folks must be the renters. Who is Senor Nate," he asked in broken English.

"That's me," Nate announced, "and you must be Pedro," Nate surmised and extended his hand. Pedro accepted the hand and shook it.

Nate introduced each of his team.

"May we go to our rooms and freshen up. That road getting here is really dusty," Nate asked.

"Si, take the hallway over there," he pointed to the left and take your pick. There are rooms for each to have a room, with the married couple sharing one," he said as he dug into his pocket, pulling out some keys. He handed them over to Nate who passed them out later when they had picked their rooms.

"Thanks, we'll get to our rooms and I'll just wander around getting use to every thing. Is that all right?" Nate asked him.

"Si, the place is yours for a month. Make yourselves to home. Lunch will be ready at one P.M. If you need anything, I will be in the kitchen. Oh, I almost forgot. The refrigidator in the kitchen and the one over there are filled with beer. The bar is right over there. Help yourselves to anything you need," and he walked back the way he would came.

"I better get going," Jose, said, "is there anything else you will need, Senor Nate."

"Yes, I understand you can get us guns. Is that right," Nate asked.

"Si, do you need some?" Jose asked.

"Yes, come sit down and let's have a cold beer," Nate said.

"I'll get the beer," Katrina spoke up. "It kind of reminds me of my old job last time we were on a caper," she said grinning. As she went for the beer, the group seated themselves at the table.

Soon everyone had a cold beer and Nate retrieves a piece of paper from the top of a desk in the living room. He seated himself and sat down at the end chair at the table. Jose sat next to him.

"Alright, listen up. With the brush and sage around here, I think the best rifles would be the 30-30 carbines. They hold seven shots and are shorter than many of the rifles on today's market. Any objections?" no one answered so Nate addressed Jose.

"Get us each a 30-30 and three boxes of shells each. You will come around in case we need more ammo?" Nate said to Jose.

"Si, I'll be out every week. You can depend on that," Jose responded.

"Ok, also get us a twelve gage shotgun for each of our vehicles and plenty of ammo. A make sure there's water canteen for each of us. The kind you can snap on your belt. Also, bring us all a hunter's type knifes and scabbards… Check with the old man, Jose and see if he has a hat for each of us. If he does not you, bring some. The sun down here is a killer. I think that is all. Can you have these here by day after tomorrow?

"Si, by noon. If that is all then I'll be going," he rose and turned toward the door.

"Oh," Nate said, "are you being paid for these guns. I wasn't given any money to pay for them."

"Si, it has all been arranged. Not to worry senor," and he continued out the door.

"Can you trust that one," Brad asked of Nate.

"I don't know. The General is the one who arranged for his help. We will trust him until shown otherwise. The General is crafty but he usually gets trustworthy people. I think the kid is all right. I have a good feeling about him," Nate said.

"Well let's freshen up and look around till lunch. Stay in the dining room after lunch and we will discuss a plan of action. I want everyone's opinion on how we do this. This is a little different from anything we have done so far. Come with ideas. I am taking a shower then a nap. See you at noon," he continued and left the group, heading down the hall.

He checked out the rooms and took the last one to the rear. He liked this one because it had and outside door from the room to the lawn. It also was near the rear exit. This was an attractive feature you never know if or when you might have to use it. He tried the keys in the other doors and left them in the locks for the others.

The furnishings were exquisite like the rest of the house. Bright colored blankets were wall hangings. Colorful pictures hung in between. The pictures were of people, flowers and beautiful women. All tastefully done. A very comfortable place to hang your hat.

The final inspection was of the bed. He sat on the edge and found the mattress was soft enough, yet firm enough for good sleeping. So far, everything was perfect. Nate hoped it stayed that way. The real test will come when they started their surveillance along the border.

Lunch was served at exactly 1 PM. This told the crew that when the cook sat a time for meals, that is when it would be.

The meal consisted of tamales, fresh fruit, and Mexican bread in a round loaf, wine and coffee.

The team ate hardy and the meal was soon over. The old couple came out to clear the table and Katrina jumped up to help. As soon as the dishes were cleared away, the old man brought out a box of cigars, real Cuban cigars.

The old man was pleased with the surprise look on Nate's face at the sight.

"The man who arranged this place for you also said you might like a good cigar after meals," he said grinning.

Each man took one as the box was passed around. After everyone had a cigar going, the old man informed him or her he would leave the box on the bar.

Very nice of the General, Nate was thinking.

CHAPTER 3

Everyone was present at the meeting to discuss how he or she would go about the task at hand. Nate had the floor and began.

"Well here we are again. Going into God knows what and we are all aware of the danger. The good thing about this mission is we do not have to kill anyone. We can but only to protect others and ourselves. The General did say he would appreciate it if we killed any terrorists we ran across. If we do not kill them, he hopes we can get in close enough to find out where they plan to attack in the U.S. This leaves us with the decision of do or do not. I will not make that decision for you. You make your own. Here we are merely Spies. You all brought along a spiral notebook to keep track of what we find. We will select our posts now and move off to our assigned position. If one of the positions gets too hot to stay there, return here and we will figure out what to do. Everyone will come back here for the weekends and rest. We can re-supply ourselves before going back. This will also give us a chance to discuss what we have learned and I will pass it on to the General. He wants a weekly report. Any questions."

"I assume we will be working in pairs. If so you'll make those assignments now or in the morning?" Delbert asked.

"That's the next item on the agenda. I will make the assignments because I know you all work well together. Here how it will go. I will pick two and they will pick where they wish to be assigned. The assignments will be from here to the Californian border or at least in that direction. I think we should stay at intervals of ten miles apart. That may change but we will try that for now. Ok, Carl and Katrina will work together because they are married. What post do you two want to work?" Nate asked.

"The one next to yours twenty miles out from here," was Carl's reply.

Everyone paused for a drink and a draw on their cigars. Everyone thinking of tomorrow and what it will bring. Nate continued.

"Don do you and Brad wants to work the next post? It's thirty miles from here," Nate said.

"Ed and Delbert will go the farthest one out. Delbert you take care of the old person. He's really too old for this kind of work," Nate smiling from ear to ear. Everyone knew he was kidding and everyone had a good laugh.

"I'll work alone and try to hook up with Sam Brown, an old friend who's somewhere in this area," he advised. "Remember if anyone is hurt or killed the partner will return here with the down comrade. I will make arrangements with the old man to call a doctor if that happens. The partner will stay here until the weekend and we will all decide what to do. Questions?"

No one said a thing.

"Oh, I almost forgot, we have to wait until Jose gets here tomorrow with the weapons. Sleep in, I have a feeling you will need it," Nate said.

Waving at Pedro at the kitchen doorway, Nate motioned him over.

"Pedro, was there a box delivered for us a day or two ago," he asked.

"Si, forgive me, I forgot. I'll get it," spoken as he turned and walked towards the back of the house.

In a couple minutes, he returned with a special delivery package. He sat it on the table, excused himself and walked back to the kitchen.

"Well folks this is the way we'll keep in touch," Nate said as he opened the box. Turning he pulled out a couple cell phones, tossed them to a couple team members and reached back inside the box. Again coming out with phones, tossing them to others. This was done until everyone had a phone.

"These are phones to keep each other informed and to call for help if need be. Inside the box are extra batteries and a list of phone numbers. Check the numbers on your phone and write your name after it on each list. This way we know who has what number. The phones are fixed so we can talk but encrypted so no one can listen in. Same as we did in Colombia. Do not use them unless you have to. We will recharge the batteries on weekends. You are responsible for your phone so take good care of them. They could mean your life. Clear?" Nate said.

Everyone nodded they understood.

At eleven o'clock, Jose drove into the courtyard and everyone came out to greet him. He opened up the back, exposing a crate of 30-30 carbine rifles. Everyone had used this rifle before and knew how to load and fire it Boxes of aminutition were transferred to each of their vehicles. Each one got a knife.

"Thanks Jose, we are in your debt," Nate said shaking his hand then he mentioned some paper targets in the front seat. They were retrived by Ed. Jose mounted up and drove away.

"About half mile to the west I spotted an opening that was flat. It would be a good place to sight in our rifles. Everyone mount up and let's go shoot," Nate said.

An hour later, they returned to the house to pick up some gear for the week. Rifles sighted to everyone's satisfaction.

"We'll see you folks on Saturday about noon. Have your wife fix a hot meal for our return," Nate told Pedro

"Si, she has a lunch packed for you to take with you. I will go get them for you," Pedro said seeming pleased he could help.

The old man hurried back inside and returned. He gave up the lunches, said good bye and returned to the house. The sun was already hot and the weather dry.

The crew was grateful for the food. They knew they would soon tire of the K-rations they were expected to eat. They had been loaded earlier by Jose. Everyone was told had to have a campsite, without a fire. A real camp-out. All had canteens filled with water and the maps showed where they could refill them. They all had their maps showing how to get where they were going and it was time.

They pulled out of the courtyard at thirty-minute intervils so as not to arouse any suspicion if anyone was watching.

Delbert and Ed were snaking thru the sagebrush at a slow rate of speed. The terrain was so that they did not dare speed or they would have torn the vehicle apart. The dust in spots was a least a foot deep. The rain a couple nights ago did not seem to have done much good. The powder fine dirt seemed to have dried out back to its powdery form.

"God, this dust will kill us. Let's stop and breathe some clean air Delbert," Ed begged.

"Ok, good idea. We are only about ten miles from our post and we can easily make it by dark. I will pull over here in the shade of this big tree and we will rest and have a drink of water. I'm as dry as a popcorn fart," Delbert returned the conversation. Now under the tree he turned off the Ford and stopped.

"Hey, Delbert, we haven't had lunch yet. Let's eat. It should still be cool. The cooler we have is a good one. We've been so damn anxious to get into action we forgot to eat," Ed stated.

They pulled a blanket and spread it out over the hood and proceed to unpack the cooler. With the blanket this way, they could sit on the fenders and place the food on the blanket. Nothing would slip off in this fashion.

"Hot damn," Ed said as he uncovered a couple cold beers. He handed one to Delbert and opened his. He raised the can to his lips and poured the cold liquid down his throat.

"Ah, that's good," he announced.

The two had a leasurely lunch and then moved on. They were anxious to get to their post and find a good spot to park before it got dark enough to use headlights.

Perhaps an hour later they came to a flat area. The area was about a mile across and was close to the border. There was really no way they could tell but according to their map they were right were they were supposed to be.

"Hey, Delbert look over there. See that big tree. Let's camp under it so we'll have the shade tomorrow," Ed said with some excitement.

"Sorry to pop your bubble, Ed but no we don't want to do that. The tree can be seen for miles around and that crossing over will head straight for it to get in the shade. Those who know this area will use it as place to meet family members. Most know you do not want to travel in large groups because that would bring attention to themselves. If gangs were robbing those coming over it would be a dead give away. I think we will find families and friends traveling in small groups to avoid them. In addition, if the Mexican police care and I do not think they do, they would spot larger groups. If they gather here at that tree and travel across the border they improve their changes of getting thru," Delbert informed him.

"Oh damn it. I'm just not thinking. Just want to get into shade. Well let us look for tall sagebrush to flop under. Will not be quite as good as your own bed but better than nothing. Any ideas?" Ed asked.

"Yeah, take your glasses and look to the east of that tree about two hundred yards. Looks like a grove of tall brush, etc. That is close enough to camp and sneak back toward that tree after dark. You agree," Delbert asked.

Ed was still looking thru his glasses and waited a couple minutes ro answer.

"Yes, I think you're right. Lets sneak around to the right and then turn straight into it," Ed suggested, "tomorrow we can look for a better place if we wish. Let us get to it before it gets dark.

Just as he got the words out a volume of shots rang out and they could hear the bullets flying by. They both hit the dirt.

"What'd you think Ed," Delbert said.

"I don't think they're shooting to hit us. Maybe scare us. You stay down and I'll find out," Ed said as he stood up. Looking around he could see three men walking towards them at a distance of about thirty yards.

"Hey gringo, you gangsters or American cops. Answer quickly or we kill you," said the tallest of the group.

"No, we are neither. We come here to hunt the deer and antlope. We are only armed with hunting rifles. Come look for yourself," Ed said hoping they would buy the lie.

"Ed, whats going on up there," Delbert asked.

"Stand up Delbert. Three people with guns and about thirty yards out and coming this way. Let us show them we are hunters. We have small rifles and hunting knives. I think they will buy it," Ed whispered to Delbert.

As they got closer, they three spred out so as not to be close to each other. To Delbert and Ed this meant they were professionals. Closer now their faces could be seen and they looked tough. The looked as though they lived out there in a cave or something. All at once they stopped.

The tall one in the middle stopped and asked.

"How many are you gringo," he said in broken English.

"Just two, no more and who are you to shoot at us," Delbert asked him. Ed nudged him.

"Damn, don't make him mad Delbert. I'd like to get out of here alive," Ed said in a strained voice.

"We are Mexican police looking for gangsters who waylay and kill our people trying to get into the U.S. We are protecting them," he said smiling.

Of the Americans neither liked this person nor his story. His smile was twisted and there was something sinister behind the smile. Ed and Delbert were both thinking the same thing. These are the bandits that are here to rob anyone crossing tonight.

"Show us your papers. My man will come over to get them and check you out. Move around to the front of the vehicle and stand a few feet apart," said the leader of this group. He nodded to the small man on their left who came forward and checked their papers. Once the task was completed he nodded to the leader.

"Your papers check out and now about the guns. Lets see them," ordered the tall one.

Delbert walked to the pickup door on the side away from the Mexicans. As he turned, he thought he heard the two Mexicans hanging back say something out of contex of police officers. A breeze was blowing in their direction, carrying sound. The tall one said something like as soon as we get their guns let them have it.

To Delbert this met to kill them, him and Ed. As he made his turn, he pretended to trip. Ed leaned over to help him up and Delbert whispered in his ear.

"They're going to kill us. I heard them say so. They are not cops, they are the bandits. When I open the door, I will toss you one of the thirty-thirtys and grab one for myself. We have to gun them down or die. Got it." Ed nodded. Both knew the rifles were loaded. They always were in hostile territory.

Both knew the risk was great but they realized without their guns they were dead. These types of men would rather go down fighting than to be slaughtered like sheep. The die is cast and action is called for.

"The guns are right here. I will give your man one to check. You'll see were just hunters," Delbert said as the other two moved in a few feet closer.

Delbert reached in and pulled out two rifles. He tossed one to Ed and quickly pulled back the hammer of his. He swung it around and fired into the chest of one the Mexican standing there. He quickly cocked the lever throwing another shell into the chamber. Swing over the hood he fired at the taller man and saw him go down. Another shot rang out and he saw the other man go down, Ed had fired at the remaining man. With all down it looked like they would live another day.

"Damn, Delbert, that was close. Who do you think they are?" Ed asked.

"Don't know but I hope to hell we didn't kill any policemen. If we did out tour of duty in Mexico just ended." Delbert responded.

"You check the bodies Ed and I'll get a shovel. The sand is soft here so this is where we'll bury them. We've got to hurry,"

Ed went through their pockets and found nothing to identify them as police. They were dirty and really needed a bath. Everything found only pointed to these three as regular Mexicans. The two breathed easier as they dug a grave. They were sure now the men were bandits. When finished with the burials, they drove to the location they have started for before this interruption. The sun was setting as they arrived.

They dug out their sleeping bags from the back of the bronco. This was going to be a long night. Their nerves were already on edge from the earlier experience.

They had decided that one would sleep and one would watch. Delbert took the first watch and worked his way over to the tree. He looked over the area and backed off about forty yards. Then he waited and waited. Ed would relieve him at two AM.

The night in the desert was beautiful. The night was dark without a moon. The smell of sage was a little overpowering but you got use to it. The stars so big and bright, some shooting stars made a great show. One could be mesmerized by nature on this desert.

Delbert jerked awake by sound from the tree area. He shook his head three or four times to clear it.

Jibber jabber was coming to him. All this in Spanish, which Delbert could not understand. He had picked up a few words from their mission in Colombia but rusty at best. Any lingo tends to fade if you do not keep using it once in a while. Delbert listened intently trying desperately to make heads or tails out of it.

From his location, he could see outlines of people. Some men and some women. He believed he saw a small child or two. They had built a fire and were just sort of sitting around as if waiting for someone. Delbert knew the border was just about a mile away. The border here was with Arizona. No river to stop them from walking across. The U.S. had built some fence along this part of the border, but not at this location.

The only two reasons for the people not moving on were they had to be waiting for someone. Perhaps the gangsters down here were late getting here or were waiting for the darkest of night before loading the folks in trucks and driving them across. If this was the case, Delbert could guess how many people would be taken across with terrorists mixed in. The question was how could they ever tell?

Delbert crept closer in an effort of seeing more and maybe hearing more words that he knew. When he stopped about twenty yards from the tree, he had a much better view.

The night air was turning cold which accounted for the fire. This is quite common in desert country. The women and three children, about

let them take care of it. I do not have their number. Your call boss," he finished, waiting patiently for a decision."

"You may have to kill the bad guys," Nate said

"Yes, but no problem. We killed three bandits getting here," was the response.

"Go for it Delbert, don't kill if you don't have to but get the enplosives. Let me know when it over and good luck," as he hung the phone.

"He said go for it Ed, but no killing unless we have to. Here is how we will do it. You go around that way and I'll go this way," he said pointing to the left. Get in, as close as you can and I will do the same. From there I will do the talking but make sure you have a bead on one of them. If we capture them, I do not know what we will do with them. We will worry about that later. Let's go," Delbert said and moved off into the darkness.

Walking was quiet in the sand and they were upon the group before they knew it. One of the illigals was the first to notice. There were only three more persons to load.

The guard holding the weapon was the first to act. He jerked his rifle to his shoulder. The last thing he ever did. This was the one Ed was watching and had already had his rifle up in firing position. The man dropped his weapon as a red hole appeared in his chest. Everyone there could see the life flowing from him. Seconds later, he dropped face down.

"Hands up," Delbert ordered and motioned this to the two remaining bandits.

They looked at each other and seeing they were covered by two men, put their hands in the air. The one who had been taking the money said something in Spanish which seem an order and the other one complied.

Ed and Delbert moved the two out by the fire. Ed searched them as Delbert covered them. Once this was done and two weapons found, Delbert spoke to them.

"Who speaks the best English?" Delbert asked.

"Si, I do. My friend speaks none. What do you want?" he asked.

"Where were you taking the explosives? What part of America were they to be used, understand?" Delbert asked.

"We do not know, senor. We were to take them to a place in the

Arizona Mountains. A man would take them from us there. We do not know where they go," the man said.

"Are you lying to me?" Delbert acting a little disappointed.

"No senor, you have caught me so why should I lie," he said in low voice as if he was embarrassed at being caught.

"Let's tie these two to that tree. Then we can let these others go after giving back their money," Delbert suggested to Ed.

"Good idea. You give back the money. Most of it is in the truck and this bastard has some in his pocket," coming from Ed.

He then turned to the two and said for them to walk to the tree. Delbert was looking in the truck and found a rope.

"Here Ed, this rope will do," and he tossed it to him.

The others were just standing around watching. None tried to neither run nor give any resistance. Most were scared and did not know what to do.

Delbert found the money in a paper sack lying in the seat. He retrieved the money Ed found on the one bandit.

"Do any of you speak English," he asked of the group.

"Si, I do," coming from a boy of about twelve, "I learned in school," he proudly said.

"Ok, son, come here. I need your help," Delbert said to him.

The boy hesitated a minute as through afraid.

"Come on. I will not hurt you. I want to give your people back your money. These bastards will not benefit from this night. Come help me and make sure everyone gets back what they gave them. Ok. I need your help," Delbert pleaded.

The boy stepped forward and the group move closer. They all understood the word money.

"Tell them to come forward one at a time and to tell you how much money they gave these two men," pointing at the two now tied to the tree.

"Si, I understand. I will tell them not to lie to get more or you will shoot them," smiling, he looked up at Delbert.

"Good idea boy,"

The boy spoke to the group in Spanish and they started a line to Delbert. They would tell the boy how much they had paid for the trip and

Delbert would pay them. Soon the money was all gone and Delbert put into motion his plan.

"Ask them if anyone can drive this truck," Delbert asked the boy.

A little more Spanish and a big man stepped forward.

"Load these people and head for the border. You can drive right into Arizona without any trouble. Drive over the desert and stay off the roads. In thirty or forty miles you should abandoned the truck and scatter. Everyone go in a different direction unless you are family. Good luck to you. Watch out for the border patrol. Do not use lights because that will tip off the patrol. Understand? Tell the rest of the people son, so they will get on the truck. Tell them to hurry. It will be daylight soon and their chances are better if they are across the border. Can you do that," Delbert finished and walked to the tree.

The boy jumped on the truck speaking Spanish all the way. The rest followed suit and waved at their rescuers as the truck disappeared into the darkness.

"What do we do with these two? Kill them," Ed said to Delbert with a wink.

"Naw, they are not worth a bullet," was the answer as Delbert reached for his knife. Approaching the two who seem afraid, not knowing what was going to happen.

"I'm cutting the rope about half into so you can get away by tonight. I do not want to see you on the border again. If I do, I will kill you. Hold still now I'm just going to mark you so I'll know you if I see you again," and with this he raised his knife and cut both across the right cheek. They bandaged the wounds and stopped the bleeding.

They all understood this cutting would leave a scar. Delbert and Ed returned to their vehicle and drove east. They had to find another place to hunt.

The sun was almost up and the sky was blood red. The two thought what their folks use to say on such an occasion. Red skies in morning, saliors take warning. Translated means a storm was on its way. Silently both wished this not to be true. After last night, they had had enough stormy weather. A quiet day and night was what they needed.

The further away from the spot of last night's trouble, the rougher the ride. The ground became rockier and small draws had to be skirted. When they reached ten miles on the speed odometer. Ed spoke.

"Up there on the left Delbert, see that draw. Drop down into it and let us check it out. I think its deep enough to hide the Bronco. Looks like it flattens out at the far end. Could be perfect for what we need."

Delbert steered in that direction and soon was traveling at an angle, down into the draw. Ed had been right. It flattens at the bottom with plenty of room for the Bronco. As you moved forward, the draw was less deep. He stopped just as the vehicle's top became even with the top of the draw. Looking out the windshield, they had a wide area of a flat just ahead. There was some sagebrush and a thorny bush growing all over the area. From here they could see for half a mile forward. To view the side areas they could sit on top of the vehicle and have unrestricted view. Tall sagebrush grew from the top, leaning over toward their parking area. This made them almost invisible from the air. The vehicle was gray in color and that helped.

"By damn, Ed, this is perfect. Maybe our luck has changed. Let us get out and build a smokless fire and brew some coffee. Maybe have a nice K-ration," his attempt at humor.

Coffee drank and lunch over they decided they had better get some sleep. One had to stay awake at all times. They discussed it and decided to sleep in four-hour shifts. Every four hours they would change over. This way they should get enough sleep to get by on. Ed, being the oldest, took the first crack at sleeping.

The day was long and hot, so it was hard to sleep. At best, it was a tossing and turning, restless sleep but better than none. Delbert had logged in almost fifty Mexicans heading north. He watched them traveling on foot thru the scorched terrain. He wondered why they did not wait until dark. It seemed they were in a hurry. Delbert figured out they must be hurrying to the border, perhaps rest then go over in the dark. Once across they could travel further and faster in the cool night air.

These were the very poor. None had coats, yet knowing the desert nights can sometime get down into the low forties. There were women and children in the group. Delbert would have been blind not to see the beauty of some of the women. He wondered what drove them to get out of Mexico and into the U.S. Life at home must be terrible for them to leave everything and go on such a march.

As they walked along, he noticed some of the men were in front and two were in the rear. Sort of a rear guard action if it became necessary. The ones he could see clearly wore shoes. At least that was a blessing. They stopped and took a half hour rest while still in the sight of Delbert. It appeared water was passed around to everyone by three women.

There is something strange about those three, Delbert thought to himself. Soon he figured out why.

They dropped off their dresses and exposed weapons. Automatic weapons. He wondered why. It was probably a muti-purpose use he would bet. One was to fight their way across the border if need be, then join a group of bandits. These could also be used against the immgration agents.

Why the dirty bustards', he thought, *sneaking across dressed as women.*

After about a half hour, they started again. It became plain the two guards in the rear were there to make sure no one escaped. They pushed the group along like cattle.

"Oh, just another half hour, please," Ed, asked as Delbert tried to wake him. "I was having a beautiful dream on the bank of a river. The water was cool and the woman naked. Oh, that is where I should be. Please just thirty minutes more,"

"No, my time to sleep. Hang onto the throught," Delbert said with a broad smile.

Ed sat up and rubbed his eyes. He stretched and got out of the Bronco. He took a hefty drink of water and walked back up the draw a few feet to pee. Returning he climbed on top of the vehicle next to Delbert.

"Anything going on, Tiger," Ed asked and was filled in on the earlier incident Delbert had seen.

"Be careful and quiet," Delbert, advised, "I think we're going to see a lot of stuff before the day is over. It might be closer to dark but it is starting to look like the whole damn country is trying to escape."

"Yeah, ever since that damn President Bush got to making deals with the son-of-a-bitch, President of Mexico, both plotting against the American people, then they came. They will keep coming as long as Bush is President. The basterd cares only about money and making money for big business. His open trade policy started it, and then they came. Cheap labor the reason for big business and jobs for the Mexicans. The Presidents are not leaders and will end up burying the middle class and they will keep the Mexicans as low class citizens. They do not even realize that in twenty years they will have so weakened the U.S. that a strong nation will be able to walk right in and take over. Then we will all be third class citizens except for the very rich. They will keep getting richer and the poor will only get poorer. If another nation does not take us, we will have a revolution and no one will be safe. There will be a blood bath such as the world has never seen. The whole world with break in fighting, atomic weapons and all. That would mean the end of the planet. A few may be sparied to reproduce and start over. Damn the rich bastards.

CHAPTER 4

Nate found his way back to the place where he had saved the child and perhaps the mother also. His mind kept drifting back to those two. He just could not help wondering if they made into the U.S. or if some other mishapt befell her. He had a hard time believing the government of Mexico would not take better care of its people. With their oil money, they could buy water-drilling equipment, equipment for planting and cultivating crops. It would take time but in ten years, Mexico could see job growth such as Europe or the U.S. had seen right after the war with Germany. This would bring them into the world community and be a country that would be attracting people from all over the world. How foolish these pigs in charge. Their only interest was power and the billions they were stealing. They were selling their souls to hell for a few short years here on earth.

The sun was down and Nate found an ideal spot close to the river for his post. A few Joshua cacti were scattered across area with the tall sagebrush.

He also took his seat on top of the Bronco. The 30-30 lies across his lap and felt good.

He was looking out towards the west and a little south. He would scan the desert first in that direction, then to the east and south. He also watched to the north. He was using a pair of his night vision binoculars, which made the job of spy much easier. They eased the strain on the eyes while giving him a clearer view after dark.

In the stillness of the night, Nate thought he could hear a wagon in the distance. This could be what they were waiting for. A wagon or vehicle of any kind could be carrying weapons or parts for a dirty bomb.

A scream pierced the cool night air and brought Nate to his feet. It came from a distance of about a hundred yards. It came again and then again.

Nate jumped down from the Bronco with a firm grip on the 30-30 rifle. He sprinted away in the direction of the female scream. Some one was hurting bad and he had to help.

Sprinting across the hundred yards or so, the screams became a whimper as if someone had given up to her fate. He slowed as he neared the spot and changed his movement to sort of a tippy-toed movement. He came up over a little ridge and saw what was causing the commotion.

A Mexican girl of about sixteen lay naked on the sand. A tall goodlooking Mexican man was just pulling down his pants. The girl was shaking and trying to roll from side to side, but could not. With one hand he spred her legs apart. She still had a little fight in her and she jerked them together and crossed them.

The rapist pulled them apart and planted his body between them, leaning forward to pentrate her body against her wishes. One man stood holding a flashlight from a few feet about them. He was also holding a pistol on a slender man of perhaps twenty. Just the facial expressions of the man told you he was somehow related to the girl. Anger in his face, showed in an awesome display of red.

Nate through the rifle to his shoulder aiming at the man on top of the woman. His booming voice echoed through the night.

"Get off her right now you son-of-a-bitch or your dead," Nate yelled.

The men all looked his way. Apparently, none of them knew of his presence until he made the statement.

The two men just stared at Nate in utter surprise. The rapist rose up, quitting what he was doing but not moving off her.

"Hey, gringo, stay out of this it is none of your affair," and he started to preform the act again.

"Last chance, stop and get up or die," Nate uttered the last warning.

A shot rang out and the man slumped forward. Nate swung toward the man above, seeing bright steel, as the man's pistol swung around in his direction. As soon as the sight on the barrel found it place, another shot was heard and silence settled in.

"Roll the pig off her and help her up," Nate commanded the young man who had been held at gunpoint.

"Si, si," he replied jumping to her defense. He rolled the man's body off her and she stood up.

"Senor, are you related to her," Nate asked.

"Si, she is my sister," was the answer.

"Help her cover up. Her dress is torn and she's somewhat exposed," Nate said.

Once covered up, she approached Nate to thank him for saving her. He nodded she was welcome.

"Now you folks can do me a favor. Bury these two pigs and then come over there. I have food and water. Would you do that for me?"

"Si, do you have a shovel, senor,"

"Yes, also over there, Come I'll show you. The girl can rest if she wishes. The digging should be easy in this sand and not take you long. Just dig a couple feet to cover them with. Come let's go.

A couple hours later, they were done with the work. The K-rations went down and the two had their fill of water. Soon after the two said thanks and again a thank you and started across to America. They wanted to be there by daylight. The sun, the bad people and the American border guards are too brutal during daylight hours.

Nate felt sorry for this group and wondered how many of this class were out there trying to get to freedom and a better life. *I am opposed to the illgal immigration going on and it is bleeding of our resourses especially in the medicial field. Yet here I am feeling sorry for the actual people doing it. This group,* "he thought, *"Would make good citizens.* He shook his head not understanding what the world has become.

Soon darkness settled in and the night became pitch black. Nate was on his perch, on top of the Bronco. He was using his night binocuars to scan the desert. Nothing moving. It was eleven P.M. Nate was sure things would start happening pretty soon.

Another hour passed without incident and Nate dosed off. A gentle brezze came up and woke him. He rubbed his eyes and listened intently. Was it a noise or the breeze had wakening him? Minutes went by or at least it seemed that way. At last, it came to him.

The sound of an engine moving carefully across the desert. Nate turned to face the noise and saw headlights coming his way from town. Putting his binocuars to his eyes, he witnessed the following scene.

The light on an older pickup truck was moving slowly across the sand. Two men walked ahead of the truck with flashlights. They were guiding a truck that was loaded with crates and boxes. They would motion the truck around little hills or soft sandy areas that would stick the truck. The truck was really heavily loaded which sparked Nate's inquisitive mind. He had to know what was on that truck.

Sliding down from his perch, he picked up a flashlight and started in the direction of the truck. He picked his way quietly thru the terrain. Without using his light, he was keeping up with the truck. Every one hundred yards the truck would stop and the walkers would have a little rest. Nate noticed Spanish was used by one of the men. Apparently the boss, as he gave hell to the two men with flashlights and the driver.

Nate worked his way within twenty yards without being spotted. He took the night glasses and picked out some letters and writing on the boxes. They were Spanish and he read them several times. He wanted to remember them. He stopped and wrote them on a piece of paper. In the dark, he was unable to see his own writing so he was guessing it was right.

The men stopped the truck and built a little campfire. Coffee was put on and Nate saw them rolling out sleeping bags. A rest stop, he guessed.

As Nate looked on, he saw four drinking cups of coffee, put out the fire and all slid into their sleeping bags. No guard was posted.

Nate sat on a rock and waited until the snoring had started. He was sure it would not be long.

It was not and Nate rose up quietly and circled around to the back of the truck. He was stepping very lightly to avoid waking anyone.

At the back of the truck, he raised the tarp. He could not see well enough and decide to turn on his light. Holding the canvass with one hand and the light in the other, he read the letters on the side of one of the boxes.

Putting the canvass down he turned and using his light to get away from the truck with urgently.

Shaking his head, he just could not believe what he had seen.

I have to get this information to the General, he was thinking all the way back to the Bronco.

"Good morning General, have you had a good night's sleep. I hope so because it's over now," Nate announced.

"What, who in the hell is this," yelled the General.

"It's the guy you always hire to clean up your messes, Nate."

"Nate is that you?"

"Yeah it's me. Grab a piece of paper and tell me when you're ready," Nate instructed.

"Ok, ok and this had better be good to wake me this early. Just a minute I have to get to my desk," answered the General.

The general stumbled out of the bedroom and into the living room as he put on a robe. By the time he reached the little desk, he was wide-awake. Sitting down he picked up the phone.

"Ok, Nate, go ahead. I'm awake now," stated the General.

"I've just come from a pickup truck loaded with heavy boxes. They all have the international sign of nuclear fision material. I am about ten miles south of the town of Ciudad Juarez and close to the river. Unless I miss my guess, it could be dirty bomb material. It is somewhat dumb to keep it in boxes so marked. This tells me someone on the border, perhaps a guard, is allowing this kind of stuff through. Thought you'd like to know," Nate began.

"Give me a good description of the truck and anyone traveling with it. Jesus, Nate this could be it. Damn the government for leaving the border open so they could come. Millions of illegals pouring in with terrorists mixed in," the General expressing his concerns and excitement.

Nate gave him a description of the truck and the men with it.

"General they are camped just a couple hundred yards from me. They are all asleep. They will start off again at daylight. Maybe you can have a plane fly off course and get a picture. Can I do anything from here? I could punch a hole in their gas tank and slow them down if you'd like."

"No, this is our first link to whoever is doing this. We will follow this vehicle and find out where it goes. We must not lose them. You stay right where you are and keep me informed. Call me when they start moving out? Great work, Nate. Talk to you later. I've got to rush," and he hung up.

Damn, I was going to catch a couple hours sleep, Nate thought, *but now I have to wait till the truck leaves. Well, if I cannot sleep I might as well wander back over and maybe pick up something that will give us an idea where they are heading. While they are relaxed around a campfire and not knowing anyone is around might get them talking. I will sneak pretty close,* he was thinking.

He took another drink from the canteen and headed back to the truck. The darkness made it difficult and the going was slow. He tripped over a couple branches of dead sagebrush. A time or two he would slide down a hump of sand and take a tumble. After these, he slowed down. No need to hurry anyway. The men were sleeping and it may be hours before they awoke and started north. By looking ahead, he used the fire to guide him. When he was in about thirty yards, he stopped. Listening for sounds from the camp on the cool night air. Hearing none, he sat down and rested.

Nate was fighting sleep. He did not dare to move around much for fear those men might hear him. He was alone and outnumbered and certainly did not want to die in this terrible place.

The camp came to life about an hour and a half before daylight. All three awoke at the sound of an alarm clock. Two built up the fire and the other dug from the truck, a five-gallon gas can (World War II army type.) and poured its contents into the truck. It seemed to fill it, so this would mean they had not traveled far to get here. Maybe. The smell of coffee was soon coming from the camp. Nate even wished he had a cup.

He eased forward and wiggled across the sand, inch by inch. At about forty feet and with the three men in sight around the fire he lay there straining to hear what they were saying. He did not understand Spanish but knew a few words. Anyone listening could pick up a few words. The smell of bacon came drifting on a breeze perked his nose. One of the men at the fire was turning food over in a fry pan. Nate assumed it was bacon. He watched as another one began cracking eggs into another pan. He could hear the crackling of the eggs. The odors from the cooking reached Nate and his stomach began to growl. The growling was so loud, Nate was afraid they could hear it. He knew this was not true but would make a good story.

Plates came out and the men sat on the ground having eggs, bacon and white bread for breakfast.

"Hey, amigos," one of the three said, "by tonight we will be close to Tucson," came to Nate. This he understood. In the same conversation, one of the men asked a question that Nate did not understand. However, a few of the words he caught. They were Diego, Navy and ships.

Another question came and the same fellow made a swooping circle to the north and ending in the southwest as he spoke. It was Greek to Nate but maybe the General and all his resources could make heads or tails of it.

Breakfast over, the men polished the pans and coffee pot in the sand, loaded them into the back of the truck and the head north.

It would be light in thirty or forty minutes as Nate headed back towards his Bronco. Reaching his goal, he seated himself in the truck seat, picked up his telephone and dialed the General.

The General having been up since Nate's call was sitting at his desk waiting for the call from Nate saying the truck had left. He had been pacing the floor which did no good at all. He wondered if Nate was still alive or dead. He knew these people were killers and would do anything to get their operations in the U.S. going. They still had no knowledge of any governmental agency having any intelligence on them. A sneak attack was what the bastards hoped for. The reason for a dirty bomb attack was to cause panic in the American people. Terrorist wished to cause fear and disrupt their way of life.

He is out there all alone looking for Sam Brown. He is alone. Why the hell did I approve his doing this," the general was thinking, *"I hope the boy's alright.* He jumped at the ringing of the phone.

"Nate it that you," the General said in answering it.

"Well you do care huh, General. Here I just thought you used me. Anyway good morning, sir, did you sleep well," Nate chuckled.

"Damn it, Nate, no fooling around now. We do not have the time. Has the truck left yet and which way are they headed," he answered in sort of a bothered note.

"Yes sir, they are about two hundred yards out, heading north. Do you have a pencil handy? I have more information," he continued on, "I overheard them talking last night. I do not understand much Spanish but I think I know where they are headed.

"God, Nate, I'd kiss you if you do. Shoot I'm ready," the General said with excitement in his voice.

"The words I understood were Tucson, Diego, ships and navy. Now I have been sitting here and thinking and I believe this means they will turn toward Tucson, Az. From there and I am only guessing, but then heading for San Diego, Calfornia. The other two words can only mean they will plant the bomb in the Navy's port, or close to it to take out the ships and the port. Get your people to working on this and see if they come up with the same conclusion. If I am right, it will save us a lot of time in preparing for their arrival. What do you think, General?" Nate asked him.

The General was quiet for a couple of minutes before answering.

"By God, Nate I think you've hit the nail on the head. I am looking at a map right now and what you say makes sense. Thanks Nate, I will see we have a reception party waiting in San Diego. I knew I had the right man for this job," he replied.

"Now wait a minute General, do go off half cocked. We do not know how they will look once they arrive there. You need to tail them and find out where they will put the bomb together or how they will sneak it into the naval yards to be put together. I think they will smuggle parts in slowly which means there are others already there to help them. Do not jump the gun and let us sweep up the whole damn gang. Put the guards in civilian clothes not military uniforms," Nate finished, waiting for a response.

"Of course your right. We will do just that. I will get the F.B.I. into this at the base and my National Guard people can follow them and report in. I do not trust the border patrol. This would not be happening if the Bush Adminstration had not opened the borders, causing them to come, by the thousands. Good work Nate, I will let you know what we find. Talk to you later, enjoy," the General said in hanging up.

Nate sat for a long time eating and thinking. Soon he drifted off to sleep.

Nate had no idea how long he slept but it was quite a while. According to the sun, it was late afternoon. He does that as he woke and stired a little. He felt cold steel against the side of his neck. He froze knowing this could only be a pistol. He mind was spinning as he tried to figure out how to get out of this situation. It was an impossible position to be caught in. He was slumped against the driver's door with the window down. He contemplated swinging around and knocking the gun away. He realized he be dead before he could complete the turn. At last, he decided he would talk his way out of this.

"Senor, please put down the gun so we can talk face to face," Nate said.

"Well I'll be damned. That sounds like a voice from the past," a familar voice came thru to Nate but he just could not place it.

"Gringo, turn around very slowly or I kill you," said the voice.

Nate turned slowly and came face to face with Sam Brown, who broke out in laughter.

"Hi, Nate you old son-of-a-bitch," Brown was saying.

Nate was able to laugh at the situation. He was in a foreign country looking for this man and he find Nate. It was somewhat funny.

"Brown, you bastard, you damn near killed me. What the hell are you doing out here"

"Same as you I'd bet. Seen the General lately," Brown grinning from ear to ear asked.

"Yeah, he's the one I'm working for and besides I was looking for you.

I think we can join forces and be more successful. We are both on the same team. You want to be my backup. It'd be like old times," Nate said.

"We could do that but you're my backup, remember," Brown replied. Walking around the Bronco, Brown climbed into the vehicle.

They talked of old times and how each was doing for the next hour. Then Brown spoke up.

"I'm not sure you want to join with me Nate, I'm not just looking I'm killing. You might say I have a license to kill. I understand you do not want that and I do not blame you. It's a dirty game but sometimes you must fight fire with fire."

"What do you mean you're killing?" Nate asked.

"I find a terrorist. I get all the information out of him I can and then I kill them." was the answer.

"Have you caught any yet," Nate asked.

"A few but none with good information. We have to find someone higher up who knows where their next attack is planned for. We roam around out here in this desert long enough; we will find just what we need.

Nate told Sam what he had discovered last night. Sam listened intently before saying anything.

"Nate, you have landed in one of the most active areas along this border. There is more action here in a day than elsewhere in a life time. This seems to be the more sympathy for the illegals right here. Our border patrol is either being paid off or they just look the other way. Some of the Bush nonsense. This strip for about twenty miles is where most of the terrorists will be coming thru. How did you know?" Sam asked.

"I didn't, I just guessed and after looking this area over it looked like the right place to set up camp, pretend to be a hunter and watch what's happening," Nate replied smiling. "It's close to town for people to get supplies, etc., plus I'm always lucky.

"Ok, if you are a hunter lets go looking for a deer. Load up on water and we will walk a ways and see what is out there. It is good deer counrty because there are farmers fields around and water if you know where to look." Sam said.

The two drank some water, picked up their rifles and headed out.

"My place is only about a mile and a half from here. I want to stop by and see if everything is alright. I have been prowling since early morning. Come on I show you my digs," Sam stated and lead the way west and a little north.

After about a three-mile walk Sam stopped. He looked around as if to locate something, and then spoke.

"This way Nate. There is a small area where's water and green grass. It has shelter on three sides by small hills. Many an illegal has gone this way. It is a good place to rest a couple days before going for the border. Poor farmers and workers usually chose this path. There are enough in every group to stop the raping and killing of the harmless. Come on, once there we'll camp for the night and watch the show," Sam advised as the trudged on.

An hour later they started walking up a hill as the sun beat down upon them. It was getting late in the afternoon and both men were tired. The sun takes a lot out of a person walking thru the desert. Nate wondered how the women and kids ever made it. Many did not.

Sam put up his hand signaling a halt. Nate stopped and waited. Sam motioned him to stay there and he went ahead. Reaching the summit of the hill, Sam dropped to his knees. He remained motionless for several minutes. He then looked back at Nate and motioned for him to join him.

Nate walked up the hill and soon joined Sam. He had dropped to his knees as Sam had done and made the last few feet crawling. Sam smiled at him and was pleased Nate still had some of the Nam training in him.

As Nate topped the hill, he raised his head to look over the summit and to see what interested Sam. He was not prepared for the sight now before him.

Before him was a group of maybe three hundred people. Mostly Mexicans.

"Remember Nate I'm a killer and I'm ordered to kill anyone I believe to be terrorists. I have spotted half a dozen mixed up in that group. They are dark in color but they are Arabs. Being in the sun a lot, they have the same color as a darker Mexican," Sam surprised Nate by this statement.

Nate stared thru his field glasses for better than ten minutes before answering Sam.

"I don't see any. They all look like Mexicans to me. God, I could never imagine how serious this problem is if I wasn't here," Nate uttered under his breath, "lets go talk to some of these people. I want to know the whole story from them."

"No, we are white and that makes us enemies. They will think we are American D. E. A. cops. There is bound to be several drug dealers in the group. The innocent will protect them until they get across the border. Most are carrying drugs for the dealers. Once across the dealers will give them twenty bucks each. Trucks will be waiting for them and the drugs will be hidden on the trucks. Nate, look at the short fat person next to the fat woman in the yellow dress. He stood at the lower end of the group and seems nervous. Just the other side of him is a tall man in a white and blue shirt. He stands out because of his height. Seeing he has a woman on his arm. To their left and a little further away, two others are just working the crowd and selling what little they could. When it gets dark, I will be wondering down that way and those will not be alive come morning. Come on Nate, I'll show you where we will spend the night," spoke Sam.

He crawled back a ways and stood up. Nate followed suit. They went back down the hill a ways, and then circled around to the left. This led them around and up to the very top of the hill. Just before they reached the top, Nate spotted the cave. It was a natural cave created hundreds and maybe thousands of years ago. It faces the backside of the hill and for this reason was out of sight and sound of the group huddled on the other side.

"I don't know if you noticed the little green patch of weeds and short bushes. There is a spring there. When I go tonight, I will fill out canteens with cool fresh water. Nate you make a small fire and put on some coffee. There is some in my backpack. I will gather a little wood for a hot meal. Beans," he announced and held up a can.

Both smiled and soon a small fire was burning under the pot. The smell of fresh coffee cheered both men in this fierce land. Nate had looked over the cave. It ran about thirty feet back into the hill. Enough of a cave to give them shelter.

After their meal, such as it was, the two walked to the top of the hill and sat watching the huddled people enduring this hardship to find a home and freedom.

They smoked and talked about the old days and how the world had changed. They filled each other in on their lives since last they'ed met.

"You know if it hadn't been for the General making a big deal about you, I wouldn't be out here. I have a lovely wife, a happy home and a business to run. He made it sound like your life was in great danger and so I came looking for you. He kinda of lied to me, the old bastard. I believe him and yet I know better," Nate said with a little contempt in his voice.

Sam broke out laughing as if he knew more to this story.

"I put the General up to it Nate. I wanted you here and my life is in danger every minute. Your's too, now that you are here. You see down there what we are up against. The Mexican government has decided to let go of its poor people and keep only the cream of the crop. By doing so they weaken our democracy, lower our wages, causing more proverty in the U.S. They know that proverty spawns hate and crime so why not let the U.S. take care of it. We donate tens of billions that we borrow from China to support the world. You would think that by now congress or at least the president could see this. Hell no, they are only interested in feathering their own nest. They do not even realize that once the good jobs have gone overseas; there is no one here that makes enough to buy the crap coming in from overseas. If they would leave it along and let the market place work it out, the whole world would profit by it. Hell no, others out there want to be the top dog but believe me they would not donate to the world. They, along with congress would take their money and run. Our congress is so dumb they do not realize by allowing big business to polutite the water and air, they too will suffer. Life can not survive without clean water and air," Sam said with such force Nate dared not interrupt.

"That's a long winded speech Sam. Careful George Bush will get you," Nate chuckled.

"Nate, I must go and take those lives so all America can sleep in peace. You go back to the cave and turn in. I will be back in an hour or less. If

I do not return, you will know I am dead. Do not come looking for me. Just report to the General. Ok. Promise me damn it. Promise you will not come looking. Keep your pistol handy tonight and every night. Bandits might find you in the cave and attack you. See you in the morning," Sam hesitated, and then turned a walked down the hill towards the group he must infultrate.

Nate went back to the cave and lay down on his blanket. He checked his 357snubnosed pistol and placed it under the blanket a couple feet away. He decides he would not think of what Sam was doing. He had his assignment and Sam had his. Both were acting in defense of America. Placing his hand over it, he fell asleep.

"Ouch," a very quiet voice coming from below the cave. Nate was awake in a flash. He reached for the pistol and placing it firmly in his grip. He moved it back next to his body under the blanket. *Any son-of-a-bitch thinks he is sneaking up on me is in for a shock,* Nate thought. He lay quiet and listened intently. His concentration of listening was so great it hurt but soon paid off.

Moments later, he felt someone standing near his feet.

"Wake up gringo. We want your money," a deep manley voice said.

Nate stirred as though just come awake.

"Huh, who is it. Sam is that you," he said.

"No, is your friendly bandito. Get up," the voice said.

Nate opened his eyes and saw two men. They were standing maybe ten feet away. They had a flashlight and were shining it on him.

"Ok, I'm getting up," he said and curled his legs under and sat up looking straight at them.His right hand was still under the blanket as Nate was using it for balance. The two never noticed.

As his hand came out from under the blanket, the 357 exploded and fire shot from the barrel. The man who had spoke was pushed backwards with the force of the bullet striking him in the chest. Hitting on his back, he slid another twenty feet and lay still. Nate jumped to his feet pointing the pistol at the other intruder.

"Careful mister, this may go off again," he advised, "hands in the air and give me the light.

"Si, senor, don't shoot," said the man as he passed the light over.

"Now I don't want to kill you so what can I do with you," Nate said aloud.

"Send me back to town, senor. I have never done this before. It was all his idea," pointing at the dead man.

"That a good idea. Take off your pants," Nate ordered.

"What?" asked the man.

"You heard me. Take off your pants," was repeated.

"Si, senor," was spoken as he did what he was ordered.

"Now your shirt," came the next order.

The man looked confused but complied.

"Now your underwear," Nate ordered.

The man complied and was now standing naked.

"Kick off the sandals and be quick about it," Nate barked.

"Town is that way," Nate pointed, "now get the hell out of here before my partner gets back. He will kill you for sure. If I see you are out here again, I will kill you so get to town and stay there. Understand. If I was you, I would run all the way. Dressed like that you might get sunburn," Nate said with a big ole grin.

"Si, si," was answered by the naked man. He turned and took off running, soon disappearing into the darkness.

That does it, Nate thought, *I am not going to try to sleep without a guard.* He pulled out a cigar and smoked while looking at the sky and listening to the night. It had cooled off quite a bit and he enjoyed the quiet of the night. The sky was filled with millions of stars and he was fascinated by the hugeness of the universe. I knew he was only looking at a small part of it. People on the other side of the world were also looking at a portion of it. It came to him once again how small man really was in the scheme of it all.

An hour pasted and he wondered how Sam was coming with his chore.

CHAPTER 5

As Sam left Nate, he walked slowly down the hill. His eyes were accustomed to the darkness and he could see quite well. He kept one eye on the ground and one one the group he was approaching. The bonfires were kept burning and gave him a good layout of the camp. He knew where one of his victims was sitting and hopefully asleep by now. The whites in the group could very well be terrorists. Some might even be Americans. In Iraq, Americans were found fighting for the Talban. Tratiors. Most of the fighters coming to the U.S. now were Arab. If only the ass in the White House had gone after the bastards in Afghanistan who were responsible for nine eleven like he did Iraq, we had cleaned them out by now. Everyone knows he went after Saddam because of his attempted assassination of his father. He lied to the world and the American people, damn his hide. His attention swung back to the matter at hand.

Most of the people were asleep as he walked thru the mass of bodies lying on the ground. He spotted his first target sleeping against a boulder at the lower end of the crowd. He was off to himself and sound asleep. The closer he got to the subject the more he looked like an Arab.

Sam worked his way up behind him, acting like he was going to the bathroom. He looked around to see if anyone was watching. Not seeing anyone looking this way, Sam dropped to his knees and crawled back to the sleeping target. He came up behind him. He pulled out his knife, one similar to the one Nate carried. A sharp hunting knife. Kneeling behind the boulder, he was ready to strike.

He moved down along side of the man and plunged the knife deep into his kidney. A silent way to kill a man. The army had taught him this. He held the man so he would not slump forward. Sam pushed his bottom a little forward and leaned him back. He stayed in that position.

Sam then searched his pockets for any paperwork money etc. Finding a billfold, folding money and paper inside his shirt, he took it all. It might just be vaulable information. Task completed he stood up and walked away.

Find a good spot to sit and survey the people with intent to spot the other three. He sat down and pretended to be one of the group. He lit a cigarette as he scanned the group.

At last, he spotted all three. One just got up and headed away from camp he supposed to relieve himself. Sam followed.

Twenty-five yards out of camp and out of sight because of the sloping hill.

Sam saw he was doing his job and walked quietly up behind him, reaching him just as he finished. The man was standing and again Sam drove his knife deep into a kidney. The man uttered not a sound and Sam laid him on the ground. He searched the body and found the same as on the first one. He to have a paper inside his shirt at the chest. This caused him to be curious as to the papers but not time to look now. It would wait until later.

The paper and money he put inside his shirt and moved away. Lighting a cigarette as he walked back to his sitting position.

The other two were lying right in the middle of the people and difficult to get to without causing a disturbance. He decided it was too dangerous and decided to head back to where he left Nate.

As he rounded the hill and came into sight of the cave, he saw a body lying not far from the entrance. The hairs on the back of his neck stood up as he wondered what it mean't. A couple steps further he saw Nate sitting on the ground looking skyward.

"Hey, you ok," he said to Nate.

"Yes, I'm fine. That friend of yours is dead and I sent one back to town," Nate said still looking at the sky.

"You can't send any of these bastards back to town. What did they try to do, steal from you? You should have killed him. He may have cronnies out there. They may come back to get you," Sam a little surprised at Nate's remarks.

"No, I doubt it. The one I sent away was a naked as a jaybird. If he is not in town before the sun comes up and he will not be. He will have a burn such as you have never seen. Even his pecker will be hunting for shade. We will not be seeing him again. Both of these are just petty thieves. One has given up his trade and the other one is thinking about it. How did your night's work go? Get any scalps?" Nate asked.

"A couple but I doubt they even find one of them. He was out a ways from the group to take a leak and never returned. The other is so peaceful just sitting by a rock sleeping. So nice and peaceful. I got some papers off each of them and I am anxious to read them. They were Arabs and fit what we call terrorists. I am sure they were fighters sneaking across with the Mexicans. I really do not care. I will report to the General. Let's get some sleep,"

"Just as soon as I drag this one down the hill a little further and hid him. You go ahead, I will be on guard for two hours then you can have a turn at it. I won't sleep without a guard posted," Nate said.

"Ok. I'll see you in two hours then," Sam replied. He rolled out his blanket, lay down, and was asleep before Nate returned from his chore.

A cool wind came sweeping across the desert and Nate pulled the blanket tighter around his body. He took a look at his watch and saw it was just minutes before he was to wake Sam and it would be his time to sleep.

He moved deep into the cave and prepared for a deep sleep. To him it seems an eternity since he had slept. Time passed slowly in these kinds of situations. Like a stakeout in the states.

"Wake up Sam," he said as he gently shook him, "your turn."

Sam woke right up and nodded ok for Nate to take his turn. Nate snuggled in his blanket in the cave and was asleep in two minutes.

The rest of the night was uneventful and as the sun came up, both Sam and Nate was awake and feeling good after a few hours sleep.

"Well, lets get back to our home base and see what's going on there," Nate suggested.

"Ok, by me I'm hungry as hell and want something that will get me thru the day," Sam agreed.

The walk started back to the vehicles, water and food on the top of the agenda. Arriving the two checked out the area before walking in. No one was around and nothing had been tampered with. From both vehicles, they dug out potatos, two frozen steaks, bread and a can of Boston baked beans.

They build a small smokeless fire from dead sagebrush and put on a pot of coffee.

In about thirty minutes, they were chowing down and feeling good about still being alive. A rest of an hour afterwards as they dosed in the sun came to an abrupt end. From a distance away, a voice called.

"Seniors, may we come to your fire. The coffee smells good and we are hungry," said a woman's voice.

Both men jumped to their guns and looked at each other. Sam moved away from the vehicles and nodded at Nate to invite them in.

"Yes, come on in one at a time. You may have coffee," he answered to the caller but held his rifle across his lap. In this position it would only take a second to have it in action if need be.

In walked a man of about thirty-six, a woman of 31 and 2 young kids, a boy and a girl.

They looked tired and hungry. The only items they had were the clothes on their backs. Both Sam and Nate felt sorry for them. Sam circled around in the direction they had come just to be sure they were alone.

"Please sit down," Nate invited and picked up some cups, filled them with water and handed one to each. They seem to drink the filled cups in one gulp. Nate refilled them and handed them back. This time they took time to taste the cool sweet water.

"Gracias," the man said. The children just smiled. They were about eight and ten years old.

Once the water was poured all around, Nate put on another pot coffee. He reached inside the Bronco and pulled out some K-rations.

"Here," he said, "eat you must be hungry," Nate said.

"Si, we are very hungry. We have not eaten for two days, gracis," answered the man.

The two kids were having trouble getting their boxes opened so Nate took one and opened it for them. Seeing this done the other one had no problem. The coffee was soon ready and Nate poured all around.

It was hard to converse with them because they spoke mostly Spanish and Sam and Nate only English, except for a few words.

Sam came in and had a cup of coffee. An hour went by and Nate noticed how tired the children looked.

"How long has it been since you've slept," he asked. It took a little to get them to understand and for Nate to understand the answer. Once it was understood, the man spoke and related the following story.

"The last time we stopped to rest and sleep some bandits came by and stole all their belongings, water and food. It had been about thirty two hours but they dare not stop for fear they might be killed if approached by more bandits because they have nothing to give them," he told them.

Nate looked at Sam and nodded his head and Sam nodded back.

"Please strech out back behind the vehicle. One of us will be up all night on guard duty and we will protect you. Those kids and your woman need to rest. Tell me what time you want to wake and we will wake you. I'll even take you to the border just before daylight so you can cross over," Nate tried to make him understand. After several minutes and some sign talking with their hands. They agreed and the family went behind the Bronco to sleep. Nate pulled out a couple blankets and tossed them over and the one he had used the night before.

In what seemed like seconds the family was asleep. Sam and Nate moved around to the front of the vehicle and lit up cigars. Sam brought over a bottle from his vehicle and the poured each a strong shot. The whiskey was warm going down and it helped them to relax. After an hour or so, Sam spoke to his partner.

"I'll be going out now, Nate and see if I can nail a terrorist or two. It will be after dark when I return but do not worry about me. I will return."

"Do you have to do this Sam? Why don't you stay here with me and I am sure I can talk the General into paying you what he's paying my crew (Nate had already told Sam about the others and where they were stationed).

"Maybe one of these days Nate, but not today. I'm one of those on the front line and in the thick of things. You remember the old days when I had to be where the action was. It's the same now.

With this, he walked over to his vehicle and soon drove out of sight towards the border but also turning a little south. The dust soon settled and Nate leaned back against the Bronco, in the shade. With rifle across his lap, he was comfortable. His only fight now was against sleep.

As darkness crept across the desert, Nate got up to stretch his legs. He left the draw and looked around the entire area for a distance of one hundred yards. Seeing nothing threatening, he returned to his camp and placed his behind on a fender. This gave him a little more height and a wider range of vision. Not that it mattered much because after dark there was not much to see. Tonight might be different because there was a moon and that will help. He couldn't help but wonder what had happened to Sam.

Nate lit another cigar and sat smoking it, fighting sleep. *Damn that Sam he was thinking.* It was his time to take the watch.

He was starting to dose when a movement caught his eye. It was some sort of animal sneaking thru the sagebrush. This brought him wide-awake as he strained his eyes trying to identify it. He didn't feel threated because there was only one. He waited. As he watched it getting closer, he decided to get down from his perch and go up on top of the bank.

Climbing the bank, he walked out about twenty yards and squated down under sagebrush. Whatever it was was not in sight but Nate could feel it. It was still there perhaps stalking him. He looked around nervously and spotted Sam about ten yards away.

Damn I show him, Nate thought as he hugged the ground tighter. Apparently, Sam had over shot his location. He waited. Finally, he stood up and spoke.

"Got you Sam. You're getting old and making too much noise. You stand and come on in. It's your time to watch as I sleep," Nate chuckled at catching Sam flatfooted.

"Well, I'm glad you're so sharp," stated Sam as he rose to full height. He walked to Nate and they both walked back to the Bronco.

"Did you get anyone tonight?" Nate asked.

"No, not tonight but I found where some vehicles have been crossing. Vehicles heavily loaded. I think they are the Mexican army. The tred are the same and there were at least four of them. Looks to me like they were using the same place for some time. I'll go back tonight and maybe find out. If my fears are confirmed, I'll have to advise the general. Now you get to sleep Nate and I'll wake you in four hours. Ok?" Sam said.

"Say no more, I'm going," Nate responded and climbed into the Bronco and went to sleep.

Four hours, right on time he was shaken awake by Sam.

"Hope you had a good sleep and now it's my turn. I'll try for four hours and then I can sleep this afternoon. Don't forget to wake your company an hour or two before daylight. It'll be easier for them to cross the border in the darkness," Sam told him.

"I'm taking them to the border before it gets light and show them an easy place to cross the river. Those people are worn out and need the rest. I'll wake you as I leave and I'll come right back," Nate told him.

"Damn Nate, we're supposed to keep them out of the U.S. not help them in. You must be out of your mind but go ahead I won't interfer."

Nate woke the Mexicans about an hour and a half before it would get light, with coffee and a hot breakfast of eggs and sausage and biscuits. They all looked rested and very surprised at the food. They all thanked Nate in their native tongue at least that was how it felt. He was able to get across to them they must hurry and eat so he could get them to the border allowing them to cross in the dark. He also got across to them he would show them a good crossing.

Soon they were on their way to the river. They again thanked Nate as they unloaded from the vehicle. Each came up to the window on the driver's side and shook his hand. He smiled and wished them luck. Shortly after starting across the river, they disappeared into the darkness. Nate sat in the Bronco for at least thirty minutes listening. He heard no shooting, saw no lights and assumed this little group made it across the river. He hoped they made it.

Back at camp, Nate parked the vehicle and kept an eye open for movement around the area. His driving out and then returning proabley discouraged anyone around. The night returned to the quiet it had been just as the sky was beganing to lighten. The sun would soon be up. Nate started another pot of coffee before shaking Sam awake.

On the first night, Carl and Katrina had a hard time finding a secure place. The best they could do was drive deep into a thicket of tall sagebrush. Neither one was crazy about the smell of sagebrush but felt they could handle it. Once parked they got out their little camper and made coffee. Because it was going to be a long night, they decided on naps. One would stay awake while the other slept. Then reverse the procedure untill dark. They assumed nothing of interest would happen until then. As it often happens, Murphys Law took a hand in what would happen.

Just as they started their coffee, a jeep could be heard coming their way. Soon a jeep came into sight with four Mexican soldiers in it. They came in by following the tracks Carl and Katrina had made thru the sagebrush.

All four jumped out of the jeep and stood with rifles ready. A man of the rank of Sgt approached them.

"What are you doing here," he asked as he approached.

"We are hunters and were told there are deer here and many game birds. Why, are we trespassing on someones property," Carl asked.

"No senor, but there are Mexicans going thru here to the U.S. Sometime Americans drive down here and take a load north for pay. We must make sure this does not happen. The Americans are mad as hell about this little problem so I must ask you if that is your purpose. If so then I will take you to jail unless you can pay. I must search your vehicle. Do you mind?" he said grining.

"No, go ahead we have nothing but supplies. No room for people you will see," Carl walked around to the back and opened up the tailgate.

The Sgt. walked around and looked in. The vehicle was packed to the gills with no open spaces. The Sgt. nodded and slammed the lid down hard as if mad for not finding anything.

"One hundred dollars for hunting our deer. You pay me now," the Sgt ordered holding out his hand.

"Si," Carl replied and pulled out his billfold. He removed five twenties and handed them over. The Sgt seemed satisfied and taking the money returned to the jeep and the group loaded up and doing a reverse turn driving out the way they came in.

"They were right in the states about money ruling here in Mexico. Even the Mexicans coming down from the U.S. says you can't get around in Mexico without paying off every cop in sight. Even for murder, a couple thousand will get you off free and clear. God, I'd hate to live here," Carl said to Katrina.

"Yeah and it gets worse when you get into the cities," she replied.

The rest of the afternoon was very quiet and so Carl and Katrina split up and made a circle around the area. They would investigate everything inside the circle. This made them familiar with their surroundings. Absolutely necessary to keep them safe. It gave them an idea where they could hide or not. In a pursuit they would know which way was best used, etc. They found nothing unusual in the area. They exchanged notes and felt the job was well done. The land around them was flat and covered with sagebrush. There were four sagebrush thickets where they could hide if need be.

"Well honey, looks like everything will be quiet. Maybe we'll get a good night's sleep. You take the first four hours and I'll play guard. You can take the second shift as guard. We do need to have a guard. We sure don't want any surprises," Carl said.

"Sounds good to me," she replied.

Just before sundown, they were finishing a supper of beans, bread, a cube steak and some coffee. They had built a small fire of dead sagebrush that gave off almost no smoke. If you were down wind through, you could smell it.

Night came quickly and Katrina turned in as the twilight turned to darkness, sleeping in the front seat of their vehicle.

Carl drank more coffee and prepared for a long night. He pulled a blanket out of the back seat of the vehicle, kissed Katrina goodnight and climbed on top of their vehicle. He had a couple cigars in his shirt pocket and decided to fire one up and suck slowly to make it last. He laid his trusty thirty-thirty rifle next to him.

As he sat there, his mind wandered from one subject to another. His marriage came to mind and he smiled. It was the best thing that ever happened to him. It was good of the General and Nate to let him bring her on this mission. During their short marriage, he had appreciated life much more. With her everyday was exciting. They had gone fishing together and he found her very good at it and she loved the outdoors. They went shooting together because he felt that currently every woman should know how to defend herself. She soon became an expert shooter. She was better with the thirty-thirty rifle than with a pistol. However, she was quite good at both.

They both wanted kids but felt they were getting too old so they took steps to prevent this from happening.

He looked skyward and wondered if there were people out there. The same question millions of people have wondered since man first appeared on earth. He looked for and found the little and big dippers. He looked for the other constilations but could not recognize any.

His eyes scanned the desert and wondered just what the General had in mind for this group. He had been around enough to know the General always had something different in mind than what he told Nate. Everyone knew and that and perhaps was why they came. Maybe they were all just curious and had to find out. Oh well, time would tell.

A cool breeze came up as the heat of the day turned from heat to the coolness that was desert after dark. It felt good for now but would soon bring the cold. This was common in deserts the world over.

He was straining his eyes at the desert and was fooled by sagebrush swaying in the wind.

After an hour or so, he began to get sleepy. He almost dozed off a time or two so he decides to go for a walk. He looked down thru the windshield of the vehicle at his wife.

She was sound asleep and probably dreaming of some far away place with waterfalls and slow moving water. Green trees would be there and she would just bend down to drink the pure, cool water. She was that way and it was wonderful to have that kind of thinking woman as his wife. It was rubbing off on him. He was starting to look at the world in the same way.

He slid down from the vehicle and with his rifle in hand; he started off toward the west.

He moved slowly thru the night. He stopped often to look around and to listen for people in the dark. On one occasion, he tripped and fell over small sagebrush. Getting up he cursed himself for doing so as he brushed himself off.

For an hour, he prowled around before thinking he should return to camp. He made a complete circle around camp and got to know the lay of the land. Important because if they need to run, at some point, he would know which was best direction to head.

He peeked in at Katrina and saw she was still sound an asleep. He looked at his watch and discovered it was time to wake her.

He gently opened the door, not wanting to scare her, and whispered. "Katrina, it's time for your watch," he said.

"Why are you whispering, Carl, there's no one for miles," she said as she stretched and yawned.

She slid out of the Bronco and disappeared over behind a clump of brush to relieve her. Returning with a couple branches of sagebrush and announced she was going to start a fire and make a pot of coffee.

"Good night, darling," Carl said, "I'm going to bed," and got inside the vehicle and lay down in the front seat.

Daylight came with the fierce intensity of the desert. Both Carl and Katrina were already up and cooking eggs and ham for breakfast. Coffee was already being savored by both. Ham, eggs and bread would be their breakfast with the coffee to wash it down.

After the meal was completed and the dishes put away, Carl mounted his perch and stood looking out over the desert fron a standing position. He could see for about two hundred yards or so. He slowly turned with his field glasses checking every inch of the land before them. Seeing nothing, he sat down and spoke to Katrina.

"Nothing moving," he said, "it's going to be a quiet day. Take a nap if you want."

"No, I don't want to," she said as she climbed up and sat down beside him.

Two hours passed and the two were taking turns getting off the truck and into some shade.

Carl was on the vehicle and Katrina was sitting down in the shade of sagebrush when a scream ripped through the stillness of the day.

Both jumped up and looked in the direction of the scream.

"Can you see anything," Katrina asked Carl.

"No, not a damn thing," he replied as another scream echoed across the land.

Katrina grabbed her rifle and started runing in the direction of the screaming.

Carl picked up his thirty-thirty and jumped to the ground and followed her at a distance of twenty yards. After they had covered fifty yards, Carl rounded a bunch of sagebrush just in time to see Katrina drop to one knee. She braced her left elbow on her leg and aiming her rifle.

"No, by God, not on my watch," he heard her say as the thirty-thirty belched smoke and he saw this scene before him.

A young woman of about sixteen was laying flat on her back with most of her clothes torn away. A Mexican army Sgt. was rolling off her to the left. His bare butt and the naked girl told the story. Another solider was just releasing her. She jumped up and ran towards and older Mexican being held by still another solider. The one holding the old man quickly turned and ran off into the brush. The man holding the girl followed him.

Carl and Katrina both approached the girl and old man. The Sgt. was dead and lay on his side. Half his head was missing.

"Are you alright," Katrina asked of her.

"Si," she replied, "thank you for coming. He was going to rape me."

"Yes, I can see that," Carl said.

"Katrina lets get the hell out of here. There may be more soliders around. We can't be caught here," Carl was saying.

"Where are you going?" Katrina asked the old man.

"The border," answered the girl, "this is my father and he does not understand English. He is grateful you came."

"Stay here. We all have to run for it before some one comes. We have a truck that has a little room. We will go get it and give you a ride to the border. It's not far," Katrina said.

"Carl you go for the Bronco. It's all packed. I'll wait here with these folks. Hurry," she finished.

Carl took off like a jackrabbit and covered the distance to the truck in no time. He walked around it to make sure they left no evidence they were there except for the tire tracks. He jumped in and fired it up and drove back to where the others waited.

Twenty minutes later, they pulled up to the border. Carl took out his field glasses and scanned the area. No border guards in sight. There was some barbwire fencing. Carl told the two Mexicans and gave them instruction on how to get into the U.S. The two took off and Carl set his course.

To throw off any pursuit, Carl drove around in circles for severals times to make it impossible for anyone following to decide which way they had gone. He then drove very slowly to the west. They hardly made a mark as to which way they were going. The ground was harder here and if they did not spin their tires this stunt should work.

"We will head west for maybe ten miles. If we see a deer along the way, we'll kill it and set up a camp that will look like we've been there for a week or more. That may throw the Mexican police off when they come out to investigate," Carl was saying to Katrina.

"I doubt if they even send anyone out. Most of the Mexican police up here are cowards. Besides, they won't want to get away from the city for long and miss all the bribes they could make. They can make none here so why come. They will proably list the killing as done by bandits and recover the body. That will end it I believe. Of course, darling we must make sure they can't identify us. Damn, I wish I hadn't had to do that but the bastard deserved it," Katrina was rattling on.

"That's ok Honey, you did it and it's done. I don't blame you and he did deserved it. The others didn't take time to get a good look at us so I think it will be alright. Relax and watch for us a deer," Carl spoke to calm her down.

She leaned over and kissed him on the cheek. He smiled as thanks in return.

They drove slowly for a good hour while avoiding soft sandy spots. All at once, Katrina whispered.

"There's one Carl, stop," coming from Katrina.

"One what?" came a reply.

"A deer. Stop." she repeated.

Carl stopped the Bronco looked in the direction she was pointing. About fifty yards was a big buck deer feeding off the top of a bush. He looked fat but they didn't care. Any deer would for proof they were hunting.

"Ok, dead eye, you knock him over. Just one shot right behind the shoulders, thru the rib cage," Carl teased Katrina.

"I have to do everything," she said smiling as she took aim.

A loud "Bang" broke thru the silence of the day as the buck fell to the ground.

"There my love, your's to clean. There are some tall bushes and a small tree right there. We can hang him in the tree for cleaning and make camp right there," Katrina said.

Carl drove over and parked in shade from the tree. It wasn't much but would do.

In thirty minutes, he had hung the deer, gutted it and covered it with a cloth to keep the flies away.

By now, the sun was getting low in the west and it would soon be dark. The deer would cool out over night and they would cut it up in the morning and put it in the cooler.

They ate a cold supper that night. Army K-rations would have to do. A little fire was built and coffee made to wash them down. They drank the coffee sitting on top of the vehicle. Little was said and each wondered what might come of the killing of the soldier.

"I'd better call Nate and tell him what we've done and see if he wants to pull us out or what. You agree," Carl asked his wife.

"Yes, I agree, he needs to know," she responded.

Carl picked up the phone and dialed the number.

"Hello," was Nate's voice over the instrument.

"Hi Nate, Carl here. I have some news you need to know that might change our plans. We witnessed a near rape today by a damn army officer. We couldn't get to where it was happening but were in shooting distance. Katrina shot the bastard just as he was crawling on top of a sixteen-year-old girl. There were two other men with him and they left running like hell. We don't think they got a look at us but they got away," Carl reported.

"Well it couldn't be helped. Did you bury the body?" Nate asked.

"No, we got out of there. There's more. When we walked up to the body, it was wearing a police officer's uniform. The other two must be cops too. We took off and disguised our trail so I doubt anyone could follow us. We are about west of where you assigned us. What do you want us to do?"

"You've done alright and I want you to stay there unless you find someone tracking you. If that happens, then come in and we'll figure out what we should do," Nate replied.

"Well, we killed a deer and hung it in a tree so we look like hunters and that will help our cover some. Now we look like real hunters. I'll bring you a steak," he laughed, said thanks and hung up.

Carl turned to Katrina and repeated the conversation. She smilled and felt relieved Nate felt that way. She snuggled closer to Carl as they finished their coffee. Like a cloak, darkness fell around them.

Neither was sleepy so they wrapped a blanket around themselves and stared into the night and enjoyed the scene the stars had going. A few shooting stars were seen and they tried to find the little and big dippers. Soon the quietness got to them and they decided one should get to bed. It was Carl's turn first. He kissed his wife and slid off the vehicle and makes himself comfortable across the front seat. He was asleep in minutes. Katrina tightened the blanket around her; made sure the thirty-thirty was close and continued watching the stars.

This job was like being on a stakeout. Nothing happens for hours, sometime days, and then all at once everything explodes. Well this was one of those boring nights and nothing happened. Both Carl and Katrina got a decent night's sleep and felt better in the morning.

A fire was built and coffee put on to boil. Bacon, eggs and bread was the breakfast that morning. They sipped their coffee slowly and enjoyed each other's company. The conversation was casual and about nothing in particular. They were still having coffee when Carl saw a four-wheel drive pickup truck coming their way.

To be prepared for anything they moved their rifles closer to themselves and waited to see what was going to happen. Once it got closer, they could read the words "Police" across the sides of the vehicle. This caused both to tense up a bit. They knew it could be about the police officer they had killed yesterday.

Thank God, they had not cut up the deer yet, Carl thought.

The oncoming truck came up along side the camp and two young Mexicans got out.

"Good morning Senor, what are you doing here." one said in perfect English as he approached Carl.

"Deer hunting and that is the one we killed last night hanging in that tree there," Carl answered nodding in direction of the tree.

"Ah, yes we noticed it as we drove up. Do you have your permit and license to do this," the taller of the two asked.

"Si," replied Carl and reaching into the Bronco he pulled out the papers that allowed the hunting.

These he handed over to the man as the other man walked over to the deer carcuss and examed it. He returned and said something to the taller one in Spanish.

The taller one handed back the papers and spoke.

"I see you have not tagged the deer yet which is a violation of the law. Why have you not done so?" he asked Carl but looking at Katrina.

"I was going to do that this morning after I cut up the deer and put it in the cooler. I did not mean to break the law. I'm sorry," Carl explained and looked thru the papers to find the tag. Finding the tag, he started to punch it in accordance to the law.

"No, no," instructed the officer, "no need to do that now. You are in violation of the law and I seize the meat."

He turned to the other officer and said something in Spanish and he walked back to the hanging carcuss and cut it down. He put it across his back and carried it to the police vehicle. He tossed it in and returned to the group.

"The fine is fifty dollars and you may pay Me." as his hand came forward and waited.

Carl pulled his billfold out of his pocket and fished out a fifty. This he passed to the officer and asked for a receipt.

"No, no receipt necessary. The fine has been paid and now my family will have deer meat to eat. You have a tag you may use if you see another deer. Good luck," the officer said grinning. Both officers got into their truck and drove away laughing.

"Whew, that was a close one," said Carl, "I thought sure as hell it would be about the dead cop."

"Hell, down here it's every dog for himself it appears. Those cops keep the meat and the fine and their supervisors are never told. They have to find their ways to collect graft from others. What a way to make a living," Katrina said.

As the day moved on, Carl and Katrina counted fifty-three Mexicans, mostly families crossing the border. They saw little of the border patrol. Once in a while, maybe every two hours, a pickup truck would drive along the American side of the border.

It would drive slowly along and on a couple of trips; they had the back loaded with Mexicans. They would take them east and these would be the ones shipped back to Mexico. Never once did they see anyone in handcuffs or with other vehicles, etc. In other words none that looked or had items that might connect them with terrorists. It seems to those watching, the border guards only took on the easiest to apprehend.

On this day the most people Carl and Katrina counted was one hundred and two.

CHAPTER 6

Don and Bradly were about beat to death when they reached their post. The roads in Mexico were something else. Of course most of the time they just wandered across the land without any roads. However the last five or so miles they were driving over farmland. Hay and grain and small truck farms.

Once they reached the river marking the border, they looked for a spot for which to watch a long stretch of the border. Here the Rio Grande was shallow which would make it easier for immigrants to wade across. Driving a little farther, they found where they could drive out onto a bluff to get the best view. The only problem they were sure to be spotted in such an open spot. On the other hand most anyone crossing here would be looking north and certainly not up.

After looking this place over for an hour or so decided, it would do. After all, they were just counting people and looking for anyone that looked like terrorists.

For the rest of the day they watched and saw not a person. The day was not as hot as the day before and they were sure to see someone crossing into the U. S.

In their spying, they did see an active U. S. border patrol. Every few minutes a pickup came down the dirty road on the American side of the border. These were two man patrols. Ever so often they would stop and park. They would walk for a distance staring at the ground.

Don and Bradly decided they must be looking for tracks of people entering the states. *At least this was their tax dollars at work* was their thinking.

Suppertime came and they backed up their vehicle on the bluff, out of sight of the border guards and out of view of the river. They built a small fire and Bradley cooked. They had cube steaks from the cooler, fried potatoes, pork and beans, with bread. Coffee was also brewed and sipped as they ate.

After the meal was eaten and dishes cleaned in the sand, they both walked forward on the bluff. They found seats where they had been parked earlier. They had the night vision glasses for watching the activity along the border. Both had lit Cuban cigars and sipped coffee as they looked on. Neither was sleepy so they both watched for a while. Both believed that nighttime was the best time to cross here. Time would tell.

About midnight, Don decided he would go to bed and relieve Bradley at three AM.

It was strange that no one passed in sight of these two all nightlong. With their night glasses, same as the military used, did not pick up even one person. Both men were relieved from watching to sleeping and such. When morning came not a soul was spotted.

After breakfast the two fired up a couple cigars and sat back to watch. They noticed a border patrol pickup truck on the other side. It would patrol east and in about an hour it came back and drove west.

"Hell, they will never catch anyone sneaking in. Too long of a patrol area. All you'd have to do is wait until the truck passed by, and then crossed over. Hell, they won't be back for an hour. Wasted time and money. The border is wide open." Bradley commented.

The next three days were boring. They counted a dozen or so people sneaking across the border but nothing compared to what the others were seeing.

The day before they were to leave to go back and meet with their teams, all hell broke loose.

It was early afternoon and Bradly and Don were out walking around an area of about two hundred square yards. It was hot and they carried their thirty-thirtys and pretended to hunt for the elusive deer.

All at once screams were heard and vehicles revving up their motors. The screams were from women and kids running thru the bush. Bradley was about fifty yards from Don and was the first to see what was going on. He looked towards the noise and saw dust flying thru the air. Standing and with his field glasses he could see what was going on.

Women and kids were running and screaming in all directions. Several men were chasing them in beat-up pickup trucks and a couple on motorcycles. If a woman stopped, one of the men would leap off a pickup or motorcycle and knock her to the ground. Mulitple rapes were taking place over the area.

Any belongings these people carried were thrown to the ground so those carrying them could run faster. Men would run and those riding motorcycles would laugh as they run them down. There was no doubt in Don's mind what he had to do. He moved in close and knelt with his rifle balanced on his knee he leaned forward, took aim and squeezed the trigger. The thirty-thirty kicked back a bit and one of the motorcyclists tumbled head over heels. His bike went flying thru the air for a short distance before coming to earth.

Just then, a girl of about fourteen came running up to him. She had seen he shot one of the bandits. She thru her arms around him and asked for help.

He motioned her to the ground as he saw one on a motorcycles coming straight at him. He through the rifle to his shoulder and again it exploded and the motorcycle and rider fell over and lay still.

By now, the rest of the men noticed where the shots were coming from. The pickup, three in all and the remaining two cycles, stopped in a group. One pointed at him and he knew he was in for it. He wondered where Bradly was.

"Crawl that way," he said to the girl and pointed in the direction of their camp.

"Si," she nodded, smiled and hurried away as fast as she could on her knees.

The motors were being revived up and they began at a high speed as they spun their wheels and came straight at him. He quickly reloaded, took aim and waited until they got closer. He had to get as many as he could to survive this charge. *Where is Bradly* kept going thru his mind.

Then to his right he saw a puff of smoke and heard a report from a rifle. Bradley was there. He took aim at one and fired. This time at the driver in a pickup. The truck went wildly out of control, hit a hump of rock and flipped over.

The other pickup and one motorcycle swerved thru the brush, making a U-turn and headed away from them.

Bradly stood up and waved and started walking his way. *God, I could kiss him,* Don thought but he sure was not going to tell him.

When they joined up Don told him of the girl he'd saved. Arriving at their vehicle, they saw the girl sitting on top of it, waiting their return.

"You made it I see," Don said to her.

"Si, senior, thank you," she said.

"You understand English," Don asked of her.

"Si, in school they teach me," she seemed to brag.

"You're safe now and may go. Are you parents out there some where?" Don asked.

"No, I'm alone and want to live in the America. You take me?" she asked.

"No, Honey, we can not but we'll help you get there. Go out there and round up all those people and have them come in. We'll build a fire and fix something to eat. Tell them not to be afraid we are friends. Would you do that for me," he asked.

"Si," she said and slid off the Bronco into his arms. He sits her down and she took off running into the sagebrush.

After about fifteen minutes, a group of people started wandering into camp a few at a time. When the girl returned, she counted forty-one people.

"Tell them they need not be afraid. We will not hurt them. We are American deer hunters. Those bandits will not be back tonight but still we must post guards. Ask if any of them have guns," Don spoke to the girl.

She rattled off a string of Spanish and waited for a reply.

Four men in the group held up their hands and spoke to the girl.

"Si, those four have old pistols but none have rifles," she relayed to him.

"Good, ask those four to come forward and tell the rest to make camp right close to our vehicle. We have two rifles and will help protect them. Have them build five or six fires around where people will be sleeping. Put on food and we have some extra K-rations for those out of food. They all need a good rest tonight and can go to the U.S. tomorrow, we promise," Don advised them.

"Si," she replied, "I'll go help them and carry wood. I will come back to here so I may sleep under your truck. Si," she asked.

"Yes, of course," both men answered at once. She smiled and walked out into the crowd.

The four men with pistols came up as if reporting for duty.

"Do you speak English," Bradly asked.

"A little," one answered.

"Ok, come with me," he motioned starting out across the desert.

He walked out some forty or fifty yards and posted the men at different locations, covering the entire area. He asked them to get comfortable and food would be sent out as soon as it was done. His instructions were they were to stay awake and if those men or others came back, they were to fire a couple shots into the air. He also told them, people from this group would be sent out to relieve them. The relief persons would not take their pistols but would merely sit with them while they slept. These would be their eyes and ears during their sleep. They would change over every four hours so the others would get some sleep. They were asked if they understood and all nodded "yes."

Bradley decided to send the girl out with the folks bringing food and water, to repeat the instructions in Spanish. He just didn't want to take a chance.

Neither Brad nor Don liked K-rations so they unloaded a few on those having little to eat. They demonstrated how they were opened and what was inside. Once they knew it was food they received many thanks. Both Americans were hoping this group would make it into the U.S. safely.

Brad built a small fire and put on some coffee. They didn't want to cook meat, potatos or bread and eat such food in front of these people. They would wait and perhaps eat some jerky and drink coffee for their evening meal.

Of course, the smell of coffee drifted along air currents and soon a couple Mexicans came to the fire. The girl had returned from her mission and was also eating jerky and drinking coffee. The two who came had their hats off, speaking to her. When they finished she told them what they had said.

"They say they are very grateful you came along when you did or most of them might be dead. They have a favor to ask. The coffee smells so good they could not resist coming forward. Could you spare a little for them?"

"Sure," Don said and went to the back of the Bronco, opened it up and reached in for a pound of coffee. It was packaged in paper for easy handling. Bringing it back to the fire, he handed it to them and thru the girl told, them this was all they could spare and they were to share it with others. They agreed and left for their space after saying many thank you.

Several hours Don and Brad, who had decided to sleep with this many people scattered about, were abruptly awakened by two shots being fired a short distance away.

Both were fully clothed as was their practice in these types of stakeouts, jumped to their feet. Don mentioned to Bard to go around to the left and he would go to the right.

Brad nodded in agreement and picking up his rifle started off slowly thru the sagebrush. He made a wide circle around to about the center of the campers. He squatted down and listened. He heard two voices whispering and looked in that direction. Two men were just rising from the ground with what looked like items. He crawled closer to see just what this might mean. As he was about ten yards out, he could see what had happened.

A couple bodies lay on the ground with blood on them. One man and a woman. Their bodies half stripped. The garments the two held were some clothing, jewelry and a billfold.

The damn vultures, he thought. They will get away with these murders. As he moved to get ready to leap up and shoot the bastards, he noticed they were looking for another victum and the conversation the two were having indicated the same.

He jumped to his feet, throwing the rifle to his shoulder and fired at the taller of the two. Levering another shell into the chamber, he fired again. The first man had just barely hit the ground when followed by the second.

Don popped out of the night and had one of the guards with him. They looked at the scene before them. Don looked at Brad and spoke.

"Did you have to kill them?" he asked.

"Yep, see what they did. They deserved to die. I doubt anyone misses them," he expressed his feelings. The Mexican guard looked on then he spoke.

"These two have been following us for a hundred miles and would attack us in the middle of the night. They always kill their victims and steal what they could. It's good they are dead," he said "not to worry. We will bury them deep. No one will ever find them."

He raised his hand and several men stepped forward. He rattled off some Spanish and the bodies were carried away.

"Hurry and lets get you people to the border. We must get you there before daylight. It's easier in the dark," Don said to the group.

With this, everyone started breaking camp and in no time, it was hard to tell anyone had ever been there. One problem existed to be resolved.

The little Mexican girl who had helped them with the language when they first came. She didn't want to go with the group wanting to stay with the Americans. For some reason she had taken a liking to them.

"Is there anyone in your group who knows this kid? Is there an aunt or uncle with you? This child wants to stay with us and even though she's good help with us understanding your language, I'm not sure she should stay," Don said to the men standing around.

"No, there is no one here who she belongs to. She thinks you are our heroes. You are good men and would not harm her. Let her stay she can be good help for you and when you return to the U.S. you take her with you. Then she finds a home and all ends well, si," one man said.

Don leaned down to talk to her on her level.

"Honey, you're a sweet girl but with us it could be dangerous and we don't want to see you hurt. Wouldn't you like to stay with this group and be in the U.S. later today? It will be three weeks before we go home. We are hunters looking for deer. Please you go with them," Don trying hard to get her to go.

She teared up a little and spoke.

"No, I will stay and help you. I work hard and can cook. You will see. Please let me stay!" as tears started to run down her rosey cheeks.

"Aw, let her stay Don. I'll look after her and between the two of us, we can keep her out of harms way. She is good help and can help us speak and understand Spanish," Brady spoke up.

Don looked up at him then turned back to the girl.

"Will you do as you're told and if bandits or soldiers come and we tell you to hide, you will do this?"

"Si, oh si," was her answer.

"Oh, alright," Don answered and the girl threw her arms around his neck and kissed him on the cheek.

"Well ok, then I must know your name," he said smiling.

"Maria, my name is Maria," was the reply.

"Ok, Maria. Where did you learn to speak English?"Brady asked.

"In school. Our teacher said we must learn it good for some day we may go to America. I want to go to America so I learn it. Yes," she said with a great big smile.

"Yes, honey you did. I'm Bradly or Brad and that fellow there is Don. You know it will be three weeks before we return to the U.S. Is that fine with you?" Brad asked her.

"Si, I have waited very long and can wait a little longer. You are good men and I will be good help for you," with this she held out her hand and shook theirs.

"Maria goes out thru the people and tells them it is time to go and hurry back. You will ride with us," Don said.

"Si" she said and took off thru the sage to make the announcement smiling all the way.

Within minutes a column was heading out towards the border. No lights were used. They had three people walking ahead and spotting rocks and other pitfalls. This close to the border and the fact lights can be seen for miles this was a slower but safer way.

Once at the border, Don and Bradly pointed out the best way across.

The leaders of the Mexican group were told to split into four groups and fan out up and down the border. Then they could try crossing three or four at a time. If they wanted to travel as a group, they could rejoin a mile or two across on the U.S. side. Don suggested they not do because they were easier spotted and followed. He told them it would be safer if the families went on alone. This advice was well received. Most of the people waved at them as they started across.

"Let's get the hell out of here just in case the border patrol is on the ball. The last thing we need is to be caught helping people cross over," Bradly said.

"Yeah, I agree. Head back south a couple miles and turn west until we find a place to camp and set up a post to view from. It's starting to get light and will be easier going now," Don answered.

"Maria, you set down and fasten your seat belt. This could be a bumpy ride," Don said.

The girl did as she was told.

They drove a couple miles south of the border, and then turned west. After about five or six miles they stopped and look over the country with field glasses. They could see hay fields to the south and figured this was good deer country. They looked and looked when all at once Bradly spoke and pointed westerly.

"I see a top of a large tree. We could head for that and maybe, at least find some shade. Can't tell what's around it but if the tree is worth climbing we would have a longer range of view. What do you think, Don?"

"Sounds good to me. I don't see a thing that looks inviting. How far is that tree from here?"

"About a mile, I'd say. Just head west and you see it in four or five minutes," Bradly advised.

As the vehicle bounced along it couldn't be helped. Dust was throwned in the air. Dust that soon would cause them trouble.

Don spotted the tree and turned towards it. A hundred yards from the tree he stopped. He had a feeling something was wrong. He picked up his field glasses and scaned the area.

"Brad, comb the area with your glasses and look for something being wrong. I have a bad feeling about this. We won't go in till we know it's safe," he said.

Both got out of the Bronco, telling Maria to stay put and walked a few feet forward. They fanned out and looked the area over around the tree. Everything seemed quiet until Don looked up the tree.

Swinging in the slight breeze were three corpses handing from a limb.

"Holy Mother of God, look up in the tree Brad and tell me I'm not seeing what I see," he said.

A minute passed and putting down his glasses, Brad spoke.

"I see what you see and I suggest we get the hell out of here now," was the answer.

"Yeah, back to the Bronco and fast," Don said.

They both turned and sprinted the thirty yards to their vehicle. Just as they came within five yards of it, two men stepped out from behind it. They were Mexicans and one was armed with a twelve-gage shotgun and the other a thirty-thirty rifle. Both weapons pointed straight at Don and Bradly.

"What is your hurry," the bigger man asked in broken English.

"This smells like trouble and we are just deer hunters and want no part of it," Don answered.

"Are you hunters and not bandits?" asked the same man. "We saw your dust and decided you may be like them hanging there. They are thieves and have paid for their crimes. Are you with them? Your dust was headed straight here and you may be a part of their gang"

"No, we are American hunters. I'll show you," Don said

He turned around towards the vehicle and yelled to Maria.

"Maria, honey, bring me the papers from the glove box," he asked of her.

"Ok, uncle Don," she answered and in no time she had a fist full of papers and was getting out of the Bronco. She walked to Don and handed them over as she looked over these strange men.

One by one, he sorted through the papers and finding their hunting licenses handed them over to these men.

"How do we know these are not forged papers? You know American criminals have come over here to steal from those trying to get to the U.S.

They are the worst of the worst and must pay for their crimes here in Mexico," the tall man said.

"Are you the police or the army?" asked Brad.

"Oh, no senor. We are vigilantes protecting our own people. Police and the army only take bribes," he answered as he pasted the papers back to Don.

"Are we free to go? We do not wish to stay here for the night," Don asked.

"Si, you go. There are several trees just over that way and closer to the border. You will be more comfortable there. There is also a spring for fresh water. These thieves will hang here a few days as a warning to others," he said and turned around and walked away. The two then started walking for the tree where their trophies were mounted.

Both Americans breathed a sigh of relief as they disappeared into the brush.

"Damn, it is dangerous down here. All this trouble and we haven't even started yet. On the weekend, I'm complaining to Nate. A person could be killed here. We could just disappear and no one ever knows it," Brad spoke out.

"Who were those men, uncle Don?" she asked.

"Oh, just some people trying to make it safe to cross the border. They are doing it the wrong way but don't have much of a choice," he answered.

Getting into the truck, they headed towards the trees that were mentioned.

It was late afternoon when they pulled into a little grove of trees. It was an ideal place. There was a little spring with a couple dozen square yards of green grass. The spring was cluttered with sticks, leaves and the like. It took only a couple minutes to clean it to make it drinkable.

All three sampled its water and found it sweet and very cool.

They backed the Bronco up close to a tree and unloaded their cooking gear and some foodstuffs. They poured out their water and refilled with the spring water. Brad took out a shovel and dug about a foot around the spring, making it wider and easier to get water from.

Once completed they took a break and sat on the cool green grass. The

94

trees limbs provided shade and they all were content on the place they had found for a camp.

The men placed their backs against a tree and watched Maria play with a doll she had brought with her. She would ask questions about America and how great it would be if she could become a citizen.

They in turn would question her on where she was from, her folks, etc.

She had come from a farm about thirty miles outside of Mexico City. Her folks were like sharecroppers. If crops were bad one year, they went hungry. When the crops were good they did well. She told them her parents always wanted to go the America but we afraid to just start out on their own. Rarely did they have money.

Then this man came along and said he would let them go with him and some others to America. Her father believed him and they started out a month ago. They knew it would be a hard trip but no one knew just how hard. He father died about ten days out. The man who they were traveling with raped her mother several times causing her to commit suicide. With both parents gone, she was on her own and committed to finding a better life.

Because she was small, no one bothered her and she worked for the man and several others. The ones they found her with treated her well and so she stayed with them. Most were good people but she's glad to have found kind uncles like Don and Brad.

After supper, they sat around having to plan what they should do and how to do it. After some discussion they decided to stay camped where they were, monitor and count those crossing the border. It had to be a twenty-four hour job. They decided to work it in shifts of four hours each. It would break up their rest but it had to be done.

When tucking Maria in for the night, she insisted on giving each a kiss.

Don and Carl were a little shy about this but finally gave in to her wishes.

After she fell asleep, they talked about her.

"What are we doing about this girl? She's very nice and pleasant. She appears to be a hard worker. I feel sorry for her losing both parents but we have no business with her. More over we are not here to help people over the border. The government's paying us to monitor how many are coming and we are to spot potential terriorist. So far, all we've done is kill people and adopt a girl. Boy is Nate going to be upset with us," Brad pronounced to his partner.

"Damn it, I know all that. I think Nate will understand once we tell him the whole story," Don answered.

"Well, let's make another pot of coffee and sleep on this. It'll look better in the morning. No need of telling Nate until the weekend. Maybe the others have had this same luck. Damn but it's lawless down here. We don't hear the half of it in the states, "Brad said.

The coffee was brewed and Don chose the first shift for sleeping. Brad poured hemself a cup of coffee and climbed upon the Bronco, complete with field glasses and thirty-thirty and coffee. Don spread his sleeping bag out near the girl and was soon fast asleep.

God, it's lonely out here, Brad was thinking. He'd only been on post an hour and was already bored with the job. He scanned the terraine until his eyes hurt. Peering thru the field glasses with such devotion caused them to tire easily. He changed his method, which helped both his eyes and his attitude. He drew his coat tighter around himself as the night drew chilly.

Another hour pasted and then another. As Brad checked, his watch he was delighted three hours had pasted and his turn to sleep was only an hour away.

Again, he placed the field glasses to his eyes and as he scanned the area, he thought he saw lights. He turned back to the spot and saw nothing. He was sure he had seen a couple small lights swinging back and forth. He put the glasses down and rubbed his eyes.

Ten minutes later, he again was peering thru the glasses. He tried to find the spot where he'd seen the lights. All at once, they were there. This time he was sure. There were two lights about ten feet apart.

As he watched the lights seemed to go off then come back on. He believed them to be flashlights. *That's some one walking,* he thought.

The lights weren't heading their way. They seemed to stay about the same distance away. As Brad watched, they appeared to be moving in a straight line towards the border. *Probably some people moving to go over the border, he thought.* Just the same, it could be something else and needed checking out.

He slid to the ground and gently shook Don.

"Wake up Don, I think we may have something to check out," he said as Don was coming awake.

"What is it, Brad, my turn to watch," he said still half asleep.

"Get up; we need to check something out. Be quiet and don't wake the girl," Brad replied.

With this, Don jumped to his feet and Brad pointed to the northwest.

"I don't see a thing," Don said.

"Keep looking. There are two small lights out about one hundred yards. I think they're flashlights and moving slowly towards the border," Brad told him.

"Damn I can't see anything. I'm getting on the Bronco," Don announced. He climbed on top of the vehicle and began a sweep of the area with field glasses. About the third time around, he saw what Brad had seen. He hurried down and whispered to Brad.

"Yes, you're right. Someone is out there all right. Funny they are moving so slow and with flashlights. Let's check them out," he stated.

They both looked down at the girl all curled up and asleep.

"She'll be ok. We won't be gone long," Don said as they picked up the rifles and each a hunting knife. They dumped shells into their pockets just in case they ran into trouble. Loaded for bear, they headed out toward the lights.

Fifty yards covered before they neared the lights, they heard voices coming from those ahead. They stopped and listened for minutes trying to catch every word. The group had stopped to rest and was cursing the way they had to travel. Some of them were speaking English and others would sometimes speak in Arabic. Don had spent some time in the world of the Arab. He didn't understand it but recognized it.

"Some of those, if not all of them are Arabs," he whispered to Brad.

"Damn, what have we fallen into," Brad whispered back, "do you think they're smugglers and are carrying weapons or worse?"

"It's more likely they are terrorists. We need to get in close and find out. Let's decide right now on if they are and carrying explosives, we destroy them. This isn't not what we are here for but by God, I'm not going to let things pass that could be going to harm my country. We'll explain to Nate later. Ok with you Brad?" Don asked.

"Yes, hell yes, I'm looking for a little excitement anyway," came the reply. "We have to be careful because if they are who we think they are, you can bet they are armed to the teeth. Most likely, they have automatic weapons and all we have are thrity-thirtys and a couple pistols. As we move in close, remember we must spot and know the location of their whole crew. I don't want to get shot in the back by someone following them."

They went on walking slowly and listening for signs that might tell them how many they might confront. Now they were twenty yards from the group they saw only four. They were huddled around a small fire drinking coffee. They stayed very still and listened.

"Damn, I don't see why we had to bring this stuff all the way from Mexico into the U.S. Damn long ways if you ask me. They are going to blow the space needle in Seattle. Why not come in thru Canada?" one voice was saying.

"Because they tried that and the carrier was caught at the border so they're trying a different way. Once in Arizona this stuff will be hidden in bales of straw and hauled to Seattle. All we have to do is get it into Arizona as we promised and we get a big payday. The Arabs will take it from there and we are free and clear," answered another.

"Right," said the other.

"Sounds like four," Brad said in a whisper.

"Yeah," Don acknowledge.

"Just to make sure, you go around to the right at distance of thirty yards and I'll go left and look for guards that are staying just out of sight. I doubt if we find any because they would also be with the fire to get some of that coffee. Be thinking how we're going to handle this. I'm with you on doing something. I know some people in Seattle that go to the needle for lunch at times," Brad suggested.

"Ok, see you on the other side. Now be quiet so we don't get caught," Don said and disappeared into the darkness.

About half way around, Don heard a commotion at the fire. He couldn't see what had happened but a cold shilver ran down his spine telling him to find out.

Getting down on his hands and knees, he crawled in the direction of the fire. He noticed those around had thrown more wood on and it was a much bigger fire.

When he was finally in sight, he gasped in terror. They had Brad who was just getting up from the ground. A trickle of blood indicated he'd been hit.

"Who the hell are you," he heard one of the men ask Brad.

"I'm just a deer hunter and couldn't sleep. Your coffee smelled so good I thought I'd come by and ask for a cup," Brad was saying.

"Liar, where is your camp?" the leader asked.

"About three hundred yards west of here. Come I'll show you," Brad said.

"No, I don't care. How did you know we were here?" he asked again.

"Your flashlights got me curious when I saw them and you moving thru the night. I just figured you were heading for the border like the Mexicans are. I'm sorry I didn't mean to disturb you. I'll go back to my camp now," Brad was saying.

"No, you won't. Give him a cup of that coffee while I think of what to do with him?" the one seeming to be their leader said.

"Oh, let me go and I won't tell anyone I saw you. We are Americans and must stick together in a hostile land," Brad continued hoping Don would soon notice the trouble he was in.

Don was sitting back trying to figure out how to get Brad out of there without getting either one killed.

After minutes of planning, he decided to go out aways and set a diversion. If he could pull it off, they both could get out without getting hurt. First, he had to get a look at what was in the wagon. Earlier, felt he knew it was explosive material.

He waited a few minutes and crawled into their camp. Most were napping. They had brought out a bottle of whiskey and after a few drinks were sleepy. Don knew this was his chance.

Crouched, he slowly moved in on the truck they were using. He approached from the rear. The fire, the four men and Brad were at the front of the truck. In fact, they were a good twenty yards away, Don noted.

The canvas was loose at this location. He pulled it open and with his flashlight, he flashed light under the covering. This was done with care and so no one up front could see. No light was allowed out from under the tarp.

Wow, Don thought at the sight before him. Boxes of dynamite were in sight. Moving around the side away from the men, he found a loose spot and looked under. Two boxes of C-4 came into sight. *Damn that's more than needed to bring down the space needle*, he thought.

Looking further under the tarp, he found a box of caps. Just what he needed to blow them all to hell after he got Brad out. He took a dozen caps, the kind that need a shock to set them off, and stuck them into the dynamite. They were placed very close together to make them easier to set off.

He then took the canvas and folded it upwards a little making an area to shoot at and covering it with white cloth. A good target. *Now to get Brad out.* He made his way to the back again. Reaching under the tarp, he pulled out seven or eight sticks of dynamite. He'd also take a couple caps and several yards of fuses.

He had to get Brad's attention so he knew if anything happened, he would make a break for it. He moved around and watched the four yawning. He noticed they had not yet tied Brad up. He knew he must hurry before they did. Picking up a couple small rocks, he pitched one near Brad's feet. One was all that was needed. Don saw a smile appear on Brad's face and he nodded.

Fifty yards out, he planted the dynamite under some rocks. He attached the caps and fuses and began stringing out the fuse towards the truck as he went. He ran out of fuse just five yards shy of the camp. Cuping his hands he lit a match putting fire to the fuse. He watched as the fire ran down the fuse and out of sight.

Seconds later, there was an explosion and pieces of rock rained down over them. Everyone was concerned about him and didn't see Bard run out of camp. He came running by where Don was and they both ran together for a couple hundred yards.

Winded, they had to stop for a rest. After they stopped and their hearts quit beating so loud, they listened. After a while, they knew they were not followed.

"Damn, I'm glad to see you Don," Brad said, "now what do we do."

"I've fixed a target to shoot that will blow that truck to hell and back and anyone within a hundred yards of it. Because you've been closer to them than I have would you like to be the one to send'em to hell," Don replied.

"Damn rights I would but what do you think Nate will say. We're down him to montor not to attack?" Brad said.

"That truck is heading into the U.S. to do damage to our people and I don't give a damn what Nate will say? We owe allegence to the U.S. and that means keeping that truck from killing our people. If you don't want to shoot my target, I will. Make up your mind before they get away," Don answered.

"Well it's too dark to shoot at a target. We'd never hit it," Brad reminder him.

"In half an hour it will be a little lighter and then we do it. Besides, I fixed some white cloth around it. All you have to do is hit it right in the middle. Target is about a foot across. We'll hit it alright. Let's get back to our rig," Don said.

Returning to their rig, they made some coffee and waited. Thirty minutes later, they decided to get to it. This chore had to be done before they crossed the border.

Don climbed on top of the Bronco and looked around with his field glasses. Brad had wakened Maria, packed their sleeping bags and other stuff in the vehicle. Maria helped and by the time Brad came down, they were ready to go. Brad had explained to her what they were about to do. She accepted this without comment, still half-asleep.

"I see they are moving out and still using flashlights. They have changed their route. They are further west than before. Come on I'll drive," Don said.

They moved across the desert floor slowly until they were a couple hundred yards from the truck. Don stopped and shut off the engine.

"From here we go on foot," he announced.

Don and Bradly were both good shots with their thirty-thirtys but needed to be within a hundred yards of the target. They walked within range and found a hole in the dirt that would accomidate both of them during the explosion. With that much C-4 on the truck, they weren't sure just how big the damage would be. They knew they might have two seconds to dive into that hole once they hit the target or no time at all.

A small pile of dirt for them to stand on next to the hole helped elevate them and give a better view of the truck. The darkness was fading and they needed to be quick. The border was just a stones throw away. Both used their field glasses to look over the truck.

"I see your target," Brad said and threw his rifle to his shoulders.

"Make sure your on target before you fire. We may only get one chance," Don said.

"Don't worry, I'll get it," came Brad's reply.

The click of the hammer coming on the weapon was deafing or so it seemed. Seconds latter the hammer dropped and the desert lit up with the explosion as these two rolled into the hole.

Within a second or two, a wind blew across them. They lay still until this stopped. Then they slowly peeked out and were shocked at what they saw.

There was a huge hole where the truck had been and not a living thing in the area. From where they stood, it looked like a giant hand had come down from heaven and removed all plants and living things for at least a hundred square yards. It looked like a barren land. It could have been the surface of the moon or some distance planet. They both knew the men with the load had been vaporized.

Standing up they got an even more frighting picture of what that much explosive could do. The vehicle hauling looked like a curled up mess of melted tin.

They looked at each other and shiverd. They couldn't help but feel sorry for the terrorists.

"Well," Don said, "let's get the hell out of here. Half the country side will be here pretty soon. We'd best not be caught around here," he exclaimed.

"I'm with you. Lets go," and they turned and ran for the Bronco.

Arriving there they found Maria in the cab and scared. She hugged them but could hardly speak.

"What, what was that explosion?" she said thru tears and a shaking body.

"Just some bad guys on their way to hell," Brady said.

"Don't worry, honey, it's all over now and we are leaving. Sit down and we'll be off," Don told her.

The girl did what she was told to do and soon fell asleep between the two men. Brad and Don looked at each other and smiled. They were becoming fond of the little one.

For about three hours they drove west and south. They wanted to get away from the border for awhile. They would set up camp further south. After all anyone crossing the border would have to go pass them even when this far from the border.

After winding around they come upon a gravel pit. It was fifty yards across and twenty feet deep. This was where they would set up camp. The girl could play in the pit while the others watched for people heading for the border. Back to montoring.

The Bronco was parked at the lip of the pit while they sat up camp in the pit. Sleep bags and cooking gear was packed to the floor and set up. Coffee was made and cold lunch meat sandwiches were served. All were hungry.

The meal completed Maria asked if she could go exploring the pit.

"Yes, shore," Brad told her, "but don't go out of sight of the Bronco. Stay in the pit, Ok,"

The two watched her go and sat back with their coffee and relaxed. They sipped their coffee as their minds were contemplating what they should tell her about why they were here in Mexico.

"Well, we are deer hunters and we had better stick to that. We don't want her to slip, when others were around and say anything else," Don suggested.

"Of course we should. The kid might slip up at the wrong time and cause us trouble," Brad agreed closing the matter.

CHAPTER 7

Further up the line and closer to the California border, Delbert and Ed had set up camp. The location was on the east side of a huge grain field. The soil here was not sand and water was available so crops were being raised. On their side of the field was a narrow strip of land that was rocky, too rocky to farm. An idea place for Mexicans to cross the border. This part of the border, like many others was not heavily patroled. Day and night one could cross without detection. It was patrolled, but only about once an hour Delbert and Ed noticed. They had timed the patrols and wondered why the guards even bothered. One sneaking across the border had only to wait and see the patrol go by and then cross over. It would be an hour before the patrol would return. Once they knew this, they backed off about a mile and set up camp. In three days they had counted over three hundred Mexicans cross over. It was like a flood of humanity running away from home. The two would often talk about this.

"God, it must be terrible living in Mexico for this many people trying to escape," Ed noted.

"Well, if you live under the heel of evil men, what can you expect," Delbert responded.

"Yeah, I know," Ed answered, "But wouldn't you rise up and overthrow that type of government. The American people surely would rather than leave the homeland. Of course we all have weapons and courage to do it with. If you hold people down so long, it takes all the fight

104

out of them. The Mexican people are a peaceful people and haven't reached that point yet. When they do there will be one hell of a revolution. It won't be pretty but it will be effective.

"Oh well, I'll leave politics to others. I have all I can do just keeping myself on the straight and narrow. I would feed these people here and not let them cross over. It would be cheaper; they would be happier and our jobs would stay with Americans. These people don't realize they are deluteing salaries and soon there will be no jobs for them. The government will have broken its self and there will be no money for health care, employment and we will be reduced to a third world country. We are almost there no thanks to the gangsters in Washington, D.C.," Delbert chipped in.

As the people passed by, they would wave at the two Americans, then not give them a second thought. Once in a while one would approached the two and ask for a drink of water. They were given what the needed and be on their way.

"Here comes a pack train of horses. Looks like they are loaded down for a long trip. They may be heading up Tucson way and those mountains. They may hide out there a while and then split up into two and threes," Ed said and pointed south so Delbert could see for himself. They were headed right for the two Americans. It was a string of twenty horses and several men to handle them. This seemed strange to both men. Of course they understood that people running away from their homeland may do weird things. In the minds and hearts these people are looking to survive, their main goal.

The caravan continued to approach the Americans. As they neared, Delbert and Ed both wondered about their intentions. Time would tell and they would wait to see. Both picked up their rifles and waited.

Two men from the group broke away and walked straight to the Americans.

"Are you the ones we are supposed to meet up with?" one of the strangers asked.

"No, we are deer hunters from the U.S. and don't know what you're talking about," Delbert explained.

"We are to meet a man who will take us to Tucson, Arizona. Have you seen such a man?" the other man asked.

"No, sorry we just arrived and so far you are the only ones we've seen. Your man must be on the other side of the border. It's straight ahead," Ed said.

The two men thought a minute and talked to each in whispers for several minutes.

"This is your campsite and it has water. Is it alright if we camp here for most of the night," one of the strangers asked of Delbert, "we'll be gone before dawn."

"No, go ahead. Take your animals over that way about fifty yards and you'll find grass and water. We'll be quiet so they don't get spooked. One of us will stay up all night just to protect ourselves from bandits," Ed said.

"Thanks," the man said and walked back to the string of horses.

"As soon as he was far enough away not to hear what Delbert and Ed were saying, Ed pipes up.

"There's something mighty strange about that group, Delbert. I don't trust them and why bring along a string of horses. Strange very strange."

"Now Ed, you are too suspicious of people. You must remember this is a poor country and most people here can not afford a car or pick-up truck. Many still farm with horses. However I believe you're right. That guy did not look like a Mexican. I wonder about him. I noticed the long tube shape items strapped to the back of a couple of those horses look a lot like missile launchers. I think the bustards are terrorists. Make sense to you?" he asked Ed.

"I didn't see any tubles but I wasn't looking. I was concentrating on the man himself. The rest looked like they were out of place and I would smear most were Arabs. What do you want to do Delbert?" Ed asked.

"I don't know yet. I could call Nate and ask but we don't have enough information for that. Nate would think we were jumping at our shadows. I think we go on a patrol tonight and see if we can find out more about this group. I'll make a note and when we get back on the weekend, we'll discuss it with the group. I'm sure the rest of our people have seen suspicious happening and people. I don't feel comfortable and will be grateful when I get back home. The Mexicans can keep this country for all I care. Let's fix something and eat. I'll fix some coffee," Delbert volunteered.

There was an occasional whinny from the horses and men cursing at them. This cursing was in Arabic language. A dead give away. The bastards had to be terrorists.

Dusk turned to darkness quickly and silently in the desert counrty. Delbert had turned in and Ed would wake him in four hours. They both would then set out on a mission on finding out just who those with the pack train were and whether they were a danger to the U.S. Both knew a dirty bomb could come across the border in this manner, easly.

At midnight, both Ed and Delbert prepared for their little patrol over to the pack train. All sound asleep quiet and even some faint snoring sound could be heard drifting across the prairie.

"Let's go in from the other side. You take one side of the camp. All we want to do is see what they are carrying so don't go into where they are sleeping. They should have guards so be careful," Delbert advise.

"Right, got you. Let's go," Ed said and turned to start the walk.

As silent as Indians they crept up to the camp. Both knew they had to stay away from the horses. They were quiet and could be spooked easily. This did present a problem for them. Most likely they had unloaded right next to where they tethered the horses.

Within twenty yards of the camp, they stopped and viewed the layout. As luck would have it the horses were a good forty yards from camp. Thru their night goggles they could make out two men guarding them. Giving attention to the area where men were sleeping they noticed the equipment the horses had been carrying was in the center of the camp. The men were sleeping in sleeping bags sort of around it. There were considerable distances between some of the men that would allow the two to sneak in and get a look at the packs. However one little noise might wake the entire camp and they would be in a hella lot of trouble. It appeared the ones at the horses could not see them. A hump of ground blocking their view of the camp.

Ed motioned to his knife and made a movement that indicated cutting open the packs.

Delbert shook his head "no". They must come and go undetected without leaving a sign they were ever there. A cut strap of fabric would tell on them. When the men loaded the packs on the horses, someone would noticed the cuts and know it was tampered with. It could be hell to pay if this happened. He motioned back they would untie straps and then tie them back. Both knew this was going to be hairy, but they might not get another chance to look. No guards on duty.

"You go around to the right and I'll peel off to the left. We'll be in plain sight of each other so if they hear us; we'll have a better chance of getting away. Let's go," Delbert whispered to Ed.

They crept into the circle. Ed found a pack that had been hastely packed and only one strap was buckled. He stopped and knelt down. He opened the strap and looked inside. Shiney cansters were packed solidly inside. The lid on them was cone shaped. At first he thought they were coffee thermals. He tried to slip one out and it was very heavy so he left it there. He noticed it felt a little warm.

Delbert stopped near a pack that was loosely covered and noticed some short pipes with caps on the ends. Both ends. They looked like pipe bombs. He found a paper with Arabic writing on it. Not being able to read it and thinking they wouldn't miss it, he stuffed it in his shirt. Another pack had weird looking metals in it also.

Now why the hell anyone would be trapsing around in this country with this type of junk, he thought to himself. Looking over at Ed he signaled he was leaving. Both men slipped out without waking anyone.

Back at camp they reviewed what they had seen.

"You know that cylinders looked a lot like you see in the movies. You know the ones they haul around radio active materials in. They could cut down spent fuel rods from a nuclear power plant and ship them that way. A border guard would never think of that if they're stopped. Under the Bush plan they might not even search them. What I wouldn't give for a Geiger-counter right now," Ed said.

"You're right but they would have to drop them from an airplane or have something to shoot it over a wide area," Delbert said.

"No, I don't think so," Ed interrupted, "all they have to do is set of a few bombs and then announce what they've done and a whole city would panic. Explosives would spread the junk thru the air. On a windy day spread it far and wide. I just know those, those things are radio-active. The bastards are eco-terrorist or worse. I wonder where they're headed. Because they're using pack animals, I'd bet Tucson, Arzonia. You thnk that's possible Delbert?"

"Yes, I do. I think the stuff I saw and thought was junk plays into that. God, I wished the weekend would hurry up and get here so we can get this information to Nate," Delbert said. "I think it's important it's worthy of a call, but lets wait till morning. They're not going anywhere tonight. Lets think of an excuse to talk to them and maybe find out just where they're headed. Might help."

The morning broke bright and clear. Delbert and Ed were both up and brewing coffee as the sun appeared in the west. Ed had the last shift and was eager to get to bed. They could hear the pack animals being readied for todays march into the U.S. The men with the horses were shouting and cursing at the animals.

"Sound like they're having trouble packing up the animals. You go to sleep Ed and I will go see if I can be of help. The shouting and cursing is not all English. Sounds like a bunch of Arabs to me. If you hear a gun shot, come running, I'll be in trouble," Delbert told him.

Rita was getting restless and came out of the truck.

"Can I go with you Uncle Delbert? I can tell you what they say. I'm good at that," she smiled as she talked.

Delbert had to admit to himself that this little girl was tugging at his heart strings. She was cute as hell and smart. She was trying so hard to be of help. He didn't want to tell her no, but had to. He'd never forgive himself if he got her hurt.

"Not this time, Honey, maybe next time. Those men are bad and I don't want you hurt. I promise to do something exciting today while Uncle Ed sleeps," he told her.

Her smile turned into a frown and little tears started forming at the corners of her eyes as she spoke.

"Darn, I never get to do anything," she said.

He didn't want her to break down and cry so he took her in his arms and gave her a hug.

"Now don't cry. You, Ed and I are out here on an adventure and have to be brave. You are brave aren't you, Rita?" he asked.

"Well, I guess so," she replied as the tears seemed to dry up, "but what exciting thing can we do out here on this old desert. It's just hot and dry and there's nothing to do."

"We can go deer hunting and if we see one, I'll let you shoot it for me. I'll help you hold the rifle and you pull the trigger," he said as a smile started spreading across her face.

"Ok, it's a deal. I'll help Uncle Ed fix breakfast while you're gone. I'm really hungry," she exclaimed.

Delbert took the last two swallows from his cup and started off in the direction of the pack train. He left his thirty-thirty behind but Ed noticed he had straped on a revolver.

Looking over a clump of sand Delbert saw what a mess the men at the pack train was having loading up the animals. It was almost as if the animals knew the items they carried were toxic.

When he was in view and the men noticed him, he raised his hand and waved. A couple of the men grabbed for rifles. One stepped out from the group and waved them away and walked to greet this stranger.

"What can we do for you this morning?" he asked Delbert.

"Nothing. I heard all the commotion from our camp and thought I might be of help. Horses are more difficult to manage than other pack animals. Your men don't seem to have the experience with horses. May I show you how it's done?" he offered.

The man was silent for a couple minutes before responding.

"Yes, please do," he answered.

Delbert walked to the first horse and told the man there to hold the horse's head in a certain way. Demostrating the technic while the first one interpered for him. He then had another man come over and showed how to do the loading. When the animal was loaded, without any trouble, Delbert spoke.

"That's the way it should be done," he advised the first man.

"That was very good. Can we load one more and I'll have the whole group watch. I am so grateful for your help," he expressed himself to Delbert.

The man made an announcement and the other men gathered round to watch. Again Delbert demonstrated how the loading should be done. Training completed, the English speaking man issured orders and the men went back to their horses.

Delbert stood watching with the leader of the group. This man offered Delbert a cigarette as they watched.

At first Delbert was going to say "no" until he saw the kind the man offered. The cigarettes came out of a yellow box. They were a little longer than American cigarettes. He took the offering and a light.

"Thanks a million," the leader said, "It would have taken forever to load those cursed animals had you not came along.

"That alright. In the desert one must help others. Don't you agree?"

"Yes," he said. Looking over the group an accident occurred. Two of the men loading dropped a load. It was almost on the horse when it came plunging to the ground. The leader ran to the two and seemed to be curseing them. Delbert saw why. Shineing cylinders were spread on the ground. At least a dozen. The fabric they'd been housed in simply ripped open scattering its load.

Delbert looked away and tried to not seem interested. He noticed the leader was staring at him. Once the mess was repackaged and loaded, the leader returned to where Delbert was standing.

Delbert was just finishing his cigatette as he approached.

"Well I must go we are going deer hunting this morning," Delbert said, "I wish you luck and I think your men will get the hang of it in a day or so."

"Yes, I again thank you," said the leader and they shook hands.

Delbert started to walk away when he stopped to speak.

"May I have another one of your cigarettes? They are new to me and very good," he lied.

"Yes, of course. Here take the rest of the pack. I have plenty more," he said as he passed the pack to Delbert.

Delbert said "Thanks" and headed back to camp with his evidence.

Back at the Bronco, Delbert related to Ed what happened and showed him the cigarette pack. Ed examed it before speaking.

"That's a pack of arab cigarettes alright. What the hell are Arabs doing in Mexico and near our border! Can only be one reason. The sneaky little bastards are here to do us harm. Let's go ahead and set up an ambush and kill the whole damn bunch. Delbert we can't let them get into the states."

"No, Ed, you just calm down. I'll call Nate and report this and let him take it from there. After all, if they are caught on our side of the border the penalties will be much greater. We are just here to monitor and to see what we can see. I agree those people are here to do us harm, but let's do this the right way. Now lets eat, I'm starved," he said.

As he turned towards the fire, Rita was standing there with a plate filled with eggs, potatoes a couple slice of bread. In her other hand was a cup of steaming coffee.

"Thanks honey," he said as he took the plate and found a place to sit and feed himself. "Have you eaten yet?" he asked her.

"No, but I will as soon as Uncle Ed sits down," she answered holding another plated loaded down and a cup of coffee for Ed. Ed took the plate and thanked her. He sat on the ground near Delbert. The two men watched her dish up a plate for herself. She then came over and sat between the two.

"It appears we've been adopted by this child," Delbert said smiling at her. She made no response except to smile.

The meal over, Delbert got the phone from the front seat of the Bronco and dialed Nate.

Ring, ring, ring, went Nate's phone. He sat down his coffee and answered it.

"Good morning, Delbert, what's going on," he said and waited for Delbert to speak.

"All hell I'm afraid, Nate. This is important and I'll need to know if we should attack a group traveling towards the border. In the next five minutes he told Nate everything that's happened and about the cigarette package. He forgot to say anything about the girl. Later, he surmised, he was afraid to because Nate might want her left behind with someone else.

She had wiggled herself into the hearts of Ed and himself. He decides to tell him later.

"Damn it. More bad news. Well I think it's time I had a heart to heart with the General and get us armed if we are to stay. No, don't attack anyone. I think I know where they are going. Tucson, Az. There are other terrorists heading that way. The General is aware of this and they are being monitored. Once we find out where they are going and who will meet them, the F.B.I. will close in. Good work, Delbert.

"Lets all head back to the hacienda today and re-group. Things are hotter here than our people know. Hurry back and start now. I'll notify everyone and we'll see you by evening. Drinks are on me tonight. Uh, make that on the General," he said as he hung up.

A ringing in his ears shook the General awake. He had just started to doze. The sat upright and looked around. The ringing came again.

"Damn telephone," he said out loud, "I should have taken it off the hook."

He reached out and picked it up. Putting it to his face he unttered a salutation to the party on the other end.

"General," Nate here, "did I catch you asleep?"

"No. hell no. You must think all Generals do is sleep. No, now why did you disturb me. I've got work to do. Now spit it out,"was the response.

"Well general, it seems this place is a hot bed of activity and my people and I am concerned. We've had more trouble at one of our posts" and he started telling the General of the recent problems Delbert and Ed were having.

"Well, you're the ones down there. What do you feel I should do about it, Nate?" he'd simmered down somewhat.

"First, do you want us to stay or not. If we stay we want more money and lots of firepower. Second we want it now. Right now. I'm not sending another person out into this desert without protection and I might even consolidate my groups into threes and not twos. They'd be better protected in a larger group. I also want a system set up so if we kill anyone, either Mexican police or citizen, we don't stand trial. You must get us out.

I don't know how you can do this but that's what it takes. You have my word we won't go out of our way to kill anyone, but we damn sure will if they pose a threat to us. I guess you'll have to get the President involved. Both of them," Nate ended his speal.

"Now look here Nate, you can't tell me what to do. These Presidents may not listen to me," replied the General.

"Talk fast and hard and they will. I think both countries want the information we can give them if we stay. We'll all be here over the weekend so if it's a go, get the weapons by noon on Sunday. By the way general is there anything special you'd like us to do, such as bomb any weapons or weapon carriers. If not then how about we capture them and bury them for retrieval later." he said.

There was silence on the line. Nate could hear the General breathing. After a couple minutes he spoke.

"I'll get back to you on that?" he said and hung up.

Nate smiled. He knew the old boy would jump to it.

Around the table all were gathered for supper. There were plenty sighs of relief. All were glad to be back to a safe area. It seemed their first week on the job had been just short of a nightmare. Everyone was telling others of their experiences and close calls. The little girl Rita sat between Ed and Delbert. Everyone had talked to her and learned she had adopted Uncle Ed and Delbert. They all had a good life as did Rita. After all the stories were told of her childhood.

Nate kept skipping away from any business at the meeting until Rita was in bed. The old man, caring for them, made her a bed in the far end of the house far enough she couldn't hear. They weren't afraid of her over hearing; they just didn't want to scare her with violent talk.

"Ok, friends, Rita is now in bed and we need to decide what to do. I'm taking a vote. Do we stay or do we go back to our lives and leave this mess as it is. How do you see it?" Nate proposed to his crew.

"I'm staying," said Delbert, "after all I've seen I think we can do a lot of good. Nate told us if we stay we'll get fire power. I'm for that. If it comes we can then kill the bastards entering our country to harm it. The terrorists we let through to the border patrol to monitor their movements inside the U.S. If we knock out those bringing weapons then they will have to find new sourses inside our borders. That makes it easier for local police agencies to follow. In fact, if we create enough hell and kill enough weapons dealers, the word will go out not to try for the border. It also means fewer guns to kill Americans. I'm staying," he finished.

"Well, hell, if he stays, someone has to stay to cover him so I'm staying," Ed piped up.

"I'm here for the duration," Sam Brown mentioned.

"Boise, Idaho would look awful good right now, but to insure it stays that way, Katrina and I are staying," Carl said and gave Nate a wink.

"Well, we're not running out on a fight. It is just starting to get interesting," said the others all together.

"I guess we have to stay to protect the two new uncles. Hell, they don't know how to raise a kid," Nate said with a smirk on his face.

Everyone had a good laugh and asked the old man to bring drinks.

A couple hours later, Nate's phone rang. Silence settled over the group. This was the call from the General they had all been waiting for. Nate took his time in picking up the phone and answering it.

"Hello, General," Nate said, "Do you have instructions for us."

"Yes, the groups of men I represent seem to feel that since you're there you might as well do something constructive. About dark tomorrow, you'll get weapons that have some power behind them. The same person will deliver them as before. The people here want you to take out those person bringing drugs across the border. I'll give you a phone number as we finish talking. When you kill and or destroy someone or a group, call this number. It will ring into a private line at the border patrol office nearest you. Advice the person answering the phone, his name is Jim, where and when you had trouble and his people will clean up and take the credit. After all that is their duty along with the illegals. They will seize the drugs and later destroy them. All this will protect your people. You are to confirm terrorists coming this way and try to determine where they are heading. This information you forward to me as usual and I'll put it to the right people to track. Hopefully this will prevent any more attacks on our turf. Got it Nate?" he asked.

"Yeah, I got it. I look forward to seeing you again Gereral, bye," Nate answered and hung up.

"Damn he's pushy," Nate said with a smile to the group.

"Weapons will be here about dark tomorrow night. When they come we will divide them and store them in the vehicles. We are to knock out drug dealers only and let the terrorists thru. He needs us to identify them if we can and get all the information on them we can. Once we kill or capture these dealers, we are to call this number and leave the mess to them. The number is on this paper." he said passing the paper down the line. Each member wrote it down and tucked it away.

"Oh, I almost forgot. Tomorrow we will reorganize our groups by making up two groups of three each. This way we have a better chance of surviving a fire fight. Katrina, I would like you to stay behind and look after Rita for us?" Nate finished with a question.

"No way and miss all the excitement. Why can't the old man and woman do that for us?" she responded.

"They can, I just thought I'd offer," came the reply.

Sam Brown spoke up after this conversation subsided.

"I'm going back out there on my own. That will make it just right for two groups with three each. I do have a mission and must get back to it. You folks work your way and I'll work mine. Just be careful out there when you're shooting, I may be close by. I'd hate to get shot in the ass by an American. I do wish you luck and I have a feeling you have plenty of that. I think that every son-of-a-bitch coming thru this area is carrying drugs. Hopefully most will resist and you kill them. That would be good riddance to bad rubblish.

The group grew silent and sipped their drinks. Sam's opinion reminded all of the serious responsibility they had taken on and that killing could very well be a part of their job. No one liked this part but could be forced to do it. Time would tell. This was where their thoughts were and of chances they may be taking.

Sunday came and everyone went their own direction for the day. All wanted to relax and live a little. Everyone was advised by Nate to be back early on Monday morning. He would be at the haciendia to receive the weapons that were coming. His day would be filled with sleeping and thinking of his true love in Colombia. In three weeks he'd be back there and making love to her. He could hardly wait.

Carl and Katrina decided to take Rita shopping in town. The child needed clothes and both throught it would be fun to take her. Both were taken with her and her adult ways. Secretly both would have liked to have a child but had never had the time. This was a chance to be a family for a day.

The rest headed for town, for drinking and chasing women. After all this was the best way to really relax according to Ed. By nine AM they were all gone except Nate and their caretakers.

CHAPTER 8

Monday was a dark and cloudy day. There were clouds that threatened rain and with it lighting. Not a nice day for a new mission to start. Nate and crew seemed rested and willing to get started. Breakfast was served around the large table and most had finished eating and were sitting back and sipping coffee. They were waiting for Nate to spell out the mission and to give instructions. This time the mission was different and perhaps a little more dangerous. Not only were they to monitor how many people were escaping Mexico, but they were to hunt down and kill drug dealers. If they were lucky the word would spread and they would quit trying to bring the poison into the U.S. this way.

This group had no qualms about killing the drug dealers. After Columbia, they could see the results in Florida and the east coast of their actions. The General was hoping for something similar on this front. The Colombian mission had completely killed the drug trade coming in from Cuba.

His mission was different because it was on land and they could be trapped too easily. Here, there were no high speed boats to carry them away from each encounter. Nate's only hope for success was to ambush their targets. They also had to identify the ones carrying drugs. The last thing they wanted was to kill innocent people. That alone would be difficult in this arrid land. Movement of people could be seen for miles in these open spaces which would help and hurt. It would hurt if people spotted them and attacked. Nate believed he had a way around this problem.

The group grew silent as Nate began speaking.

"Well, it looks like we're ready to go and I have a few suggestions. First let's get Rita out of here. Katrina would you take her to Pedro's wife. She has agreed to watch her for us. Explain to her why she can't go with us and we'll see her in a week. I'll wait till you get back," Nate started out.

Katrina rose from her seat and asked Rita to come with her. The child had heard Nate and seemed to understand. She left the table and went with Katrina. The two disappeared into the kitchen. Katrina returned to the table in five or six minutes without Rita.

"Ok, you all have packed you vehicles with the new fire power and covered it so it is not easy to uncover. Larger chest with ice have been packed with frozen deer meat. As you've seen, a couple deer heads have been mounted on your Broncos. Your fire power is now great. We have hand held missiles, six all together. Use these only when you must because when they are gone, they're gone. Don't throw away the tubes when you're through with them. We want no evidence its Americans doing this. We now have automatic weapons and lots of ammo. You must be careful on picking targets. We don't want any soliders or cops killed. To start with we will bury any bodies and we'll find a spot to bury the drugs. We'll all put them in the same place so they'll be easier to retrieve. I have the number of the U.S. Border patrol station and will call it in after every two or three raids. Just so you'll know we have suspensions a couple of their agents are on the take and they plan to catch them. I just want you to know so if a couple comes upon you, they may not be friendlies.

"Ok, about 20 miles out and two miles from the border is a lone tree. Behind the tree is a hole. Kind of a slopeing hole about ten feet deep. When you recover drugs take them to that spot and dump them in. Cover the poison with a foot or so of sand. Your movements must be at night so you won't be spotted. Is that clear?" Nate asked.

All nodded yes, as he went on.

"All your movements should be at night if possible. This way you won't be spotted. You are to call me after every strike and give me details.

I will relay this information to the General and to the border patrol. Clear?" again heads nodded.

"All right boys and girls, lets get going and find a good spot you can work from, change it often and pick places you can see for some distance. See you back here next Saturday morning. Good hunting," Nate finished and took a big swallow of black coffee before rising from the table.

They all rushed to their vehicles and fired them up. Nate had made assignments earlier. Ed Chaney, Delbert Osborn and Don Hopkins would be one team. Brady Jacobs, Carl and Katrina would be the other team. Sam Brown and Nate would work alone as a hit and run team.

Little known to the group as to the whereabouts of little Rita. Rather than staying with Pedro, she had gone out the back door and had sneaked around to the corner of the house. She peeked at the vehicles and spotted the one Carl and Katrina were about to get in. Keeping a couple bushes and a vehicle or two between herself and the group, she ran to that vehicle unnoticed. Reaching up she opened the top part of the back. Placing a foot on the trailer hitch she propelled herself into the vehicle and on top of sleeping bags. She turns around and quietly closed the opening and laid down flat. She was quite sure no one would notice her. Just as she was situationed, the vehicle started moving. She smiled knowing she had pulled it off and was going along for the ride. Little did she suspect danger ahead?

The vehicles peeled off to go in different directions. Some aimed further west than the others. They moved slowly so as not to throw up dust clouds in case anyone was watching.

Delbert and his group were going the farthest to the west and in miles. This meant they would have to find the tree for the drug drops on their way out. This was their first point to discover and remember for trips back. Finding it they marked it on a map just in case. It was just as he described. On the back side was the hole for burying their loot. After completed, they headed west again. They had decided among themselves not to get any closer to the border. The last thing they needed was someone getting suspicious of these Americans. The thirty-thirtys they carried in the cabs of the trucks and dressed as hunter's right down to the red shirts.

Carl's team reached the area they were to monitor first. They stopped and got out for a look around. Rita felt the vehicle stop and heard voices outside. She knew they had reached the area they were assigned to. Wiggling around, she reached the latch on the back window. Tugging on it she finally opened it. As it came open she lost her footing and slide to the ground. The sudden hurt caused her to cried out.

"Ouch," her voice was heard around to the front and sides of the Bronco.

"What's that," Brady said and went to check it out. Katrina and Carl followed.

"Why you little devil," came Brady's voice.

Carl and Katrina came into view just then. Rita was getting up and dusting herself off.

Katrina walked over and helped her.

"What are you doing here," Katrina asked her as the other two looked on.

"I wanted to go with my new uncles not stay home with those old people. I can help, honest I can," she said as her lower lip started to sag. A cry was coming and Katrina knew it.

"You guys go on and find us a place to hide and I'll handle this," Katrina said while gestering with her hands.

Being shooed off by two women, the men walked back to the front of the truck. They scanned the surrounding country side they found little to be happy about. After minutes of looking Brady noticed a hump a couple hundred yards away.

"Hey, Carl looks a little south at about two hundred yards. See that hump in the desert. It looks like part of it is a tall bunch of sage brush. Might be a good place to hole up. See it?"

Carl looked and looked before finding it.

"Yeah, let's walk down there and see if it will work," he responded back to Brady.

Katrina and Rita came around the truck in time to see them starting out on their walk.

"Where are you going?" Katrina asked.

"We're checking out a place for us to camp?" Carl answered back.

"Why don't you drive?" she asked.

"We don't want a lot of tracks going there to give us away. If it is good enough we will be going to and from it a few times a week. The fewer tracks the better. We'll sweep the tracks with a bush to make them disappear every time we make a move, etc, Make sure Rita stays and understands what we are about. Ok?"

"Ok, she will be alright as soon as I explain to her why we are here. You guys go ahead and I'll tend to Rita. She's such a darling little girl but still a child and so far doesn't understand. I'll teach her. Go."

The two men reached the area they needed to and looked around. They discovered the patch of tall sage brush covered about a five acre plot of land. This was perfect for their needs. The sage thicket, while not being large would give them some room for movement if needed.

They walked back and forth until they had covered and inspected every foot of land.

On the back side they noticed a ten foot piece of ground that had green grass growing on it.

"Hey, Brady" said to Carl, "look at that piece of ground that's green. Means there is water here. Let's take a look."

Reaching the spot one planted a boot in the middle of the grass. It sunk down over a foot.

"Damn, I think you are right Brady. Let's dig this out and see if it is a spring. Could we be so lucky," Carl said aloud.

"We don't have a shovel," Brady reminded Carl.

"Well, we do at the Bronco. Let's dig it out by hand just so we know we've found water. You dig from that side and I'll do it from here." was Carl's reply.

They dropped to their knees and began pulling sand towards themselves. They soon realized the deeper they went the wetter the sand. At a foot and a half they could squeeze water from the sand.

"I've seen enough," Carl advise after a few minutes. "There is water here. Let's go get the Bronc and move in here."

Arriving back at the vehicle and the girls, the men told them what they had found and they were moving there.

Brady drove them the short distance to the sagebrush grove. Looking for a good place to park, they had found a twenty foot area about a hundred feet into the brush that had no growth. An idea place to park. They cleared a narrow pathway from the outside to this interior spot. Once completed they drove in and parked.

Katrina sat Rita down and explained they had to be quiet so no one would find out they were there.

"I understand," she replied, "I'll be very quiet."

They set up camp and the women prepared a meal and they all rested.

An hour or so later they put one on top of the Bronco to start monitoring activity.

Carl was the first on watch so Brady cut small sagebrush and started swinging it across their tire tracks to obliatering them. All signs of them being there, erased.

A family of six walked by about an hour later. Some of the kids were barefooted. All their clothes looked to be old and half worn out. They looked exhausted to Carl. They looked so tired they might fall over at any time. Carl had to wonder at what was so bad in their homeland; they would go to all this trouble. He knew that many had heard stories that in America the streets were paved with gold. Not true of course, but maybe a job was waiting for those who would make it. Most never considered many would die along the way.

Rita climbed up and Carl helped her sit where it was comfortable at least for a while.

"Uncle Carl," she started, "is all the people walking for the border the same as I was?"

"Yes, honey, they want a better life for their kids. It's a shame that the government doesn't spread the money they get from oil to create jobs. Then the people would stay home and build Mexico into a beautiful country. The whole world would help. It is better all these folks stay home and live better. The government has much money but those in power steal it for themselves. There is nothing left for the people. Many die early," he finished, looking at her and curious how much this little girl understood. "Do you understand all this?"

"Oh, si, my mother and father talked about it all the time. Since I was a little girl," and she smiled up at him.

He smiled back but said nothing.

The rest of the day was that way. Fanilies going north. Most all were dressed in rags All looked hungry and on their faces a look of desperation. Nothing remotely resembling hope.

Rita and Katrina played silly childrens games and did well at staying quiet. They had leveled off a spot of ground and spred blankets over the area. This made a nice place to sit and play games. Brady could see they were getting bored. He also knew Carl and Katrina needed quality time together so he came up with an idea. His shift was about over and some daylight was left.

"Rita lets you and me stretch our legs and let Uncle Carl and Katrina guard the camp. Would you like to?" Brady asked.

"Oh, yes, let's do," she said joyfully.

Brady took her little hand and they headed south to see what they could see. They walked about a mile and were enjoying the time together. Rita was like any other kid and was full of questions. She would pick up rocks and ask questions about them. Questions like where they came from and what kind of rocks were they. Brady could only wing it and try to answer her questions. In the end he had to tell her he wasn't sure to most of her questions.

"I'm sorry little one but I just don't know," he finally announced to her.

"That's ok, Uncle Brady," she would say and squeeze his hand.

A little further along them heard strange noises coming from their right. Brady stopped and listened intently in an effort to make out what was taking place.

He spoke to Rita in a low voice and told her to stay.

"Why, can't I come?" she answered back. "I'll be very quiet, can I go with you?"

He agreed to take her but she must be very quiet.

"There may be bad men over there so please be quiet," he said and crouched down and started in the direction of the noise. As they moved along, the noise grew louder.

Finally he knew what it was. Another ten feet and he gazed upon a scene he'd not expected.

"Close your eyes and don't look," he told Rita, "and stay here, I'll be right back."

He crouched even lower to the ground as he moved forward. He got within twenty yards from a horrible sight.

Three white men had torn the clothes from a girl of about eighteen and were raping her. One man was holding her down by her hair with a hand over her mouth. Another was holding her legs down and apart. Still another, smaller man was just getting off her and was trying to zip up the zipper in the front of his pants. This was the last thing he'd do on this earth.

Brady stood up and shot him in the forehead. His other shot took off part of the head of the man holding her. The third man jumped up and went for the gun hanging at his side. He was too late for Brady finshed emptying his revolver into the man's body. He was dead before he hit the ground.

The girl curled up where she was not realizing she was safe and waited for the worst.

"Rita, come here honey quick. I need your help." Brady hollored. The words were hardy out his mouth when Rita appeared. She had been watching all the time.

"Yes, Uncle Brady what can I do?" she asked.

"Get down next to her and tell her she's safe now and not to be scared. We are here to help. The bad ones are dead and give her your sweater to cover up with." Seeing this would not be enough, he peeled off his outside shirt and gave it to the girls. He turned and looked away as they covered the naked body of the girl.

As he looked away, facing north, he noticed a head of a horse watching him. The animal was about thirty yards and seemed curious of what was going on.

Strange, Brady thought, *he'd not noticed the animal there earlier.*

"You girls wait here Rita, I'll be right back," he said and started in the direction of the horse.

Hearing running steps, he dropped to the ground with revolver in hand, cocked and ready to fire. Discovering it was Carl and Katrina, he lowered his weapon.

"Brady, what the hell's going on" Carl asked as reaching the scene.

"Those three were raping that girl so I sent them to hell. I don't know anything else except there a horse over there and I'm going to check it out. Katrina will you care for the girl? Come on Carl lets see what we find over there," pointing in the direction where he'd seen the horse.

Both men, with guns in hand proceeded in that direction. As they came close they saw an old buckboard style wagon. The bed had been extended to carry more. A horse stood near by and another was tied to a wagon wheel.

No one was around that they could see. To make sure they wouldn't Be bushwhacked, they searched the area before feeling comfortable enough to inspect the wagon. It was pile high with many items.

Back at the wagon, they started unloading it. First items coming off was camping gear, sleeping bags, little gas range used by sportsmen, etc. Then they found wooden boxes with foreign writings. Neither could read it and the mystery deepened. They pried the top off one of the boxes to find four five gallon containers. When one of the containers was opened it contained a yellowish powder.

They both scratched their heads not knowing what they had found.

In the middle of the wagon and towards the front, was twenty sticks of dynamite. This was well concealed. Had they not unloaded the entire wagon this would not have been found. There was a mattress wrapped tightly around it. The mystery deepens every time they unloaded or opened a container. Other gear they could not identify was found in cardboard boxes.

"Damn if I know what we have here but it's not legal. We'll let Nate figure it out. Let's go bury those bastards so they won't be found," Carl said.

"Right," Brady said, "we'll let Nate figure it out. Let's load the wagon. It's coming with us."

Arriving back at camp they checked on the girl who was raped. Katrina met them and advises she's was ok, but in shock of what happened. They were told she was an orphan and on her way to America in search of a better life. Her name was Jasmine.

Katrina was curious about the wagon and Carl explained they thought it might belong to terrorists. The yellow powder kept nagging at him. He knew he'd seen it before but where? It was an uneasy feeling he had about it and its use. He knew he knew but it just wouldn't come to him.

The women started fixing something to eat and busyed themselves with building a small fire and took the two burner stove out of the vehicle to cook on.

"Come on Carl. Grab a shovel and let's bury the bodies before the sun bloats them. One big hole should do it. This is sandy soil and shouldn't take long," Brady said.

They dug the grave to the east about twenty yards, making two trips, before they decided it was far enough from camp. The digging began in earnest.

They stopped to rest a few minutes later. As he took a drink of water it hit Carl.

"Damn, Brady, I know what that yellow powder is. It's uranium and it's radio active. As soon as we plant these bodies we need to move the wagon farther from the camp. By god, I think we have the makings of a dirty bomb," Carl said almost under his breath.

"Are you sure," Brady asked.

"Yeah, I saw some in a museum once. It's what they make atom bombs out of," was the reply.

"The hole is almost done and I'll finish it. You go move the wagon and call Nate. Tell Nate we want someone here as soon as possible to take it off our hands. Tell him to move fast and ask for instructions. Tell him we killed the bastards who were hauling it. To bad we didn't know. We could have taken one of these fellows alive and maybe he would have told us where it was headed," Brady said.

"Yeah, you're right. Damn it anyway,"Carl showing his concern.

Carl took off for the wagon and Brady finished the burying. Once the wagon was moved and parked behind some sagebrush, he felt better. He gathered the girls and Katrina around and explains the wagon was dangerous and they were not to go near it.

"Do you all understand?" he quizzed them.

All nodded their heads yes.

"Nate here," came over the line as the phone was answered.

"Hi, Nate," Carl replied, "I have something very important to tell you. We had an incident this afternoon," and he went into the details of what happened.

"Anyway, we buried the men and then to look over their wagon. Nate, I once saw uranium in a display in a museum. This wagon contains about three hundred pounds of the stuff. I think it was headed into the states for use as a dirty bomb. I have no idea where or how it will be used. I'm quite sure I'm right and I need you to get someone down here to take the stuff. Sorry I had to kill the bastards but I didn't know what I'd find in the wagon. In fact I didn't even know there was a wagon until I started looking around. What do you think?

"I think you may have stopped a terror attack. To bad we didn't get the men alive but don't worry about that. The important thing is you got the wagon. Give me directions to where you are and I'll call the General right now and have the stuff picked up. Good job, Carl. I'll get back to you," Nate said as he closed the conversation and hung up.

Carl related the conversation to Katrina and they settled down to wait for the returned call. Supper was cooked and sleeping bags and a blanket was spread out. The three hunked around the fire and only little Rita was active. Her childhood chatter was kind of soothing to the others. Kids are great even in a time of stress and danger.

128

Saturday morning came like all others with a promise it would be hot. Nate's team was all at the hacendia by noon.

After all the greetings were said they all moved to the large dining room table for food and cold beer. They would report to Nate after they satisfied their hunger and thurst. He didn't mind and was not in a hurry. He had a surprise for them all that might take some back home. He was staying after he thought over the new request of the General's. When he started this assignment he knew in his gut that more would come of it. He wondered when the general received the new request. Recently or did he know all along. From his past dealings with the general he knew this man could lie to get things done his way. Nate knew he'd never find out but again promised himself and his wife this was the last assignment.

"Listen up gang," finally came from Nate, "I have information for you. Carl, the uranium you found on that wagon was in fact uranium. It had been thru a process that enriched it making it more radio-active. If mixed with other materal and was set off with an explosion of some force, it would have the effect of a dirty bomb. It would make an area unlivable for some time. How long is not known. When it goes off it could kill a few thousand people in a downtown area. The General wishes you hadn't killed the people with it. He would have loved to have them put through a C.I. A. discussion. By what you did might scare others off but he doesn't think so. It looks like somewhere a large attack is about to happen. We think this was just one of two or more loads of the bad stuff. It is only reasonable they would send more than one load just in case one fell into the wrong hands."

Nate sighed with relief when he got this all out. He noticed the team was glancing from one to the other with a question on their faces. *Well now I'll give them the bad news,* he said to himself.

"What do you think we've gotten ourselves into boss? It kind of looks and sound like world war three is about to start right here," Carl said.

"Well here's the word I get from the General. He, of course is interested in terrorsts coming over the border to attack. We have now proved that. The load I found and being trailed by the F.B.I. and local police agencies. This group is still camped outside Tuscon, Arizona. They're still there and appear to be waiting for something or someone. It could be that load Carl caught was what they were waiting for. Well, we have that load and there may be another coming. If so, we have been ordered to leave it alone except to follow it. Yes, you heard right. We are to follow it right into the U.S. The C.I.A, the F.B.I. and the General feels something big is about to go down and they want us in on it. By following these people maybe we can figure it out before someone gets hurt. It also puts more of our people where we might need help. It's going to get dangerous people and you weren't hired to do this type of work. If any of you want to leave, say so now. There will be not hard feelings. If you stay your salary will double and it may take longer than a month. Sleep on it and let me know in the morning. Any questions," Nate finished, "and I'll tell you more in the morning. Go to town and let off some steam if you'd like to. World War Three is not starting here if I can help it. I'm staying."

A couple got up and went to the kitchen. When they returned they carried cans of beer. The rest of the group seemed to be in shock. A quiet had drifted over the room as what Nate had told them started soaking in. The beer was placed on the table as some started reaching for them. The popping off of the tops broke the silence. The ping, ping sounded loud in the stillness of the room.

"What are we going to do with Rita if I chose to go on this mission? She needs someone besides these old folks here to care for her," Katrina broke the silence.

"I'm glad you brought that up," Nate answered. "You are not going with us this time. The General said he would find someone just across the border for her to stay with. An American couple. It will be your job to sneak her over and then come back here. We may need you and we'll leave one of the phones. When our work here is completed you and Carl can decide what to do with her. I think I can arrange to have her legal so you can keep her or turn her over to the legal system to place her with a family."

They all had a big meal and most were headed into town for some fun. This new information was a hard bit to chew on and they all needed to give an answer by morning. Each chewed it over in different ways. Carl and Katrina both thought it would be nice to have Rita as a daughter and discussed it quietly in their room. But there was a lot to think about and after discussions each fell silent and drifted into thinking separately. Nate wanted to go back the Columbia and his beautiful bride. These were the type of thoughts each were having about the future. All thought of how the future might change if America started having terrorest attacks on a regular basis. Here and now they might have a chance to deter any future plans of attacking America. Here and now was important. Each knew no one else was available to do the job if they turned it down. What were the consences if this was not done successfully and now?

By midnight they were all back at the table drinking beer. None were drunk and no one had a good time in town. The mission that lay ahead was so serious they couldn't relax. A decision had to be made. Each thought what the others would think of him if he didn't go, etc. Damn the General anyway. Most suspected he knew this when he recruited them. It had all been a gimick to get them in place making it easier for them to say yes. Most wondered why they just didn't use the army and station it along the border. They had equipment that was susficated and chance of success more certain.

Well at least the beer went down smooth.

"I really don't know right now. No one has said anything and I gave them until tomorrow to give me an answer, General," Nate responded to his question on if the team was going to take this last assignment.

"It's really important they do this for their country, Nate. I can't tell you just how important this really is," Nate replied.

"I know, General, it must be serious for you to be calling this late or this early. What is it about three AM in Washington? After breakfast I'll ask them for a decision. You can't push them General or you'll lose them. Just leave this to me. I'm staying so at least you have one. Now get some sleep and let me do the same. Goodnight, General," Nate signed and turned off the phone.

No one got good nights sleep that night. A lot of tossing and turning was had by all.

The next morning everyone was a little cranky and out of sorts. They kept moving around a lot. Most even went into the kitchen to get the food and coffee. The coffee was going down at a rapid rate. After several cups each, the team seemed to settle down. Cigars were lit and they leaned back and waited for their leader to spcak. The wait wasn't long.

"The General called late last night and wanted me to share some facts with you. To date, this year over five thousand Mexicans and six border guards' have been killed along this border. Mostly in and around cities like Tijuana and that town across from El Paso, TX. There's street fighting in the daytime the same as at night. There are beheadings and twenty to thirty people at a time. Folk's things are bad. If Mexico implodes all hell will be to pay. We will see lawlessness like never before. Now this new mission will do nothing to help that situation, but terrorist must be discouraged now. If just one group gets thru, more will come. It important we stop them dead in their tracks so the world will have nothing to do with it. Terrorists will be killed as soon as they enter the country. Now we have two groups that are merging not far from here and waiting. We've been very lucky to have spotted them. Now it is urgent we find out where they are going. If we can find that out and stop it, we may postone the inevitable.

This is why the General needs us and I hope you've made up your minds to stay and help me. I'm staying. I'd would, like it better to be in Columbia with my wife. Perhaps in thirty days I will be. This will be dangerous work but you've all done that before. I feel this is so important I'm willing to die trying to stop these bastards. Let me know. I'm going to walk around, smoke a cigar, drink a beer and be back in a few minutes. I need your answers then. Go or stay, it's that simple," Nate finished.

Quiet again settled across the room. Everyone looked at each other, wanting someone to go first. Finally good ole Ed Chaney spoke up.

"By God, I'm staying. I'm not about to let this war spill over into the states. If it can be stopped, then it must be right here on the border. If I have to kill everyone one of the bastards then that's what I'll do. I'm not too old to fight for my country.

Again it was silent.

Next Delbert Osborn spoke.

"Hell, me too, Ed I'm with you. Let's go get'em and get this show on the road.

This did it. The ice was broken and everyone was staying. Katrina spoke in favor of Carl going, but was a little miffed at having to stay back with Rita.

"Katrina, this phase of our operation is going to get dangerous real fast you did a triffic job in Colombia but I don't want you hurt. This is a different ball game. You can be of help by taking care of the child and I'd like you to nose around the city and see if you can gather any information for us. You can leave Rita here on any evening excursions. I want Carl to be alright with this. We won't be coming back on weekends until this is over. Could be a month or more. What do you say Carl?" Nate finished.

"Well I'd rather be home in Boise, but I know she can handle this so it's ok with me," was the answer.

"That settles it. We leave at dawn tomorrow morning. Delbert, you and Ed hold on and I give you your assignments now. That's all folks and I thank you. This may get rough but now we know it's for God and counrty and not just for ourselves. Go to town and blow off some steam but don't get arrested," Nate finished.

Nate, Ed and Delbert remained at the table while the rest took Nate's advice and headed to town.

"I need you two to get across the border and head for Tucson, Arizona, and find that camp. You are to report back by phone when you're in position. You will follow them where ever they go. See if you can figure out where they're going and call it in. Guys we must know as soon as possible where their attack will be. If this can be done we'll have one hell've reception committee waiting for them. Handle everything your way, but don't get caught. If we fail here, other planned attacks will happen. Every local police, sheriff's offices, etc have been notified. The F.B.I. has moved agent's into the area and will assist if needed. All those agencies have been told to stay out of our way and to take no action on their own. They will come in only when we need them. Ok, that's it. I going to get a cigar and a beer and watch some TV after I call the General," Nate finished and stood up.

He went into the kitchen for the beer and picked up a cigar on the way. Next stop was the living room and TV.

"Hey, General, I have some good news for you. My team is truly American. Everyone of my team members have agreed to stay and enter this fight. They've been briefed and are ready to start out tomorrow morning. Is there any thing else I need to know. Have you left out any little tidbit I should know," Nate said as the General took his call.

"I'm going to stay as a floater so I can be mobil and circulate from area to area. Once this thing starts moving I may need to re-enforce someone. I'll give you a day by day account of our actions every evening around six our time. OK?" Nate continued.

"Yeah, that's fine," said the general, "and I'll call you if I need more information or need it earlier. Remember Nate, the Mexican police are not your friends. They are so corrupt they'll take any side for money. If they try to interfer with your mission, kill and bury them. They will never be missed.

Good luck and here's hoping you find what we need. Good bye and good luck," said the General as he hung up.

Most were up early and had the coffee on when Nate arrived at the table. After breakfast was served Nate made further assignments.

"Don, you and Brady go out where Carl and Katrina were last week. They can tell you how to get there. I want you to patrol ten miles to the West of there and five miles east. Now remember you are still hunters of deer and you must not raise suspicions. Play it cool and visit with people. If you spot something don't take action. Report it and I'll report it to the General. The rest of you do the same. Ed and Delbert may get help from the F.B.I. but I want to know what's up before they do. I'll let the General make the hard decisions for us. Delbert and Ed you take the post I had. This should be the hot spot so be careful. All of you be careful. Katrina knows her job so that leaves Sam Brown. He's not here and is a different matter. Don't interfer with him but help him if he needs it. He's a friend and works alone. Understood? Saturdays we may still meet here and rest on weekends. Depends what happens. Play it by ear."

All nodded and the meeting was adjourned. Everyone sat quiet sipping coffee and digesting the information they had received.

Everyone drifted away to their assigned positions after gasing up and filling a couple five gallon cans for emergencies. Nate did the same and drove off into the desert. His team wondered if he was going out to find Sam. They were betting he was.

Nate drove several miles criss-crossing the desert looking for signs of people. He found several places where people had walked but when he checked closer he determined no heavy loads passed this way. Deep inside he felt heavy gear would be needed to carry out an attack on American soil. He overlooked the fact that this was a modern age and everything was being more compact and lighter. During this trip he would learn this fact.

It was a dull day except for his movements across the sand. As night was falling, he decided to camp at dusk and began looking for a bunch of bushes or sagebrush he could pull into and at least halfway hide himself. He finally found one and pulled into it. Here the soil was firm and he did not sink into the sand. This was always an important consideration because you never know when you might have to get out in a hurry. It would be not only embarrassing but possibley fatal. His position was about two miles from the border.

The night was uneventful and Nate got good nights sleep. In the morning he lit a can of "heat" to heat coffee. In a short time the coffee was boiling and he poured a cup. It was a good, strong black coffee. The kind that would stay with you a while. He climbed upon the front of his rig and looked around as he sipped his coffee. As he peered out through the sagebrush he saw what looked like people moving his way. They were coming from the south and had to be Mexicans heading for the border. His cup ran dry so he climbed down to refill. Back on the top of the rig again he noticed the group of people had disappeared. Getting out his field glasses he scanned the area where he had seen them before. There was no sign of them.

They couldn't have gone far in two minutes. Where were they, he was thinking to himself. They had to be out there somewhere. He continued his scan and coffee for thirty minutes and decides to go on foot to where he had last seen them.

Climbing down from his view point the put out the can of "heat" and put his coffee pot away. He put a holster and revolver on his belt. He picked up the thirty-thirty rifle and began his walk.

Perhaps a hundred yards from where he had seen this group he noticed the entrance to a little draw. It looked as if the draw deepened as it ran westward.

Nate slowed his step and began to slouch over as he got close to the mouth of this draw. He stopped many times to listen for any sound or voices from the group. They had looked like farmers and he found it unusal they would hide like this.

Just arriving at the draw he stopped. This time he heard a baby cry. The cry soon ended as if someone had placed something over its mouth. Nate peeked around into the draw he saw it was quite deep. A group of people we huddled around a small smokeless fire. A pot hung over the fire and Nate picked up the smell of beans cooking.

Nate lay on the hillside awhile wondering what to do. It was quite apparent these folks were not terrrorists. He decided just to walk in and be friendly. Maybe this way he'd find out something that was going on out in the desert. He picked himself up, dusted off and walked into the draw.

A few steps and he were within their sight. At least half a dozen Mexicans moved their heads around to see who he was. The noise of his walking must have tipped them off. That was fine with Nate and he threw

you. When you get to the river water your animals and I get there in time to take you across," Nate replied.

With this the group moved out and Nate packed his bedroll, cooking items and coffee pot. He was ready to move out. He decided to do one last thing and call the General. He may need help getting this group over the border.

CHAPTER 10

"Good morning General," Nate said with a smile when he heard the General forcing himself awake.

"Stop that grinning Nate. I know it's you now what the hell are so important you bother me at this hour," growled the General.

"I need you to get a hold of the border patrol and get me cleared for crossing. I'm sure they will see us coming and that's fine. Just have them give us a slight look over and let us go. This will put me in real good with the Mexicans and I might learn more. Oh, I almost forgot to tell you, I traveling with them," mentioned and waiting the cursing he knew would come.

"You're what," and a string of curse words flowed down the line to Nate's ear.

"Figured it was better this way and safer too. Just get the border patrol informed and have them make it look good but not to search us. Ok," Nate came back

"OK, ok, how soon will you be at the border?" questioned the General.

"We are there now so get cracking I'll stall some and wait until dawn which comes any minute now," Nate threw at his boss and quickly hung up not needing a response.

Nate fired up his Bronco and headed after the Mexicans. Nate caught up with the group at the river. The river was low and Nate was grateful for this. The animals were already drinking, strung out along the water's edge. Nate waved at the men as he arrived. Once they realized it was him they waved back. Nate decided to go over to the U.S. side. He wanted to make sure the coast was clear and that there was not quicksand along the river. They didn't have time to pull and animal out if it stepped into quicksand. He drove into the water and kept a close eye on the bottom. It was gravel all the way across, for which he was grateful. Reaching the other side he continued up the bank until he was on top. Reaching this point the looked back towards the Mexicans. They were looking at him, waiting for a sign to come over. He waived for them to come on. The man he had delt with started first with a donkey and a cart. The last twenty feet was the worse because it was the steepest. It took only twenty minutes for the crossing and soon they were all safe on the American side.

They waited ten minutes to catch their breath before heading north. They were just about a quarter mile of a mile inside the country when a group of border patrol officers drove up. Nate swallowed hard hoping the General had made his call. If not they could all be sent back across the border after everything was convencasated? This would blow the whole operation if that happened.

Four border patrol officers dismounted the jeep they were riding in and drew their weapons. They placed themselves around this group so it appeared they had the group surrounded. Every one stopped in their tracks. An officer with Sgt. Stripes on his sleeve ordered everyone to put their hands up, in Spanish.

The Mexicans obeyed as Nate got out of the Bronco. Both feet firmly on American soil, Nate approached the Sgt.

"Where the hell do you think you're going," bellowed the Sgt. as he pointed his pistol at Nate.

"I need to talk to you alone, Sgt. Can we do this?" Nate inquired.

"Why talk. We caught you coming into the U.S. illegally and you're under arrest. I see you're running human cargo. This will get you twenty years in prison. Stay right where you are," barked the Sgt.

"Sgt.," came a voice from one of the patrol officers, "a radio call for you. It sounds urgent. Do you want to take it?" he asked.

"Yes, hell yes, but watch these people. Make sure this one doesn't get away. Take the keys from his vehicle and be careful. He looks dangerous to me," remarked the Sgt.

The Sgt. walked back to the jeep and took the mike and headset. He began talking and looking back at Nate.

At that moment Nate knew the General had gotten through. *Damn near too late. Another few minutes and the whole caper would have been blown. It was important these Mexicans didn't find out Nate was attached to law enforcement,* he throught.

Silence hung over the traverlers and the patrol. Nate noticed the fear in the eyes of the Mexicans and was sure they were not breathing. Five minutes passed as the officer argued with someone. He couldn't hear a word but felt the General had came thru for him. Finally the guard put down the mike and yelled at Nate.

"Hey, you, come here," indicating he meant Nate. Nate walked the distance to the patrol vehicle.

In a friendlier and quieter voice the Sgt asked Nate if he was Nate Armstrong.

"Yes," was the reply?

"Well I've been ordered to assist you in getting across the border but was told to make it look good so no one suspects you as a government agent. I propose you and I make it look like you are bribing me. This is one thing the Mexicans understand. To get anywhere in Mezico you damn near have to bribe everyone. The men will do a damn poor job of searching just to put the frosting on the cake. I don't know what you're doing but good luck," said the Sgt. With this Nate took out his billfold and pretended to pass bills to the Sgt.

"Let me go tell them about the search so no one runs for it. Ok?" Nate asked.

"Yeah, sure," the Sgt. replied.

With this Nate walked back to the Mexican he'd been dealing with and told him that they would be searched but not to worry. The search is just to make things look good.

"Did he take money from you?" asked the Mexican.

"Yes, but don't worry I can afford it. Just tell your people to be calm and not to run. Ok?" Nate asked.

"Ok," came the reply. The man walked down thru the group speaking in Spanish. Finished he waved to Nate.

The border patrol officers moved quickly and patted down the men only.

"Ok, get them out of here," yelled the Sgt.

"Let's go," Nate told the older man who gave an order in Spanish and the caravan move north away from this place.

A short distance away from the border, Nate decided it was time to find out the old guy's name. Nate stopped his vehicle along side him.

"Say, old timer what is your name. Mine's Nate. We are going to spend about three days together and it would be nice to use our names. You agree," Nate said.

The old man stepped close to Nate's opened window and extended his hand.

"Si, my name is Manuel," he proudly stated as the two shook hands.

Twenty minutes passed and Nate became restless. He decided to go on ahead and find the easiest path to take. He was anxious to see if the General had heard anything from the others on his team and he wanted to give him, his location.

"Hey, Manuel, I'm going on ahead and find the easiest way to go to Tucson. We need to start turning to the right up ahead a bit. I'll return in an hour. Just follow my tire tracks. Ok?" he told the old man.

"Si, senor, we will follow you" came the reply and Nate drove off as a pathfinder.

The land was fairly flat as he picked his way along. About five miles he stumbled across and old road. It looked as though it hadn't been used is years. Nate knew that in this country the sand and the wind could cover tracks in just a few hours and hide any usage. He stopped and got out to inspect it closer. He walked up and down this old road trying to find any use of it in recent days. He did not fine any sign until he got the idea to kneel down. On his knees he bent to with a couple inches off the ground. In this position he blew softly to move the sand about. He spent several minutes until he found what he was looking for. When he blew and the wind blown sand moved, he noted a tire track. Continue blowing opened up a larger area showing a couple feet of the tire track. He blew some more to remove all the sand in the track. This done he could tell it was fairly fresh. He stood up and looked. He thought he knew what type of vehicle made the track. His guess was a four wheel drive. Possibility a 1 ton pickup truck with dual tires on the rear. The finding of this track was not proof of anything but did show this old road was being used. His best guess was hunters or dirt bikers. With this he mounted up and called the General.

"Hello, Nate," answered the General to the ringing of his phone.

"How did you know it was me?" Nate inquired.

"Because the others have all reported in and it had to be you. What's going on?

Nate told him he was guiding the Mexican caravan towards Tucson and would drop off when they were in five miles of the city. He gave his position as best he could and waited for orders.

"Just keep you eyes and ears open and keep me apprised. Have fun Nate," the General said as he closed the conversation by hanging up.

Nate smiled at the way he and the General hung up with each other. It was almost like a game where they had to see who could hang up the fastest. He made a mental note to ask the General the next time he talked to him.

In the meantime, Manuel was wondering why this American was being so helpful. Maybe it was time to ask him. It's not that Manuel was concerned but that he had not considered the Americans willing to help illegals coming into their country. *Yes,* he thought it was time he asked him.

Nate, not wanting to get too far ahead of the caravan decided to turn back. He was about ten miles out ahead of the group and he didn't want to risk losing them. Heading back he stayed in the old road. Not really being in a hurry he drove at a speed of twenty miles an hour. He kept his eyes open on this drive looking over the landscape for signs of traffic. He had felt a moment of emergency in the General's voice on that last conversation. This was quite unusual for a man of his experience. Nate felt this man was so sure that an enemy of the U.S. was about to attack and he felt helpless to stop them.

Nate soon came upon his group who were taking a break along side his tire tracks. He pulled up to where Manual was standing and stopped.

"Hey, Manual I have good news. This old road goes at least ten miles and maybe into Tucson. I didn't follow it all the way but at ten miles it was still going in that direction. We should make good time. Do you know what day those balloon races are taking place? I do hope we make it on time," Nate expressed his feelings.

"Not exactly?" answered the old man, "but I need to talk to you senor."

"Sure jump in here where it is cooler and we'll take a little ride while we talk. Your voice sounds serious and my guess you don't want the others to hear. Come on," Nate said.

"Si, senor, you are correct in your thinking," came the answer as the old man walked around the truck and got in. Once he was seated Nate drove slowly to the north.

Nate could feel the old man was uptight and concerned. At a little rise in the ground Nate stopped the Bronco with it facing south. From this point they could see and watch the others. The old man was slow to start, not being shore of his ground. He didn't know how this American would take what his was going to ask.

"It is very kind of you to be helping us, but I'm concerned with your interest in lowly common phesants. We are just poor people seeking a better life and yet you have jumped in to help. Would you tell me why?" The old man stopped talking but was looking intently into Nate's eyes.

Nate assumed this guy could read your eyes for any sign of lies, mistrust, etc.

"I have told you the truth about wanting to see a balloon race. They are great to watch. All are different colors and huge once blown up and floating into the sky. Is that not enough to satisfy you?" Nate asked.

"Normally yes, but in a time like this when your people are so against us coming into your country it seems unusual. Most Americans hate us for the taking for jobs Americans won't do. It's odd that one would want to help. I'm responsible for those people over there, (pointing at his group) and need to know if there is another reason why you do this. Understand, I don't mean to insult you but I must protect my people," he finished and waited for an answer.

Nate knew he must answer quickly or it would appear he was lying. Perhaps it was time he told him. He and his people seems honest and good people and maybe he could find out even more if he told the truth. Anyway he had no time to think about it. He had to answer and now. He chooses the truth.

"I'm working for the U.S. government. I'm here to stop the flow of drugs into our country and terrorists who wish to harm us," Nate blurted out.

Nate watched for a reaction from the old man. The first he saw was a moment of fear flash in his eyes and across his face. A calm look came across his face as he looked at Nate.

"You tell the truth, senor?" was posed to Nate.

"Si, I swear," Nate responded, "but I'm not here on imigration issues. You and your people have nothing to fear from me or my team. I fear you have been lied to and were asked to bring in contraband to be used in an attack. We don't know where and attack might happen and you are not to blame. Others have also been used by the criminals who wait for you in Tucson. My mission is to follow them to where an attack is to happen and stop it. You understand you have nothing to fear from me. I need your help to prevent this from happening."

Nate saw anger rise in his face and could not tell if it was for him or the others using him. It took five minutes for the redness to drain from his face. A very quiet five minutes as Manuel throught this over. Then he spoke.

"Senor Nate, you are telling me the truth. I can tell from your eyes. You must promise me my people will not be hurt or sent back to Mexico," a statement rather than a question.

"Yes. Once you meet these men outside of Tucson and deliver their items to them, you are free to continue on. I could even call ahead and clear the way for you. We are just after these criminals before they kill Americans. You have come all this way to become Americans and this is your first duty to help protect your new country. I just ask you not to tell them about my traveling with you or that they are being watched. Will you agree to this?" Nate offered his hand.

"Si, I agree and will not even tell those traveling with us. You tell me what to do and I will do it. I do wish to become an American," Manuel answered.

Nate breathed easier. He and Manuel joined the carrivan. He let Manuel out where he had picked him up and the group began its walk to Tuscon.

Nate knew the General would never have approved of telling Manuel as he had done but it was his life not the General's. This group of Mexicans might just be to key to unlock where an attack was to take place. Nate felt comfortable with this group and had no doubts of his decision.

Evening was settling in and the group set up camp. The animals were cared for first, then the people. Small fires were started for warming up beans, and coffee. The night was clear and would be cold.

The next couple days were uneventful and for Nate boreing. Never had he traveled so slow and with nothing to do. At times he would go ahead to pick a route and after that was done he would drop back and follow the carravan. Often he would stop and talk to Manuel. Some of the older folks would grow too tired to go on. Nate would pick them up and travel along close to their animals.

Two days out of Tucson, the boredom was broken. The little group was entering hilly country. They could only see a short ways ahead. Small hills and gullies reduce visability to a few hundred yards. Most were lulled almost asleep, except for the movement of their feet. Nate would dose for a few minutes then move to catch up. It was at one of these times as he was just coming out of the fog of sleep. He had started up his Bronco and looked up. About a thousand yards ahead, a herd of cattle came boiling over a hill, heading straight for them.

Nate saw Manuel way over to the left side of the donkeys. He could see and hear which was running for all its might. Manuel, not knowing what to do started running for the carravan.

Nate could see he'd never make it and dropped the Bronc into gear.

Tearing thru soil as he headed for the old man, breathing hard. Reaching where the old man was, he suing the vehicle around in from of him. This put Nate between the cattle and Manuel. The old man, seeing what Nate was doing took two huge leaps and grabbed the door handle on the passenger side. In a second he had opened the door and swung inside. With this Nate dropped the Bronco into another gear and spun it around. Doing this put him in front of the donkeys and the other Mexicans at an angle. The old man, now understanding what Nate was doing, leaped out and began hollering at his people. They understood and rushed to the Bronco and hit the ground. None of them let go of a donkey and they prayed.

The barrier Nate had made with his vehicle forced the running animals to go around it. It was over in a matter of seconds. The dust and dirt was so thick Nate couldn't see if any were hurt or not. It took a couple of minutes for it to clear and Nate could see the little group getting up from the ground. They were covered with dust and dirt but the old man yelled at Nate all were unharmed.

As Manuel walked up to Nate, who was now standing on the ground, and kissed him on both cheeks.

"Thank you senor, you saved my life. Thank you, oh thank you," Manuel kept saying. The rest of the Mexicans came up and shook Nate hand with great joy. There was excitement for survival. All were happy to be alive.

Nate had to smile at their excitement. Looking towards where the herd was heading and they were out of sight. Nate could not remember if any cowboys were with them or not. After all he had been busy.

The Mexicans decided it was time for a break, built some small fires and put coffee on. Manuel found a bottle of tequila and brought it over to Nate.

"Would Nate honor me by having a drink with me? I owe you everything, yet all I have to offer is a good drink," Manuel said and raising the bottle continued, "This is fine liquor, my friend."

For the next hour they rested, ate beans and tortillas, hot coffee. This was topped off with the liquor. Nate had to agree with Manuel that this was fine liquor.

"Manuel, I'm going to go ahead and find you a camp site for tonight. I'll then take a little nap before heading back. Keep going straight ahead and in a couple days we'll be in Tucson.

"Si, enjoy your nap," came a response and a great big smile.

CHAPTER 11

At a slow speed, Nate drove off blazing a trail that would bring this group into Tucson, Arizona. He knew the Mexicans would follow his tire tracks so he drove in a straight line. As straight a possible. He stopped from time to time to enjoy the scenery and take a drink of water. The liquor had tasted good and was well received. After all one does not face death every day. During these quiet times he wondered what the rest of his team was doing and what they are finding.

After a few miles he was driving across some hilly country. He stopped for a smoke. He'd been craving a smoke for quite a while. He was reserving his supply till he got close to a city. In Tucson, he would replenish his supply. It was during this, he glanced at a hill that was perhaps a hundred yards away. He noticed some green bushes and green grass.

With this sighting, he straightens up. His little group was running out of water and the anmials were suffering. He shiffed gears and headed over to the area. Pulling up to the green spot he noted a wet spot of twenty yards across.

By damn, he throught, *how lucky for us.* The pool of water was about twenty yards across, forming an almost a round pool. He dismounted and walked to the tempting sight.

He knelt near the edge of the pool and bent to drink. The water was cool and sweet to the taste. The water was good. After drinking his fill he took a shovel from the back of the Bronco. He walked a couple yards out from the pool and drove the spade into the ground, leaving it standing straight up. He looked around and found deer tracks but no other sign.

There that's my marker, he said to himself, *this will make it easier to find.*

He drove much faster going back that he did coming out this way. In minutes he was back. He drove up to Manuel and spoke.

"Manuel, Manuel," he spoke in an excited voice. "I've found a spring up ahead where we can camp and water the animals and fill out canteens. It is good cool water and we can just make it before dark. I think it would be good if we camped a couple days and rested up. In a day and a half we will be in Tucson.

The old Mexican wiped his brow before showing his gratitude.

"Thank God," he started, "I wasn't sure we would make it. I'm getting too old for this stuff but at least I'll die with freedom. I thank you for your help, senor. Some day maybe we can repay."

"Unload the cooking gear and throw it in here and I'll go on ahead with two or three of your people and have fresh coffe and some food waiting when you arrive. You should be there in about an hour," Nate informed him.

"Yes, yes, we are all tired and need food and water," Manuel said in an excited voice.

He stopped long enough to tell his little group. The news perked them up and they began unloading a few items used for cooking. These they rushed to the Bronco and handed them to Nate. Nate placed them inside and soon was ready to go.

"Manuel get me a couple to go along with me," Nate reminded him of his need for help.

"Oh, si," was the reply and the old man pointed at two men and spoke to them in Spanish. The replied by the nodding of their heads. They came forward and got into the truck.

"See you in about and hour. Follow my tire tracks and you'll come right to us," Nate said and got in the truck and drove away.

At the spring, Nate cleared away some of the brush while the other two built a fire and unloading the needed gear for cooking. The coffee pot was the first item to go on the fire and in five minutes they were sipping coffee. The atmosphere was of happiness and things to look forward to.

Nate filled all the water containers he had, wanting to fill them before their donkeys got into the water. He knew from experience the mess animals can make by just wadeing into the spring.

Nate's timing was about right on the travel time for those walking. In just about and hour and a quarter, Manuel and his group came into sight. The people all came forward to drink their fill before bringing the donkeys to the water. Most also splashed the cool water over their heads. Some even stripped off their shrts and threw water on their bodies. A joyful time for all. Next the donkeys were brought on and they too, drank their fill before being staked out for the night.

This being a special night they had more than just beans. Ham was sliced and one man mixed up bread and builds a make shift-oven over the fire. It was a simple matter of piling stones so the heat would stay at an even temperature. A piece of metal was scrubbed and biscuit batter was place on it. He then took stones and sealed the front opening. He left a small hole where he could peek in and see when they should be taken out. This was their evening meal.

After the meal was completed Nate and Manuel sat on the ground, leaning back against the truck. Nate brought out a couple cigars and offered Manuel one.

"Si, gracis," he said.

The night was clear and a bright moon lit the desert like a light does in a room. The air was cooling fast and many of the Mexicans had gone to bed. These two just sat and lost in their thoughts. Neither, it appeared, wanted to break the silence. After a half hour had passed Manuel broke the silence.

"Mr. Nate you have been good to my little group and you are what you seem to be. I've been thinking about how I can repay you for your kindness. I've thought of my conversations with these men I'm meeting and only one word sticks in my mind that didn't make sense. The word is Diego. This word didn't make sense the way they used it. I must have missed something in the way they used it. Does it mean anything to you?" he finished turning to Nate.

"Diego, um, Diego," he hestitated then went on thinking out loud. "No the word makes no sense to me. Keep thinking and try to think how they were using it. Well it's getting late and tomorrow we will part. I want you to know Manuel that you have been very kind to me. I've enjoyed our little jount across the wilderness. I hope you become an American citizen because America needs you. God bless and help you on your way."

With this they shook hands and Manuel joined his group and Nate curled up in the Bronco.

Nate had a fitful night's sleep and couldn't understand why. The name Diego kept coming thru his mind. He could only assume this was the leader of those who would cause us harm. As he tried to sleep, his mind kept running that name. He throught he'd heard it before but he wasn't sure. His constant tossing a turning went on through the night. Come the first light of day he gave up on sleep and got up. Everyone else was asleep so he built a small fire and put the coffee on.

Halfway through his second cup, Manuel appeared and extended his cup. Nate poured and the two settled back to enjoy the black brew. They were silent and together enjoyed the early morning. Some birds sang and some just flew from cover to begin the search for food. It was peaceful giving, the time to recharge and prepare for the day. The quiet time every human being searched for. It was so quiet that neither wanted to break the stillness of the time. Both were thinking of each other but neither spoke.

Manuel knew he would miss this American who had been so helpful. His thoughts also drifted to his people and those who traveled with him. He knew not where they would land and put down roots. He knew he'd never forget this man. He could only hope there would be more like him where he decided to relocate to. He knew of the tensions between the two peoples. Many hated Mexicans for coming and taking away American jobs. He knew of the killings along the border among the doppers and gangs who wished to control the drug highway into the U.S... He had heard of the five to six thousand killed in this fight just this year. He understood the hatred on both side of the border. His thoughts were that someday and soon both sides would identify between the evil and good ones. He knew his people could help in this fight if given the chance. Many Mexicans would put their lives and the lives of their families in danger if called upon. His mind relaxed as he wished for and remembered the peaceful time he had lived through. Not much was needed then. A belly full of food and a good woman to love was all that was needed to make a man happy. *Alas, those days are gone forever, a shame. The world moves too fast and with too much hatred. Greed,* he feared would doom them all.

Nate was thinking of what was ahead and day dreaming of home. He also wondered why people couldn't just live and be happy. Greed would kill them all sooner or later. He also was trying to figuring out what Manuel had told him. Every sort of plan of attack he could think of made no sense. He did take into consideration the groups wanting to attack the U.S. were insane and would think nothing of killing themselves. The bastards think they can hide behind the Coran when even their priests, the non-radical ones, are against violence. Only the the twisted minds of those craving power believe in killing. What they don't realize is that there will be no seventy some virgins waiting for them. Only the gates of hell are calling them forward.

"Tis a beautiful morning my friend," Manuel finally spoke.

"Yes, my friend it is. Too bad we can not enjoy this peace all the days of our lives," was Nate's reply.

"Si, but then we would not realize how wonderful it is. God gives us hard time so we will recognize the good times. We need the hard time to enjoy the good times. A fate man has brought on himself over the years," he answered.

"You are right, but it is sad," Nate remarked.

"Si, but I think we will camp here for a day to freshen up before going on. You say in a day we will be near Tucson?" Manuel asked.

"Si," Nate replied "but I must go on ahead. I will show you how to get to the camp you're looking for. With a stick Nate drew a map in the sand for Manuel. The old man understood and thanked Nate for his kindness.

"Now remember, not a word about me. Ok?" Nate said.

"Yes, senor, I remember, I won't forget," came the answer.

The rest of the camp was stirring and other fires being built. Nate and Manuel refilled their cups and put on another pot. Nate knew they would be around with beans for breakfast and he wanted none. Damn, he wanted a good old American style breakfast. He planned on getting one as soon as he could get to town, but for now he'd enjoy the coffee.

"Where do you think you'll be going now you're in America," Nate asked Manuel.

"I have a cousin in San Diego, in Calfornia. He will meet me in Tucson and we will fly back to his home. He says he has a job for me taking care of lawns," came the reply.

"Good, I'm glad you have folks that can help. I'll go now," Nate said as he rose to his feet. Manuel got up and looked at him.

"Good luck to you, senor and please stop this attack you mentioned," at this he paused seeing Nate was intent on going.

"A minute senor," Manuel said and walking up to Nate handed him a piece of paper.

Nate looked at it found it was a phone number.

"What's this?" he asked.

"The phone number where I stay. Call me sometime and someday you may come see me," Manuel said before walking away.

Nate threw a couple things in the Bronco, shook hands and mounted up. He fired up the vehicle and drove off towards Tucson. He drove a couple miles and stopped. Excitement was building within him and he had to report in.

"Good morning General, Nate here. Where am I to meet my crew and has anything happened I should know about?"

"No, nothing interesting as far as I know now. Osborn and Chaney are out near the camp of our terrorists and will monitor their movements. Menlow Park is on your side of town and the rest will meet you there. I'll get word to them now. How long before you get into Tucson?" asked the General?

"About an hour I think. What's next General?" Nate asked.

"Nothing till our suspects move and then we'll play it by ear. Your team is to rest up and relax, I'll tell you when it time to move out. Enjoy," he said ending the conversation.

"Wait; wait," Nate said, "what about rooms for us?"

"Oh, didn't I tell you. Reservations are being made as we speak. I wasn't sure when you'd be in so I waited till you got here. I must be getting old because I thought I told you," stated the general.

"Ok, thanks and I'll relieve those out at the camp if we're here more than two days. Osborn and Chaney needs some time in town, too," Nate told him.

"Well if the people you came in with have the stuff needed to carry out their mission, they'll be gone by morning. Just let me know. We have time on the satilite each day for tracking these bastards. I'll very the times each day so we can be sure of where they're going. Now behave when in town," he signed off and Nate's phone went dead.

Nate dialed and waited for someone to pickup. After three rings Delbert's voice came over the line.

"Hello, Nate, what's up," he said.

"That's what I'm calling you for. Any movement from our little friends?"

"No, they seem to be waiting for something and are acting like campers. Nothing interesting," he advised Nate.

"Well, the people I've been traveling with may have what they're waiting for. They should be there by mid-afternoon. The rest of us will be staying at the Menlow Park Hotel. That's on the west side of town. You stick with this group and call me if they start moving out. If they don't go by morning, I'll relieve you. I'm going out tonight and raise a little hell after a bath in hot water and a shave. Tomorrow will be your and Ed's turn to stay in town. I'll tell you when I see you what the Mexicans I came with brought for these bastards.

"Ok, boss, just don't forget us and have fun, Bye," and he hung up.

That evening the team had all arrived. They had showered and shaved and dressed in clean clothes. All were in a good mood and ready for a decent dinner and a few drinks. There was a sense of joy of being back in the good ole U.S.A. Their spirits would tell you they also sensed their job, in this mess, was coming to a close. They may be right and then again they could be wrong. They all met in the dinning room for dinner.

Everyone asked where Delbert and Ed were and Nate told them they were on stake-out.

In public they could not speak in specifics, only in riddles so the public couldn't figure what they were even talking about. They laughed and talked as through on vacation and that was exactly what they wanted represented to anyone listening. They still had to be careful about their mission. You never know who is listening.

Everyone ordered a large t-bone steak, after all the General was paying and for whiskeys.

After the steaks were devoured, they sat back and chatted. Whiskey was poured but not drank in a hurry. A couple lit cigars and leaned back just to listen to the others. Nate was enjoying the company and realized this was always the best time of any mission. The getting together afterwards. He also knew this one was not over yet and this get together was an extra bonus to them. He'd said a little prayer, asking to get them all back home in one piece.

Katrina noticed the look on Nate's face and decided to breakup his thoughts.

"Hey, Nate the group you came in with, where were they going when they left here. Further north I'd bet. Did they say?" she posed the question.

"I'm not sure except some will stay here and some mentioned Oregon. The old man has a nephew coming here to take him the San Diego," as the words fell from his lips he knew where the attack would take place. *Holy cow*, he said to himself, *I've got to call the General.*

He jumped up and rushed out of the room. He went directly to the elevator. He was delighted and alarmed at the same time. Once in his room he dialed the General.

"General, Nate here. Can you talk?" he asked.

"No, just a minute and I'll be with you." Nate could hear a chair scrapeing the floor as some one pushed back from a table. It was supper time and he would have bet the General was eating and with other big shots.

"Ok, Nate what is it. Your timing is terrible. I was having a nice dinner with friends. Well what is it?" he demanded.

"I figured out where the attack will happen. The term we thought was a man maybe. It's not. I believe its San Diego, California. The bastards are going to hit San Diego. There is one hell-of-a marine base there, but remember we are dealing with terrorist and that can mean only one thing. They're going to hit the navy base. Holy God, man they are going after the navy," Nate said but was unable to hide his excitement.

"Now calm down Nate and tell me how you know this?" asked the General.

"My gut tells me?" Nate answered.

"Oh, hell man, my gut tells me I'm hungry if that's all you have to go on," was the response.

"No. General, you have to believe me. They're going to hit our navy base at San Diego. It' got to be. Nothing else makes any sense," Nate said.

"Ok, let's say you're right. I can't just notify the base without more information. I sure they'd laugh if you told them your gut told us. When can we say more precisely and can you say about when this will happen?" inquired the General.

"No, not right now, but maybe when this group moves out of Tucson. I'll keep eyes on them and you continue observation via the satellite. See you General," Nate signed off.

Nate was a little displeased with the General's attitude at the information and yet he knew it was right. He would have to get more information of a concrete nature before you alerted the navy base. After all the F.B.I. and all local law enforcement would have to be notified. He knew he'd have to be patience. He was sure they could nail these bastards when the time was right. He wished he could shake the feeling of a looming disaster. This conversation over and he returned to the dining room. This time he really needed a drink and a cigar.

The team looked up as Nate entered the room. All were wondering what had happened that caused him to leave the table so fast. He could tell by the look on their faces so he decided to tell them. They had a right to know.

He ordered a drink for the whole table and waited till they were served. After a sip, he leaned forward. He checked the tables around them and most were vacant. Only one over in the corner had people. They were two people, a young man and a woman in their early thirties. They were oblivious to what was going on around them. Their hands were all over each other and Nate was sure they would soon depart to a room upstairs.

The rest of the crew, feeling something important was coming, also leaned forward and were quiet.

"I just got off the phone with the General and I think you all have the right to know what it was we talked about. I told him it was my opinion that an attack on American soil would occur at the naval base in San Diego, California. I wanted him to notify the base and he said no. We need more concrete evidence than my gut talking to me. This means we'll just have to wait and see. The direction they head in will tell us more. Just be aware and report to me anything you think is suspicious. This group could also be a decoy and others are to do the attack. God help us if that happens. This group could be on to us, but I don't think so. Do you think I'm right? Just nod your head if you do. If you don't, I'd like your opinion," Nate finished, leaning back and waited for an answer.

The waiting was unbearable as he waited. It seemed hours pasted when in fact it was only a very few minutes.

As he looked down the table, the nods began. It was unanimous. Nate smiled to the group and took a healthy puff on the cigar. He motioned the waiter for another round of drinks. Nate knew he'd sleep better knowing they were all in agreement with him.

"Tonight you're on your own. Go to town and have some fun. We may have to pull out tomorrow. Depends on the group camped out. If we don't then two of you will have to relieve Delbert and Ed so they can have some time off. If anyone needs money, stop by my room. Don't get drunk and I don't want any trouble with the law," Nate finished.

He sucked in on the cigar and blew a perfect smoke ring. The air conditioner's air grabed and blew it across the room before is disappeared into thin air. He again leaned back and took a sip of the whiskey.

One by one the team got up from the table and drifted off. Nate moved to the bar for company. As are all bartenders, this one was entertaining. He had a couple more drinks and left for his room. Inside the room he clicked on the T.V. took off his shoes. He had brought back a couple beers and proceeded to open then, then dialed his wife.

CHAPTER 12

Next morning Nate awoke at five thirty as usual. He made his trip to the bathroom and coming back, he stopped to make the in-room coffee. Clicking on the T. V., he turned to a news station. The coffee finished perking just as the commericals were through and the news coming on. With a full cup, Nate listened and watched. News always seems bad, except once in a while.

The news was over and coffee gone, he decided to shower and head downstairs for breakfast. He was sure some of his team was up and maybe even waiting on him.

Half hour later Nate walked into the dining room and saw Brad and Don sitting next to the windows at the far end of the room. He wandered over and sat down.

"Good morning, I trust you both slept good. Those beds were the best I've slept on since I left home. I'm actually looking forward to this day," Nate revealed to the men.

"Yeah, the beds were great. They must have been new. I slept like a baby," Brad said and Don nodded in agreement.

Nate ordered steak and eggs, toast and coffee. Don and Brad followed suit as they were only having coffee when Nate walked in.

Within minutes the rest of the crew was seated around the table and ordering. Everyone was in a good mood and seemed to look forward to the coming day. They chatted about their homes and experiences since they were on a mission together. If one was listening in it seemed they missed these missions even if they were always putting them down. Most had even said, after every mission, they would would never go on another. Truth being they loved the excitement and the threat of danger.

About half way through the meal, Nate's phone rang. To himself he wondered who might be calling this early. Had to be either the General or Delbert and Ed.

"Good moring," he said in answering it.

"Hi, boss, Delbert here, can you talk?" a question posed.

Nate looked around and found they were alone in the dining room answered.

"Yeah, why, what's going on?" he questioned.

"Well, as you know, the Mexicans you came with unloaded stuff from the donkeys and the Arabs have now loaded it into a big old truck. The truck must be a left over from the forties. An international five ton rig. It has tall side boards with canvas over the top. The sucker was fully loaded and a little wobbly. The Mexicans have cleared out and these folks are packing up to leave. What should we do? Do you want us to follow them or what?" Delbert asked.

"I'm sending a couple others out there to relieve you. Wait till they get there and they'll take over. Just pay attention which way the go. I have an idea they will travel west along an old dirt road. It's the one I came in on. I believe they are heading towards San Diego, Calforina. When you are relieved come on into the hotel and have breakfast with me. I'll fill you in then," Nate said.

"Ok, boss, keep the coffee hot," he laughed before hanging up.

"Carl, you and Katrina go relieve them so they can have some breakfast. Just tail those we are interested in and I'll call you in an hour or so," Nate said.

Carl and Katrina got up, left the table and went out to their Bronco and headed out.

In roughly half and hour Delbert and Ed walked in. Both were dusty and hungry. They joined Nate and ordered steak and eggs for breakfast, with coffee. Nate waited until their appetites slowed before he told them where they were on this mission and his thinking on where these people were going.

"San Diego. Holly molly that would put a crimp in everything. Are you sure boss," Delbert's response.

"It's my gut feeling and the General doesn't believe it. I know I'm right but can't prove it. This makes our mission even more important. If I'm right we have to stop it before they are in place, what do you think?" Nate asked.

"It's very possible," said Ed "there's no better place on the west coast if they want to instill fear in the people. God, I hope you're wrong. We should know in a day or so by the direction they're traveling."

"Any change in what we should be doing?" asked Delbert.

"No, we monitor and report. Once we know where and perhaps when this attack will take place, we'll attack them. The hell with the General. He's too concerned about fall out in politics; I'm not. The only thng is we have to be right and time will tell us on that point," Nate replied.

"Damn, we might have some fun on this trip after all," Ed put in his two cents worth.

"Maybe, but remember this is a dirty bomb and if it goes off over San Diego tens of thousands of people will die. Also we have no protective gear to handle the crap," Nate reminded them. "Half our pacific fleet will be in that harbor at one time or another. Even the ships will not be useable if this happens. The dirty bastards are really trying to hurt us this time. If this happens it will make September eleven look like kids play. We have to stop it regardless of what the General thinks. If I come to that decision, are you with me," Nate asked even though he knew the answer. Everyone nodded yes.

"Ok, you two have a night in town and leave in the morning. Everythings paid for so no worries there. In the morning you follow the rest of the crew behind our suspects. No hurry, but catch up to them tomorrow evening. I'll meet you all there and we'll see what it looks like and I'll devise a plan for the following. We can't stay bunched up and let them spot us. We'll have to spread out across the desert. Remember we'll have a satellite as a guide. Enjoy fellows," Nate said as he left the table and headed out of the hotel.

In thirty minutes Nate was on the outskirts of town. A short drive and he found the old road he'd came in on. He noticed tire tracks going out the same way. A close look showed a heavy truck and some smaller tracks. This would be his team following the truck. Nate stopped to make a call to the General.

"Good morning General," he said into the phone when he heard the General's voice.

"Hi, Nate, how are you this morning. Do you have any information for me regarding last nights talk," said the General.

"No sir. This call is to tell you we have moved out following our suspects. They are heading due west on the old road that has little use. I have a feeling this road is used by smugglers, dopers and such. Anyway we should come to a paved highway soon heading north and south. If they turn north we know we're wrong. If they go across and continue west we'll know we are right. I still bet my last dollar on it."

"I know Nate and I have an awful feeling you're right. I've had nothing on my mind except this all night. I hope you're wrong but in the past you've been right every time. Tell me what I can do to help?" asked the General.

"Well, can you still get time on a satillite for us. It would shore be nice if we could use it to follow this group. I'm afraid they will notice us and ruin our whole play. Pictures taken from up there when they meet up with their compardies would be helpful. You do expect a bloody fight when we go to take them out, don't you," Nate advised him.

"Yes, but by then we'll have the F.B.I., Federal Marshalls, state and local police to help us. The navy's shore patrol will also be involved. God, I can't stand this waiting. Let me make a call to those controlling the satillite and I'll get right back to you," signed off the General.

Minutes went by before Nate's phone rang.

"Yes, General, what did you find out?" questioned Nate.

"Well, it took some talking to but yes we've got time on the satillite. Once I got to the General who's in charge. He had to run it past the President. When he was told how serious it was, he gave permission that it would be for our use only. We can use it in any manner we wish and it will be kept secret. What's first Nate?" he asked.

"Zoom in on our little group. We are about ten miles above the border, traveling west. By now the target is about an hour or so out of Tucson. It's slow traveling so I'd guess the target is about thirty to thirty miles out of the city," Nate answered.

"Got it, I'll get right back to you if the satillte is on this side of the earth. If not it may be a few minutes," said the General.

Nate speeded up until he caught up with his team. He motioned them to stop. They stopped and Nate got out of his Bronco to meet them. All of his team got out of their vehicles and waited for him to speak.

"I just talked to the General and we have use of the satillite for as long as we need it. He's checking right now to get us pinpointed so they can find the suspects when it comes around this side of the earth. As soon as he calls we can take our time following this gang. I don't want to take a chance they might spot us and desert the project. Its best we catch them now and maybe stop their idea of attacking us. If I'm right and they suceed in this dirty bomb mission, they will shore as hell scare our people," Nate finished.

They brought out coffee and cigars and waited.

Thirty minutes later Nate's phone rang.

"Yes, General," he said and listened for a couple minutes. After he hung up he told his team they were about three miles ahead of us. He also told of a paved secondary road about twenty miles ahead. Nate agreed with the General this would be where they turned north if they were going to. If not, then we'd guessed right and San Diego was the target. They waited a few minute longer before taking off tracking the enemy.

They followed at a slow pace of keeping the target those few miles ahead. It was a grinding slow process and dirty. A wind had come up and caused them to close their windows. This done the heat became their enemy. They were forced to open the windows, and then the dirt and sand blew in. Soon they were all cursing the southwest desert. Thankfully, they knew they would soon be entering fertile, irrigated soil.

Throughout this little journey, the strike force, as they started calling themselves, slept in their vehicles and ate cold food. By using Canned Heat they did have hot coffee which made the trip bareable. Because of their use of the satellite, they maintained a distance of four to five miles.

They knew at that distance they could catch up fast if anything happened. Nate was always fearful of being discovered. No one wanted that to happen and expose the whole operation. Included in that fear was a feeling that if this group didn't arrive where they were to start the attack, a secondary group may be held in reserve. If so they had no idea where they were or how many there were. This was the group they had to stay close to.

Nate's phone rang and he answered it.

"Hi, General, what's up?" he asked.

"You were right Nate. They didn't turn north when they reached the secondary road. Looks like San Diego is where they're headed. This road will take them into San Diego, on the south east side of town. They won't be far from the Mexican border. Any ideas?" he asked.

"Yeah, keep that satellite trained on them as much as you can. When we start hitting city traffic, we'll move in closer. If we lose them we'll need you to find them for us. I've a gut feeling they'll turn into Mexico and set up camp. Fewer activities on that side of the border. As I recall the land if quite level and perfect for landing and taking off in balloons. Now I'm going to let you make a decision. Do we want to inform the military at the bases around San Diego bay? Keep in mind how they will react. My guess is they'll over react and blow it. You know as well as I do that the terrorists are watching and any change will tip them off. If that happens we'll miss them. They may even move the attack else where. You know the military mind better than I do. What do you think?" Nate posed the problem to the General.

Dead silence was heard on the phone. Nate could hear him breathing but that was all. A couple minutes went by before he spoke.

"Damn it, Nate, what do you think we should do. Either way we'll be damned if we do and damned if we don't. They do need time to evacuate if a bomb goes off. It'll take a several hours at least. If we don't give them enough time and it does go off, we'll be blamed for the deaths. If we wait and the bastards find out what we're up to, we never catch them and people elsewhere will die. You're right about the military, they do over react and that would tip off these bastards. What would you do? I need an answer, damn it," he said.

"It looks like we have to take a chance and tell someone. Can you discuss this with the president?" Nate asked.

"Maybe, but do you think that's wise. He may not be as willing to take the correct action as we will and if people die, he'll be blamed," he said.

"That's true but if no one dies and we stop the attack, he gets the credit. We all have to take a chance once in a while. That's life," Nate responded.

"Ok, I'll see if I can get in to see him. I'll tell him it's of national interest that we talk. I'll get back to you, Nate. Be careful," he said and added a goodby.

An hour passed and Nate had an uneasy feeling about this mess. He was sure the President would leave it up to them. He really didn't want to make this call. Damn the General. He's always getting him into these situations. Well time will tell. He lit another cigar and waited.

Two and a half hours later, the phone rang. Nate looked at it, not really wanting to answer it. It rang four times before he reached for it.

"Hello, General," he finally got out.

"Hi, Nate, I wasn't able to speak to the President. He's locked up in another situation and will be all day," Nate was informed.

"Ok, that may be good for us. While I waited I thought up a plan that will help. It's not the entire solution but it will save hundreds of lives if pulled off. He needs to let you talk to the commanders of these bases and lay out the following plan. Navy ships are always going out on maneuvers. As soon as we know what date the attack might occur, the navy needs to be prepared to go out to sea on a manuvers. Not the whole fleet but most of it. They can also load up with soldiers and marines. That will make it look like they're going out to play war games. So that it doesn't look too suspicious they need to leave two days before the attack. That puts the burden on us to find out the date of the attack. I think I have someone who could do this for us. The marines and the soldiers should be granted leave, told what's going on and advised not to come back until its safe. The shore patrol and MP's from the marines will be our operating force. We don't want to tell them until the day before. We must keep it quiet.

Those leaving on leave must depart base slowly, by tens and twenties hourly. This makes it look like normal leave and hopefully not tip off the terrorists. The navy needs to have four or five very fast boats, armed with machine guns, ready to go. They'll need flares and night googles. In fact anyone staying should have night googles, including our people. We have the 30-30's and have some automatic weapons and side arms. That will do for a start, don't you think General?" Nate finished.

"My lord, you have been doing a lot of thinking haven't you. I'll keep trying to get to him. I'll run this pass him and see what he thinks. Thanks Nate, I'll get back to you," said the general in closing.

"Wait a minute. Make damn shore you stress that this operation is on a need to know basics. If we scare these people off we may never find them again," Nate advised.

The next day the General was in the oval office along with the Secretary of Defense. The secretary was there at the bidding of the President.

"Gentlemen, gentlemen come right in and please be seated." greeted the President.

"Now General Scofield will tell us about the mission going on out west and what so concerns you. Both the Secretay and I understand this is to be on a need to know basics and will be kept top secret. Tell us why this mission and what have they found that so concerns you?" asked the President of the United States of America.

"Well sir, in aiding the Department of Homeland Security, I sent three teams out along the border to monitor how many Mexicans and perhaps terrorist are illegally coming into our country. Over a period of two weeks, we have counted hundreds of Mexicans coming. This of course is of no surprise to us but we have found a group that appears to be planning an attack on the military bases at San Diego, California. So far it looks like they are putting together a dirty bomb. We can't be sure yet but my main man on site thinks so. Arabs are involved. My teams are sitting on them awaiting a call from me regarding instructions," advise the general.

The Defense Secretary cleared his throat, as if to speak.

"Wait till he finishs," said the President.

"Our idea is to plan a way to evacuate the bases slowly so the bastards don't get wise and call it off. Our way might do that and save thousands of lives but leaving thousands at risk. I know his plan and will be happy to fill you in on it. Keep in mind we don't yet know the date of the attack. I've been thinking since talking to him yesterday and my belief is the attack will come in four days, April 11. The attack on the World Trade Building and this one just might of April 11. For some reason the 11th seems to mean something to these people," added the general.

"My God, the people have been right all along. What is it you need from me? We need to stop it from happening. Can we move in and capture them now?" he questioned.

"No sir, we can't. They are not all there yet. We believe they will attack from the air," said the general.

"My God, from the air again," exclaimed the President rather loudly.

"We think so, but this time by balloons, colorful balloons. No one would suspect it but we know they have balloons brought in from Mexico by donkeys. We've seen them." said the general.

"Balloons, balloons, the sneaky bastards," as he phrased it. After a couple minutes passed and everyone in the room could see how serious this matter was.

"What is it you need of me?" asked the President.

"I need permission to imform the military leaders of the plan to evacute most of the soldiers and sailors and marines stationed there and make sure it is kept secret. Perhaps the Secretary of Defense could issue some order. If this is possible, I'd have my man go there and instruct those who need to know and to make sure they follow the plan. Would the President like to know the plan?"

"Yes, but first this man of yours, is he reliable. How well do you know him etc. and why should we take his plan and not divise one of our own? Is he that good?"

"Yes sir, he's that good. I can give you everything you need about this man and you can run your own check, but he's good. He did a lot of covert operations in Nam; he helped slow drugs coming in from Colombia a couple years ago. I'd stake my life on him," said the General.

"Ok, tell me the plan?" said the President.

More discussion was had before the meeting ended. The General got what he wanted and permission to have Nate go to San Diego. He smiled when he thought how Nate would take the fact that he was going to inform the brass at San Diego and lay this on them and not him.

The phone rang and Nate stared at it. He knew it would be the General. He wasn't quite sure he wanted this conversation. For one it might not be what was needed. He hated politics after the goof-up on the Viet Nam War.

Washington was always wanted to micro-manage what should be left up to those in the field. Would this new president be that smart? The ringing didn't stop and he knew it had to be answered. *Well let's get this over with,* he thought and picked up the phone.

"Hello, General, did he buy it or should I go home?" was the way Nate answered it.

"No, Nate he was very receptive to your plan. In fact he is issuing orders as we speak that you will come by and give them instructions they are to follow to the letter. He's not one to micro-manage so you're it. It's your plan and you set the time for a meeting. You say who's to attend and they will be there. When do you want to be there? You have anything at your disposal you need. Give me a date and time you want to be there and I'll see to transportation. If you know, give it to me now so I can get started. Ok?"

"Aren't you going with me? You're a general and I'm a civilian. They may listen to you. I have to talk to generals and colonels, etc. Why would they believe me? You'd better come," Nate said.

"No, my boy, it's all yours and they will listen. When the President speaks, they listen. When do you want to go? Time is getting short so hurry a decision and let's run with it. I trust you and so does he. How about it Nate?" spoke the General.

"Damn you General, I don't like talking to the brass. If I must, I must. I need to be there by ten oclock tomorrow morning. Get me out of here now. Notify whom ever you need to, to get all command officers, at the level of colonels and above. I need a room that is sound proof in a building that is cleared of all personel and people. I'll want guards, two or more at each door into the room and building. Is that clear?" he ordered.

"Yes, quite clear," answered the General. "Anything else?"

"Yes, hurry it up, I'm going out for a steak and a couple drinks in San Diego. Get me into a hotel close to the base and have me picked up at nine am. That should do it General," Nate finished.

"Ok, a chopper will be there in an hour. Be ready," said the general and the call were terminated.

Using his phone, Nate called Delbert who was up ahead. When Delbert answered he was advised to get a driver for Nate's Bronco.

"I'll fill you in when you get here with a driver," Nate responded to questions.

Soon after, Ed and Delbert arrived. He filled them in on his trip to San Diego. The plan was for Ed to wait right here for the chopper's arrival with Nate. Ed could catch up after he departed. Nate requested Delbert keep him advised of their movements.

"Don't press those up ahead. Keep your distance and remember you can call the General to keep tracking the terrorist. I should be back by one Pm tomorrow. Are we clear," asked Nate.

"Yes, boss," Delbert replyed. Ed got out of Delbert's vehicle and into Nate's.

With the whirl of chopper wings Nate was spirted away and in a short period of time was deposited at the naval base. The admiral who was the commanding officer was waiting at the helo-pad for him.

"Good afternoon, sir, I take it you must be Armstrong," he said as he shook hands.

"Yes, thanks for meeting me. Have you been told why I'm here?" Nate asked.

"Not a damn word except that I'm to help you in any way I can and that when you speak, you're speaking for the President. I surmise it is important. I'm curious as hell. Oh, here we are," he said indicating they had reached his office.

Once inside and having reached the admiral seated there, waved Nate to a chair.

"I'm Admiral Jones, Mr. Armstrong, would you like a shot of whiskey. I understand you being here is in the best interest of the United States and it is a matter of national security," he said as he reached into a desk drawer. From the drawer he pulled a bottle of Crown Royal and two shot glasses. He filled both and handed one to Nate across the desk.

"Thanks Admiral," Nate said, "lets forget about the Mr., I just Nate and I'll call you Admiral. Ok by you," Nate said as he tossed down the whiskey.

"Fine with me. Here let me refill your glass and then you can tell me what's so damn urgent. With the President, I picked up an indication of excitement in his voice. When he told me how serious this was, I was surprised. It was almost like war would soon be announced. Am I right?" asked the Admiral.

Nate noticed the seaman had not left them yet. Proablely because the Admiral had not excused him.

"Tell your man he'll have to go and we'll get down to business," Nate said.

"Oh yes, you can go seaman and I want no calls or interuptions until I say so. Understand. Keep everyone away from the door and you stay at your desk," he ordered.

The seaman saluted and left the room, closing the door behind him.

Nate thought for a minute, wondering just how to phrase the situation. He'd sized up this officer and came to the conclusion he was not an ass kisser as are many high ranking officer. This one came up through the ranks he'd bet. Good this is the type of man he liked to deal with.

"First you've been told this is top secret. Right?" Nate asked.

"Yes sir, I have been in no uncertain terms," came the answer.

"Ok, I'll tell you a little now and more in the morning. You are very close to being correct that war is about to happen and you are the target. Not you personally. This base is going to be attacked by Arabs with a dirty bomb if I can't stop it. You do understand what that means?" Nate stopped to see how the man was taking it.

"Holly hell, when?" asked the Admiral as he leaned forward.

"We don't know for sure but my crew and me maybe able to find out if I can find a gentleman who can find out for me. I have a telephone number and will try to call him this evening. We do know it will be soon. Now here's the kicker. We can't attempt to evacuate everyone. I'm telling you now that we will try our best to stop it, but any earlier attempt could mean they would only go somewhere else. We would lose them and we'd have no idea where they'd go. The White House and I feel the best way to stop them is here. I need to have a meeting in the morning at 1000 hours with all lead personnel. We must get word to them quietly so rumor won't get out. This applys to all branches of the military," and was intrupted by the Admiral.

"My God we have the army, navy and marines stationed here. A few flyers from the airforce. It would take three days to get them all out."

"I know that. We must get a head start on it and make it seem normal. You can start by anouncing a war game at sea and move most of the fleet out starting after my meeting. You must not say a word to anyone because that would cause a panic. My team has the terrorists under observation now. We can't move in on them because others are to join them. You and the officers must trust me. A tall order I know. If we get this done right we'll kill the terrorist and save the base. Understand," Nate concluded.

"My God, it can't be done!" coming from the officer.

"Yeah, I think it can. When your fleet sails tomorrow night you take as many people as you can. Take the entire Navy and some marines if you have room but you must load them carefully. All they need to know that it's a war game they're going to and that was the reason they weren't told. You were told of the officers I need to talk to tomorrow morning were you not?" Nate questioned.

"Yes and they have been advised," he replied.

"Good, now would you please get me a ride to my hotel? I've slept in the desert for days and I need a shower, a good steak and a couple more whiskeys," Nate expressed his needs.

"Certainly," replied the Admiral pressing a button for the seaman.

In moments the seaman appeared, reporting in the usual manner.

"Yes, sir, how may I help," he spoke as soon as he entered the room.

"Get our guest a car and take him to his hotel. Have the shore patrol do it and remind them to pick him up in the morning at nine hundred hours," ordered the Admiral.

"Yes sir," he replied and turning to Nate said "right this way sir."

Nate thanked the Admiral, shook hands with him and left with the seaman.

In the outer office he was offered a seat as the seaman picked up the phone and dialed. He spoke a few words and hung up. He turned to Nate and advised him his ride would be right there.

Nate didn't feel like sitting, so he remained standing until the outer door opened and a Lt. entered. The black band on his sleeve showed he was a shore patrol officer. He looked at Nate and said.

"Ready if you are, sir."

Nate followed him out to the jeep and climbed into the back. In ten minutes they were in front of the Horton Plaza Hotel.

"You're to have me picked up at 0900 in the morning, right," Nate reminded him.

"Yes sir, that's my orders. Good night sir and have a pleasant evening," he saluted and drove away.

Nate registered and headed into the restaurant. It was nice and recommended by the hotel staff when he registered.

He was shown to a table and waited until a server arrived. It was only a couple minutes before she was there. She was a woman in her early thirties and clad in a see thru top and tight panties. Very attractive, making him think of his wife. Damn, he'd be glad to get back home. He knew this would be his last mission and he was so looking forward to retirement.

He ordered a steak and a couple whiskeys.

"No, hurry on the steak he said but bring the whiskies now, if you will," he said.

"Yes, sir," she said smiling and turned away to place his order.

Nate leaned back and began people watching, a favorite pastime of his.

CHAPTER 13

Nate awoke early on this very important day. He had butterflies in his stomach and was nervous. He had a bad night, with little sleep. In a couple hours he would be standing in front of generals and adminrals. Hell, he'd never been in this position before and right now he was praying never again to be. He wished he had the time and date of the impending attack. He didn't and that would draw speculation from this group. His thinking was maybe this gang of murderers had picked April 11. Maybe the 11th held some special meaning for Muslims. He'll get the General working on it. *In fact I'll get him started on it right now,* he thought to himself. He reached for the phone and nearly jumped out of bed because it's ringing scared him.

"Good morning, it could only be you at this hour, what's happening," Nate said into the phone.

"Nothing unless you have something on that end," came the reply.

"I was just going to call you and run something by you. I believe you have the resources to check this out for me. I would like to have it before I go before the brass. In thinking this mess over I was thinking perhaps April 11 might be the day of the attack. What do you think?" Nate posed knowing full well he'd not given enough information to him.

The conversation got serious.

"Why that date, Nate. What would be the foundation for your comment?" was the General's serious reply.

"Well, September 11 was the last attack and now April 11 is coming right up and that made me wonder. It's just a gut feeling. Would you check out the 11th of every month and see if you can find a connection. It could be a holiday or a date something happened in the Muslim world. Anything at all that might have been taken serious by the militants in that society. That's all, a gut feeling," Nate said.

"Sure, I'll check it out but I doubt I have it by the time you speak on the problem. Nate make sure no one is allowed in the room with you and the command officers. You can imagine what would happen if word of this sneaked out. We'd have a mass exodus from thoses bases and once it reached the city it would be unstoppable. You can only imagine the death toll. It would probable kill as many as the bomb. We must keep it a secret. I have faith in you boy, take care of this for me," coming from the General.

"I'll do my best General and you get me that information as fast as you can. Call me anytime because I need to share it with this group. Now I'm going to have breakfast," Nate replied.

Now this conversatin was completed, Nate finished dressing and shaving, he made his way to the restaurant. Entering he found a nice table by the windows and seated himself.

He barely seated himself when a blonde waitress come over, handed him a menu and filled his coffee cup.

"I'll be right back to take your order," she said smiling, "you'll need to look over the menu," she said smiling.

"No, I don't need any time I know what I want. Give me a short stack and two scrambled eggs and more coffee. Thanks," he said.

"Yes sir," she said politely and headed for the kitchen.

When the pancakes arrived he truly enjoyed every delicious taste. He savored the maple syrup, with very mouth full. The real butter was a calm pleasant flavor and the cakes themselves had a nice flavor. Once he was finished he pushed the dishes away and lit a cigar.

Perhaps fifteen minutes later, a white navy car pulled up in front of the hotel. A young man got out and came into the building. Nate recognized the young sailor who had dropped him off last night. As he entered, Nate waved at him.

The young man saw him and came over to the table.

"Good morning, sir. I trust you had a good night," he said.

"Yes, it was ok. Have a cup of coffee, I'm not ready to go yet." Nate said as he slid the extra cup his way.

"Thank you, sir, don't mind if I do," he said with a cheery smile.

Nate waved to waitress over and asked for coffee for the young man.

"Well young man what have you planned for the day. Something exciting I hope," Nate pressed him.

"I'm to stick with you all day, sir. Maybe tonight will be exciting for me," he said and hurried to say, "I don't mean that to say your not exciting, sir,"

"No offense taken and lets knock off the sir. I was never in the military and don't wish to be," Nate said, also smiling. He liked this kid who tries so hard. The navy needs more of his kind.

"Do you know your way around town, son?" he asked.

"Yes, was there someplace you want to go perhaps this evening." asked the young sailor.

"How much do you know about my visit here, sailor," Nate asked.

"Not much, just that I'm your driver and I'm to get you to the base before ten," he said glancing at his watch.

"It's time to go, sir, if you want to get there on time."

"Ok, let's go," Nate said throwing a ten on the table and heading for the door. The young man hurried to get ahead of him and open the car door.

"Relax sailor, I know you'll make it. Besides I take pride in having Generals and Admirals waiting on me for a change. Excites you a bit to do it?" Nate asked.

"Yes, sir, it does, it's cool but don't tell anyone I said that," he replied and started the car.

Nate chuckled and leaned back and enjoyed the ride.

It took thirty minutes to get to the base and through the gate. They pulled up in front of a fairly large building.

"This is it sir. If you'll follow me I'll show you to the Admiral's office," said the sailor upon opening the car door for Nate.

"Lead the way, I'm right behind you," Nate informed him. "Say what is the Admiral's name?"

"Admiral Perkins, sir," came the answer as they entered the building.

Two Shore Patrol officers were stationed at the door. They checked the sailors ID and asked Nate's for his. Nate showed his drivers license. One of the officers spoke up.

"You have no papers for entering here. How do I know you're to be allowed here? Wait here," he ordered

With this he stepped to a wall phone and dialed. Almost instantly his call was answered. In a couple minutes he returned.

"Sorry for the wait, sir, but I had no paper work on you. You may go in, the Admiral is waiting for you," he said.

"No problem, I understand," Nate said and followed his driver. Down the hall and the sailor opened a door and entered. Nate followed, closing the door behind him.

A chief petty officer jumped to his feet and saluted. He had been seated at a desk.

"Mr. Armstrong, you may go right in. The Admiral is waiting," he announced

Nate opened the door and stepped into an office. A grey haired man looked up from a desk. He looked Nate over before speaking.

"Mr. Armstrong, it's a pleasure," he said stepping around his desk and shaking hands with Nate. "Have a chair, sir. Excuse me a minute.

He opened the outer door and gave orders to clear the outer room and he wanted no interruptions.

"We still have a few minutes, sir. Would like a cup of coffee and I'm very curious as to why you're here. I hope you can enlight me. My orders came from the White House to give you assistance you need and to assemble all the command on base. I've set the time for our meeting for ten hundred hours. We have twenty minutes and I'd like to know what's going on. Here's your coffee," the Admiral said passing over a cup filled with a dark liquid.

"Well, I will give you the reason I'm here but any other information will have to wait till our meeting. I'm sorry but that's just the way it is. We can not take a chance of a leak. You were informed of that fact weren't you?" Nate questioned.

"Yes, I was and we'll handle it in that manner. Surely as commander of this base I'm entitled to get a little information now. I'm curious as hell why we are treating a citizen as someone in charge of a military base. I'm just curious," the Admiral expressed his feelings.

"Yes sir, I'll tell you now but I just want you not to react as you might. Fasten you seat belt Admiral because you won't believe what you're about to hear," Nate said.

He watched for a reaction from the Admiral. Face muscles tighten was the only reaction Nate noted. That's about all he expected of a career man with this rank.

"Your base is about to be attacked by terrorists with what we believe is a dirty bomb. That's why I'm here. I'll explain what you need to do and what not to do," Nate said.

"Holy damn, you must be kidding. I don't believe it," he expressed himself.

"Call the President, he does believe it and I'm the one who stumbled on to the mess you're about to confront. But don't worry until I tell you what we have and I can tell you we have these people under observation. My team is sitting on them right now. The best and hardest thing we must do is not to cause a panic and yet do certain things. We can't have rumors running all over the place. You can imagine what would happen if rumors got into the city. We'd never be able to control the mass exit," Nate replied.

"Well, it's about time, lets go down to our soundproof room and you can inform us on our duties in the face of such an attack," said the Admiral.

The two men rose from their chairs and walked out the door. The Admiral advised his aid where he'd be, but he was not to be disturbed unless World III broke out. He was serious and a frown crossed the face of his aid. He knew this was serious.

Down the hall and a turn in the hallway and they were at the room. The Admiral entered first, then Nate. Everyone in the room jumped to their feet.

"At ease," barked the Admiral in a milder voice than usual. This was noticed by every officer there.

"Be seated, everyone," also word from the Admiral, "this is Mr

Armstrong and he's here today to speak for the President. You can not write anything down what you hear and there will be a time for questions later," he said looking at Nate. Nate nodded yes for agreement.

Nate stood up and was wrestling with how to start. He decided to be direct as would be any officer in the military.

"Gentlemen I'm going to drop a hot rock in your pants and expect nothing except total, and I mean total cooperation in this mater. First I'll tell you that for years I've been doing covert operations for our government. Because of my current mission and information I've come across information that tells me your base is going to be attacked by terrorists with a dirty bomb. You've all heard of a dirty bomb so there is not reason to explain it to you...We know who these people are and have them under observation. The problem we have is that they've not yet broken the law. They've come in thru Mexico. As far as we can tell, they are suicide bombers. Yes, they are Arabs but fit right in with the Mexican race. They are the same color, light brown and that makes them hard to spot. They blend in and many even speak Spanish. You all understand how sneaky these bastards are. If they suceed in the attack it will be worse than Peral Harbor. We don't know when it will happen but it will be soon. Your jobs will be to evacuate these bases without alarming anyone. My job will be taking out the sons-of-bitches before they get to you. Now you must follow my instructions to the letter. Those who can be will be given a five days leave. The ships will go to sea on the pretense of war games with Canada. That will explain why every ship that can operate under its own power leaves port tomorrow. I can not stress enough that in no way can these people watching you catch on to what we are doing. Understand?" Nate said at the top of his lungs.

"Now my guess would be our attackers are not smart enough to realize what we've done until its too late. I'm sure all of you can see what damage a successful attack would do to the morale of this country. OUR country.

This has to be a smooth operation or it'll come back to bite us in the butt, so play it cool and don't let on we are in too much of a hurry. With my information I believe the attack will be on April 11. That's two days," and Nate hesitated to get a feeling of the crowd.

Everyone in the audience drew a deep breath. You could almost feel the air being drawn from the room. Everyone looked at each other with deep frowns. The same question on each mind. How are we going to do this under the restrictions?

"Any questions so far," Nate asked of the twenty or some odd group. A hand went up from the middle of the group.

"Yes, what's the question, Nate asked.

"Do you know sir how are they attacking, by what method I mean? Do you know sir?" one asked.

"Yeah, I believe it will be by balloons. They have been carrying at least 3 all across the Mexican desert. Don't worry about that, it's my job to stop them. Your job is more serious. If we let this leak out, we'd never be able to handle the panic. That would be your job so make it simple, Keep your mouths shut and do what we must," came Nate's reply.

Admiral Perkins raised his hand and waited for Nate to finish answering.

"Yes, Admiral," Nate said.

"If all this is true then why is a citizen carrying the ball? What General in Washington are you working with?" he asked.

"General Scofield, sir," Nate answered.

"Before we put anything into operation I will have to talk to him. Even if the President requires this, I want Scofield. I can see where a dirty bomb could do this nation great harm by attacking here but I think the military should be running the show," the Admiral finished.

"Call him if you like, but you are running the show. The burden for this whole operation is on your shoulders to pull it off. I'm just the messenger with the information. I was right out of town a ways and it would take much longer to fly him out here from Washington. I'm the guy responsible for catching or killing these terrorists. His phone number is 202-567-0271. You best get calling because he and the President expect your fleet to start out of the harbor by daylight tomorrow. I know it takes a while to supply those ships and a while to get up a full head of steam. I'd suggest you call a reporter and tell them you're going on manuvers. This will be in the morning papers and will not give away what we are really doing. Now before you go off half cocked remember those ships will only be out to sea three days or four days. That is if we're right and the strike or try to strike's on Sunday. Yes, gentlemen, Sunday. Continuing, "The rest of you gentlemen must give leaves to as many as you can that are not really needed. You must do this to several hundred of your people by early Sunday morning. You must do them in waves so you don't have thousands leaving at a time. The waves of military personal must be close together but not being so obvious that it's noticed. I'm shore we are being watched. If those bastards check on to what we're doing, we'll blow the whole operation and they will move on to some other target. We can't let that happen. We must capture or kill them all, here and now," Nate finished.

An officer up front raised his hand.

"Yes sir," Nate acknowledge him.

"Why not let them know they're expected so they go after another target. This is a juicy one for them and odds are slim we pull this off. They would find lots of targets that are not so well fortified. Also they would have fewer people to kill but still enough to scare the nation," he finished.

"Yes, you are right, but the problem is we might lose them. Anyone here ever tail someone?" Nate asked.

A couple hands went up.

"Those who just raised their hands can tell you it does happen that even best of law enforcement officers can and have lost sight of those they are watching. When this happens you go back to research hoping to find a trail. This can take hours or sometime days. By then this type of group could disperse and be anywhere in the country. They could also strike anywhere and kill Americans. We don't want that. Now we know where they are, we must stop them. So far they've broken no laws so we can't go in and kill the bastards. No, we must nail them here and now. Ok, I believe all of you know what you must do and will do it. Adminral Perkins will call Washington and have his answer in minutes and tell you it's a go. That's all I have to say. Let's get to work," Nate said as he turned to leave.

"Thanks Admiral," Nate said as shook hands with Perkins.

"Where are you going now, Armstrong?" came a question.

"I'm going back to my team and wait. I'm hoping we get evidence enough to kill these bastards. I do have a hand yet to play that might get us the day and hour of the attack," Nate advised.

"Here's my number if you need anything and call me as soon as you get these people. OK?" the Admiral asked.

"No, sir I won't do that. General Scofield will. Good bye Admiral and good luck. I'll have the seaman take me back to my hotel. Thanks," and he turned around and walked out of the room.

Nate called Delbert on his way back to camp, curious if anything had happened.

Once Delbert was on the line, Nate asked if anything new had happened.

"No, not yet boss, except four more men have joined up with the first group. Carl is working his way up as close as he can. He thinks he may be able to get close enough to hear a conversation," Delbert reported.

"Damn it, he doesn't know their language. How can that help?" Nate said, cursing under his breath.

"Don, come here," Nate asked now back at camp, and Don came over to find out what Nate wanted.

"Don, do you think you could crawl in behind him and get Carl back here without being discovered? Damn it, Carl knows better than go in where he might be discovered. He could have at least waited until dark, damn it," Nate still fuming.

"I think so, I'll try," Don replied and left camp.

Nate lit a cigar and filled a glass with whiskey. He took a seat in the Bronco. He had problems to work out and he needed to be alone… The main issue was to figure out what day and time of day these Arabs were going to strike. He knew with that information it was going to be hard to stop it. All eyes in Washington were on him. He felt uncomfortable in this position but knew fate had placed him here and there was nothing he could do about it. He knew the one advantage he had were the balloons. They were huge and colorful. From a distance they could watch for them.

Lifting the cup to his lips he took a sip, then another, all the time trying to figure out how to start this conversation.

Manuel introduced the nephew to Nate. This time Nate sized him up. He didn't detect any problem but proceeded with caution.

"Manuel, what we are going to talk about is very secret. Does your nephew have to be here to hear this?" Nate asked.

"Oh, no, he does not have to be. I thought he might help," Manuel said being embarrassed. He spoke to the nephew in Spanish and the man got up and moved to the counter a ways away.

"Manuel, it would be of great help to this country if you could remember if you heard dates or times the people in question might attack. Any at all. Even if you don't think its necessary please let me decide," Nate said almost begging.

Manuel throught and thought but just couldn't come up with an answer.

"They talked much around the campfire and some during the day, but I can't remember if times or dates were mentioned," he said.

"Lets just sit here and drink our coffee and see if anything comes to mind," Nate said.

Nate was hoping beyond hope something would come from this meeting. He just had to be sure of the time and date. He was sure he was right about the date but the time was needed. *God, help us,* he said under his breath.

A half hour drug by and still nothing so Nate decided something else.

"Manuel, what I'm about to ask you to do is something dangerous and you don't have to. You understand that?" Nate said, "If I showed you where they are camped and took you there do you think you could find out for us? They know you and if you went in with a story you couldn't find your nephew and you needed money. They know and trust you. Ask them if they have work for you for a couple days. Tell them you would do any kind of work for money to eat on or any thing you want to tell them. You must be aware they will kill you if they find out what you are doing. You may have to stay a couple nights. Do you think you could do it for us?" Nate said hopefully.

Deep wrinkles appeared across the brow of the old man as he thought this over. He appeared to be in deep thought and Nate stayed very quiet during this period of time. The old man turned his head towards he nephew then back to Nate.

"Yes, senor, I will do this for you. You have welcomed me into your country and it is now my country. My family is living here and it is a good life and I must do what I can to keep it safe. I would kill these people with my bare hands if you asked me to. What you ask in not much and I will do it. When do you want me to start," he said.

Reaching across the table Nate shook the old man hand and thanked him.

"You tell your nephew what ever you want and I'll wait outside in my Bronco. When you are ready we will go to police headquarters. I will have someone pick you up there and take you close to the camp. Thank you my friend," Nate expressed his thanks.

The two got up from the booth and Nate tossed a ten dollar bill on the table. He walked passed the nephew and out to the truck.

The old man stopped at his nephew and they had a conversation in Spanish. It seemed a heated one to Nate. He noticed, thru the window, the younger one kept looking out the window. Finally they finished and both came out to the truck. The old man got inside and waited for the younger one to close the door. The nephew looked across at Nate and spoke.

"You will bring him back safe and sound. I don't want him to go but he says he must repay you for accepting him as a human being. As a fellow human being and not as just a Mexican as so many of the whites do. He believes this is now his counrty and he does this for the country. He won't tell me what it is you want him to do, but that it is important so I accept it."

"Yes, he will be fine. I'll have him back on Sunday at the latest," Nate assured the young man. At this they drove away.

Arriving at police headquarters, Nate and the old man walked in and told the desk officer he were Armstrong.

"Go right in sir," the officer said, "he's expecting you."

"Thanks," Nate said and walked thru the door marked, Chief.

As Nate crossed the floor to the desk of the Chief. He noticed the man behind the desk was in his mid-fifties. He had dark hair and appeared to be built like a Sherman tank. As he rose up to greet Nate, Nate was sure of it. This man was about five seven or eight inches tall and builds like a wedge. He had broad shoulders and narrow hips. When he stood, he stood as if he was being attacked. His feet were planted so he could not be off balance. He appeared to be ready for anything. He surely wasn't a man to be taken by surprise.

"Nate Armstrong, I'd guess. I'm Fred Still, pleased to meet you," he said sticking out his hand. Nate shook hands before he spoke.

"I'm sure that by now you've had a call from Washington regarding myself and a team. That right," he asked.

"Yes, that's true and I'm damn curious. Have a chair and we'll have a chat," said Still.

"I've cleared the outer office, but let's check," he said walking to the door. Jerking the door open, he looked out, and then closed it.

"I've a Sgt. outside that has orders to keep everyone outside while I'm talking to you. I understand this is top secret and is on a need to know basis. I'm all ears so shoot. What the hell's going on that is of so much interest to Washington," he said.

Nate leaned back a little and looking straight at the man, began his conversation.

"Your area is about to become a target for a dirty bomb to be set off by Arab terrorist. They are here already here. I think they will try to get it set off on Sunday, April 11. That's this Sunday. I have a team watching them right now for any move but we have a problem,"Nate let him have it full bore.

The chief just looked at him for the longest time before he entered the conversation.

"What the hell kind of problem. Just move in and kill the bastards. I'll come with you with some of my men and we'll make short work of them," he spit out in a half notion, but hostile tone.

"I wish it was that simple Chief, but we can't do that," Nate stressed.

"Why the hell not?" was his response.

"Because if they catch on to us knowing about them they may not strike. They may just fold their tent and go elsewhere and we don't want that to happen. We know they are here now, but if they run and disappear into the woodwork, we may not find them again. If this happens the bomb will go off and world war III may have started. We must stop this strike and kill'em here. We can't jump too soon but we shore as hell can't jump too late. Right now all we have is they are in this counrty illegally. There may be others just waiting to see if this group's successful in this attempt. If this one fails the others may go home. That's asking a lot but could happen."

"Son-of-a-bitch," he breathed almost under his breath. Silence followed as both men sat looking at each other.

Nate broke the silence.

"I know chief, it's a bitch but that's it in a nut shell," Nate injected into the conversation.

"Just what does Washington want me to do? How will we ever get the people out of the San Diego area in two days? Do you realize the panic this will cause when the word gets out? Even some of my officers, firemen, etc may leave their posts just to save their families. God, Armstrong what a bomb you've already dropped on me. Oh, Lord helps us all. Well now I've got all that off my chest, do you have any plans or ideas how we handle this," was the Chief's response.

"Well kind of. I'll give you and only you the location of these people and I would like to have you shut down or be ready to close a few roads when needed. I'd like you to call the sheriff and have his people help. Come up with some type of emergency that won't cause a panic, but yet serious. Increase patrols across the city in key areas that might help out. That will be up to you. Give the sheriff the real reason and remind he must keep it a top secret. I would suggest that when I call you that these bastards are on the move, you'll be ready to move. Most of the planning will be your baby to control traffic, etc." said Nate.

"Well you're just full of surprises today aren't you? Damn I wished you'd not come today. I was so looking forward to a relaxing weekend. Well we'll just have to deal with it. What else do I need to know?" said the Chief shaking his head.

Nate could feel the hatred in Ed's voice as he talked.

"Calm down Ed, it could be his way of getting more information. They know this man and trust him. Let's watch and see what happens. If they start breaking camp we'll know they have found us out and are leaving. If that happens we'll have to follow them. We're through with supper and are starting back now. Don't do anything foolish. I'll be there in fifteen minutes. Don't go back and stay at camp. We'll set up patrols later. Have you eaten?" Nate asked.

"No, hell no. Can you bring me something?" he asked.

"Shore, how do you like your steak," coming from Nate.

"Medium rare," was the answer.

"Got you. See you soon," Nate replied as he hung up.

Everyone had heard the conversation and was finishing up quickly. Nate ordered another steak to go and for the bill. Nate soon received the steak and laid a hundred dollars on the counter as they left.

CHAPTER 15

Back at the camp, the small group waited for instructions from Nate. Ed was having a time composing himself.

"What do you think the old man is doing?" he spoke to Nate.

"Hopefully he's playing it the same as you or I would. I wouldn't sell this old man short just yet, Ed and you calm down. This will do us no good. In case he's told on us, we will set out a guard tonight. I don't think they would come after us. If he told on us, they would disappear into the fabric of our population and be hard to find. That's why we must take care of them here and now. Not sure when now will be, but damn soon. Listen all of you. We've been in tough places before and we all know some times we're wrong. I can name you a dozen in Nam that helped us when some of us thought they were on the other side. Same thing here. One thing is for sure they would never take him with them and we can get to him if need be. Now lets all have a couple shots of whisky and we'll send someone down there. If anything urgent comes up, l will let you know. Just make sure you sleep with your clothes and boots, just in case. You know, like the old days," he smiled and looked around the team. All brave people but this nuclear threat would scare anyone with common sense.

"Brady, you sneak down to their camp and see what you can see. Don't go in close enough to get caught. Take your time going. Its pitch black and you dare not use a flashlight. Don't fall and for heavens sakes don't get caught. I'd think they'd kill you in a minute. See what the old man is up to and report back by daylight in the morning. Ok?" Nate asked.

"Sure, boss," he said tossing down his shot of whiskey, picked up his thirty-thirty, slipped on a jacket because of the cold in the desert at night and walked off into the darkness.

"Ok, everyone it's time to turn in. This could be a short night," Nate advising them. He mounted the Bronco and slipped inside to sleep. He rolled down the driver's side window so he could hear what went on in the darkness. The rest of the team dosed the fire and had gone to bed.

Ed was the first one up and building a fire. He put on the coffee pot and sat near the fire. He looked towards Nate's truck and noticed some movement. To himself, he thought he'll soon be up. Ed was right because as soon as the coffee started boiling and the odor reached Nate, he rolled over and sat up. He knew the first one up would be Ed. If not Ed it would be him. They were both early risers.

Nate opened the door and stepped out and on to the ground.

"Good morning, Nate," Ed said, "did you have a good night?"

"No, it's hard sleeping in a vehicle or I'm getting to old for this nonsense," was the reply.

"This is going to be our last gig isn't it. We're not kids anymore, Nate. This you should remember before you say yes to the General again. That is if we survive this one. Looks like we will, but only time will tell. Come on and have a cup." Ed handed him a cup of the black brew.

"Yeah, I know. I have a beautiful wife waiting at home for me and here I am sleeping alone. I must be crazy to even want to come on these capers. Well maybe this weekend will end it. If not, I think I will quit anyway," Nate said as if into the air.

"Yeah, sure and the hell you will. If the General asks and your woman lets you come, you'll say yes. You love the excitement to much. Remember who you're talking to Nate. We've been together too long for you to convince me," replied Ed.

"Yeah, guess you're right. We've been thru a lot together, haven't we?" Nate said.

"You bet and it's been good for us but now is the time to settle down. If I had a woman like yours, I'd never leave home,"Ed said with a big grin.

By now the rest of the team was starting to stir. Leaning against the Bronco, Nate enjoyed his coffee.

Just as dawn was breaking, Manuel and Brady came walking in.

"Boy, that coffee smells good," Brady said as he walked over to the fire and helped himself. He also filled a cup for Manuel and passed it over to him.

Nate waited till they had found a seat and had taken several sips of coffee before him questioning the two.

"Well, Brad, what did you find out?" Nate asked.

"Let Manuel go first. He's the one who found out things. I was just along for the ride.

"Ok, Manuel, did you find out when and what day they plan to attack America?" Nate asked looking at him.

"Si, senor they plan the attack for Sunday. They didn't say the time in front of me. It seems they are unsure what time the ones will show up with something call plutonium. The ones with this are out in the desert somewhere, but fairly close. This plutonium seems to make people sick and has made their journey very hard. Two have died on the trip. They will stay in the desert until the balloons are inflated. When the balloons are ready to go, they will send up a flare. Then they will rush in and load the stuff on and be ready to take off in minutes," Manuel related to them all.

"Do you have any idea where these others are hiding," Nate asked and the old man looked south and pointed.

"Somewhere out there, senor," he said, nodding towards Mexico.

"Damn," replied Nate, "this means we need to scour the desert and find them. I'd rather catch them on the ground than after they're airborne."

"I'm going to call the General and the rest of you get ready for skunk hunting. I'll be with you shortly," Nate addressing his team.

"Senor, I would like to help. May I go with you?" asked the old man.

"No, Manuel, we are grateful for what you have done. You stay here and get some food and sleep. If I need you it will be this evening. Ok?" Nate replied.

"Si, senor," he said.

Nate dialed the phone and waited. His wait was not long. On the first ring the General was there.

"Hello, Nate, what's going on. Have you been successful? Did you take any alive, etc, etc." an excited and anxious voice asked.

"Slow down General, I do have some news and we are getting closer," with this he brought the General up to date.

"You can understand Nate, how up-tight the President and some of us are!"

"Yes, but you have to trust us to get this done. My crew and I have never let you down yet. This is a lot more important and we'll get it done. Relax, I'll keep you posted. We are going to start out over the desert and see if we can locate where the bastards are hiding. If we do, they are dead and we'll move in on those with the balloons. Have faith," Nate advised as he hung up on the General. He knew the General had a short fuse but he controls himself after he gets the first words out. *He knows what we are up against and for once he doesn't have full control over a situation that may panic the nation,* Nate was thinking.

Nate asked his crew over and briefing them on what he wanted to do next. Once they had gathered round he spoke to them.

"Well gang, Washington is really up-tight and is asking; we hurry up and resolve this situation. We all know we can't, but that doesn't help how they feel. The security of our nation is in our hands. I don't like it any more than the rest of you, but here we are. The responsibility is on our shoulders. What we are going to do the rest of today and tonight is to fan out across the desert and see if we can flush our quary. I could get help from the military but I'm afraid they would spook the bastards and they would get away. So go in pairs and take your side arms and your thirty-thirty rifles. No automatic weapons. Continue posing as hunters. Take canteens of water and some food. I'll help you layout grids for the search. We have to go slowly and if you come upon this group and have no doubt, kill them. I don't want a fire fight between you and a dozen Arabs. Understood? First I'm calling the Chief of Police and asking for some radios. This will make it possible to talk to all parties involved in this action. I think it's important. It will make it possible to call for help and assistance if need be. The phones we will use for our communications only. You guys get out the map and fold it into the section that shows this part of the country," Nate said.

"How far down south?" Delbert asked.

"Oh, about ten miles in three directions and over to the sea," Nate responded.

Nate broke away from the group and entered the Bronco. This would provide silence for his conversation with the chief.

The Chief's phone rang at a time he was just about to pull his hair out. He resented the fact he had to take orders from a civilian. A thirty year veteran as a police officer, he felt he was better qualified. Of course he knew nothing of Nate Armstrong's background. If he had, he felt a little more comfortable in this situation. Nate's career made him an expert in this kind of a fight and a fight there would be.

"Chief Still," he answered.

"Mr. Armstrong is on line one Chief, should I put him thru?" said the Sgt. working the front desk.

"Yes, any time he calls put him straight thru, we can't afford any time lost," was the response.

"Hello, Armstrong, what can I do for you?" He questioned.

"Chief, I need radios for each man I have. Seven will do and I need them yesterday." Nate sprung on him.

"Seven radios, what the hell for?" was the answer the Chief fired back.

"We have information that the people with the radio-active material is out here in the desert, but in hiding. My people will comb the area for a distance of ten square miles. We don't have much time so hurry. Make sure they are fully charged and send extra batteries for each. This ties us into your system and we won't take the time to dial. Make sure you inform your radio operators to put us straight thru each time we call. Also your command officers to obey my calls. This is going to be a life or death situation and quick, decisive action is needed. Ok," Nate asked.

"Ok, I'll get the radios out right away. I'll get one of the traffic choppers to fly over there in the next half hour. Hold a minute," stated the Chief.

"No, don't send any choppers. We can't afford to spook this crowd and they are sure to see the choppers and our mission will be comprised. Send a car and I'll meet you at the highway and Ocean Drive. Ok?" Nate said wanting an answer.

"Sure, just a minute so I can get the radios and have the Sgt. run them out to you," said the Chief.

Nate could hear the orders for the radios being given. The Chief was barking orders before he came back on the line. He finally spoke again into the phone.

"Ok, they will be there, what else?" asked the Chief.

"Nothing right now and thanks. We're going to see if we can flush our targets from the brush and kill'em. We would like a prisoner but my people won't take any chances to capture one. I'll keep you informed. Has the navy started moving the ships out?" Nate asked.

"Yes, in fact we have several out to sea already. They are are loaded with sailors and marines. The Admiral thought it would be better to load up every man he could and take them out that way. If thousands of the military were out the front gate on leave, it might look suspicious," said the chief relaxing a little. He was a man of action and things were starting to happen. His kind of action.

After hanging up, Nate got out and walked up to where the map was spread out over the hood of his vehicle.

"You guys got this divided yet," Nate said with a slight smile.

"Waiting for you boss, but we can show you how we think the areas should be divided. Care to see?" Delbert said.

"Sure and lets hurry. I need to go meet a policeman. He's bringing radios. Show me," and all attention was directed at the map.

With a lead pencil, Delbert drew three lines on the map and hesitated to explain.

"This seems to be a good way to do it," he said as he pointed to the area in question and continued.

"I figured Don and Carl can swing down the center, facing south along the ocean and inland at least two miles. The balloons are closer and this might put them right into the action first. That's what I figured you'd want. Ed and I will swing around to the left, facing south and sweep down that way four miles and two miles wide coming back. Each team needs to stay close to his team mate and know where he is at all times. This leaves you Nate, to be a floater. You can sweep back and forth thru all the areas. Remember guys, if you stumble upon this group unexpectedly, they will try to kill you. They have nothing to lose. They are suicide bombers and expect to die. Let's make their dreams come true and help them greet their God. I'll just bet there are no seventy virgins waiting for them. If so, I doubt they could handle three," he finished as laughter erupted from the crew.

"Wait a bit. I'm going for the radios and we'll leave when I get back," Nate informed them. He got into the Bronco and drove off towards the highway.

As he approached the highway he noticed a white car parked on the left side of the road. He smiled because he knew it was a police car from a distance away. There were no markings on it but once you've seen a police car, you've seen them all. He pulled along side and nodded to the officer behind the wheel. Both cars had their windows down and they conversed thru them.

"Good evening Sgt., I'm Armstrong. Do you have something for me?" asked Nate.

"Yes sir," and he opened his door and got out of the patrol car. He walked to the rear and opened the trunk. Nate followed.

"Here are your radios and in the bag are the extra batteries. Six radios and extra batteries. That's what you ordered right?" coming from the Sgt.

"Yes, that's fine and tell the Chief thanks," Nate said as he shook hands with the Sgt.

"Sounds like you folks are going to have a wild time out here," spoke the Sgt.

"Hope not," said Nate, "but you could be right. You folks in the city ready if they sneak thru our hands?"

"As ready as we can be on this type of operation. As much as I would like to be out here with you, I hope you stop this thing from happening. This will be the exciting end of the mission. If these bastards get into the city, there's really not much we can do," explained the Sgt.

"Yeah, you're right. Well, I've have to go now. Good luck to you Sgt," Nate expressed his thanks.

"You to, sir," was the reply and Nate placed the radios in the back and drove back the way he had came.

Nate was deep in thought and about a mile from from where he'd met the Sgt., a man walked out in front of the Bronco. This surprised Nate who romped on the brakes and slid to a stop.

The man just smiled and walked around to the passenger's side and opening the door got in.

"Hi, Nate, how are you?" he said and Nate found himself staring into the face of Sam Brown.

"Damn you Sam, I could have killed you and I'm fine. What the hell you doing here?" Nate said in a raised voice.

"Just came by to keep you company and join the fun!" he exclaimed. "The General told me where you are and here I am. He said you'd be grateful for my help so let's hear that part," he said and waited for a reply.

"Well, it's true we have a real mess on our hands here and can use all the help we can get. Where the hell have you been all this time and where's your transportation?" Nate questioned.

"Oh, I've been roaming around having the time of my life. I've seen to it that several tons of dope failed to cross the border and a couple of big guys are being interrogated in Washington right now. Might lead to shutting down a massive program in the drug trade. My vehicle is out there a-ways," he replied and pointed out to the desert.

Nate just shook his head.

"Ok, Nate fill me in before we get to your camp," Brown asked.

Nate talked the rest of the way back to where his team waited. He went into details of what was going on. Sam listened intently without interrupting so much as once. After the briefing Sam spoke.

"A sad shape of affairs in the world today, Nate. Why can't humans just leave each other alone and live a happy life," he said quietly almost under his breath.

"I don't know Sam, I don't know." was Nate's quiet reply.

Nate pulled into camp and both he and Sam got out of the rig.

"You all remember Sam. He's here and will be going with me. Delbert show him the map and explain while I pass out the radios," Nate said.

The group walked with Nate to the back of the Bronco. Nate reached in and started pulling out radios. He handed each one until everyone had one. I

"The batteries will assure you have enough power till late tomorrow morning. Everything should be over by then, God willing. Ok, any questions," Nate talking. None came forth.

"Ok, folks, it a tall order but you must cover your sections with a fine tooth comb. Every square foot must be covered by daylight or shortly there after. The signal to return will be the filling of the balloons. If you've found nothing by that time, report in. We'll need you here. If you've found the ones with the stuff to do the damage, take'em. Remember radation kills so if you take any, bury it and mark the spot. Someone properly dressed to handle the materal will get it later. Don't stay around it long. Well, get going and good hunting. Let's see if we can stop this attack tonight. On the radios if you need the police or the military use the co-sign of Armstrong" Nate explained and motioned Sam over.

"Lets grab a couple canteens of water and I'll grab some beef jerky and crackers for eats," Nate said. Once loaded he turned around and found everyone had walked away and started their search. He and Sam followed suit and in a matter of seconds were out of sight of the camp.

Nate and Sam walked along at a distance of fifty yards apart. This way they could see each other as long as it stayed daylight. After dark they would have to rely on their instincts, same as the other teams. Even now in the dusk of the dwingling daylight, it was a strain on the eyes to keep track of each other. It seem impossible to Nate that this would accomplish anything but they had to try something. The night goggles helped courtesy the Navy. Just sitting around doing nothing and relying on grabbing these terrorists at the balloons in the morning, was kind of dumb. By then it might be too late.

About twenty minutes later Sam and Nate had parted to cover more area. Nate saw a fire burning up ahead. A thought went thru his head that this might be it. He wondered if Sam had seen it and soon dismissed this idea. Sure Sam had seen it. He knew Sam would be closing in on the fire on the right side. He chose the left side as he grew closer. The fire was now about a hundred yards ahead and appeared to be a campfire as he had thought. More than likely it was set and being used by Mexicans coming to America. The ground in this area was getting a little rough and a little more small brush kept trying to trip him up.

Sam on the other hand was going thru the same experiences and had to move very slowly to keep from falling. He didn't want to fall and create any noise that might be heard at the campfire. He decided to crawl the last fifty yards and he wondered if Nate was doing the same. He smiled at the thought and knew Nate was. These two had worked in Nam together and could almost read each others minds. Damn he hoped this was the terrorist's camp and they could end it right here and now. Slowly he proceeded in a crawling position.

Nate was proceeding in a crouched manner a little further in, but finally realized that crawling was the way to go. He dropped to his hands and knees and moved on.

The two were within thirty yards when they saw two men sitting around the fire drinking coffee. Both hesitated for a few minutes and waited to see if any more people appeared. It'd be a shame to jump in there only to find yourselfs surrounded by half a dozen men.

Satisfied the two were the only ones in the camp, Nate and Sam stood up to walk the rest of the way. Nate looked over and saw Sam from the light of the fire standing about twenty yards out. Sam smilled and nodded. The two walked into the camp and spoke to the two men sitting there.

"Good evening," Sam greeted them, "that coffee smells real good. Can you spare a couple cups?"

This startled the two and they jumped to their feet and reached for rifles lying near by.

"No, no, we mean you no harm, just two lost guys trying to get back to their hunting camp," Nate said as he looked over the two. They appeared to be Mexicans and looked kind of tired. They were dusty and Nate hoped they understood English.

The two stopped and relaxed at this commet.

"Si, you may have coffee. Cups right there," said the smaller of the two.

Nate and Sam edged their way over to the coffee pot and bent over to pick up cups to fill. At this moment they noticed two other men coming into camp. They looked beat and from the way they held rifles and were looking over Sam and Nate. Trouble loomed.

"Oh, oh," Sam whispered, "I think we're in trouble."

"I agree," Nate answered, "are they Arabs," as he filled the cups and straighted up.

"No, don't think so, Mexicans," he whispered back.

The two men who had just entered camp pushed past them and picked up cups for their coffee. It was very tense in the camp as neither party seems to know what to do about each other. Finally the dirtiest and meanest looking Mexican spoke.

"Drop your rifles, senors and put your hands in the air."

Nate and Sam were just finishing their coffee and looked in his direction. Both reached the same conclusion at the same time. Four rifles were pointed at them and they had no choice. They dropped the empty cups and dropping their rifles, putting their hands in the air.

"What's the hell's the meaning of this," Sam said as if insulted.

"What it is is a stickup. Empty your pockets and stay right there," the order came from the same man.

They followed the order and once their pockets were empty they were told to back up a few feet. This was done and one of the four moved in and collected the money on the ground. He also picked up the wallets and relieved them of their cash. This completed, the wallets were dropped back to the ground and the Mexican backed up a few feet.

"You senors may pick up your things but not your guns. We will seize them so you won't hurt yourselfs," said the Mexican giving the orders and with this thru back his head and laughed.

Nate and Sam walked the pace or two and reaching down, picked up the remaining contents of there pockets. Straighting up them were ordered out.

"Now get out of our camp and don't come back. America is that way," he said, "and don't come back or we kill you."

Nate and Sam walked off into the darkness in the pointed direction, fuming as they walked.

CHAPTER 16

After walking a few hundred yards the two stopped and sat on a couple rocks they had bumped into in the darkness. After a short breather, Nate spoke.

"We can't let the bastards get away with this," words from him to Sam.

"Hell no, let's goes back and kills those bastards right now. I'm ready," Sam replyed.

"Oh, we're going back alright, but not right now. Let's wait a while, and then go back. They all looked beat and once they drink a little and fall asleep, they'll sleep very soundly. Then we teach them a good lesson. You catch a half hour nap, Sam, then I'll do the same," Nate suggested.

Sam laid upon the sand and fell fast asleep.

Nate's anger was slowly disapating as he enjoyed the quiet of the still night air. His mind was racing with thoughts of what might happen tomorrow and he shivered at the thoughts. Mankind had finally come to the point of destroying themselves. Rather than just sitting back and enjoying each other and families, we are choseing a violent path. *God help us all* was in his thoughts. His thoughts shifted and returned to home and his wife. *For sure when this caper was over and he survived,* he thought, *I'll never again leave that darling person. They would run her club and be very content and happy the rest of their lives.*

All at once his mind jumped back to reality.

He realized he had fallen asleep only seconds ago. A noise or something had brought him out of it. He looked around and saw nothing but the pitch blackness of the night. Glancing at his watch he saw it was time to wake Sam. With the toe of his boot he nugged him, then stepping so he'd not be hit if Sam came awake fighting. With so little sleep it was possible Sam wouldn't remember where he was until he was completely awake. He was right to do so as Sam whirled around, still lying on the sand.

"Where am I," he inquired of Nate as he saw him standing there.

"Stand up Sam, my turn to sleep," Nate reminded him.

"Oh, right, right, I'm getting up," and with this he stood up and stretched his arms and blinked his eyes. At last he was fully aware of his situation.

Nate laid down upon the ground and fell asleep within seconds. The day, while not strenuous physical work, his mind had wore him out. An hour's sleep was welcome. A quiet snoring came up from where he lay and Sam seated himself to wait out the half hour before they would be on the move again.

Thirty minutes later Nate felt a shaking and was immediately awake.

"Come on Nate time to go to work," Sam was saying.

"Ok, I'm coming," was Nate's response as he rose to his feet.

"How should we do this, Sam," asked Nate.

"Lets just sneak right up to their camp and steal the weapons and shoot them whle they sleep," Sam replied.

"No Sam, I don't want any bloodshed. Damn you're getting mean in your old age. We'll grab the weapons and take them prisoner. We'll search them for our money and just so they don't follow us, we'll take their boots and that'll teach the bastards. Are you game?" Nate asked Sam.

"Yeah, yeah, I think you're getting soft Nate. Have it your way, I'll go along but if they resist, I'll shoot. Ok?" he said

"Yeah, that's ok." Nate said and started walking back towards the camp.

The only guide they had back was the fire and it had grown smaller. Luckly the red cinders shown for quite a distance and was good enough to guide them, once they were in sight of the camp.

"Lets crawl the last twenty yards," Nate said to Sam, "just to be sure they are asleep."

Soon they were approaching the area and dropped to their knees. Slowly they crossed the space between themselves and the Mexicans. They stopped and counted the sleepers. All four were sawing logs and unaware of their late night visitors. Sam motioned to Nate and they stood up and walked the few steps to where their rifles were leaning against an old beat-up Chevrolet truck. This they must have brought in after Nate and Sam had left earlier. They checked to be sure the rifles were loaded and decided it was time for a rude awaking.

Sam fires a couple shots close to the sleeping bodies. It was amazing how fast they came alive. They jumped to their feet only to find guns pointed at them.

"Put your hands up and don't move or we'll kill you," ordered Sam.

Once they were all standing and awake, Nate began searching their pockets for the money taken from them. All the money was counted and only the stolen dollars were put in his pocket. The rest was dropped to the ground and a slight breeze moved it away.

"Take their knives, Sam," Nate said. Once this was done both Nate and Sam smiled at them.

"You want to tell them Sam or should I?" Nate asked of his partner.

"Oh, let me," came the reply.

"Now your bastards remove your boots. We'll be taking them too," he ordered the group.

The one who had spoked to them in English spoke.

"You can't leave us in this country without boots. Its, its cruel." he started saying.

"Shut up or I'll shoot you. Take off your boots right now," Sam repeated.

All the time this was taking place, a man in the front seat of the truck was watching. This man had come with the truck after Nate and Sam had left there earlier. He was thinking how he could help his friends escape from these Americans. The only way he knew was to jump out of the truck and have his pistol trained on them. They would have to drop their rifles and his friends would then kill these American dogs. He smiled at the thought. He knew he had to be fast or it would never work. He knew he had to chance it. He prepare to spring out the door. He drew his pistol and half stood at the door. He lifted the handle and shoved on the door. The door hesitated a second but made a noise. It finally flew open and the man jumped to the ground.

Nate and Sam both heard the noise from the door and swung around to meet the challenge. Both seeing the man fired their rifles at the same time. The man fell dead just several feet away.

Both men swung back and found that none of their prisoners had moved. They left the camp carrying five pairs of boots. The dead man would not need his, but the others might so they too had to be removed.

Sam and Nate strolled out of camp, kinda of cocky. They knew they would not be followed by anyone without boots. Several yards away Sam posed a question.

"What the hell are we going to do with these boots? This many pair are hard to carry?" he questioned.

"We get another two hundred yards behind us and we'll bury them in the sand. Most of this soil seems hard. Watch for some soft soil, sand and we'll do it. It has to be soft because all we have to dig with are our hands. All we need to do is lay them a couple feet deep," Nate replied.

They reached a sand dune a few minutes later and all but stumpled over it.

"This will do," Nate said and both dropped to their knees and began pawing at the sand. Minutes later the boots were under-ground and they stood up.

"This was a no good plan and we're going back to the Bronco. I'm going to call the rest of the crew and tell them to do the same. Either we flush them out with our vehicles or grab them at the balloon area tomorrow. Damn, I wish we could get this over with tonight but it seems impossible. You agree?" Nate asked Sam.

"Yeah, stumbling around in the dark, someone could get killed just falling over this brush," he smiled as he said it but of course Nate could not see the smile due too the darkness.

He pulled the raido out of his back-pack and triggers the broadcast button.

"Nate calling his team. Respond by clicking your radios, no verbal required. He counted the clicks and knew all had answered.

"Discontinued your foot search and get on with it in your vehicles. If we can't flush'em out tonight, we'll set up for tomorrow. End of transmission," he said and released the trigger on the radio.

"That was short and sweet, hope the bastards were listening on a police band," Sam spoke up.

"It was short and sweet and I doubt they heard it. Remember these are Arabs and not to bright," Nate replied.

Back in the Bronco, Nate and Sam stopped long enough to have a good drink of whisky. They sat talking about the days gone by and their experiences. This was a good rest for them and there was never a doubt they truly liked each other.

Meanwhile Delbert and Ed arrived back at their Bronco and rested a bit. Ed pulled a bottle of whisky from under the seat and they both took a swig. Their walk in the dark was uneventful and they were glad to be back in something with wheels. They to sat a while and talked of days gone by and their hopes for the future.

"This going to be your last trip doing this type of work Ed or are you going to continue," Delbert asked.

"Hell I don't know. I'm getting old and Nate may not want me again. I just don't know," came the response.

"Nate says he's through with this covert stuff. He's declared he's staying home with his cute wife and just enjoy life," Delbert stated.

"Yeah, I know but he said that after the Colombia caper and here he is right back at it again," Ed said.

"Well, let's move out and drag thru this patch and see if we find anything," Delbert said. With this he fired up the engine and dropped it into gear and slowly moved out.

The lay of the land was hilly and bumpy and it was a rough ride for Nate and Sam. The darkness didn't help but still they pushed slowly on. Keeping the lights on bright allowed them to see always ahead and helped with Nate being able to weave back and forth between the little hills and bumps. They stopped often to listen for other vehicles. An hour of this somewhat tedious adventure and they needed a rest. They had a swallow of whiskey and lit a cigar. Nate had remembered to bring some along.

"This is a bitch, Nate and we're not doing any good. Should we turn back?" Sam asked.

"No, I don't know about you but I dare not try to just sit still and do nothing. You just keep looking for movement out there and I'll watch my driving. I''d hate to run upon one of these bumps out here and turn over. Then we'd have a mess. Well let's get on with it," Nate said and put the Bronco into gear and started the slow movement again.

Soon there after Nate realized they had gone five miles and turned to the right for a half mile. Again he turned right and started back the way they had come. Reaching the northern end of their search section they stopped to eat a sandwich. It was a quiet night, no moon and as dark as the hubs of hell.

They ate in silence, each with their own thoughts of tonight and what might be tomorrow. Both wished this night to be over and tomorrow started. Nate thoughts were of those balloons and how to stop them without anyone getting hurt. He knew the enemy would have automatic weapons. No way could they put eight or ten people out of commission with that kind of fire power, without getting hurt.

Delbert and Ed were getting tired of this little game and would stop more often. They had brought along large thermos of coffee which helped keep them awake. The bumpy countryside helped in this regard. They were jousted, bounced and tossed about to the point of weariness. On one of these stops, Ed noticed something in the distance.

"Look Delbert, south and a little to your left. I thought I saw a light flickering. I'd say it was about a half mile. Hard to say really with this country so flat. Half mile at least," he blurted out, hoping he was right. He would take anything to break the monopoly of this night.

"I'm looking," Delbert answered, "But don't see a thing yet."

Silence fell over them as Delbert strained to see what Ed had drawned his attention too. He knew Ed was not prone to announce something that wasn't there. He strained and strained his eyes till they hurt. Then all at once he saw a glow in the dark right where Ed had said.

"There it is again Delbert," Ed spoke in hopes Delbert saw it too.

"Yeah," Delbert said, "I see it. A red glow. I wonder what it could be. A lone lantern maybe. Hum, this is interesting."

"Call Nate on the phone, not the radio. If it is our little group of terrorists they may be listening to the police band radio. Everybody does these days," Ed explained.

"Ok, hold on a minute till we see it again. My eyes might be playing a trick on me. I want to make sure we are seeing something," Delbert said.

The two, now on the edge of their seats, waited minutes that seemed like hours.

"There it is again," Delbert announced, "now I'll call Nate."

Picking up the phone from the seat, he dialed Nate's number. It was answered on the first ring.

"Nate, Ed here and I have spotted something a half mile away. It looks like a single lantern in the night. Has a red glow and that's all we can tell from this distance. What do you want us to do?"

Nate was silent a couple minutes as he weighed their options. Delbert was getting impatient with the wait and just as he was about to say something, Nate answered his question.

"Leave the Bronco behind and go in on foot. Don't use any light or they'll see you. Sneak in close to where you saw the light. Remember don't do anything till you report back to me. If you can prove they have radio active material then we will assume it's our group and we'll all get together, including the marines and attack them. Delbert you make damn sure you're right though. If we jump someone who is not the terrorists, we will have exposed our hand and we might as well go home. Good luck partner," Nate ordered.

"Don't worry boss, I'll call you soon," Delbert responded and hung up.

He turned to Ed and repeated his conversation with Nate.

"Well at least we get out of this truck and out in the fresh night air. That should keep us awake and the exercise will do us good. Let's have a cigar first and then go. That will give us time to finish our coffee," Ed said and proceeded to unwrap a cigar. Finished, he placed it in his mouth and put a lit match to it. Delbert followed suite and silence again took over and they finished the coffee without a sound.

Ten minutes later, they left the Bronco and started the treck across country. Every few yards, one would trip over an ant hill or low growing brush. It was slow going with their trying not to make noise. Within fifty yards of where they could see the light, Delbert dropped to his knees and motioned Ed to do the same.

"From here on in we crawl, Ed, and no talking. Hand motions only," Delbert whispered to Ed.

Ed nodded in agreement and they began the slow creeping to where they could hear and see what was ahead.

It was slow going over and around humps in the darkness. Ever so often one or the other would place a bare hand on a sharp item. He'd have to bite his tongue to keep from holloring out. Damn it hurt. Both could feel a sticky substance on their hands and knew it was blood. Not serious but damn uncomfortable. They stopped just short of where the fire illuminated the surrounding landscape. From here they could see inside this little camp. One man sat near the fire with an automatic weapon across his knees. A couple more were zonked out in sleeping bags. They had an old truck which was parked to one side. There were barrels stacked on the back of the truck. A strange cargo for being out in the desert. A couple of boxes and some miscellaneous items were piled around. Near the fire were a frying pan and a couple pots, like the kind used for cooking. It all seemed quiet and comfortable way to be. No hint of violence except for the automatic weapon.

Ed nugged Delbert and pointed out it was an automatic and drew a question mark in the air. Delbert shook his head that he didn't know.

A closer examining of the one sitting up disclosed Arab dress. This son-of-a-bitch was advertizing he was Arab. How dumb could you get? Then they both remembered they did not know they had been discovered and felt relaxed. To their way of thinking, they would want to die in their native dress.

Delbert motioned to Ed to back up and return the way they came. He didn't want to take a chance on waking the one on guard duty.

Crawling back fifty yards was just as grueling as when they crawled in. Fifty yards back from the camp, Delbert stood up and spoke.

"Did you see the barrels on the back of the truck, Ed?"

"Yeah, why barrels I wonder?" came the reply.

"Because they are easy to pack and you can get a lot of stuff in one. I think we've hit the jackpot. Inside those barrels are the dirty bomb materials. They can run the truck right in among the balloons, grabbing the stuff inside and be off and running in just two or three minutes. There are enough of them. I think I'm right. Hot damn we can get this over with tonight and everyone can sleep in, in the morning," Delbert said, "I'm calling Nate right now."

"Yeah, Delbert what's up?" Nate's response to the phone call.

"I think we've found the terrorist and the dirty bomb material. It's a small camp with only three men. All we could see was one atuomatic weapon but you can bet there are more. Two were asleep in sleeping bags so we saw no arms for them. But as you know in our experiences you always assume they are all armed. Let's raid the damn camp and put an end to this mess tonight, boss."

"Wait a minute Delbert, let's not jump the gun. If you went back to the Ocean Drive, could you find your way back there?" Nate asked.

"Yes, hell yes. We will drive in a straight line back and when we join up I'll just follow my tracks back. Let's do it Nate. It's time to take these so-and-so's out," Delbert said, almost begging.

"Ok, drive back to the road and I'll drive up and down the road until I find you. Sam is hot to trot also. In the meantime I'll call Don and Bradly and have them sneak down to the balloon area. If we do this right we'll have them all by daylight. I want to size up the situation first and if you're right I'll call in the standby marines to help. God, would the President be happy if we could end it now. Ok get started."

"You drive Sam, I've got to call the General and get the go ahead," Nate said as Sam took the wheel.

"Good morning General," Nate said to the answering of the phone on the other end. "I hope you slept well up to now because you won't get any sleep till this is over. Delbert thinks he has found our little group of rats. He's taking me out there in a few minutes. If this pans out and I feel these are the people we're looking for, do I have your permission to attack and end this mess tonight?"

"Yes, hell, yes, but don't jump the gun. You must make sure you're right. Get a gieger counter and check out radiation. If no radiation, no attack. Understood," ordered the General.

"Where in the hell am I going to get a gieger counter this time of night? Any ideas," Nate barked back at him.

"I could fly one out to you but that will take four hours at the least. Someone must have one out there. Get a hold of the military and your friend the Chief of Police and make them get you one and get it quick. Hurry now and I'll sit right here and await your next call. Oh, and just so you know young man, I haven't gotten any sleep yet this evening," said the General.

The phone clicked in Nate's ear and the conversation was over.

"Son-of-a-bitch," Nate exclaimed to Sam, "he wants us to use a Geiger counter to confirm this is the group we're looking for. Son-of-a-bitch, where are we going to get such a thing in two hours, Sam. The sun will be coming up and we can't use the darkness to hide in. Son-of-a-bitch."

"About the only thing you can do is make some calls and find one," Sam replied.

"Hell of a lot of help you are, but you're right," Nate agreed.

"Chief Still," said a voice on the other end of the line when Nate dialed a number.

"Hi, Chief, Armstrong here. We think we've found the group we were looking for, but there one little problem. The General wants us to verify they are carrying a hot load with a gieger counter. Where in the hell can we find one this time of night?"

"Well, you've come to the right place. My department has one for emergencies. I'll grab it and be right out. Where are you located exactly?" asked the chief.

"Come out to Ocean Drive and start for the ocean and I'll be parked along there. You can't miss us. Oh, and Chief, don't wear a uniform," Nate added.

"I won't I'm already dressed down in dungrees and ready for action. I can't see letting you have all the fun," he smiled when he said it not knowing how it would be received. The conversation over, he hung up.

"Damn," he hung up Nate said to Sam. I wasn't through talking," he dialed again.

"Yes, Armstrong," was from the Chief answering the phone.

"You hung up too fast I had more to say. Once you get to Ocean Drive, have your men close it. Have someone call the marines and get those standing by loaded in their choppers but not to move out till they hear from me. Got it," he ordered to the Chief, with a smile. Thinking to himself, *I'll show him whose boss.* He continued, "And hurry we only have a couple hours to verify before the sun come up. We need the darkness to get close enough to check their load,"

"Yes boss," replied the Chief with a smile.

CHAPTER 17

Twenty five minutes later the Chief, with the Geiger counter arrived. Nate and Sam were standing outside of their vehicle. Delbert and Ed sat comfortably in theirs.

"I knew you couldn't do this without me," he said as he stepped outside his unmarked police car.

Nate smiled at the gull of this cop, but didn't say anything to unset him.

"Hi Chief," Nate greeted him; "you got the device?"

"Yeah, here it is," he said lifting a black box looking gadget, with a handle on it, from the seat of his car.

Nate looked it over before saying a word. All this time he was formulating a plan to get this used and get back safely. He knew the Chief would want to be the one who used the box. Not wanting to upset him he decided to assign him and Delbert to go into the camp.

"Delbert, you and the Chief go in and sneak up close to the camp and try to get close to the truck to test with the counter. I assume the Chief knows how to use it. Take a reading and back off and lay low about three hundred yards back this way. Call me on the phone and give me the results. If you detect radiation you stay right there and I'll bring our people in and we'll capture the bastards. Look around and get a count of the enemy if you can. I'd hate to go in with our small force and find fifteen or twenty terrorists with automatic weapons facing us. While we work our way in, lead by Ed, you can go back in close and to the back side in case they try to get out that way. We need to get everyone. Don't let any get away. Kill'em if you have to or take them prisoners. Clear on that, Delbert?" Nate requested.

"Sure, lets go, Chief, jump in my rig," Delbert said and Ed, who was listening, got out and gave the Chief his seat.

"Hurry, Delbert it will be getting light soon," Nate exclained.

"Right boss," came Delbert's reply and he pulled out and started south.

Delbert stopped in the same place he'd parked earlier and the two got out.

"Now chief, we'll be crawling in the last few yards so we must be quiet and no talking. Hopefully they are still asleep and won't know we're here. When we get to where we can see the inside of the camp you taper off to the left side and work your way to the truck. God, I hope we can end this tonight," Delbert informed to policeman.

"Me too," answered the Chief, "and got you on what to do. I assume you'll be watching the figures in the camp and will warn me if trouble looks to be starting. Right?"

"Right. Now let's get going and no talking," was the response.

As they neared the camp, Delbert stopped and listened. He was seeing if he could hear any talking in the camp. After a couple minutes they proceeded as he heard nothing but snoring. All was quiet.

They stopped at twenty yards of the camp behind a clump of brush. Delbert waved to the Chief to go to the truck and take the test. The Chief nodded and crawled off to the left. Delbert looked into the camp and everything looked the same. The same Arab sat sleeping with the weapon across his lap. The minutes creeped by and it seemed like a lifetime the Chief had been gone. In reality it was closer to five or six minutes.

In the meantime the Chief had reached the truck and turned the Geiger counter on. He could hardly believe his eyes at the reading. The machine went wild and the clicking was loud. He quickly turned the clicking down and looked again at the dial. It laid all the way over which indicated the reading was much stronger than the machine could record.

The load was one hot hombre. Freezing the dial, so Delbert could see it, he started his crawl back towards Delbert. As he turned he looked towards the rear of the truck. Two legs emerged from within and as they touched the ground, the rest of the man appeared and stood up. He was yawning and that gave the Chief time enough to take a step in that direction and hit him with the butt of his pistol. He hit him hard and heard bone breaking inside the man's skull. He holstered his weapon and grabbed the man before he fell. He drug him over a sand dune and kicked a little sand over him. *Damn,* he thought to himself, *if they find the body they will know we've been here.* He also knew if they attacked right away they would have prisoners and it would matter. He had to get back to Delbert and warn Armstrong.

Five minutes later he was coming up along side Delbert. He made hand signals they had to talk. Delbert shook his head and turn and crawled back the way they'd came.

Back to the vehicle the Chief showed Delbert the reading on the counter and told of the killing.

"Holy, God, its way stronger than I imagined," Delbert exclaimed.

He grabbed the phone and called Nate.

"Nate, this truck is hotter than hell. The Geiger counter went off the screen. I wouldn't want to be around that truck very long. I think we've found what we were looking for. You should know the Chief had to kill one of them or blow the entire caper. Should we go back and get in place for the attack?"

"Yes, this is what we've been waiting for. Get around to the back side. We're coming," Nate explained.

It was just getting daylight as Delbert and the Chief got into place. Nate had called the Admiral and told them he was ready for the marines and to hurry and get them here. Nate wasn't sure he'd need them but he'd rather have them. Having a strong force and find out they weren't needed was better than going in weak and find out they were needed.

Nate called Delbert for instructions.

"We're in place, Delbert and the marines are on their way. You and the

Chief take a bead on any one in their camp with an automatic weapon. You'll know when we move in when you hear choppers overhead that's the way the marines are coming. They've been told of your position and ours so stay there. Don't move in. You can take out those you can see with the automatic weapons and anyone who tries to escape in your direction. It would be nice to capture one just to see we've done the right thing. We need all the intelligence we can get. Washington will want to know. Keep that in mind when the shooting starts. Needless to say, but don't take any risks. A prisoner would be nice. I'll hang up now because I think I hear choppers coming in. Yeah, I see them now, goodby," Nate said as he hung up.

The choppers came into sight and Nate knew it was time to go. If they waited too long everyone in camp would be awake and it could get bloody.

"Come on Sam, it's time," Nate said and he jumped to his feet and ran forward into the camp. Sam was but a step behind him.

"Hands up, all of you," Nate yelled to the two men he could see standing in the camp. They were looking at the choppers and we still caught them by surprise. They had only moved to a standing position but Nate knew in seconds they would be over the surprse and would start firing.

With two men faceing them with drawn pistols, the two jerked their weapons to a hip high firing position.

Oh oh, trouble, Nate thought as he fired his weapon. At the same time he heard the crack of a rifle and both men dropped face down to the ground. He knew Delbert and the Chief had joined the party.

Marines were dropping all around them, scaling down ropes into the camp.

"Looks like you beat us to it, Armstrong," said a Captain from the Marine Corp. Is this the lot of them or are there more?" he questioned.

"Have your men scout around for a couple hundred yards and see what you find. We really need a live one," Nate instructed.

"Right," came the reply and he raised his hand to his men and motioned they follow him.

The Chief and Delbert came in and the Chief being nosey wanted to see what was in the truck. He walked around to the back end of the truck and opened the canvas. He jumped back at what he saw and yelled.

"Here's another one," came the shout.

"Don't kill him," Nate shouted and rushed around to where the Chief stood, pistol drawn.

Huddled in the truck was a small man. Clearly he was an Arab and looking scared. Nate drew his pistol then spoke to the man.

"Get down here and keep your hands in plain sight," he ordered the man.

The man shook his head and shook his head. Nate took this to mean he did not understand. Nate motioned for him to get down by waiving his pistol in that direction.

Finally the man understood and came slowly out of the truck. He sat on the bed and slid to the ground from there. He immediately threw his hands in the air and spoke for the first time.

"Don't shoot me. I intend you no harm," in English. By this time the others had gathered around.

"Delbert you and the Chief get up there and check for a bomb. He may have set one just waiting for us," Nate ordered.

The two jumped up into the cover bed of the truck and did a hurried search. They knew these people were suicide attackers and would like to take someone with them to heaven.

"No, no bomb, I mean you no harm," repeated the man.

"Move around front where there's better light," Nate ordered and the man obeyed and walked around front near the fire.

"No, bomb boss, just five, fifty gallon drums" came Delbert's voice from inside the truck.

"What's in the drums?" Nate replied.

"Don't know yet. Give me a minutes and I'll find out," Delbert said.

"Ok, let me know as soon as you know. I'm going to interrogate this man and it would help," Nate finished and turned to the prisoner.

"One of you seach this guy while I hold a gun on him. He could hide a bomb under those clothes?" Nate asked.

Sam stepped forward and did a search of the man and finding nothing, he shook his head to Nate.

"Sit down, sit," Nate ordered the prisoner.

"What's in those barrels?" Nate asked as he remembered the Geiger counter report.

The man sat on a rock and looked at Nate smiling. Finally he spoke.

"No bomb. Nuclear material for bomb making. In each barrel there is a fuse to explode it over city from balloons. A great victory for Islam," he said and continued smiling at Nate.

"What's so damn funny, buster. I could have you shot right now. Do you understand that," Nate trying to get through to this man.

"It is too late to stop it so I'll tell you," the man took a deep breath and continued, "I'm already dead. With the nuclear radiation for days I have been killed. Shoot me if you want it will make my sacrifice much greater if you do. May God's will take me home in a matter of days. I am smiling for that reason and because there is another load of nuclear particles arriving at the balloons now. They will be loaded shortly and out over your precious Navy base. Hundreds will die and San Diego will be no more. Ha Ha Ha.

"Son-of-a-bitch," Nate stated loudly. He was thinking *is this true or is he lying to us. If it's true Brad, Carl and Don should be seeing it right now. They've not called me so I don't think its happening.*

Nate dialed and waited for an answer.

"Hello," Brad answered.

"Brad is there any activitive around the balloons yet?" Nate asked.

"No, we are at about forty yards and the only movement is they are starting the balloons fires, but that's all. Why?" he questioned back.

"We have caught a group with nuclear material and they say there's more coming. Are you sure no one has entered their camp with a truck of van. Maybe a wagon?" Nate asked.

"No boss, nothing, I'll let you know as soon as we see anything," Brad answered.

"Ok, I'll see if I can get anything more for this guy and get back to you. Maintain your current positions and I get back to you. Bye," Nate signed off.

Nate was disturbed by this and had to wonder if the Arab was playing him. After all they were killers and very unlikely to tell the truth. But that grin. The son-of-a-bitch had that silly grin on his face. Nate had to fight back an impulse to wipe it off his face. The only thing he hadn't tried to persuade this man was torture. The Bush administration had approved it and by God maybe it was time he did. Nate knew he was not the kind of man that could do this, but at times he sure felt like it. He pushed the thought aside and decided instead to try more conversation and kindness. He had some time because no one has yet arrived at the balloons.

He walked over to the coffee pot on the fire and poured himself a cup. He waved the pot at the prisoner and asked if anyone wanted a cup. The man who spoke broken English nodded and held up a cup. *Ah*, Nate thought, *maybe now we can get somewhere.*

Nate sat down on the ground to talk. The marines and the rest of the crew stood around uneasy and uncomfortable doing nothing. They were patient and understood what Nate was doing.

"Ok," Nate started, "just where are these others coming from. All their land routes are blocked and still you say they are here. Where in the hell is here?"

The man had taken his cup and placed it to his lips and took a swallow of the black brew. He then looked up smiling.

"You have just answered your own question," he said.

Nate's brow wrinkled as he tried to understand what this man was saying. Then it hit him like a ton of bricks. *The ocean, the ocean that was the only other way. Damn and they had over looked it. All eyes were on the land and these sneaky bastards are coming by sea.*

Nate stood up and walked away a few yards and asked the Chief to come with him.

"Do you know the shoreline around here?" Nate asked of him.

"Yes, of course, I've been sailing up and down this coast line for years. Why?" he answered.

"How is the shore line immediately west of where the balloons are," Nate asked.

"Kind of rugged. You have about thirty yards of sand and then cliffs. The cliffs are about one hundred feet high," he said and now he was aware of what Nate was thinking and continued on, "but they would have a hell of a time getting anything like those drums up the cliffs.

"Is there a place where the land slopes towards the sea?" Nate asked the Chief.

"Well, yeah. About a mile south from where the balloons are the cliffs down there are only about fifty feet high but no boat has a chance there. There are under currents and cross currents that would push or pull you into the rocks. There are plenty of rocks. A boat wouldn't have a chance," he finished.

"Maybe not the size of boat you use to but maybe small row boats. These could rise and fall with the waves and maybe make it. Remember these crazy fanatices are already dead because of their exposure to the radiation. Maybe they had training to over come just such an experience. My way of thinking is that may be why they are late. That one guy seems to think thay should aready be loading the balloons with their poison. When I called my people, no one had showed. It could be because they are having trouble getting up the cliffs. I'm going to run this by this guy and watch for a response. If he reacts the way I think he will, how long before we could get a coast guard cutter down there?" Nate asked.

"Forty to forty five minutes I would guess," came the answer.

"Ok, lets go back and I'll spring it on him," Nate speaking almost to himself.

The two men walked back, stopping in front of the English speaking man. Both sized him up and stared down upon him seated on the rock. The Chief had stepped to one side and watched intently waiting for Nate to ask the question.

"We've figured out your little scheme. Your buddies are coming in from the sea. They are landing about a mile south from where the balloons are. The game's over so you might as well tells us the rest," Nate said with a lot of conviction in his voice.

The onlookers saw the man's jaw tighten and his face contorted in a red glow. Both the Chief and Nate knew they had struck a nerve. Nate dialed the group watching the balloons. It was answered on the first ring.

"Yes, boss," Brad said upon answering the phone.

"The rest are coming in from the sea Brad. They are late according to our information. These people think they are already at the balloons and loading. That's not true, right?"

"Right," came the answer.

"Alright, here's what I want you to do. You take Don with you and head down that way. I believe they are having trouble getting up the cliffs. They should be about a mile from your position. Get there on foot as fast as you can and report back to me. Take no action on your own unless you are fired upon first. Got that?" Nate fired at him.

"Got it, boss, we're on our way. The line went dead as he hung up.

Nate then dialed the Admiral and waited.

The phone was answered with a lot of commotions in the background. It was hard to hear but Nate recognized the Admiral's voice.

"Admiral, this is Armstrong. We believe the group hauling the other load of nuclear material is landing about a mile south of where the balloons are. It's where the land slopes downward towards the sea. The cliffs there are only about fifty feet high but with rocks and cross currents. Water is dangerous. The coast guard should know of the place I'm talking about. Tell them just to spot them and take no actions until I get there. Once they are on the way, I'll be in touch by radio. Got it?" Nate said.

"Got it," was the reply.

"What's all the noise about Admiral? Nate asked.

"It my people getting out to their posts, etc. It sounds like action is coming pretty soon. I want them in place before that happens. Good luck Armstrong. Stop it down there if you can!" answered the Admiral.

The Arab who spoke English started laughing again. This time it was louder and more jovial. It was like he knew a secret that the rest didn't.

Nate, annoyed by the laughter, just had to find out what the hell was so funny. He pulled his thirty eight from it hoster, walked over to the man and gave an order.

"Open your mouth, you bastard," Nate said and the man did as he was told.

Nate pushed the pistol inside his mouth and pulled back the hammer. At this time he had the entire camp's attention. The men standing around looked on. Terror filled some eyes and the rest watched with their mouths open. All were shocked but none moved forward to stop him.

"You tell me what's so damn funny or I'll blow your brains out. Do it now," Nate threatened and pulled the pistol out, but kept it near the position.

The man laughed a couple times before answering.

"Our leaders told us the Americans were stupid. I shall tell you again that I do not fear death. I'm already dead to my people. The radiation is killing me. Even though we have just a little with us, I've handled it too often. You see, we are what you call the decoy. We have a total of ten pounds of the material in the drums. The rest is just sand. The real high grade material is with the others coming in from the sea. They are already on to the balloons. Alli is with us and I shall be a marter. Ha Ha ha ha.

"You're the dumb son-of-a-bitch because you told us everything and your people have not yet made it to the balloons. They are having trouble coming up the cliffs. When we give a press release, the whole world will be told you were weak and not a marter, but a coward. You and your whole crew will be branded as traitors, who gave away the information that was used to stop you. Your whole family will be rounded up and murdered. Now that's what I call a dumb-son-of-a-bitch and not a laughing matter," Nate told him. He holstered his weapon and turned around and walked away.

No more laugher was heard as the man fell to the ground. Sam knelt down to the man and took his pulse. There was none. The man was dead.

"Well, that's that. Chief, you and the marines find the barrel that is radioactive and pour the rest out. See if you can find anything in their clothing or equipment where they got the substance. It's supposed to be ground up nuclear rods. Spent fuel rods. That means they either came from Iran, Pakistan or North Korea. I'm sure those in Washington would like to know. When you get the material make sure you have protective clothing to handle it. I can't believe it's been ground into powder. Too hard to handle. Probably into small pieces that can be carried by the wind. I can't believe it would be in large pieces. Too easy to find and clean up. You handle it with the others. Sam and I need to get out to where the others are coming ashore. Tell the Admiral to make damn sure the choppers are ready to go on a moments notice. I think we'll need them," said Nate as he reached out to shake the Chief's hand.

Sam was already in the Bronco waiting to go.Nate jumped in and they sped off in direction of the ocean.

"Well, Nate it looks like we're going to catch the bastards with their pants down. God, I hope they are still coming up the cliff when we get there. I'd love to pick off a couple hanging in mid-air," Sam said with a jovial voice.

"I hate to spoil your fun Sam, but you not going to do any unnecessary killing on my watch. This is my game and you'll do as I say. Understand," Nate said as he looked over at him.

"Yeah, yeah, I understand, but all these guys deserve to die for this little game they started. We didn't ask for it but by damn we'll finish it," was Sam fairly quiet response.

"Yes, I know they do and by being around the material they're bringing in they are already dead. Just living shells of what were men. Not good men but men never the less, men.

"Watch out for that bump Nate," Sam yelled at his partner.

Nate not having seen the huge bump jerked the wheel as they were half way over it. This put the vehicle off balance and it started to turn over. Nate jammed on the brakes and the Bronco slowly rolled over on it's side.

The two men scrambled out the open windows on the driver's side. Nate went first and when his feet hit soild ground, he reached back in for Sam. Sam was just sitting dazed, seemly not knowing what had happened. Nate grabbed him by an arm and pulled him out the window.

Sitting in the dirt, both men just sat there looking at the Bronco. After about five minutes they looked at each other and shook their heads. Both knew this could and would make them late in arriving at the ocean.

"What the hell now boss," Sam's sarcastic remark add insult to injury for Nate.

"Shut up and let me think," Nate said. After about five minutes Nate reached back inside the vehicle and grabbed the phone. He dialed and waited for an answer.

"Admiral, Armstrong here. I had an accident cutting cross country and need your help. Can you send a chopper out here with a cable strong enough to right an overturned vehicle," Nate yelled into the phone.

"Yes, we can do that. Hold on a minute and I'll get one started," replied the Admiral, "and quit yelling in my ear. I can hear you fine."

A couple minutes went by, which seemed like and hour for the two waiting.

"Ok, Armstrong, are you still there," asked the Admiral.

"Yes, we shore can't go anywhere," Nate responded.

"Ok, give me your location and I relay it to the pilot. Just where are you?"

"As near as I can tell we are about three miles south and a little east of where the balloons are. Tell the pilot to swing to the east and come in from that direction. He's not to go close to where the balloons are," Nate finished.

"Right, got you. He should be there in about ten minutes. Good luck," the Admiral fired back and hung up.

"Well there's not much to do except wait for the chopper to turn us right side up," Nate said grinning.

"This caper is starting to look like the keystone cops. Every which way we turn, we hit a snag. It's got to smooth out soon or we're just wasting our time," Sam replied.

"Delbert and the others will let us know when those coming by sea have arrived. Delbert is a good leader but he'll call me before he does anything but observe. It won't take too long to get there once the Bronco's back on it's feet. Let's have a shot of whiskey and a cigar," Nate announced and reaching inside the vehicle found the bottle. Sam pulled the cigars out of the glove box and they both sat down on a clump of dirt. Each lit up and had a good swig from the bottle. There wasn't much to talk about so they puffed away in silence.

Minutes later they heard the swish of the chopper as it arrived and sat down a few yards out. Nate ran out to meet it and Sam stayed where he was.

"We need you to flip our vehicle over on it's wheels and hang around till we get it started," Nate instructed the pilot.

"You guys doing a little speeding in rough country were you," laughed the young pilot. "Just stay out of the way and my men will handle it. We've done this before."

Two men jumped out of the back carrying a cable. They ran to the truck and began working the cable under and around it. The chopper lifted off and moved into position over it. The pilot put the chopper within six feet of the Bronco. The two with the cable hooked it to a metal loop on the bottom of the plane. Once the connection was made, the two jumped off and moved away. One waved in an upward motion and the pilot slowly moved the chopper up. It was a slow move and kind of delicate for this kind of operation. The Bronco slowly righted itself and the pilot moved it over a few feet so it was on flat land. He let it down and the two men with him rushed back under the chopper and unhooked the cable. Both then move out from under and waved the pilot away. The chopper moved out a few yards and again sat down. The pilot then waved to Nate to go to the vehicle and start it.

Nate did so and found that after a few tries the Bronco started. He waved at the pilot as Sam got in and they drove away. The experience over, they had more serious things to do.

CHAPTER 18

After a bouncy, rough ride across country, Nate pulled over and stopped. He picked up the phone and called Delbert.

"Where are you located?" Nate asked.

"Right where you told us to be. We are on the lower end of the slope. Where are you?" Delbert responded.

"Damn if I know. We are approaching the ocean somewhere south of the balloon staging area. Can you give me any guidance that would help me find you? A focal point, a clump of rocks or something. I don't want to run right into them and have them spot me," Nate finished and waited for a response.

"It's just as you said. When the land starts sloping downward, to the south, we're at the lower end of the slope. The only thing I remember that might be of help is there were two cows getting up to graze. We'd be about five hundred yards below them. Do you see any cows?" Delbert told him.

"Hell no. Those cows could be to hell and back by now. Anything else?" Nate's response.

"No, it was still dark when we got here. We stumbled over lots of things getting here. Just so you know the terrorists are here. We are watching them right now. They are in some rough water and having a hell'va time trying to get ashore. Hurry we may need your help," Delbert explained.

"Be right there," Nate said and hung up.

"Ok, Sam, as I drive you watch for two cows and tell me when you see them," Nate asked of Sam.

"Cows, what do you mean cows? I thought we were looking for terrorists. You change your mind," Sam said with a chuckle.

"No, damn it. Delbert said that was the only thing he could identify on the way down here. Now keep you eyes open. The terrorists are trying to get ashore now. Delbert and crew are keeping an eye on them till we get there," Nate said as he started the vehicle moving again.

All at once he felt they were going down hill. Looking ahead he saw they were on the slope. Then he saw them. Two cows grazing off to his left. *Thank God,* he said to himself.

"There are your cows," Sam delighted in saying.

"I see them," Nate responded.

Soon the vehicle Delbert had been driving came into view. Nate pulled over and stopped. They got out with their rifles and started the walk down to meet their crew and the terrorists.

Nate slid in beside Delbert and gazed over the edge. The ocean below was like a devils charm. In the center of it all was two small boats being slamed around. Nate counted three drums in each boat and two on rocks at the shore line.

"Those two on that rock, I assume were on the boats?" Nate whispered.

"Yes," Delbert replied and you don't have to be whispering. We could shout and they could never hear us over the noise of the ocean."

Nate looked the situation over and asked everyone to back off a bit so they could talk.

They backed off about ten yards before standing and walking back another thirty yards to avoid the noise.

"These bastards are crazy. They may die before getting ashore with the other three drums I spotted.

"Yeah, but you have to give them credit for even trying," Sam piped up.

"I'm calling the General and tell him what's going on and ask if we could take them now. Just the four of us could do it. My only concern would be if the drums fell into the ocean and sank. Sea water would be corrosive on metal and would sooner or later eat through the drums and the radio active materal would maybe poison the fish. Wonder how badly it would be. There's a hell of a lot of water out there and maybe it would be deluted so that it wouldn't do much damage. I'd better let the General find out," Nate finished and dialed.

"Hello, Nate, what's going on out there. We are about to go crazy here in Washington. Have you found the bastards and are they in custody. Come on man, spit it out," ordered the General.

"We caught a group that turned out to be a decoy. They had radioactive materal with them but not in the amount they would need to do this job. The men with it were convinced they were as good as dead from handling the stuff. I'm not sure that's true. I turned them over to the marines and they should be on their way back to camp. Do me a favor and call the Admiral and ask him to get the prisoners started on treatment. I think they can be saved and if so we may get vaulable information from them. They think they are marters. Wonder what they'll think if we keep them from dieing and they would then become outcasts. Their group would try to kill them just to keep their mouths shout. Anyway do it. Now the good news. We are laying on top of a cliff watching some Arabs trying to unload five drums similar to the ones the decoys had. One they have on shore and because of the heavy tide and current, are have one hell'va time. My question to you is can we take them now, before the get unloaded. There it is possible we could dump one or two of the drums into the ocean. As rough as it is here, frogmen could never survive in this surf. They'd be beaten to death on the rocks. You need to find out if we lost a drum on two in the ocean, what kind of damage would the radio-active materal on marine life. The drums might even break open when hurled against the rocks. I need to know before we try. See if you can find someone who would know. Be sure you tell them that we have no idea how much of the poison is in the barrels, as yet. Hurry we need the information," Nate said.

"Sure thing, I'll call you with the information. Bye Nate and good work," signed off the General.

Hanging up the phone Nate was faced by three people who wanted to know what he'd learned.

"Ok, ok, the General is trying to find out about the drums. We now watch and wait. A couple can take a nap if they so chose. I'll watch what is going on below," Nate said.

"I will too," came from Sam.

"Me too and another me too," came from Ed and Delbert causing a smile to light up Nate's face. To himself he was saying, *how anyone could go wrong with a crew like this.*

The four walked back to the cliff and again laid on their bellies to see what was going on below. Nate kept the phone next to his ear so he could hear it if it rang.

As they looked over, they saw the crew below had landed another drum. All said a short prayer that the General would get back to them soon.

Half and hour went by before the phone rang again. It was the General.

"What's the word General?" asked Nate.

"Don't let the drums get away from you. We would have a disaster in the ocean around San Diego for decades. The metal of the drums will be corroded long before they would be turned into a reef. Use your best judgement on when to take them and be careful. The President says to tell you what a great job you are doing and your crew. He is concerned about the drums," was related by the General.

"Ok, I'll get back to you as soon as it's over. You can all breath easier because we will do it right," Nate responded.

"Anything else?" asked the General.

"Yeah," Nate said, "has the decoys been evaluated yet and will they die," Nate asked.

"Yes, they have been evaluated and they did not get enough exposure to kill them. They will be sick for a couple, three days but not deadly. Why do you need something from them," asked the General.

"Damn rights, I want something from them. Once we get this handled I'll want to talk to them. Specially the English speaking one. I have them all kept in solitary confinement and they are not to speak to anyone. I want

241

to interrogate them without them getting together on a story. Will place them on a suicide watch. They want to die and become marters and we must not let that happen. Ok, general?" Nate asked.

"Ok, you got it, Nate and thanks," answered the General.

The conversation over, Nate went back to watching the scene happening below.

The sea was throwing waves hard against the rocks, making it difficult for the small boat to remain steady. There we now two men on the rocks and two in a boat with two more drums. The two in the boats would tie a rope around a drum and push it overboard. The two on the rocks would then pull it to shore. They had a hell've time in getting it on the rocks where it would sit comfortable. The men in the boat was taking a beating and barely staying on their feet. As the last drum was pushed overboard, a wave rose over the boat and washed one overboard. The other man was busy trying to staying in the boat and the man was washed out to sea after being battered into several rocks. He then floated out with the tide. There was no doubt by the Americans, he was dead.

Nate knew that the three remaining men would have to climb the cliff and would soon be arriving on the bluff where they are laying. As he watched he saw the man in the boat tie the rope to a bundle and cast it overboard. It floated and was easily pulled to shore. He wondered what was in the bundle. Realizing they must move back a ways, he motioned the crew to backup. One by one they did as instructed. At ten yards back they stood up and walked to where Nate was taking them. He had stopped at a place where there was a clump of land that rose above the flat area between them and the edge of the cliff.

"Ok," Nate started, "they will be coming ashore soon. I want to see how they get the drums up that fifty foot cliff. I'm sure that bumdle has something to do with it. We need to stay hidden until the last drum is up here. Then, on my command, we'll take them into custody and arrange for transport. We might as well let them do the work of bringing the drums up here. Wait for my command. Let's take them alive if possible but we really don't need to. The decoys were captured will proably talk once they know they will be shamed in their country. No matters today. That works in our favor. If you have to shoot, shoot to kill, but don't if you don't have to. Ok, men we lay down here untill the drums are up here. I'll give the word to jump them. Spred out some so we can take them from all sides," Nate said as he lay behind the rise.

The grass was damp from the morning dew. It felt good with the fresh smell of grass. In a matter of minutes one of terrorists stuck his head up over the bank and looked around. Satisfied the coast was clear he pulled himself up and stood looking back over the cliff.

He uncoiled a rope from around himself and dropped one end down towards the ocean. A couple minutes later he was pulling something up. The bundle appeared and was pulled back from the edge a bit. From the bundle he pulled a long iron stake which he pounded into the ground. He then tied the rope to it before going to the bundle. Undoing the canvass from around it, he exposed lumber. He quickly worked the lumber into what is called a jack. It's used to lift roofing material onto roof's etc. It was ingenius in how it was constructed and so easy set up. There was no need for nails and fit together well. He then placed a pulley on the end pointing out to sea. It appeared to be hung on metal straps.

Taking a cable from under the tarp, he picked up a cable and pasted it thru the pulley. He then pushed the jack out to the edge of the cliff. When he had it in place he picked up metal straps and more of the long spikes. With these he went to the long tail of the jack, placed the straps, three in all, over the tail and proceeded in driving the stakes thru holes in the straps. These were what would keep the jack from falling forward into the ocean. They countered the weight of the drums so they could be lifted without the jack tumbling over the Clift.

"Look, Delbert," Nate said, "they have thought of everything."

"Looks like it boss," was the reply.

Apparently the two men below were to tie the cable around the drums and they pull them up. The man on top was the one to take them off. The Americans watched with amazement as they watched the drums lifted, the top man swinging them while they were in air and setting them down a few feet inland.

It took less than twenty minutes to do this. Once done the other two came up and the three pushed the jack over the Clift and into the ocean.

The men were ready to go and some even started to stand. Nate waved them down. Something was wrong. *Just how the men would get the drums to the balloons,* he was thinking. He didn't have long to wait.

The whirl of chopper blades coming from behind them was quite evident of what was going to happen. Nate turned to look just as a burst of gun fire came from the chopper and bullets bit into the soft soil.

Nate jumped up holloring at the men.

"Shoot the damn thing down. Delbert you come with me. We need to capture those with the drums," Nate yelled and was up and running as bullets plummed around him. He glanced back and saw Delbert right on his heels.

The three men at the drums didn't quite know what was happening. They just stood as if in a trance. Finally one figured it out and turns around and ran the few feet to the cliff. He didn't hesitate at the edge. He just threw himself over. Death rather capture was how he felt.

At ten yards, Nate leaped into the air, aimed at the one who seemed to be the boss. He hit hin hard before he knew what was happening. Nate guessed he was a slow learner. Of course he'd not been a jungle fighter as Nate had been.

Picking himself up from the ground, Nate dusted himself off and for a moment his mind took him back to those days in Nam. An exact same type of situation happened to him then, the only difference then was he killed a Vet Cong warrior. This guy was not going to be so lucky.

Returning back to the present, Nate looked skyward and saw the helicopter making another run. He saw that Delbert had the other Arab down and tied up. Nate dropped to the ground just as the chopper plowed another couple rows, in the ground around him. He could hear the rat-rat-tat of the machine guns and hugged the soil even tighter. Once the guns stopped he jumped up and looked to see if everyone was ok. Delbert, Sam and Ed all reported they were.

Nate walked back over to his prisoner just as he was coming around.

Nate took handcuffs to restrain him before he awakened fully. Nate helped him sit up. The chopper apparently decided it had done enough damage decided to flee.

Nate triggered the on switch of the police radio. He broadcasted the incident and a discription of the chopper. Several police and fire units acknowledge they had received the broadcast.

Kneeling beside the Arab, Nate asked him a question.

"Was the chopper the way you were going to get the drums to the balloons?"

The man shooked his head as if to say he didn't understand English. Nate tried again.

"Do you speak English?" Nate asked.

Again he got the same response. Delbert asked his prisoner the same questions and got the same response. Nate knew the one he was holding was the leader and would be the one for information. Nate still felt the need to hurry. He didn't know why, but tension was growing inside him. He decided to speed this up so he drew his pistrol and placed it about three inches in the man's mouth.

"Now, damn you, you speak to me and answer my questions or so help me I'll blow your brains out. Understand," he made a motion of the gun going off and the man's head with it. The prisoner just smiled.

Nate pulled the hammer back and asked again. The man just smiled. Having failed, Nate removed the gun and holstered it. As he did the man spoke?

"You Americans are futile in your attempts to make us talk. You see this is a suscide mission and we want to die. We are already dead because of the exposure to the radio-active material we've been around for a month. We have many virgins waiting to attend our needs so your threats we wish you to carry out. Marters we will then be," said the man.

Nate looked at him with discuss as he replied.

"You stupid bastard, we have foiled your attempt to attack us. This type of failure will be seen by your God as inferior and not worthy of martyrdom. You will go to hell for your efforts and your family and friends in your homeland will be murdered. Of course you know that, don't you?"

For a moment Nate saw the smile wiped away and a very serious frown replace it. Then as quickly as it left, the smile returned and the man seemed at peace.

Nate couldn't figure it out. He had a dreaded feeling they had not heard the last of this mission. He radioed in to police headquarters for some mode of transportation for the drums.

Chief Still himself answered.

"Boy, I'm glad you boys nipped this in the bud. I'll have a five ton truck there in thirty minutes and a fork lift to load it. Good show, Nate," was said with gladness in his voice.

"I'm signing off Chief and will call you by land line. Armstrong out."

Nate dialed his number and received an immediate reply.

"Still here," was the way the Chief answered the phone.

"Ok, chief, here's what we need. There should be an atomic energy group in San Diego. If so, call them and see if they will receive this materal. It's radio-active and can't remain as it is. They may have the way to handle this stuff. If they need a higher authory to approve what needs to be done, get them the General's number and let him handle it. After all why should we do all the dirty work," he stopped to chuckle a little then went on. "If you don't have the equipment, call the Admiral and get them to do it. We'll wait here and ask them to make it quick. We need to get back to the balloons as fast as we can. I haven't heard anything from my guys watching them so I think we're alright. I just want to get this thing wrapped up so we can get some rest. OK?" Nate asked.

"Run the Geiger counter over these drums, Sam and let's make sure they are hot," Nate said.

"Sure, will do," Sam responded and he left the group to get the counter and do the test.

Minutes later he returned and reported to Nate.

"Hotter, a fire cracker, Nate," was the report.

"Ok, everyone take a brake. It could be an hour before we get out of here," came from Nate and everyone found a comfortable place to sit and relax.

Cigars were lit and a comfortable feeling settled over the group. Nate however was uneasy. That feeling that all was not right seemed to bug him. Finally he decided to call Brad and Don watching the balloons. He just had to know that end of the mission was secure.

Dialing he waited for the third ring before someone answered.

"Brad, here," was the answer.

"Hi Brad, this is Nate. How's everything where you are," Nate asked.

"Quiet, too quiet, you know it's like a thunder storm ready to break, but doesn't. It just keeps building and building and could blow at anytime. These creeps have the balloons all filed with hot air and it's apparent they are waiting for something or someone. No one has gone near this group and nothing's been loaded. How goes it with you?"

"Good, but like you I have a very uneasy feeling. We captured three men and sized their cargo of four drums of radioactive material. This must be what your group is waiting. We'll be as much as another hour before we can transport the drums. Keep a close watch over those ballons. Don't let any of them float away. If they try, go in shooting. Understand?" Nate asked.

"Yes. Don't worry we won't but I will be glad once you get here. So hurry up boss," Brad finished and the two hung up.

The sun has risen in the sky. Nate was getting uncomfortable with the wait. He knew the men could handle this and he could go at anytime. It was just a matter of pride that made him stay. Being responsible, he felt he had to wait till the drums were loaded on a truck. Then he could report to the General, they were. Even though he often felt he had been set up by the General and not told the truth of the missions he took on, he'd never file a false report. Time drug on.

Two hours it took the truck to arrive. It finally pulled up and the loading began. Nate's uncomfortable feeling grew worse. It was getting on towards mid-day and the balloons had not yet tried to take off. *Something was not right,* he kept thinking.

Finally the last drum was loaded and secured. Nate spoke to his crew.

"Come on guys, let's get out of here. I don't like the idea it's getting so late and the balloons haven't even tried to take off. You'd think they would have aborted by now. Of course you can never tell how the Arab mind works. Come on lets go," he said as he mounted the Bronco and fired it up. Everyone loaded up and they were on their way.

A short time later they arrived at the place where Brad, Don had parked. Don was waiting for them. He greeted them with a wave and waited for them to dismount from their vehicles.

"Well Don, how goes it?" Nate asked as soon as his feet touched ground.

"We're a little uncomfortable with this whole thing," he replied before going on.

"It seems they are waiting for something and I'm not sure it's for the ones you took down. They keep looking at Ocean Drive as if someone was coming from that direction. That's not possible is it, boss?" he finished looking into Nate eyes.

"No, it's not possible. The police have blocked that road and are not allowing anyone down here. Let me check and see if the road block is still in place," Nate said. He picked up the police radio.

"Armstrong to the road block on Ocean Drive," he said as he keyed the mike, waiting for a response.

A minute went by before a response, which bothered Nate. Of course, he was on edge and not very patient at this stage of the game.

"Road block, to Armstrong," came a reply, "go ahead."

"Are you ok and have you had anyone trying to get pass you?" Nate asked.

"No, no one. It's dead with no traffic. Over and out," was the answer.

Nate laid the radio down and pondered what he should do next. He and his crew could continue surrounding the group with the balloons and wait for what might happen. They could attack that group, take over the balloons and set up a trap for who ever they were waiting for. At the very least they could confirm if the ones they captured are the ones being waiting for. He was about to settle on the last idea when his phone rang. He answered it.

"Armstrong, this is still. There is something wrong. I can feel it," he started.

"Me too," Nate said I've had a bad feeling for the last couple hours. I wonder what the hell they're waiting for. I've been thinking of moving in and taking those with the balloons. But, damn it, I want to make sure we get them all. It's obvious they are waiting for something or someone. What do you think?" he asked the Chief.

"I think somethings come in to your area by Ocean Drive. That radio call you made to the road block stinks. They are four of my best men and they would have used our police codes. Something has happened to my men. Be on your toes and get into range of those balloons. Something's about to pop. Do you want to take some help back to the road block or should I. You're closer and can make it quicker?" asked the Chief.

"We'll do it. I'll let you know what we find," Nate answered.

"Delbert, Sam, we've got a run to make. Don you get back to our crew and tell them to be on their toes. Somethings about to pop. Don't take any chances. Go," Nate said.

"What's wrong, boss?" Delbert said as he got up close.

"Chief Still thinks there is something wrong at the road block. The officers I called did not respond by their code. We need to check it out. Those balloons have been inflated for two hours at least and yet no one has tried to get close to them. Come on, jump in, we need to check that road block quickly. You two lay down in the back and leave the back door open. Have your rifles and your pistols ready to go. I don't like this.

Delbert and Sam did as requested and Nate took off for the roadblock.

Minutes later Nate came in view of the road block. The two police cars were parked at an angle across the road as taught in the academys. The space between the fronts of the cars was just wide enough for a car to pass through. This is common because a road block with cars is not intended to wreck anyone. The idea behind the open space was to let the car get up close and stop. The space, to most people, would look small and not provide room to pass through. As he drew closer he could see people in the front seats of both cars.

Now close enough to see police hats on the men and the tops of police shirts. He could make out the badges on their shirts.

"Get ready, we are coming upon them. At first glance it looks ok. There's something wrong though," he said to Delbert and Sam.

He stopped the Bronco ten yards out from where the police cars were. Not one of the cops got out to approach them. *Very unusal,* Nate throught. If these were real cops they would be out of their cars and waving them through or to stop. Nate finally realizes the other thing that bothered him and which convinced him to speed through them.

"The cops have their hats on. If they were real cops, they wouldn't. Also there's supposed to be four cops on this post, not two. This is a warm day and we whites would have our hats in the seat. Arabs, being from a hot climate wouldn't because they are use to covering up from the sun. I'm going to run thru them. Be ready to shoot because I'll stop just pass them. My actions should bring them out of those cars shooting. Shoot to kill boys and stay low. I'll bail out and help when the shooting starts, "Nate said as he accelerated and the Bronco leaped forward.

Nate had been right. As soon as he started moving, the men in the cop cars came boiling out of the cars. They had police hats and shirts on, but their Arab atire was worn below the shirts. Apparently they didn't expect anyone by that would require they get out. They proably throught they could just wave people away. *Well by God they were wrong,* Nate said to himself.

Nate was able to snake the Bronco thru the opening, between the two cars just as the fake cops started shooting. *Damn, automatic weapons,* Nate throught as he slammed on the brakes and bailed out.

He hit the dirt rolling, with his revolver in hand.

The two were totally taken off guard by the movements of the Americans and were shooting wildly about. Their actions showed they were excited and unable to calm down.

Nate saw one run to his side of the road. Nate had stopped his roll and was ready. Being on the ground gave him an advantage of being a smaller target. Nate raises his pistol and fired twice. The man folded up like a bale of hay and fell to the ground.

The shooting stopped and Delbert yelled at him.

"You ok, Nate. We got the bastard on this side and noticed you nailed the other. It's safe to come out now.

Nate stood up and walked up to the man he had shot. He felt for a pulse and found none. *Another Arab got his wish to die a marter,* Nate thought.

He joined Delbert and Sam in the middle of the road. Sam had just straighten up from checking the dead man they had shot.

"He's dead," Sam exclaimed, "I wonder what they did with the real cops?" he said, almost to himself.

"I have a feeling we will find four dead bodies somewhere around here," Nate said.

"I'll look over this way," said Sam. He started out to a small hump of dirt some fifty feet off the road. As he reached to top of the hump, he stopped. Below him were four bodies laid out across the land. They couldn't be seen from the road and did not appear to have been dead long.

"I've found them. Nate, call the Chief and tell him to send the meat wagon. All four are here and dead. It doesn't seem they've been dead very long," Sam reported.

"Chief Still, please," Nate said in answer to his call. A minute passed and he came on the line.

"Chief this is Armstrong. We came to check the roadblock and found four officers dead. You need to send the meat wagon and some more men to man this location," he waited for a response.

"What the hell. All of them dead. Son-of-a-bitch. All were good men too. Damn it, damn, it. This time I'll send several and roadblock material. Have you determined how they died?" asked the Chief.

"No, I'm in a big hurry to get back to the balloons. Nothing going as it should. Everyone can get on the radios and to hell with call signs. These people now know we are on to them. We killed two of here. Have the medics bring enough transports for six bodies," Nate said.

"You say you got two of them. Good for you now get this mess cleaned up in a hurry. Hell, it's damn near noon and we thought this would be completed long before now. Oh, call the General he's called for you just a little while ago," said Chief Still.

"Ok, will do and I'll be heading back to the balloon area as soon as I do. I'll leave two of my men here but they only have thirity-thiries. Can you bring them a couple automatics? Hell, bring enough for all seven of us. I have a feeling this is coming to a head and I want my men armed. Do me a favor and call the marines and advise them to be ready on a moments notice.

They will soon get a call to move in," Nate said and hung up.

"Well, good morning Armstrong," said the General, "now tells me what the hell's going on. You should have had that mess cleaned up hours ago. Fill me in so I can advise the President. He's getting nervous."

"Well if he was here he'd be even more so. We just had four policemen killed and we killd two Arabs. They know we're here but still they make no attempt to take off in the balloons. Someone is still coming," Nate said and advised the General with the rest of the facts before signing off.

CHAPTER 19

Nate crawled into position along side Brad. Brad nodded hello with his full attention still focused on the balloons and the half dozen men handling them.

"Anything new, Brad?" Nate asked in a low voice.

"Nothing boss," he replied in almost a whisper. "These men are getting jumpy. I don't know what the hell's going on. Somehow their plan has backfired or something. You have any ideas?" he asked Nate.

"No, not really, but I think it's about time to take them out. You heard about the roadblock didn't you?" Nate questioned.

"Yeah. That tells me the men you caught coming in from the ocean are not the only ones here. Where the hells are they and why not move in. If they are monitoring the police band, they know we're here. You don't suppose they are so dumb they'll not doing so?" Brad asked with a frown.

"Hell, I don't know and that's my problem if we move in now and not get all the radioactive material, we're screwed. Washington is getting nervous and so am I. The roadblock situation is what I don't understand. If they are coming from the highway, why not do it at the same time you take out the cops. It's dumb to take them out and then wait for someone to arrive. Your odds of getting discovered are greater.

Just then the radios blared out with an announcement from the police. "A five ton farm truck just ran the roadblock and is speeding towards the balloons. There are several drums on that truck. Armstrong advises us on action you want us to take."

Just then the phone rang and Nate answered it. It was Delbert.

"They ran right through us boss. Neither I nor Sam is hurt and we are in pursuit of the bastards. We are coming straight at you. Looks like the fun will began," he said.

In a second Nate knew it was time.

"Move in, move in, he blasted over the radio. Kill or capture the bastards. Chief get the Admiral to release the marines. Get them here quick," Nate instructed.

Hooking the radio to he belt he looked over at Brad.

"Let's go, son. Keep your head down," Nate advised.

Nate jumped to his feet and looking down at the balloons he saw the men in attendance leap into the balloons baskets as if ready to go as soon as the truck arrived. He looked to his right, toward Ocean Drive. In the distance he saw the top of the truck's cab. Both he and Brad had jumped into their vehicles and headed towards the balloons. He increased his speed and Brad was keeping up. Lookng towards the ocean he could see the other guys rushing in. The men in the baskets began shooting.

"Zig, zag, Brad, thru his open window," Nate yelled.

Brad did as ordered and saw puffs of dirt coming up from the ground around him. Nate abandoned his vehicle, now in close as did Brad. They dove to the dirt. His other men were doing the same. After all the rapid fire of automatic weapons could spray bullets over a large area.

Nate took aim with his thirty-thirty and plugged one of the men who had stayed on the ground. Just then the truck roared into the space occupied by the balloons. The men leaped from the cab and also began shooting. A couple men from the truck grabbed sacks, out of the drums, and headed for a balloon. He dropped it in the basket and returned to the truck and started the procedure over again. This time he made it just ten feet from the basket before he was cut down. The man in the basket jumped out and grabbed the sack and threw it into the basket. He then ran for the truck and returned to the basket with another sack.

Delbert and Sam had just arrived and stopped on the edge and took a quick look.

"Lets ram that truck and see if that won't give us an advantage," Delbert to Sam.

"Hell, yes, anything, lets get in there," was his answer.

Delbert floored it and headed for the truck. Knowing his vehicle didn't have a chance against the truck, Delbert swerved at the last minute. He hit the driver's door and that stopped the gun fire from there. The door of the truck was ripped off and landed some fifty feet away. They came to a stop and both rolled out and begain picking a target.

More sacks were removed for the passenger's side of the truck. That side was more protected than any and several of the short runs to the balloons, just feet away. Nate counted six in all made it to the basket. The balloon started lifting as to men dropped the sand bags.

"Don't let that get up. Shoot the bastard down," Nate yelled at the top of his lungs.

Everyone turned their fire at the one lifting off. It was gaining altitude. The men had ducked down and there was no clear target. Nate jumped to his feet and ran to Delbert.

"Where's your flare gun, Delbert," he yelled.

"Under the driver's seat," came the answer.

Reaching the Bronco, he reached under the seat. His hand felt the gun which he quickly pulled out. He saw the flares and grabbed two.

Nate ran to the passenger's side and loaded the gun. He aimed the flare at the balloon and fired. The target was over three hundred feet up but Nate knew the flare would go higher.

The flare ripped right through the balloon. It causes the material to catch on fire. The balloon stopped gaining altitude and sort of hovered a couple minutes. Before crashing to the ground. The fire was short lived and went out when it hit the ground.

The whirl of choppers was deafing, but welcome. Marines were sliding down ropes and the shooting stopped.

The other balloons had loaded sacks and were attempting to take off. A young marine ran for it and grabbed the side of the basket as it started lifting. Someone inside the basket fired a pistol point blank into his body and he fell back to earth.

"Stop that balloon. He has dirty bomb material on board," Nate yelled at everyone.

"Don't shoot," yelled a Marine Captain.

He walked over along side of Nate and pointed skyward. A chopper was settling down over the balloon.

"What the hell is he doing?" Nate asked.

"Watch," was the only reply he got.

The chopper moved over to one side and then slid in close allowing the blades to barely touch the balloon, ripping a wide gash in the material and it came crashing to the ground. Two marines ran and took a man into custody. They yelled he had a broken leg, but was otherwise unhurt.

A movement caught Nate"s eye and he turned his head in that direction. He saw the truck driver sliding down the hill towards town.

He wanted that man. He would be the only one that could tell him where they got the radio-active stuff. He wanted him bad. But he could leave right now. He had to issue instructions that would take five to ten minutes. He stared at him until he went out of sight. He would remember this man's face and how he was dressed. He got a good look at his face as he turned to look back at them.

"Ok, Delbert, you stay here and help with getting this stuff safely out of here. Call the Admiral and get any nuclear facility near here to handle it. They should have containers, lined with lead, which is the best method of handling. Tell them to get the lead out. In minutes, this place could be crawling with sight seers. The noise we created was heard a long ways away. Set up an area around here of about forty yards and keep everyone out. Use the marines, everybody helps.I'll keep in touch but I'm going after the truck driver with Sam. Now, I've got to call the General and tell him the danger is over. Jump to it Delbert," Nate said, then turned and walked around behind a vehicle.

"Hi, General, how's the pressure in Washington. Has everyone had a heart attack by now," Nate asked when the phone was answered.

"Damn it, Armstrong, this is not a game. What have you got for the President? It had better be good," was the crustly answer given.

"The danger is over General, We have prisoners and some are dead. One got away but I'm going after him with Sam. All the drums containing the poison are in our hands. You might call the Admiral with any nuclear site information in this area. They will have the equipment need to dispose of it. That's what needed. My men will help until this is cleaned up. As soon as I get off this phone, I'm after the one who got away. Right now he's got almost an eight minute start. Anything else, General," Nate finished.

"No, I don't think so. Great job my boy. Good luck on the hunt. Call me when you're through," said the General.

"Oh, before you go, General, find out if there's a mosque in the area. Shore as hell, he'll want to hide in one. Call me when you find out. Catch you later General," Nate signed off and turn to Sam.

"Sam, come here," he said.

Sam came over around the vehicle and stopped near Nate.

"Yeah, boss are we going hunting?" he asked

"I thought we would. Do you know that driver by sight?" Nate questioned him.

"I think so," was the answer.

"How about picking him out of a crowd? Could you do that?" Nate kept pushing.

"Not if he changed clothes. Up close yes, but not in a crowd," came the answer.

"Ok, for the most part of the time, we'll stay together. Make sure you have plenty of shells for your pistol because that's all we're taking. Oh, and Sam, we need him alive. Ok. I know you prefer the other way but not this time. Understand," Nate instructed.

"Ok, alive it will be. Trust me," answered a smiling Sam.

Remembering something, Nate dialed the phone. He needed to talk to Chief Still. The phone was answered by an officer and he was transferred to the Chief.

"Hello, Armstrong, congrats on the way you handled that situation. All of us can relax now and get back to normal," was the greeting.

"Well most of you can relax but not all of you. You need to be aware one of the terrorist in on the loose in this end of town. He was the truck driver who brought in the real load hazardous material. Sam Brown and I are starting after him now. If you know of a mosque in this area, get me an address. Its proably better we use our phones not your radios. Also I don't want anyone integrating the prisoners. That my job and someone else might jeopardize us getting information. Is that clear," Nate said with authority in his voice. He knew how police were and didn't want any spoilers in this action.

"Hell, Armstrong, you take all the fun out of it. I was going to do it myself after I get a little sleep," came the response.

"No, don't. I'll let you sit in on it when I get there. First I need to capture this one. Alert your men that we are on foot and they are to assist us in finding this guy. He'll want to go dead and become a martyr, but we won't do that. We must take him alive because I believe he has the information we need. Tell your men not to get jumpy and shoot at us. We may be going thru backyards, up alleys in through homes even," Nate said.

"Ok, go for it. I'll call you when I get that address. Good luck," came the response.

"Sam lets go," Nate said as he strated down the hill. Once at the bottom they noticed footprints heading across a sandy street. They were out in the boondocks of the city. It wasn't the best part of town. After they walked three blocks, they came upon some kids playing ball in the street. They stopped to talk to them.

"Hi boys, did you see a dirty, dusty man go by here a few minutes ago?" Nate asked.

"You mean a guy who had a rag wrapped around his head?" one kid piped up causing Nate and Sam to smile.

"Yeah, that's him. Which way did he go?" Sam jumped into the conversation.

"I saw him go up the street two blocks and cut over to the left. Seemed like he knew where he was going," another kid heard from.

"Thanks kids," and Nate handed the kid a five dollar bill, "for ice cream."

"Sam, cut over to the left and be careful. This guy could be laying in wait for anyone persuiting him. I'll keep going up here for four or five blocks, then cut back and join up with you. Do go fast and wait for me," Nate said no uncertain terms.

"Right boss," came Sam's reply and he turned to the left and cut over from the street he was on. Nate proceeded straight ahead and with caution. He knew in his heart this one would rather kill Americans. It seemed that the way the Arabs lived and degraded their women, showed hate was more prominent in their hearts than love. *Our religion teaches love, not hate, in all our types of religion. If their's was a true religion it should teach love, not hate,* he thought.

Having gone five blocks, Nate turned to the left and walked over a couple blocks. He found Sam waiting on the corner.

"See anything, Sam," he asked.

"No, not a damn thing. You know down the street there," Sam points, "is a small business district. He may want to mingle with people. I'll bet we find him in a saloon. What do you think?" he answered.

"Possible, but no alcoholic beverages are allowed in their countries. But you're right he needs cover and more of the male Arabs drink when out of country. Lets move along and see if there's one up ahead," Nate replied.

The two walked another four blocks and shore enough there was a little business district about three blocks long. Right in the middle of the second block was a sign that said, "Ruby's Bar & Grill."

"There she blows," Sam said, "let's hurry."

"Are you thirsty Sam?" Nate asked smiling because he knew he was.

"Ok, once we get there you take the front door and I'll take the back. Remember we nail this bastard first, and then we drink. If he still has that head dress on he'll be easy to spot," Nate reminded him.

Arriving at the bar, Nate departed and walked around back. He kept his hand on his gun sort as a comforter. He eased his way thru the back door, making little noise. He nodded at an employee as he went thru the back room and into the bar. He saw Sam walking slowly thru the place and looking every man over. Nate knew with the killer instinct Sam had he'd spot him if he was there.

Both came together in the middle of the bar and Sam shook his head. Nate had to agree, having looked over the couple dozen people there.

"Hi folks, I'm with the Feds. and we are tracking a man who tried to blast San Diego with a dirty bomb. Now we stopped that from happening and he took off runing and we need to catch him. Anyone see an Arab running or walking thru this area. Can you help us?" Nate asked.

Right away, the employee Nate had passed in the backroom spoke up.

"I did about six, seven minutes ago. I was out back when he came by. What drew my attention to him was he was taking off his head gear and tossed in our garbage can. He was dark skinned and could have been an Arab. He also asked me if I knew where Baker Street was from here."

"Yeah," Nate said "that's him."

"What did you tell him?" Nate asked, hardly able to contain himself.

"I told him sure; I knew where Baker Street was and directed up the street about ten blocks and a couple to the left. I figured he was going to that funny looking church over on Baker Street. Seems like it an arab church," he said.

"Thanks," Nate said and turned to Sam.

"Lets have that beer now Sam. I want this guy to think he's safe in a mosque. Let's let him catch his breath," Nate said as his phone rang.

"Yes," Nate said in answering.

"Nate, this is Admiral Perkins. The General wanted me to inform you that there is a mosque on Baker Street. The number is 10132, Baker Street. Do you know where that is? I can direct you.

"Yes, we are just a few blocks away from there. One of the citizens told us. I'll get back to you. Thanks, Admiral," Nate replied. He then dialed the police.

"Chief, this is Armstrong and I need you to send backup to the mosque at 10132 Baker st. I'll be there in five minutes. Will you do that?" Nate asked.

"Yes, and I'll tell them you're in charge. Get back to me as soon as you catch the bastard. The newspapers have gotten wind of this and I'll have to give them some sort of statement so hurry," Chief Still answered.

"Here we are risking our lives and he's worried about news reporters," Nate said and winked at Sam at the same time.

"He's got to be hiding in that mosque. Now's the time we find out if those here legally really want to be Americans. I'll bet we have trouble getting him out of there," stated Sam.

"You could be right," Nate said, "let's jog the rest of the way."

They picked up their pace and rounded the corner onto Baker street and were across the street from the mosque.

They stood watching the front door and waiting for the backup.

"You go around back and nail him if he comes out that way. I'll wait here for the police," Nate said.

Sam left Nate, crossed the street and went around to the back of the building.

In minutes police cars showed up and dozens of police piled out. Nate waved down a Lt. and motioned him over.

"I'm Armstrong, Lt. and I have a man around back. We are looking for an Arab who we suspect went in there," pointing at the mosque, "you been briefed on why we need him alive."

"No, hell no, I'm always the last to know," stated the Lt. Nate filled him in on the details.

"Ok, we'll surround the place and you take charge," and with this the Lt. called over a Sgt. and gave him instructions. In sixty seconds or less the building was surrounded and the Sgt. returned to them for further instructions.

"Lt., Sam and I have no arrest powers so we'll need you or the Sgt. to go in with us," advised Nate.

"Ok, the Sgt. will go with you. Would you like a bullet proof vest?" offered the Lt.

"No thanks," Nate responded.

"Do you have one on Sgt.?" asked the Lt.

"No, I'll go with the guys like I am. Hopefully it won't come to a shoot out," the Sgt. answered.

"Let's, go," Nate said as he started across the street. The other two followed close behind.

As they were approaching the door, it swung open. A man of about fifty five or so stood in the opening.

"Yes, gentlemen can I help you," he asked.

"Yes," replied Nate, "you are harboring a felon and we need to talk with him. Would you bring him out and do we need to come in to get him?" Nate replied.

"We harbor no such person. Only a brother in need of sanctuary. He told us the police might be by and he had done nothing wrong. We are disturbed that you would bring this kind of force for a man who has done nothing wrong. Perhaps you need to explain," said the Muslin.

"He leads a group or terrorists on an attemted attack on this city a little while ago. Two of us saw him run from the scene and tracked him here. We mean to take him in and I would advise you not to resist. We mean you or your mosque no harm, but we will take him with your permission or not. Do you understand?" Nate asked.

"Yes, I understand. I'm an American Muslin but my faith in God is greater than in what you say. In America, don't you need a warrant to force your way in here. I believe we have rights here and I encourage you to show me a warrant. If you have one, show me. If not, go get one," he said.

He closed the door and was gone from sight. Nate eyed the door for strength in case they would have to break it down. As he walked back across the street, he dialed the Chief.

"Still, here," came the answer.

"Armstrong, here. I need you to get someone to a judge and get us a search warrant for the mosque. Entry has been refused. Tell the judge it's a matter of national security. If he has any doubts, have him call the General. I'll call the General as soon as we hang up to advise him. We need it fast and will stay in place until we get it. Have an officer deliver it quick. We have the place completely surrounded so no one can get out. Hurry man, hurry," Nate said in closing.

He dialed the General and gave him the information. He thanked Nate for the call.

"We need a search warrant Lt. and I've got the Chief working on it.

Keep your men in place and tell them no one leaves the mosque unless I get to talk to them," Nate said.

"Got you, Sgt. pass this along to our units," instructed the Lt.

"Let's get comfortable it could be a long wait. Depends on how convinced the judge is on the national security issue. If I know your Chief Lt., he won't quit until he gets it," Nate said, just to have a conversation.

Time passed slowly when you're waiting and watching the clock. Anyone who has ever waited in a train station or an airport has experienced it. Nate lit a cigar and hopped up on a car fender to smoke it. Some one had slipped away and returned with coffee, which helped.

An hour went by before a police car came screaming up the street, coming to a screeching halt in front of the mosque.

Two officers jumped out and rushed over to the police Lt.…. They handed him a piece of paper, which he unfolded and read.

"It's the warrant, Nate so we can go in," he stated.

"Notify your people we're going in and to be on their toes. Remind them this guy is to be taken alive. We need him," Nate expressing concern.

"Do it Sgt.," the Lt. said and started across the street with Nate and Sam. He also motioned to three other officers to follow. Reaching the door, Nate knocked loudly.

The door swung open and the same man stood facing Nate.

"We have the warrant," Nate advised and pushed past him. The Lt., being right behind Nate handed him the warrant and proceed inside with the other officers.

"Fan out guys and check every nook and cranny in this place," Nate told them. Nate had stopped just inside and spoke to the man at the door.

"You can make this much easier if you just take us to the man," he said.

"The man is not here that you are looking for. This is our church and people come here to pray. It is a sanctuary for people in trouble. We do not mean to violate any of your laws, but we do nothing the Catholic Church does not also do. Why do you search for this man? Is he bad or perhaps he is a victim. Why are you so intent on catching him? Perhaps if

I knew, I would more likely to help you," he said while looking Nate in the eye.

The man seems sincere and maybe he would. Should I confide in him more than I have already? What this man is wanted for and would he feed the information to the press. If the press gets ahold of this and publishs it, we could still have a panic, Nate was thinking.

'If I tell you will you keep it a secret and tell no one and will you direct us to him. He needs to be taken off the streets. You have to believe me and cooperate," Nate argued with him.

"If I do not know his crime, I can not help," answered the man.

"Are you a citizen of the United States and do you love this country," Nate asked, thinking he might take advantage of the man's need to be an American.

"Yes, I have been here ten years and love my new country, but what has that have to do with this," he inquired.

Nate looked him over very closely. This guy was cool and not yelling about his rights and Nate considered telling him. He seemed honest and maybe he felt strongly about the safety of his new country. It was worth a try.

"Ok," Nate said, "I'll going to trust you to keep a secret. What I'm about to tell you must stay with you. You must not repeat it to anyone. You understand?" Nate asked.

"Yes, I understand. Now you have me very curious and a little concerned," he said.

"Ok, God help you if you don't keep it a secret," Nate started. "This morning early, the man we are looking for and a group of others attempted to explode a dirty bomb over San Diego. The rest are in custody or dead. He seems to be the leader and we need to stop him before he does more damage. If the news media gets ahold of this and prints it, we may have a panic on our hands. That's why it's a secret. Now tell me where this man is so we can catch him before he gets away. Remember he cared nothing about you and your church. He knew it was here but was willing to kill all of you and thousands more of Americans citizens. You must help us, he's a terrorist. He cares not for you or anyone, he's a traitor to your religion. The Curran does not teach what he's doing. In fact it's against it," Nate pleaded.

During his explanation, Nate noticed the man's jaw tighten and held that way right up to the end. He took it as a good sign.

CHAPTER 20

"You, of course are correct. My religion does not accept murder and I will help you. Please keep my help confidential. Perhaps some in our group would be apposed to helping you. Come I will show you where he went," said the man as he turned to go thru another door.

Nate, Sam and the police Lt. followed. They went down a stairs to the basement. They entered a large room where only rugs covered the floor. Not carpets, rugs.

This must be their prayer room as well as the main room upstairs, Nate thought.

"On the left side wall you see that brightly colored carpet," the man asked Nate.

"Yes," Nate replied.

"Move the carpet aside and you will find a door leading into a tunnel. The tunnel goes across the alley and comes up under a shed. He went that way and once out he would have headed for the warehouse district across town. Please stop him for my people's sake," he pleaded.

"Notify your men about the shed, Lt. and that one of us will be coming out of it. We need to make sure he's not still in there. Who wants to go?"

"I'll do it," Sam said, "see you over there."

Sam stepped thru the door and was gone. The others closed the door and Nate stationed one to stay and the rest left and went across to the shed. Althrough their wait was not long, everyone was on edge. They were quiet and waited for any sign of activity in the tunnel. Within five minutes after they arrived at the shed, they heard Sam's voice coming from under the shed.

"Don't shoot, it's me," Sam shouted and came scrambling up from under a sheet of galvanized tin that lay on the floor. As the tin moved aside, all could see the hole and Sam's head poped up. He was grinning as he told them the terrorist was not in there.

"It's as I thought but I was hoping we could end it here," coming from Nate.

"Well you're thru with us, Armstrong, so I'll pull my men and we'll be out of here. Call when you need us. I'll be at the Chief's office until this is finished. You heading for the warehouse district?" he asked.

"No, I'll see you back at the Chief's place. Have him bring the prisoners to his jail so I can interrogate them," Nate advises.

"Will do, see you there in a few minutes," answered the Lt.

All the way to the Chief's office Nate kept running questions thru his mind. He knew these terrorists were willing to die as martyrs than talk. He needs to be sharp in questioning them. It was anyone's guess which was the weakest and who was not. *Problems, problems and more problems*, Nate thought, *this assignment had nothing but problems.*

At the police headquarters, Nate sat down with a cup of coffee and jotted down some questions he needed answered. He tried to be crafty at this so he could come in the so-called-back-door and trick those he interrogated to disclose any kind of information. He desperately needed information and quickly. Once the driver who got away had time to catch his breath, he be off and running else where. They had to move quickly. The coffee helped clear his mind and a plan soon took shape. *He'd get the bastard or die trying*, Nate was thinking.

In talking to the Chief, Nate discovered there was an Arab speaking officer on the police department. This was a relief to him and made it much easier. Now he had the means to do the questioning and keep it within the department. He felt sure this would be done without leaks to the press.

Before questioning Nate felt he should get a meal under his belt. His whole crew was hungry and needed a little rest.

"Sam, tell our crew to get in their vehicles, we're going for a good old fashion dinner. I need to speak to the Chief a minute, and then I'll be right with you," Nate advised.

"Alright," Sam replied in a jubilant voice.

Nate went to the Chief's office and caught him just as he was leaving.

"Chief, I need a favor," he started, "could you have one of the prisoners put in an interogation room. I'll have a go at him when we return from eating. Also I need the officer down here that speaks arabric. He'll be my interpetor for questioning."

"Can do. It will take a while to get the officer because he's off duty. How do you want him; in uniform or plain clothes?" asked the Chief.

"Plain clothes, I think. I might want to play a little game on the prisoners. Yeah, plain clothes."

"Ok, it'll be about forty five minutes to an hour to get him here," came the response.

"That's fine. We are going out to eat and will be gone at least that long. Put the first prisoner in introgation. I want him to look at four walls and wonder just what's going to happen to him. Gives him time to think. It might make him prone to worry. He may realize death is not coming to him today and I'll squeeze him."

"You got it," replied the Chief, "I order it before I leave for a meal myself. The wife called and said it's ready. I'll be back in time to watch the interviews. Maybe I'll learn something. Eat hardy; it may be a long night."

Nate could not help but notice the change in the Chief's attitude from their first meeting. Apparently he's satified Nate and crew knew what they were doing.

Nate left the building and waved to his people. They mounted up and drove off down the street with the other Bronco following. Turning to the left when reaching the highway they returned to the restaurant they had eaten in the day before. Upon entering, they asked if they could be seated all together at one table.

"Yes, of course," replied the waitress to their request. Tables were pushed together to accommodate.

They sat down and Nate ordered beer all around. He told the waitress to put it all on one tab as he was paying the entire bill.

"It's the least I could do. We'll all have a trying day and the General is really the one buying. He just doesn't know it yet," Nate grined as he said it.

The rest of the crew laughed and sat sipping their beer. They had told the girl they wanted a couple beers before ordering food. She nodded, she understood and left them alone to talk and drink.

After a couple beers had been consumed, Nate motioned the waitress over and said they were ready to order.

All ordered the same. Steaks and all the trimmings. These were hungry people.

Thirty minutes after the food arrived, most were finished and pulled out cigars. They all ordered another beer, pushed back their chairs and relaxed. About half way through the cigars Nate spoke to them.

"Well men, it's time to say goodby again. This has been a time consuming mission but so far we have won. I'm sure the President and the General are very thankful for our work. All of you head for home except Sam and Delbert. We are staying to try to fine out where the nuclear stuff came from and then we'll be out of here. We have the police force on our side when we need them, so the rest of you can go. You may all find a room for tonight and fly out tomorrow. In less than a week you'll all receive your pay plus a twenty five thousand bonus. You all should know that this is my last mission. I'm getting too damn old for the type of work, so you won't be hearing from me with any work offers. I have a beautiful wife in Columbia and that's where I'm staying. She's much nicer to sleep with than where I've slept on this mission. If any of you need another mission, call the General, but leave me out of it. I want to thank you for your dedication to the team and to America. Most Americans will never know what you've done for them. You're all invited to my place anytime you want to come visit and I may drop in to your homes. Keep in touch and God bless you all. So long. Come on Delbert and Sam lets get going," Nate said and dropped two, one hundred dollar bills on the counter to pay for the food.

God, it had been a long day and now it's getting dark, Nate thought as he pressed the gas pedal down and headed back to the police headquaters. He was anxious to get to those damn camel drivers.

Back at police headquaters, Nate was shown the interogation room. Not yet ready to tackle the man sitting there, he walked back to the main office. He took a seat at a desk and began thinking and writing out notes to sort of guide him. He knew the only thing these people knew was torture and pain. The acceptable program was to shame them into confessing and throw themselves on the mercy of the court. Didn't always work here and he doubted it would work on Arabs. He also knew he needed to get the information from him so the government could take some action against the nation furnishing the radio-active junk. He doubted this one had that kind of information. He was aware this wasn't really his duty to do this. Washington could send the F.B. I. to do this. Nate didn't want to wait and thought the quicker the better. He didn't want that driver to get away. He knew he'd have to be on his toes and grab at anything this guy might slip up on. That would be hard to do with an interpreter. He thought of using brass knuckles and beating the truth out of him. He decided against this. It just wasn't his way of doing things. On the other hand he could lie like hell to him about letting him go for the location of the driver. *Naw,* he would not buy this so why try it.

All at once he remembered something he'd heard many years ago. The one thing Arabs feared more than anything in the world. The thing they feared more than their God or clercs.

Leaning back he knew this would work if he presented it in a firm, believable manner. *Yes,* he thought, *this was the method he would use.* He knew he'd have to work up to it and act out a part he'd done before with this thing as the last resort. He'd waste a half hour then pull this on him.

To get himself ready, he'd have another cup of coffee and a cigar. He walked over to the coffee pot and refilled his cup and returned to the table.

"Can I help you with anything?" asked the desk Sgt.

"No, thanks, I'm just stalling for time. It has been my practice to let the person to be interrogated wait. The more they look at four walls and think about what is about to happen, the softer they get," Nate answered.

"Yes, but this is an Arab and it might not work," explained the officer.

"I've got nothing to lose by doing so. Let him worry a little longer," Nate said as he sat down at the table. He lit a cigar and sipped his coffee when it hit him. Where in hell was the interpeter?

"Sgt., I am waiting for an officer to interpet for me. Do you know how long it will be before he gets here?" asked Nate.

"Oh, he's back in the squad room. You ready for him?"

"Yeah, get him out here and would you have someone pick me up a box of those little wooden matches," Nate said.

The Sgt. picked up a phone and spoke briefly before hanging up. A man came out of a backroom and approached Nate.

"You Armstrong," he asked.

"Yes, are you my interpeter?" Nate answered.

"Chuck Edwards at your service, sir," smiling he sat down across from Nate.

"But you're white, I was expecting an Arab type fellow," Nate added.

"Yeah, that's what most people say. I assure you I'm what you need and I'm good at it. I lived in the Middle East for four years and learned the language. I'm ready when you are," he said.

"Ok, but before we go I want it understood that I'll do all the talking, you just explain to me what he says. It's very important. Also when we go in you need to tell him that I'm from the government and explain your position. Clear," Nate said.

"Yes, don't worry, I know the rules. If you go a little tough, don't worry about it getting repeated. What goes on in that room stays in that room, except the confession? Ok?" came the answer.

"Good lets go," Nate said and the two got up to leave.

Just at this moment the Chief walked thru the door.

"Oh, good you've not started yet. I'm going to witness the interogation to see how you government people work. Don't worry I won't get in the way. I'll be behind the mirror. Let's go," said the Chief as he started down the hall.

As they reached the room, the Chief entered a room adjacent to interrogation. Nate and Edwards entered to the surprise of the man sitting there. He actually jumped a little when the two entered the room.

"Ok, tell him who we are and why we are here," Nate advised the officer.

This was done and Nate seated himself across the table from the Arab. Edwards took a position in a far corner and leaned against the wall.

"I want to know who you are and where you come from." Nate asked and it was explained to the suspect.

A string of foreign words came forth and Nate waited to have it explained to him.

"He says he came from Iran and he told me his name. Let's call him, Hussein," Edwards advised.

Nate thru back his head and laughed loud and long. A part of his technique.

"You know we got to you before you were exposed to enough radiation to kill you. You will live unless I kill you here. When the word gets to your home country that you failed, you will be dishonored as will your friends. Tell me now what I want to know and I'll see to it they will never hear how miserly you failed. Understand," Nate asked.

Nate waited for this to be explained before he went on.

"You have heard how some of our troops, with the help of the C.I.A., water boarded prisoners and even did some torturing of people like you," again Nate waited for this to be explained to him.

"I want you to tell me the name of the driver who got away and where we can find him," Nate said.

The interpeter and the Arab had a long discussion before Edwards turned to Nate.

"He says he will tell you nothing. Torture him if you wish, he will not tell," Edwards stated.

"Tell him we know him and where he is from and I'll see to it his whole family is murdered if he does not talk and then disgrace for failure will go to other members of the family. His uncles, aunts, nephews and such. Does he want that to happen because of his stupity," Nate ordered.

Again a long conversation between Edwards and the prisoner took place. By the tone of it he knew the man was refusing to coorperate with them. He was racking his brain for a way to get thru to this bastard. A plan began to find its way to the front of his brain as he wondered if it would work. He would first try another method.

"He refuses to help us," Edwards said to Nate.

Nate went into the hallway for a moment and was joined shortly by the Chief from the room next door. This is where, from the window inside you can watch the interrogation.

"Tough nut to crack?" asked the Chief.

"Yes, but I think I have a plan of attack that will work. Give me your gun," Nate ordered.

"You can't kill him," said the Chief in a loud voice.

"Give me your gun, I said," Nate responded.

The Chief reached for his snub nosed revolver, a thrity eight. He passed it across to Nate who opened it up, dumping out the ammo.

"That should make you feel more comfortable," Nate said grinning from ear to ear as he handed over the shells.

Nate went back into the room to try again. The Chief ran to his room, not wanting to miss a thing.

Once inside the room Nate held the pistol so everyone in the room could see it. He walked around behind the prisoner who now seemed very nervous. Nate bent over him and placing the end of the barrel into the man's ear.

"Tell him I will kill him now if he doesn't tell me what I want to know," Nate told Edwards. The sentence was translated. The prisoner began smiling and actually calmed down a little. This Nate had expected of a suicide bomber. If he died here he would be a martyr.

The translation took place with no results. This was told to Nate who bent a little closer and spoke.

"You greasily little bastard, I'm going to kill you and have your body wrapped in a pig's skin and buryed out in the desert. You could never go to heaven if wrapped in a pig skin and buryed that way. I'm going to kill you soon if you don't start talking," Nate said as he looked up at Edwards and nodded for the interpertation to take place.

Edwards even seem nervious as he spoke the words. Even he thought Nate was going to kill him. He rattled off the words and started backing up. He didn't want any blood to splash on him.

As the words fell on the ears of the prisoner, Nate could see a facal change from a smile to one of extreme horror. Nate had heard the Arabs had this fear. It had even been in a picture show Nate had seen earlier in life. *By God, it is true. The actually believe they could never go to heaven if this happened to them, he was thinking.*

The man started talking at a fever pitch. He was talking so fast Edwards could not keep up. He did catch enough to relate to Nate he would talk. Anything but this type of burial was the man's thinking.

"Calm him down if you can. Tell him to relax. I'll go get coffee for all of us. Ask him if he wants coffee and how do you take yours?" Nate asked.

"Just black for me. Hold on a minute and I'll ask him," Edwards said.

A string of words passed between Edwards and the prisoner. Edwards looked over at Nate, smiling.

"He'll have black coffee and he thanks you a thousand times for not burying him in that way. I'll stay with him while you're gone," Edwards stated.

As Nate closed the door behind him, he almost collided with the Chief.

"I'll go with you for the coffee. Armstrong that was the greatest piece of work I've seen in years. How did you know about the pig skin? I would never have thought of that," the police chief asked.

"I've done extensive reading plus in Viet Nam, the method of intergation seems to be to find out what those you seek information from, fear most and use it against them. The crazy bastards don't fear death so you find other methods. I remember when I was a kid, in movies; the French Foreign Legion used a stunt where they said they dipped bullets in pig fat. The information was allowed to be over heard by a native spy.

The spy took the information to his people who were about to attack the fort. After they had gotten the information, the attack was canceled. Saved a fort and a couple hundred brave lads. I did not know if it was true but I thought it was worth a shot. Some time you can learn from movies. Let's get that coffee. I want to get right back there before he realizes I wouldn't kill him," Nate explained.

The two hurried to the Chief's office and filled three coffee cups and Nate started back with them.

Nate entered the room and handed the prisoner a cup. He put on a mean looking face so he would not pick up on Nate lying about killing him. Nate wanted this man to fear him and therefore give out the information requested.

Edwards took his cup and went back to stand in the corner. Nate sat down across from the Arab and put his feet up on the table. He drank his coffee, but staring at him the whole time.

Nate was taking his time and enjoying the coffee. So was Edwards. The prisoner drank his slowly but didn't appear to be enjoying it. In his place Nate didn't think he'd enjoy it either. All knew the questioning would start again.

Minutes later it did just that.

"Edwards, ask him for the name of the driver that got away," Nate instructed.

The question was posed to the man who seemed to struggle with an answer. Finally he answered to Edwards, but kept his eyes on Nate for any response. Edwards nodded and spoke to Nate.

"He does not know his last name. His first name is Alli and he's from Saudi Arabia. This whole plan was his idea and he was given the honor of executing the plan. Now that it has failed, he is disgraced and will try anything to get back his honor. He is a dangerous man and while in your country will try to kill many that is what he said," Edwards reported.

"For this plan to get this far he had to have contacts with people here. I want to know who helped and I want to know now," Nate said in a loud voice for the benefit of the prisoner.

Edwards nodded and spoke to the man. The prisoner took a deep breath and it appeared he was thinking.

"They will kill me if I tell. Please don't bring the rath of Allah down on me. I plead for mercy. Please do not force me to tell," he said franticly.

This was reported to Nate who just smiled.

"Tell him this. He was the one who started this attack on America, with the help of others and now you must face American justice. Like it or not you must pay for your crimes. I will ask the courts to be merciful because you cooperated with us. That's the different between your country and ours, we can deliver mercy. Now answer the question and give us the names of who helped and where they are. If not," Nate pulled out his pistol, "we still have the pigskin."

Apparently he had forgotten this little item and upon hearing this he went into a long string of words. Edwards just shugged his shoulders. It all came faster than he could keep up. Nate waited.

Finally he stopped and they waited for him to calm down. Looking around the room, the prisoner could read the faces of those with him and knew he'd not get any relief from them. He knew he must talk. Some twenty minutes later, Nate and Edwards had compiled a dozen names of a sleeper cell of terrorists in San Diego. Other information obtained was this cell planning attacks if this one had been successful. Now they will wait a year or two before trying again. Nate and Edwards both had written down the names and addresses. Nate excused himself on the pretense of coffee and a bathroom call. He stepped out the door into the hallway.

Again he came face to face with the police chief.

"Just the man I wanted to see," Nate expressed his pleasure of seeing him again. He torn off the page he'd written on and handed it to the Chief.

"Get this to the F.B.I. a.s.a.p. and your department can help. You'll get the credit for a round up of terrorists if you don't let the feds take all the credit. Ok by you?" Nate explained.

"Hell, yes. Looks like a busy night and maybe tomorrow," related the Chief.

"No, it has to be all at once. Each house must be hit at the same time or these bastards will disappear and we'll never find them. I'll call the General and tell him what's going on. He can also help with the F.B.I. if you need it. Now go and earn you pay, I have a ring-leader to catch," Nate said with a smile.

The Chief had come to wonder if the smile was just a smart ass way of gradeing his conduct. Anyhow he did not dwell on it. He turned around and headed out. Nate followed him to the coffee pot, and then returned to the room taking the pot with him.

After entering the room he pours each a refill of the black brew. Setting it down, he turned to the prisoner.

"You have done well up till now and I hope you're wise enough to continue," Nate said and waited for the translation.

The man now was smiling and nodding his head yes. He seemed to get more pleasure out of the coffee this time.

"Where is the truck driver hiding? I know you know and now's the time to tell," Nate said.

The man froze with the cup to his lips. Nate could see he was deep in thought and was scared to death, almost. He knew he was between the devil and the deep blue sea. Either answer or wait for reprisals from his people, or don't and a pig skin overcoat awaited him. He realized he must talk. So far the Americans had been kind to him, but he knew this one called Nate would carry out what he had said about the pig skin. He chose to talk.

As they say in law enforcement he spilled his guts. Nate thanked him, told Edwards this was his prisoner and walked out. Up front he stopped at the Chief's office.

"I have the information I need Chief and will be heading out. Get someone to relieve Edwards. I want him with me. The truck driver is hiding in a warehouse on the docks. Can I have the loan of ten men; I don't want him getting away," Nate explained.

"Sure, hell, yes, wait with your men out front and I get you a crew," came the response.

CHAPTER 21

Nate, his crew and ten policemen surrounded warehouse # 16 on the waterfront. They had gone in quietly in unmarked police vehicles and the Bronco. They all wore bulletproof vests and had brought along a few canisters of teargas. They were loaded for bear and damn serious. After all, what happens here could prove to be a deterrent against other tries? Nate was thinking this and it was what kept him determined to catch the son-of-a-bitch. At the station Nate had made it clear that this man must be taken alive regardless of what happens. He explained why and got nods of approval from the cops.

Nate was hoping there would be no automatic gun fire. Too many people could be hurt and it would lower the odds of taking Alli alive. The General had been informed of this action and approved. The time had come to take this man down.

On a bull horn, Nate issued an order to those inside.

"This is the police and everyone in the building is to come out with their hands in the air. No weapons or we will start shooting. Alli, you come out first," Nate said and handed the horn to Edwards. He repeated the order in Arabic. All was quiet inside the building. They waited and nothing happened.

"Repeat the order, Edwards and add a few brutal words if you want. Just get him out here," Nate instructed.

Again the words went out in Arabic and again they waited.

Damn it, Nate was thinking, *looks like we going to have to go get him. I really don't want to because some one may get killed.*

"One more time Edwards," Nate said and no sooner was it said, than it was done.

The men were getting hyped up and anxious to go. It was plain to see the police were men of action and hated waiting.

Nate was thinking of a plan that might work.

"Delbert, you and Sam come with me. We're going in. Edwards you take charge if I don't return. Clear," Nate finished.

"Clear boss, hurry back," was the answer.

Nate grinned at the comment and started across the drive. He arrived at the man door and was joined by Delbert and Sam.

"Well, men here we are again. Looks like we need to flush him out. Follow me in and one of you go left and the other go right. Ok?" Nate asked.

"Sure, lets go," came from Sam.

Nate tried the door and it was not locked. He nodded to the men and pushed door to open and hurried inside as did the other two. They fanned out as directed and slowly moved thru the warehouse. When they reached the office for the building, about the middle, they carefully went in. It was a room with windows all around. Inside they found a desk, chair and a cot. The cot showed use and lifting the blanket, Nate felt the sheet under was warm.

"Damn, fellows, it appears he saw use coming or was told we coming just minutes ago. The sheets are still warm. Fan out and lets get him before he gets away," Nate instructed.

One went down the right and one down the left side. Nate went down the center where there was little cover. He crouched and moved slowly, looking from side to side not wanting to overlook a thing. They soon reached the back side and a man door there. They stepped out in time to see a motor boat coming out from under the building.

"Get the numbers off that boat. That's our terrorist I'd bet," Nate said in a very disappointed voice.

"There is a trap door back there about forty feet, but I opened it and looked through it. I saw no one so I closed and came on. He must have been right there just feet from me. I'm sorry Nate, I goofed," coming from Sam.

"I got the numbers off the boat, Nate," Delbert butted in.

"Good, let's let the police run them for us and maybe we'll have someone who's helping with his getaway," Nate said and headed for the police Lt.

"Run this for us, Lt," Delbert asked as he handed over a piece of scrap paper.

"Sure, we'll know in a couple minutes," came the Lt's response.

Nate lit a cigar and tried thinking of where this man could have gone to. The appropriate place would be a mosque. He wondered if there was another one in town.

"View Drive, number 23710," blurted out the Lt. "The boat is registered to a Harvey Downs at that address.

"Good work Lt," Nate told him, now I have a question for you. Are there any other mosque in the city and where are they located?" Nate asked.

"I don't know, but let's call the Chief and he can find out for us. You think he may be going to another mosque?" asked the Lt.

"I don't know but it's a good bet he did," Nate answered.

The call was made and they were told they'd find out and get back to them.

Some fifteen minutes later Nate's phone rang.

"I've got the information for you. The address is 27000 View Drive. Does that help?" asked the Chief.

"It sure the hell does. That's only four blocks from the boat owners place. Chief, can I hang on to your men till we raid this place and can you get a judge to issue a search warrant for the mosque?' Nate asked.

"We'll do what we can. Move slowly and maybe we will have it by the time you get there," informed the Chief.

"Great, we will take our time. Don't want to be in place until the warrant is issued. Have someone run it out to us. I'm sure who ever is in charge of the mosque will demand to see it. Thanks Chief and Nate hung up.

One of the policemen pulled out a city map and found View Drive. It was located northeast of the city, close to the city limits. The city was spreading in that direction but it was still sparsely populated around that area. The map showed several vacant lots. This area was a little bit isolated and was a perfect place for a mosque. Nate felt good about this and was confident this was where their fugitive was hiding. Just then the phone rang. It was the General.

"Armstrong, what's going on out there? We're all getting nervous as a whore I church. When can we wrap this thing up and get some sleep. Have you caught the driver or not. If not where is he now or do we know?" said the General in a disturbed voice.

"We think we know where he is. He's hiding in a mosque and we are waiting a warrant before we hit the place. Leave me alone General and I'll get him. When that happens, you'll be the first to know. Ok?' Nate answered a perturbed voice.

"Yeah, yeah, yeah," said the General.

Nate ended the call by hanging up. He gathered all the men around him and told them of the new development and the mosque across town. Everyone was anxious to go. They were all given the address and told to move slowly. He was being careful so as not to arrive early before the warrant arrived. Vehicles were fired up and they started across town.

"We have the warrant and it's on the way," explained the Chief in a call thirty minutes later, to Nate. Nate's group was just ten blocks away from the mosque when this message was received.

Now armed with the warrant, Nate passed the word by radio to surround the mosque. He knew that he didn't really need possession of the warrant, just the knowledge it was issued to search the place.

In his message to surround the place he also instructed that no one was to leave or enter the place. The trap was set and it was time to see it sprung. However the method used this time would be different. The police and Nate's men were told to be in close and when the front door opened to let him in, they were to enter through any door or window on every side. Nate had it this way in hope of trapping the suspect inside and maybe taking him with out firing a shot. With everyone in place Nate walked up to the front door and knocked. Delbert was covering one side of the door and Sam the other. Each had automatic weapons. This time if they couldn't catch the bastard, they were to kill him and all who harbored him. This order came straight from the White House.

They waited a couple minutes and knocked again. A couple minutes later the door swings open wide and a cleic of about fifty five stood there, in the open doorway. He was dressed in some sort of robe, looking impressive.

"Yes, gentlemen what can I do for you," he said in perfect English.

"We have a warrant to search this place. Here's your copy," Nate said as he rushed passed by him and into the mosque. Delbert and Sam followed with there guns at the ready.

"Wait, wait, sir," yelled the man, "This is the same as your churches. Anyone can seek sanctuary here. You have no right and your guns are not allowed."

"Delbert take this person and sit him down and keep him quiet. Sam come with me but be careful," Nate directed and the two moved forward down the hallway. They looked into a couple rooms as they went. Soon they entered the main room. Around forty people were kneeling on rugs, facing the front of the room. They were all repeating something in Arabic. A prayer it seemed. The two stopped in astonishment.

"Wait Sam, till this is over. All these are dressed in robes and anyone of them could be cover for our man. It's funny I don't remember their religion to have meetings at night. Let's wait till the police join us. We will then search everyone as they go out. Be ready for him the make a run for it. Catch him alive if we can and if not we'll put him out of his misery," Nate instructed.

Soon police were coming into the room from all different directions. They stopped when they entered and looked to Nate for directions. He held up his hand and motioned everyone to stop and wait. They did but all kept their weapons raised for action if need be.

Those kneeling soon became aware there was something going on. They quit praying and started looking around. Seeing police banishing weapons, they stood up. They seemed surprised but Nate wasn't buying that.

"Delbert bring that man here," Nate spoke loudly down the hallway.

"Coming, boss," Delbert replied and the two came forward and soon stood next to Nate.

"Tell them we are looking for Alli and if he comes forward the rest may go. If he does not, we then must search each one on their way out. Tell Alli to come forward now and this will end. Understand?" Nate asked.

"Yes, of course, but the person you are looking for is not here, but I will tell them," and he started rattling off the words in Arabic.

As he spoke a murmur went thru the crowd. First it started low then became louder as the group got mad because of these intriguers. They started to stamp their feet and Nate feared they would soon attack.

"Tell them not to get violent or we will shoot. If they will look around they will see automatic weapons capable of killing all of you. Tell them to form a single line and start this way. They will be searched by the police and they are not to resist. Tell them now," Nate ordered in a raised voice.

The man did as he was told and the crowd quieted down and began forming a single line.

"Two of you police officers come here and search everyone one. They are all men so no problem there," Nate again instructed.

Once the procedure started, Nate whispered to those doing the search, to seize any weapons, etc. and if any were found, those carrying are to stay in that room there, pointing down the hall. I will look at everyone's face. *God, I hope he's here*, Nate said to himself.

It was a slow procedure and taking time. Nate was getting nervous and starting to think he was wrong. Just then there was a fury of excitement and the back of the line. Nate moved quickly to find out why. As he turned to look, he saw the face of the man he was pursuing. He was dressed in Arab style clothing.

Nate scrambled to get back to him but was blocked many times by the people. They would step in front of him; throw their bodies in his way. Anything to slow him down.

One of the policemen yelled for help as Nate neared the end of the line. He saw his man running down a narrow hallway in the back. The policeman staggered to his feet and Nate saw the blood dripping from the hair line. He reached him and asked what happened.

"Don't bother with me. Get the son-of-a-bitch. I'm alright and I'll send you help. Get him," he said excitedly.

Nate ran down the hallway and found a door at the end. He hesitated, and then slowly opened it. The firing of a weapon was heard and bullets riddled the door Nate was holding. He jumped back and pulled his pistol. Two cops joined him as backup. Again, he pushed the door open and heard footsteps running. He dove thru the doorway and down the steps. The two policemen followed. It was dark in this basement. The steps had ended and all was quiet. Too quiet. Nate motioned to the policemen to spread out and look for their suspect.

"Be careful, he's like a caged animal and will kill you. Rember he is a suicide attacker. Now he's fired on us gives us the right to kill him. I want him alive but not if it risks our lives," Nate whispered to them.

The three spread out in this large room and found nothing. There was another door and they stopped just short of opening it. Again the firing of an automatic weapon rang out behind the door as bullets ripped the wooden fabric of the door. They waited and listened. They could hear nothing but still they knew he was there waiting.

Nate told the cops a plan of attack.

"I'm going to get on my knees at the door. He's firing about waist high which should allow me to crawl thru and surprise him. It sounds like that is a smaller room. I'll call out when I have him dead or alive. One of you pushes the door open and I'll go. Be quick or you might be hit," Nate said.

The policemen nodded in agreement and one moved on each side of the door. Nate dropped to his knees and was ready. He took a deep breath and nodded. One cop pushed the door open with a bang. Fire from an automatic, spit through the doorway.

Nate went thru in a fast crawl, quickly moving to the right side of the door. He heard what sounded like cursing and the weapon fell silent. The next sound was metal hitting the concrete floor. Nate waited and listened.

A sound of a window opening across the room came to his attention. He jumped up and yelled at the cops.

"Come on in, he unarmed and trying to get out a back window."

Nate rushed forward in the dark towards a faint light coming in from out side. He reached the window and found his suspect stuck in the window. With his clothing, his hips were too large to pass thru. Nate smiled and grabbed his feet. The other two joined him and they easily pulled the suspect back inside. He was fighting and cursing until one of the cops smacked him ove the head with a sap. He went down like a sack of spuds to the floor. They handcuffed him and found a light switch.

The light came on and the three found they were standing in middle of weapons rooms. Hundreds of automatic and rapid fire weapons were stacked everywhere. Boxes of ammo were stacked in one corner.

Nate grabbed one of the cop's radios and triggered the mike.

"Lt. don't let another one go. Keep all those son-a-bitches inside. Inform the Chief we've found hundreds of weapons and ammo. These basterds were going to start a small war. Get us some more men and we'll need trucks and hand carts to move all this stuff. Tell the Chief to get his ass down here. This is where he takes over and we go home," Nate advised.

He picked up his phone and dialed the General.

"We got him, General," Nate said when he heard the General's voice on the line.

"Great Armstrong, I knew I sent the right man on this mission. Has he told you anything yet?" the General eagerly asked.

"No, we just got him. I'm still in the room where we captured him. The police are just taking him out. I'll interrogate him soon and let you know. I'm waiting for the police chief to arrive. I'm in a mosque and there's a room here full of guns. I believe this is a sleeper cell we stumbled into. I've ordered all people here to be detained until we know what's going on. Hell there's enough arms and ammo to start a small war. You might want to notify the local F.B.I. I think the chief will, but they might want to send someone out from Washington. We do have an officer who speaks their lingo and has been very helpful. Got to go General, I think I hear the Chief coming," Nate reported.

Sure enough, as soon as Nate hung up, the Chief came through the door.

Looking around at the weaponry, the Chief whistled long and hard. Looking at Nate he spoke.

"Damn, I will say this for you Armstrong. When you're around, there's never a dull moment. Good work. I saw the bunch upstairs and I'm holding everyone till I find out what this is all about," he said reaching out to shake Nate's hand.

"I can tell you what's going on here. It will come out that this is a sleeper cell for terrorists. I believe your city was picked just because they are here. If the attack had been successful, this crowd was set to take over and establish a foothold in America. This mosque is probably just outside the targeted area. There are perhaps hundreds of Arabs living or coming here to join in. You best be careful and on your toes. You my friend have just entered the new war. A War on America. I wish you luck. I'm going back to the station and interogate our captive criminal. I'll let you know what I find out. Hopefully it will be helpful," Nate said and turned to leave. Halfway to the door, he stopped and turned around.

"Oh, I contacted the General and I think he'll be sending some agents out here from Washington. I think you'll have plenty of help. See you Chief," he said going thru the doorway.

One hour later he entered the introgation room with Edwards. The prisoner was being guarded by two policemen. He was handcuffed and his feet shackled.

"Take off the handcuffs; the shacklers will be enough," Nate told the officers. They obeyed and Nate asked them to leave. They did and entered the observation window in the room next door.

"Tell him this Chuck. You came here to become a martyr and made a mess of everything and even lead us to a sleeper cell. For this I thank you. Boy are you going to be killed in very brutal ways if I get you released in your country. I'm going to give you a chance to stay here in our prisons if you cooperate with me," he pauses for this to be explained to the man.

Edwards told the prisoner in his own languge. As he did Nate watched the man's face for any changes. He turned red in the face and spat at Nate. He rattled off several lines and jumped at Nate.

His jump was short and Edwards and Nate sat him back in his chair.

"Tell the bastard if he tries that again, I'll have him beaten," Nate said winking at the officer.

The translation took place and when Nate looked upon his face he saw only pure hate. *He's going to be a tough nut to crack,* Nate thought.

The prisoner settled down and slumped forward in his chair. In his mind it would be best if he just sat that way and said nothing.

"You tell me what I want to know and I'll get you a lawyer. As a terrorist you have no rights but I'll honor them anyway. We can not leave this room until I find out where you got the dirty bomb material. Was it from North Korea or from Iran? It has to be one of them. That's all I want to know," Nate raising his voice, "which one was it?"

He waited and motioned to Edwards to repeat it to Alli.

A conversation took place between the officer and prisoner. There was some back and forth talk that lasted a couple minutes.

"He says he will tell you nothing. He called you several names that were not very nice. Do you want to know what they were?" asked the officer.

"No, I'll forgo that, thank you," Nate replied. He lit a cigar and went into a deep thought process. *I've got to come up with something, a gimick, something that will make him talk,* was his thinking. *I can always use the pig burial trick.*

Getting up he left the room and went up front to the coffee pot. He filled three cups and proceeded back to the room. Entering, he gave one to Edwards and sat on in front of Alli. He sat down and began sipping the black brew. Edwards was doing the same but the prisoner just looked at it. Then he suddenly picked up the cup and threw its contents on Nate.

Nate jumped back as if shot in a surprise reaction. He almost fell over backwards as the liquid covered his shirt. He leaped from his chair and went around the table. He pulled his pistol and placed it against Alli's head.

"You son-of-a-bitch, I'll kill you myself if I have to," and Edwards translating as he spoke so as not to lose any of the meaning.

Nate pulled the hammer back on the thirty eight as it rested against his head. He was tempted to do just that but knowing it would get them nowhere. He relaxed the hammer and placed it back in his holster.

"No, I won't kill you because that's what you want. You would be celebrated as a martyr for trying this attack on America. The fact you were not successful would make no difference if you were killed. No, I won't kill you, but I'll make you wish you were dead,"Nate said to him and Edwards repeated in Arabic.

The prisoner showed not sign of stress or worry. Nate's guess was he thought he had us in an uncompromising position. He smiled to himself as he thought of the bural in a pig skin. To make sure that stunt worked, Nate figured he would need him tired, exhausted and worn down so he would put him through what he expected. Torture was out and so were beatings so he would fall back on methods he used in Nam. He would keep him awake for many hours and not feed him. This would be the pain he would feel. He looked over at Edwards.

"Do you have anything planned for the next forty eight hours, Chuck?" Nate asked.

"No, what do you have in mind," Edwards answered.

"We're going to play his game of wait and see. In Nam we broke many a tough commie with the methods we are going to try. The danger has passed and what we are trying to do is get information of who provided this group the material for this attack. First we don't feed him for forty eight hours. During that time we'll keep him awake and I need you for that. If we can break him down to a point that he doesn't know what to expect. Tired and hungry works in our favor. Once he's that way then I try the pig skin trick like on the other one. You game?" Nate asked.

"Damn, rights, I'm game. After what this idiot and his pals tried today, do what you have to. I'm with you," came the response.

"Ok, first we'll put him in solitary confinement for a few hours. You go home and get some rest and I'll sleep on the cot back there. Take your time and I'll see to it he's kept awake by the desk Sgt… When you came back, bring a lunch. It's going to be a long secession."

Having all but forgotten about Delbert and Sam, Nate went up front to the Sgt's, desk.

"Have you heard from the Chief on how they are coming on the weapons? I have two men working with them and need to speak to them," Nate advised the Sgt.

"Your men are on the way here now. No, the Chief and our department are nowhere thru loading the weapons and bringing in the people they arrested. There's something like thirty to forty. It will be late tomorrow before we process all people and guns," said the Sgt.

Just then the front door opened and in walked Delbert and Sam.

"Hi, guys. Is the fun all over for tonight?" Nate asked grinning. The two looked beat and butts dragging.

"Fun, did he say fun?" Sam aiming the question at Delbert.

"I believe he did. Weren't you having fun? For us it was a walk in the park," was Delbert's response. All of them laughed including the desk Sgt.

"Well guys, you can both get a room and let's go get something to eat. A cold brew will puts us all in a good mood. In the morning you can both head for home. I'll call the General and have our money deposited directly to your account, Delbert. I'm not sure about you Sam, so I'll let you handle it. Let's go eat," finished Nate.

CHAPTER 22

Nate awoke with a start, next morning. His brain still half asleep he forgot where he was. Swinging his feet off the cot and sitting up he became fully awake. He put his head in his hands and recalled the events of yesterday. Now awake he stood up and stretched. He could smell the coffee drifting back from up front. It was then he realized he was fully dressed. He had crashed last night, fully dressed. He walked up front. As he opened the door to the main office, the Sgt. spoke.

"Good morning, sir, I trust you had a good sleep. Sit down and I'll pour you a coffee," he rose up from his chair to get it.

Returning, he handed a cup of the black brew to Nate.

"Thanks, what time is it," Nate asked.

"Ten AM," came the answer.

"No, you must be mistaken, Sgt. I never sleep that late," Nate said a little unsure of himself.

"Check the clock on the wall. Edwards called and said he'd be in about noon, if that's alright," mentioned the Sgt.

"Yeah," Nate said as he sipped at his coffee. He was feeling better with each swig.

"I'm going for breakfast and will be back in an hour or so. Tell the Chief if you hear from him," coming from Nate.

"Sure, but it will be tonight before he calls. He only got out of here an

290

hour ago. I guess that mosque situation is a real mess, huh," the Sgt. digging for information.

"Yeah, it sure is," Nate responded and fill him in on the entire situation. Finished with the story and the coffee, Nate went out to the Bronco.

He again drove down to the little restaurant on the highway to feed his stomach and to stop its growling. In the super market next to the resturant, he replenished his supply of cigars.

"Is our guest still awake," Nate asked upon returning to the station some hour and a half later.

"Yeah, he is. He's begging to be left alone so he can sleep and he's noisy as all get out," replied the desk Sgt.

"Ok, I'll take over from here. Thanks and send Edwards back, when he comes in."

Nate lit a cigar on his way to interogation. He had it going nicely as he entered the room.

The prisoner jumped to his feet not knowing what was going to happen. *A good sign*, Nate thought. *He's getting jumpy. That's good.*

Nate sat down and pointed to the corner. He was meaning for Alli to stand there. The man just shook his head and walked over and looked at the corner. When he started to leave Nate yelled at him.

"Get back, get back, you are to stand there understand?" Nate said.

The man just shook is head and started to sit down.

"No, don't do that. Stand there," Nate tried to get through to him. Finally he got up and walked to the corner and stood there. By this he hoped to teach by illustrating the desired effect. The prisoner still had a puzzled look on his face, but walked over when Nate motioned him to. At times Nate wondered if this one was acting or if he really didn't understand English. Seems funny a person would be sent here not knowing a word of English. He did understand and stayed in place after Nate returned to his chair.

The room was getting filled with cigar smoke and Alli's eyes started watering. He sneezed a couple times and motioned to Nate to put out the cigar. Of course, Nate totally ignored his request and smoked on. He had learned several years ago that sometimes a little irritant was better than pain.

He sat there looking around for about forty minutes when Edwards entered the room. He carried a couple cups of coffee and handed one to Nate.

"What's happening, boss" he greeted Nate.

"Tell this guy he's to stand in that corner until we tell him he can sit," Nate said.

"Years ago in Nam, we figured a little discomfort was better than pain in getting someone to talk. Thought I'd try it on this one. He thinks he's tough. We'll see. Make him stand there until he gets wobbly and is about ready to fall. Then and only then can he sit. Don't let him lay down. By tomorrow evening I'll try our little plan and see if it works. Have you heard how the Chief and the boys are doing with all those guns and all those other prisoners," Nate asked.

"I know the Chief doesn't want you back here unless you're on vacation. He curses the increased workload. You know they took those people from the mosque to three different stations to process. All together there were thirty seven not counting the dozen or so who we released before you had us hold them. God, do you think they are all terrorists?" asked Chuck.

"Yeah, I do. They are all guilty of harboring a criminal and should be punished. They all knew about the guns, etc. This country is going to have to get tough on this kind if we are to survive. I'm serious. I only wished we could roundup those we released, but it's to late now. Well at leaset we have several of the sleeper cell and this bastard" Nate finished and put his cigar out. He concentrated on the coffee.

All night long, Nate and Chuck Edwards took turns keeping the prisoner awake and on his feet. They finally gave up on the standing and let him sit. To do otherwise may have resulted in his falling. They had no desire for him to have a mark on himself when he appeared in the courts. After all they were not C.I.A.

Finally they had him where they wanted him the following evening. First Nate decided to go to dinner first. Nate needed to fill Edwards in on any plan for his next performance.

Back to the little restaurant they went for a leasurely dinner. The desk had arranged to have the prisoner watched by a uniform officer during their absence. The Chief had also returned to his office and wanted to watch Nate's tactics. This being a new world since nine eleven, he was wise enough to understand this was not to be the last time he would deal with Arabs again. Very possible.

After the meal Nate and Edwards talked about what was ahead.

"I'll work around to the pig skin. It has to be done just right to be convincing. In other words I have to convince you that I would do as I say as well as him. You must react as though you believe it. If you do then he will. How this will end I don't know but don't be surprised at any thing I do. You can and should react as though believe I would do as I say. Just don't believe it. Ok?" Nate asked.

"Yeah, sure, you have already taught me a lot and I'm here for the long haul. I don't think this will take long and we can all relax," Edwards responded.

"Yeah, in thirty minutes after we start, we should have him talking up a storm. I'm hoping he tells us of other sleeper cells in this country. I want you to get me and throw away gun without any chance of being traced to us or your department. I have a plan to end this and how that will be best for all involved," Nate expressed his feelings.

"How are you going to do that with a throw away gun? I'm curious," asked Chuck.

"Can't tell you. It will spoil the surprise and may tip off the prisoner and therefore it would not work. You just have to trust me and go along with anything you see me do or say I'll do. At one time you will be left alone with him and I want you to relate to him what a dirty bastard I am. Tell him anything to convince him I've used the bamboo shoots under the finger nails, loped off heads, etc. Tell him I'm the dirty one the government calls on to get information from hard core traitors and terrorists. Tell him many do not survive. OK?" Nate asked.

"Sure, I'm just anxious to get started and get this over with and go home to my family. Thanks to you and your crew we can all sleep tonight. We are grateful you know," Chuck's way of saying thanks.

"Ok and one more thing. When you interpret this time do it with a little more feeling. Raise your voice when you came to words where I do. Act mad as hell at him for being as stupid as getting caught and things like that. Can you do that for me? It will be more believeable," said Nate.

"Sure, no problem," he replied.

The two got up from the table and walked to the cash register where Nate paid the bill. Then out to the Bronco, and back to police headquarters.

Back at the headquarters, Nate asked Edwards to go to the prisoner and he would follow as soon as he talked with the Chief. Nate approached the desk Sgt. who waved him on in to see the Chief.

"Good evening Chief. I trust you slept well after all our excitement yesterday," he asked.

"Like a baby. Knowing the main threat was gone helps a lot. Thanks to the way you handled things all of San Diego can sleep better. Problem is they don't know it," replied the policeman.

"Ok, Chief. We are about to round the corner and end this thing for good. I need you to do something for me. I take it you want to be in the room next to intergation and watch the whole thing. Right?" Nate asked.

"That's right. What I learn may come in handy next time something like this happens. What do you need?" he asked.

"I need to handle the tape recorder and only tape what the prisoner says. I'm going out on a limb or two and don't want it recorded. I believe you understand. I know you understand that our national safety is at stake and this may call for extreme measures. Of course the courts don't need to know what we used to get the information. If they did know they may throw it out. We don't want that. Will you do this for me?" Nate asked.

"Hell, yes. Lets get started," said the Chief raising from his chair and heading for the door.

Nate and the Chief walked down the hallway and each entered a different room. Nate to interrogate and the Chief to observe.

Before the door closed behind either, the voice of the desk Sgt. was heard coming down the hallway. It was tense and filled with excitement. They both closed the doors and hurried back to the front area. The Sgt. met them and pointed out the window.

The scene on the street before them was a little bit chilling. Cars were parking along side each other, not paying attention to the marked parking areas. Two men were emerging from each one. There were six in all, so when all were parked, Twelve men stood there. They wore black hoods and Arab dress on their bodies. Nate was heard from first.

"Hell, that's the bastards from the mosque that were released prior to finding the guns. They're after Alli," yelled Nate.

"Sgt, get on the radio and call in the patrol units for help. Call the swat squad and tell them to hurry, we are under attack. Hurry before they cut our communtrations. They all have automatic weapons and are surrounding the building. Get Edwards up here. Come on Nate lets get armed," coming from the Chief.

He dashed into his office and opened the desk drawer. Reaching inside he found the keys to the gun cabinet. He moved to it and unlocked the door. Reaching inside he grabbed an automatic weapon and a couple clips of shells.

"What do you want Nate, help your self," as he rushed back to the front. The Sgt. had finished his calls and approached the gun cabinet. Nate chose a twelve gage shotgun and a box of shells. He dropped the shells on a desk and broke it open. He filled his pockets with shells and joined the others at the front. Edwards joined them and all returned to the front loaded for bear.

"You get back on the desk Sgt," the chief ordered, "and relay messages to me as the others arrive. I don't want them barging in and some getting killed."

Some one outside let go with a bull horn.

"We don't want any trouble but we want Alli. He's a friend and has done nothing wrong. We are willing to take him if you don't give him up. You have two minutes to decide," was a voice making this demand.

"To hell with them," said the chief, "I can tell them now."

With this he opened the door a crack and poked his weapon thru. He fired a volley right thru the parked cars. Two men fell over and glass flew thru the air from windshields and side windows of the cars.

Those outside responded by automatic weapons firing at the building.

The glass windows came crashing in and everyone dove for cover. Desks were turned over for protection. The desk Sgt. was further back into the room and out of the line of fire. He continued working the radio and finally made an announcement to the Chief.

"Chief, I have twelve, two man cars heading in. The first should be here in five or six minutes. The rest a little longer. Any special instructions on how they are to come in," he asked.

"Yeah, have them use the cars to block off the street and leave one man at each end. The rest leave their cars outside and walk in. Make sure they are armed and tell them the attackers are wearing black hoods. Advise them there are twelve of them. I don't give a damn how they take them, but take no chances; they are a group of suicide bombers. I don't think they're going easy. Kill them if you have to," the Chief told him.

Nate aimed at one of the attackers as he attempted to crawl up to the building. He took aim with his pistol and fired. The man yelled with pain, then rolled over dead. Another one was gunned down as he stood on a roof across the street. The Chief took his automatic weapon, pointed it in that direction and let go with a burst of bullets. The attacker fell forward off the roof and to the sidewalk below. He remained motionless and it was assumed dead.

The screeching of tires announced the arrival of uniforms. A couple of attackers had to risk bullets from the office or from the street. They made a bad mistake of running into the street and firing at the officers. The two were gunned down with shotguns carried in the patrol cars.

"Tell the uniforms to wait right there until more arrives. It shouldn't take long to mop up this bunch. I think we've already killed six," he yelled to the desk. Sgt. The order was obeyed and the message sent out.

From their place in the office, which is elevated above the street, Nate ans Edwards had a vantage point. They were looking down somewhat on the attackers, who had to hug the ground when trying to move forward into the building. One made it to the steps before being blasted by Edwards. Three shots were placed about an inch apart in the man's chest. He fell inside thru the broken glass door. He never moved.

Edwards crawled over to him and checked for a pulse. There was none which he announced to Nate and the Chief.

More tires came screeching in and it seemes that cops filled the street. Noise of breaking glass filled the room.

"Damn," said the Chief, "we forgot the back. There's a window in the supply room. I'll take care of it," and with this he leaped to his feet and ran thru the door into the back,

Moments later shots rang out. Four altogether.

"Sounds like pistol shots, must be the Chief," Edwards said.

By this time police had spread out around the building and some coming in the front door. Shots were heard around back and across the street. Then a deathly silence settled in. A police Sgt. came in from outside and gave us the all clear. He then walked over to Edwards and handed him something. No one noticed except Nate who assumed it was the throw away pistol.

"Yeah, you were right. The body count is twelve. All dead. Is everyone ok in here?" he asked the Chief.

"Yeah," was the answer? "but you'd better call the coroner right away Sgt.," he said addressing the desk officer. "Also have the uniforms keeps sightseers away until the coroner gets the mess cleaned up. Better call the city shop and tell them we will need a clean up crew, once the bodies are removed. Tell them its glass and blood removal. They need to send someone around to estimate what's needed to repair this place."

"Come on Edwards, lets get back to Alli. He's probably going nuts hearing all the shooting," Nate called across the room. He then started down the hallway with the officer right behind.

Once they reached the room, Nate stopped.

"Is that the throw away weapon the uniform gave you, Chuck," Nate asked.

"Yeah, you want it now?" questioned Edwards.

"Yes, I'll take it," Nate replied.

"Can I ask how you're going to use it?"

"You can. Just watch and see," Nate answered. Turning around he unlocked the door and went in.

The prisoner jumped and starting jabbering at Edwards who was answering him.

Nate guessed it was about the excitement up front. They finished and Edwards faced Nate.

"He concerned about the shooting and I told him what it was. I told him that a dozen of his buddies were killed and none got away. I told him to sit and you were going to complete the earlier conversation. He's all yours boss."

Having finished Edwards walked to the far wall and stood, waiting for Nate to start the questioning.

"I'm going to make this short and sweet for you. I'm not going to waste any more time on the B.S.…. He's what going to happen. If you don't tell me where the radioactive material came from, I'm going to kill you myself. I'll then have you wrapped in a pig skin and buried in the desert. No one will ever know where. You country will be told of your failure here and your friends and family will disappear over time. That's how your country deals with failure aren't it?" Nate waited for Edwards to explain.

The look on the prisoner's face was precious. He turned from a suntanned complexion to white, then red and then to purple. Apparently this piece of scum was fearful of the pig.

"Tell him to write down on this pad," Nate tossed him a legal pad, "where the stuff came from and I want the addresses of any other sleeper cell he knows of. If he doesn't then I'll kill him and bury him as I said. He must do it and do it now," Nate said and at the same time he pulled out the toss away and laid it on the table in front of him.

For a minute, Nate thought he was having a heart attack. After a couple minutes he regained his composer and started writing like the devil himself was after him.

For several the minutes, Nate and Edwards watched the man writing like his life depended on it.

Edwards wasn't sure what Nate was up to but was certain this was yet to be over.

After fifteen minutes the prisoner laid down his pencil and told Edwards he was through. Nate was told.

"Edwards, take a look at it and see if he's done as I told him," Nate said.

He did as he was instructed and after reading it he looked up at Nate.

"He's told everything you asked for. The radio-active material came from North Korea, to Iran and then to the port right here in San Diego. It was easy to retrieve from the ship here. He's told of sleeper cells in San Franciso, Seattle, Chicago and New York. He's named names and how many in each cell. Yeah, he told you what you asked."

"Good," Nate said. "Now tell him this. He's played straight with me so I will with him. He wants to become a martyr and not a tratior so I'll fix it for him to be that martyr."

Nate went on.

"You take this pistol," Nate passed the throw away pistol to the Arab. "It's not loaded and this officer and I are going to leave this room. The next people to come in will be F.B.I. agents. You stand against that wall, with your back to the door. When it opens and someone speaks to you, you slowly turn and point the gun at them. They will fire and kill you and you become a martyr. I'll advise the press of your bravery and your country will never know otherwise. Understand," Nate said and nodded for Edwards to translate.

Edwards waited a moment to let this soak in. He didn't like the sound of it.

"Are you sure you want to do this. It is about the same as murder. I'm not sure I can do this," responded the officer.

"I can understand that. You just think for a moment that this animal was about to kill tens of thousands of Americans. The courts are such these days you can never be sure what will happen. He doesn't deserve to live in my book. More important it will send a message to these radical bastards that we will not stand for their killings. We really need to make them think they will be killed as soon as they arrive here. I think this will send a message. Once he's dead I plan on wrapping him in a pig skin and sending him home. His government will take care of the family of a tratior. Once the F.B.I. gets thru with the raids on the sleeper cells, his buddies will put two and two together and know it was him that squealed. They will punish many family members and friends. That alone should warn others to stay the hell away. Now if you don't want to be a part to this, go home. Just remember what we do here is keeping your family safe a little longer. There is no doubt in my mind that sooner or later we will be fighting bastards like these, often and on our shores. Go on home, I'll get someone from the University," Nate finished.

"No, I'll do it," said the officer as he began addressing the prisoner.

Relief seemed to sweep across the Arab's face as he was told the plan. He smiled and thanked Nate for his humanity.

"Come on Edwards, lets go," Nate said.

Both left the room and started down the hall. Coming out in what was left of the lobby, they saw two suits.

"F.B.I. I'll bet," Nate whispered to Edwards. Edwards nodded in agreement.

The chief came out of his office and seeing Nate grined.

"I can't say it hasn't been fun, because it hasn't been. You finished with the arab?"He asks Nate.

"Yeah, these agents come to take him in custody. He's in the interrogation room," Nate said. "Be careful he's a sneaky bastard and dangerous."

The two thanked him and walked down the hall. Edwards looked at Nate.

"Let's go get a drink," Nate asked Edwards. "Would you like to go with us Chief? I figure I owe you."

"Damn rights you do," responds the Chief as two shots were heard coming from interogation.

One of the two agents came running up the hall shouting.

"The bastard had a gun and we've killed him," he said.

Nate smiled at Edwards and said, "Well there goes Alli to meet his virgins except they won't be there. Besides he could never handle that many girls. We did him a favor.

In the following months several raids were made. The sleeper cells in New York, San Francisco, Seattle and Chicago were taken out. They were big raids where several hundreds of persons were taken into custody. Each raid made the headlines and told of the conspiracy being hatched by these groups.

The government took notice of the lax security at our ports and took steps to tighten it.

Across the Arab countries reprisals occurred against people who had been in good standing in the radical movement. This alone assured the U.S. and its allies of much fewer attacks. The world breathed easier because the information gathered from these raids told of other cells in other countries. Raids overseas also gave up several hundred Islamic radicals.

Alli arrived in Bagdad, in a pig skin, but went unclaimed for over a week. The government ended up taking him to the desert and burying him in an unmarked grave. His family soon vanished from the earth. No one was sure of what happened to them, but many believe their own kind killed or drove them from the country. Either way they dare not identify themselves for fear they'd be punished.

Hopefully this will set back the global terrorism a decade or two. Violence begets violence and those killers that want to destroy our way of life to be free, shall feel the full wrath of free people.

Nate went back to his life with a nice big check for his efforts and the thanks of the President of the United States of America.

Sitting at their breakfast table in Colombia Nate was reading of the raids and the repercussions. He smiled and poured another cup of coffee.

This book is pure fiction but does raise the question of secure borders. Had the Bush administration not sold out American jobs for cheap foreign labor to benefit the large corporate farms any such attacks may not happen? However, without secure borders, any actions like the one described in this book can happen at any time and could be successful.

Wake up America.